W9-BMN-648

PRAISE FOR
Gossip

"The three days I spent with *Gossip* were the high point
of my month. If only more novelists approached their craft
with the imagination and skill of Christopher Bram,
literature might well achieve what it needs to survive in a
world of cyberspace and *Nightline*—a much larger share
of the scandal market."
—Robert Plunkett, *New York Times Book Review*

"Bram's a wry, subtle, and compassionate writer whose
insights into human nature grow more impressive with each
book. His characters, by turns self-dramatizing, noble,
and petty, are observed with a gentle but
scrupulously honest eye."
—Joe Keenan

"Gay politics, Washington politics, and the corrosive effects
of trash-toned media drive Bram's fifth novel. . . .
Bram maintains wit and suspense all the way through
the crackerjack surprise ending."
—*Publishers Weekly*

"A closely wrought psychological portrait of both a
descent man and the sharply divided gay world he inhabits.
Bram makes a bold, imaginative leap with considerable
skill in this new tale."
—*Kirkus Reviews*

CHRISTOPHER BRAM, one of America's best-known gay writers,
is the author of five previous novels, including the acclaimed
Father of Frankenstein (available in a Plume edition). A widely
published film and book critic, he lives in New York City.

Also by Christopher Bram

Surprising Myself
Hold Tight
In Memory of Angel Clare
Almost History
Father of Frankenstein

CHRISTOPHER BRAM

GOSSIP

A PLUME BOOK

PLUME
Published by the Penguin Group
Penguin Putnam Inc., 375 Hudson Street, New York, New York 10014, U.S.A.
Penguin Books Ltd, 27 Wrights Lane, London W8 5TZ, England
Penguin Books Australia Ltd, Ringwood, Victoria, Australia
Penguin Books Canada Ltd, 10 Alcorn Avenue, Toronto, Ontario, Canada M4V 3B2
Penguin Books (N.Z.) Ltd, 182–190 Wairau Road, Auckland 10, New Zealand

Penguin Books Ltd, Registered Offices:
Harmondsworth, Middlesex, England

Published by Plume, an imprint of Dutton NAL,
a member of Penguin Putnam Inc.
Previously published in a Dutton edition.

First Plume Printing, April, 1998
10 9 8 7 6 5 4 3

 REGISTERED TRADEMARK—MARCA REGISTRADA

The Library of Congress catalogued the Dutton edition as follows:
Bram, Christopher.
Gossip / Christopher Bram.
p.   cm.
ISBN 0-525-93914-8 (hc.)
ISBN 0-452-27338-2 (pb.)
I. Title.
PS3552.R2817G67   1997
813'.54—dc20

Original hardcover design by Jesse Cohen
Printed in the United States of America

PUBLISHER'S NOTE
This is a work of fiction. Names, characters, places, and incidents either are the
products of the author's imagination or are used fictitiously, and any resemblance
to actual persons, living or dead, events, or locales is entirely coincidental.

To Ed

Author's Note

This is a work of fiction. For the sake of verisimilitude, however, several real publications, organizations and public figures, including some journalists, are named. They have been used fictionally throughout. All statements attributed to actual persons are purely imaginary.

Many friends, colleagues and insiders generously helped me with facts and ideas. Chief among those whom I can name are Draper Shreeve, Mary Gentile, Mary Jacobsen, Jim Jones, Will Meyerhofer, Ed Sikov, Cedric Tolley, David Fratkin, Patrick Merla, John Niespolo, my editor Matthew Carnicelli, and my agents Edward Hibbert and Neil Olson. Thank you all.

They met in cyberspace, made love in Washington, New York and Miami, and ended their affair on the six o'clock news. One could say that William O'Connor and Ralph Eckhart had a very nineties relationship.
> —Maura Morris, "Strange Bedfellows," *Village Voice*

I should have known better. I was thirty-four years old. I'd made peace with the who, what and where of myself. I did not crave importance or fame. Nancy thought I might be depressed. She would, but she may have been right. We'd been each other's sounding board, witness and back scratcher since college.

I went down to Washington to see Nancy Wenceslas. She was feeling unhinged in her new life and wanted my help. "I seem to need a mental health visit, Eck," she admitted sadly. So I went. The other thing began as a lark, a diversion, a harmless stumble. But the stumble became a fall, a long slide down a slippery slope that later landed me in the public white noise. You probably think you know all about me, if you ever caught my name.

The world is full of other people's words.

"Hear about Keanu and Geffen? Woo woo."
"In your dreams. Wishful thinking by some old fag."
"I hear Klein pays beautiful men to humiliate him."
"Gee. I never have to pay for that."

"Proposal: Clinton is Bush with a Southern accent and est training. Respond."

"Who said that? You're an idiot cynic to say that. After the last Republican convention?"

"But he's right. Talk is cheap. All the nice talk from the Crats hasn't changed squat."

"My dears. If you want to talk like newspapers, go to a room and leave the rest of us to our fun."

What sounded like a party had almost no sound at all, only the sporadic dice-like click of my computer keyboard. Our sentences were silent, instant, words jetting across the screen, lines scrolling into oblivion. Once you grew accustomed to it, Gayworld was no stranger than talking on the telephone. You stopped seeing the format, abbreviations and misspellings:

The Cardinal: Who th f is Gefen???

But I was a newbie and still found the chatline odd and metaphorical, an elastic black hole, a computer game of words. I often felt like I was talking to imaginary spirits on an electronic Ouija board, with only the example of my friend Peter Hirsch to assure me that these people were real. Peter had introduced me to Gayworld, goading and coaxing me into the future with the promise of bold new freedoms.

The dark green ether was honeycombed by rooms much like my own, mostly in New York, with occasional aliens dropping in from other area codes. I sat in my shadowy shoe box five stories above East Ninth Street, beneath my overloaded bookcase and a ceiling that shed yellow eggshells of paint. A cold November rain beat against the glass and slurred in the leaky window frame, but there's no weather in cyberspace. It was the Tuesday night before my trip to D.C. and I'd turned on my computer to chat before bed, like dropping into a bar, only I didn't have to get dressed. I wore a ratty sweater and the gym shorts I sleep in when I sleep alone. Peter said that when his boyfriend Nick was out he sometimes sat naked at his keyboard, not for sex—one used the phone lines for that—but simply to remind himself that he was more than a bombardment of electrons.

Everyone had a handle, a pseudonym, so it was like a masked ball in the telephone system. We were an eclectic mix of fantasy egos: the Cardinal, Billy Budd, Tom of Chelsea and Shanghai Lily, who was Peter—"It took more than one man to change my name to Shanghai Lily." Peter had met most of the regulars and reported that they tended to be techies and nerds. A nerd manqué myself, I was in no hurry to meet anyone. I enjoyed remaining mysterious. Torn between pretention and camp, I became Sergeant Rock, which seemed a good joke, although people who didn't know me had no truth to rub against it.

"Mr. and Mrs. Clinton appear to be making enemies left and right. (Pun intended.) What do you New York types think of that?"

There was a new handle on the screen tonight: Thersites. He insisted on talking politics, but only Billy Budd rose to the bait. Our preferred subjects were movies, books, gossip and computers—the medium was often the message here.

"My dear Thirsty. I rap my fan across your knuckles," went Shanghai Lily. "Politics nix."

Dry and soft-spoken in life, Peter was a tyrannical hostess in Gayworld. And his camp side, which peeked out in an occasional "dear" at the bookstore, ran wild. He was forty-two, a former actor-singer who worked with me at Left Bank Books, although we'd known each other before. I'd gotten Peter the job a year ago when he needed to get on group health insurance. He was okay now, but still carefully rationed his time, energy and passions.

I couldn't remember who or what Thersites was. A character in one of Plato's *Dialogues*? I pictured an older man in the boondocks with a classical education and too many magazine subscriptions.

"Anyone going to Hell this Friday?"

"No way. Got caught in the darkest back corner last time."

"The elephant's graveyard," I quipped.

"Bingo. You never know whose clammy butt you're pawing."

"I prefer Tunnel of Love at Wonderbar."

"More like the Broom Closet of Love," I typed. I knew the clubs well, but hadn't visited them in months.

"Whatcha doing this weekend, Sarge?"

"Going to DC to see a friend."

"Woo woo."

"A friend from college," I explained. "A woman."

"I have tickets to Rigoletto," announced Billy Budd.

"SOSO," typed someone else—same old same old.

"And I take the flying boat to Bermuda on Friday for bridge with the Duke and Duchess of Windsor," said Shanghai Lily.

I knew that Peter was scheduled to spend Friday at St. Vincent's for his monthly tests. "May you come up trumps every time," I told him.

A longer entry crowded the screen:

"You say that you are coming to Washington, Sergeant Rock? What a coincidence. I live in DC. You sound like an intriguing fellow. Would you care to meet for coffee while you are in town?"

Thersites. He'd been drafting the invitation while the conversation moved on.

"Thanks but I won't have time," I quickly answered.

"Don't be shy, dear. Go meet him," said Shanghai Lily. I could just see Peter smirking lewdly at his screen.

"Please, Sergeant. I meet so few people F2F"—face-to-face.

"Do it, Sarge."

"Go get him, tiger."

"What else is there to do in DC?"

Everyone jumped in, a pack of computer yentas determined to see Sergeant Rock, who never met anyone, actually make a date.

I couldn't think clearly in the cascade of input. "Can we step into a room and discuss it?" I told Thersites.

"Certainly."

I brought down a box and clicked myself in.

"Wish me luck, gentlemen." Thersites clicked himself in with me. I clicked again.

The others would see our box sucked to a dot while an empty field filled my own screen. I needed the space to think. Because, despite myself, I was already tempted. What else *was* there to do in D.C.? I expected several long, heavy conversations with Nancy, but she would be busy during the day, and coffee with a stranger, even a stuffy old man, might break up an idle afternoon.

"Hello," he began.

"You live in DC?" I was stalling. Being alone in the digital dark with a stranger had a disturbingly erotic quality.

"I began in Maryland but now live in the District."

"I might like meeting for coffee but don't know my schedule yet," I typed.

"Mine is quite flexible."

"Give me your phone number and I'll call when I'm in town."

"I'm afraid I can't do that."

He must have a boyfriend or, more likely, a wife. "What if I give you the number where I'll be?"

"When are you most likely to be free? Day or night?"

"Day I guess."

"Then why don't we meet at the zoo? Do you know the National Zoo?"

"Yes."

"Let us say four o'clock, Thursday afternoon, the zoo."

The zoo made it comically wholesome. Maybe he was literal about having coffee. He must be retired if his schedule was so flexible. Talking with a real New York homo might be enough for an old Southern gentleman.

"OK. If I'm free."

"Excellent."

"What if something comes up and I can't be there?"

"That's a chance we must take."

"You don't want a number where you can reach me?"

"Let's leave it like this. For the suspense. (Gentle laughter.)"

He made it easier for me to stand him up. "Suit yourself. Where in the zoo? It's a big place as I remember."

"The reptile house."

"What cage will you be in?"

"(Hysterical laughter.)" Only the most literal man would regularly type in his stage directions. "Shall we meet by the pythons?"

"OK. What do you look like?" I typed.

"Ask me no questions and I'll tell you no lies."

"How old are you?"

"Ibid."

He spoke in footnotes. A retired academic? "But how will we know each other when we meet?"

"It adds to the mystery."

I decided to take no chances. "I am 34. I have a shaved head. I am more Mr. Clean than Sergeant Rock."

"Stop! I refuse to read what you wrote. I want us to surprise each other."

"(Sigh.)," I typed mockingly, although the irony wouldn't transmit. "All right. I will be there if I can."

"Excellent."

"I will look for a male who is looking for a male. Am I right to assume you are male?"

"(Gentle laughter.) Most definitely."

"I feel like Kitty Carlisle."

"Who?"

"Never mind. Shall we rejoin the others?"

"I will say good-bye. Until Thursday at the reptile house."

"See you Thursday. If I can make it."

His cursor blossomed into a square, the black bar blinked and he was gone.

Back in the main room, the yentas were hungry for details:

"Who is he?"

"You meeing him?"

"Ask me no questions and I'll tell you no lies," I replied.

"Did you at least learn what a Thirsty-ditty-do was?" said Shanghai Lily.

"Not yet. There's a good chance I won't."

"Puss puss puss," someone chided.

I told everyone good night and booted down. I took out my date book and lightly penciled, "Reptile house, 4 pm." If it was a joke, Thersites had a very private, cryptic sense of humor.

When I replaced the computer jack with my phone jack, the telephone promptly rang.

"So why not meet this guy?"

After the silent words, Peter's velvet voice was so startlingly physical that I could *hear* his long, deadpan face, his lanky frame, his elongated fingers.

"I don't know if I'll have the time. I'm not going down there for fun, you know. Nancy needs my help."

"You are such a frigging Boy Scout," Peter said. "You know, most people, if a friend sold out, would write them off as a lost cause. They wouldn't take time off to go hold their hand."

I frowned. "That sounds like Nick talking."

Peter clicked his teeth, embarrassed to be caught with a borrowed observation. "It is. But he has a point."

"Come off it, Peter. Nancy's a good friend who needs to see me. And she didn't sell out."

"Okay, okay. She seemed nice enough the few times I met her." He quickly disowned the charge. "But you know Nicky. Power corrupts. They're all crooks or cowards and D.C. is closet city."

"Nick underestimates Nancy. And she's out down there." So out that she suspected she was known as the Other Lesbian, to distinguish her from the assistant secretary at HUD. "Nick wouldn't be so scornful if he still had a little power."

"I won't argue with that," said Peter. "He misses his glory days on the barricades."

"I respect his anger," I claimed. "When it doesn't turn self-indulgent." I liked Nick—I once liked him very much—but couldn't forgive his constant sniping at Nancy.

"When you coming back?"

"Saturday. So I'll be there at breakfast on Sunday."

"Well, tell Nancy hi. And seriously, if you meet Thirsty, I want to hear the gory details."

"There'll be no gore to share, Peter. See you Sunday."

2

The brick hulks of dead factories and high stride of power-line pylons swung across a cold blue sky in my window. It was a weekday afternoon, the train half-empty. I had two seats to myself and sat sprawled with *Can You Forgive Her?*, the first novel in Trollope's Palliser series. I loved to read on trains. It was like time tripping. I especially enjoyed visits to the nineteenth century, not because it was more restful than the present but because it seemed thicker, more solid and knowable, its people embedded in a dense cake of custom and conscience.

I was not quite of the decade. I preferred Victorian novels to new movies, trains to planes, Fruit of the Loom to Calvin Klein. I owned a computer only because a friend had left me a Mac in his will. On the other hand, there was my head, which I'd been shaving for a year. Not razor shiny, but once a week with electric clippers, a haircut that ranged from five o'clock shadow to a skullcap of springy brown velvet. I did it first for the novelty, then continued because it saved twenty dollars a pop at the barber. And it provided instant distinction, easing the chore of proving myself cool or queer or artistic. My skull had a nice shape and the brain can be a sexy organ. I was not who I looked like but I knew who I was. The distance between appearance and reality gave me more room to breathe.

I began to think about Nancy once we passed Wilmington, but with more curiosity than fear. I enjoyed being needed yet knew she'd need me only so much. This trip was for Nancy, yet I didn't see myself as a Good Samaritan. I looked forward to escaping the cramp of New York knowingness, and to spending a few days with my oldest friend.

Nancy had phoned a week ago, sounding frantic yet amused by her panic, which was her style. She did not plead or whine. She gave no single cause for her emotional crisis, but cited work, stress and loneliness. "I need a reality fix," she said.

"You must be in trouble if I represent reality."

"You better believe it," she said with a laugh.

I offered her two days of vacation available to me before the Christmas rush began, plus my Friday and Saturday off. We often took holidays in each other's troubles. When she broke up with her first lover, I went down to Philadelphia to provide distraction and continuity. She came to New York to do the same for me when Alberto went into the hospital for the last time.

"I need a reality fix myself," I said. "And I want to see life in the new regime. You're my window on Washington, Nance."

"That's all I am these days. Glassy essence."

"Dissociated sensibility?"

"Out the ass."

Our friendship had a highly literary bass line. We'd met on the school literary magazine at Chapel Hill, when I was going to be a poet, Nancy a teacher and critic. Our ambitions were perpendicular yet complementary; we extended each other. Not that anything literary came of either of us. Twelve years after college, I no longer thought of myself as an unhatched Yeats or Stevens, but as the capable head of shipping and receiving at a bookstore near NYU. And Nancy worked on Capitol Hill.

She was not in Congress. She wasn't even a politician. You may have seen her on CNN during a Senate hearing. You've certainly seen people like her, the aides and staffers lining the wall behind the men whose very public faces have the half-animate familiarity of life-sized Muppets. Women senators are too rare to look like cartoons, and the staffers are clearly human, young unknowns anxiously waiting for a split second of celebrity when they pass a document to the boss. The guys can be quite cute, as many of us discovered during the Anita Hill hearings.

Nancy didn't go to Washington until a year after Anita Hill. It was a surprising move for a Ph.D. with a dissertation on codes of lesbian desire in Emily Dickinson. Unable to find a tenure-track teaching post, she'd taken an administrative job at Penn that included writing speeches for the dean. A gift for snappy phrases that Nancy herself dismissed as "the thousand clichés of light" caught the attention of the president of Bryn Mawr, a former state representative who'd decided to run for the Senate. She hired Nancy as a speechwriter and, when she won in an upset that pundits ascribed to female anger over the incumbent's cross-examination of Hill, took Nancy with her to D.C.

"Does your crisis have anything to do with Melissa?"— the lawyer Nancy had been dating since August.

"Oh no. That's turned out to be purely social. We squeeze each other in once a week, if we're lucky. If either of us had time to meet someone new, we'd quietly disengage. Just as well. I can't be myself with her. You know me, Ralph. I have to present a tough front. Which brings out the pathological liar in me. Even with Melissa."

"It's not pathological. It's just—"

"Neurotic. Okay. I'm a neurotic liar. Who's become an institutional liar. Because everyone here is like that. Nobody can afford to show themselves in a bad light. So there's nobody who can make me honest."

Nancy wasn't as fearless as she pretended. Her dishonesty was mostly in her own mind, although she often found it hard to tell a story without giving herself the last word she only wished she'd delivered.

"And that's why I need to see you, Ralph. So I can be honest for a few days. Plus we'll have fun. You're not visiting a basket case. We'll talk and do coffee, talk and do tea. Just like the old days."

When I thought about Nancy in her absence, I almost always pictured her as she was in college: a galumphing girl in overalls with a squashed haystack of frizzy hair, emphatic elbows and, under her eyes, the crepey circles of a debauched courtesan by Edward Gorey. Only the circles remained, but I retained the old mental photograph, as if it were the true Nancy, the real Nancy, my pal and equal. New York friends couldn't believe that someone like me knew someone in Congress. I enjoyed confusing their assumptions. I didn't envy Nancy's new importance or feel judged by her success. I was proud to know someone who did work so far beyond my capabilities.

But I was happy with my own life. I had a job rather than a career, yet preferred it that way. I passed as an adult at Left Bank Books. Only Elaine, the manager, and Howard, the buyer, had been there longer. I'd recently been promoted to assistant manager but two other people had the same title and, except on Sundays, when I ran the store, my domain was the basement. I liked working down there in the clutter, bad lighting and old-fashioned smells—the cocoa-like cardboard, the sour curdle of wet pasting tape. I enjoyed the reverse snobbery of being a manual laborer in letters. Lugging and tossing heavy boxes kept me in shape without joining a gym. And I did not take the work home with me, which left plenty of psychic space for the rest of life, such as reading and activism and affairs of the heart. I hadn't attended a political meeting in months, and even my last routine romance was over a year ago, but I was having a spell of downtime and knew I should enjoy it while it lasted.

The sun was setting as the train flew over the rivers that empty into Chesapeake Bay; a shadow train raced across the orange fractals of water and sputtered out in the woods. Then came suburbs, then the white lights of the railway yards and, in the distance, the bald dome of the Shrine of the Immaculate Conception.

I already knew Washington, the stage set if not the life backstage. Growing up in North Carolina, I once thought it was the Big City. Now I enjoyed its artifice. Union Station was a vast neoclassical shopping mall. The Metro seemed spookily smooth and civil after the bang and stink of the New York subway, the homogeneous white-collar crowd exotic in the theatrical lighting of coffered basilicas buried below the earth. I rode up from the depths at Dupont Circle in the long cannon of an escalator toward an oval light like a gibbous moon. The moon opened into a city of traffic and rattling leaves and half-deserted sidewalks.

Nancy lived a few blocks away in a tall turn-of-the-century monstrosity called the Cairo. She wasn't home yet but had left a key with the doorman. I let myself into the apartment that looked much as it had when I'd helped her move in, what Nancy called Bachelor Wonkette. She sublet it fully furnished from a weapon-systems salesman who'd gone home until the next election. Her chief contributions to the decor were stacked newspapers, government reports and, on an exposed brick wall, the framed print of an Emily Dickinson daguerreotype that I gave her for her thirtieth birthday. The iron-spined, Bambi-eyed poet looked startled and amused to find herself in Washington. We were up high enough for the illuminated dome of the Capitol to be visible in the window over the sofa.

I was in the kitchen making tea when I heard the front door.

"Eck!"

"Nance!"

I swung around the corner and we embraced. Her loaded briefcase clobbered my shoulder.

"You're here! You found your way okay? Sorry the place is a mess but I worked until midnight last night and had to run out first thing and—welcome!"

She flung off her coat, bounced on her toes and punched me in the arm. The blond tomboy from college was hidden in a tweed suit, her frizzy hair tamed in two short wings. Not quite boyish and definitely not butch, she was entirely Nancy. The circles under her eyes, permanent crinkles of lizard skin, brought a touch of melancholy to her face.

"Let me catch my breath." She dropped into a chair to untie her plump running shoes. "You hungry? I'm famished. I'm taking us out to dinner."

"You don't have to do that."

"But I want to. I made reservations at Trumpets around the corner. So you can see queer Washington first thing."

"Do I have to dress up?"

"Oh no. You look fine. Nice to see a guy who isn't starched and pressed. They'll think I'm conspiring with radicals."

The kettle in the kitchen whistled. I went to turn it off.

"We can have tea when we get back," she called out. "I'm all yours tonight. All day Saturday too, but Thursday and Friday are going to be hectic."

"No problem."

When I returned, she was sitting quite still. "I feel better already," she said in a softer voice. "Just seeing you and knowing I'll be able to talk. Do I seem crazy to you?"

"No more than usual."

She grinned. "Oh good."

"But why Trollope?" she said out on the cold windy street. She knew my habits and had promptly asked about my train reading.

"I don't know. Because there's so much of him. Because I've already read George Eliot and Dickens."

"And he's good?"

"Very. In a sane, leisurely way. And nothing too terrible ever happens."

"Maybe that's what I need these days. Sane and leisurely."

We went down to a black glass door below street level

and entered a restaurant. It was like stepping into homosexuality, first the lighting, then the microwave hum of men alert
to the presence of other men, although I quickly learned that
their attention was not necessarily sexual.

We were checking our coats when Nancy grabbed my
arm. "Ding!" she said. "Want to meet Bob Hattoy?"

"You know him?" Even I recognized the name.

"You'd be amazed at who I know."

I followed her toward the bar, where a tall, lean fellow in
glasses held court with three or four other men in tailored
suits, one with a red ribbon.

"Bob!" said Nancy, thrusting her hand at him.

"Nancy! Hello. I've never seen you here."

"Came tonight for dinner with a friend from New York.
Bob, this is Ralph Eckhart. Ralph, Bob Hattoy."

"An honor," I told him, which he accepted as a perfectly
natural thing to say. I resisted the urge to praise his speech at
the Democratic convention and tried to remember what he'd
done since.

Introductions were made, an automated round of smiles
and handshakes. "Ken and I already know each other," Nancy
pointedly told the man with the ribbon. "Don't we, Ken?"

Hattoy and Nancy shared pleasantries about Senator
Freeman, Nancy's boss, until the maître d' told us our table
was ready. We were halfway across the room when Nancy
growled, "Did you see Ken Walton's face when he found out
Bob Hattoy knows me? Ha!" she crowed. "The little prick
won't even return my calls. What do you bet he phones first
thing tomorrow?"

We sat at our table, an isle of light in a pool of islets,
before Nancy noticed the confused look I gave her.

"Oh God. You see what this town's done to me, Ralph?"
She gave a comic moan. "I am losing my soul."

"I didn't think that. I'm just surprised that you of all
people have to play that game."

"I know. But it comes with the territory. Pecking orders
and food chains. The court of Louis the Fourteenth with fax
machines."

We ordered quickly to get rid of the menus. Nancy launched into a discussion of her job, the overload of duties, the trial of playing housemother to the junior staff, the amount of effort required to accomplish the smallest thing. She was ferociously cheerful about it, even humorous, but let me see the panic underneath.

"I've gotten so caught up in the game, Ralph, that I forget what real life is about."

"Love and work," I reminded her, a pet phrase of ours.

"But that's my problem. I'm nothing but work here. Everyone is. So I try to get from work the personal meaning that one can get only from love or friendship. It leads to—abominations."

"Your politics don't give you a grip?"

She released a long sigh. "I've begun to wonder if political beliefs are like algebra. Something you study in school but never use in life. It's not how we imagined, Ralph. The good-guys-and-bad-guys stuff doesn't cut it here. It's more office politics than party politics, much less social conviction."

I nodded knowingly, without being sure we knew the same thing. I'd lost my faith in ideology too, although it could still kick in when I least expected.

"But being gay hasn't been a problem?"

"God no. Just look." She gestured at the room. "We're in every bureau and department in town. We might not all be out on the job. Old habits die hard after twelve years. But most people know. Nobody cares. Except Republicans, and not even all of them. The only problem I've had is with the interpersonal, things you have to ignore when you can't use the G-world."

"Such as office romances?"

She laughed, very loudly. "Oh no. Work-environment stuff. Unfun." An intern had reported that another intern was making homophobic jokes. Nancy called a meeting to lecture everyone about sexism, racism and homophobia, only to learn it had been one mild joke, and the whistle-blower was the joker's bitter rival.

"What was the joke?"

She rolled her eyes. "How many lesbians does it take to change a lightbulb?"

"One, and it's not funny?"

She nodded. "You see why I think I may have over-reacted?"

We laughed. We could both be so earnest yet always saw the comedy in our zeal.

"How do you feel about Senator Freeman now?"

"Ixnay," she said. The waiter had appeared with our food. "Oh, but this looks delicious," she told him. "I should be more careful," she said after he left. "This place is ear city."

I lowered my voice to ask, "Then you've become disappointed with her too?"

"No! Not at all. I admire her, I respect her, I'm thrilled to work with someone of her caliber." She stuffed a baby carrot in her mouth to stop what sounded like a press release. "No. I—" She spoke more carefully around her food. "I get frustrated. We don't work as closely as before. Kathleen's as swamped as the rest of us, and there're days I don't even see her. Last night, for instance. When I knew I'd be at the office late, rewriting her speech for the AMA convention in Pittsburgh. I needed to run a new idea by her on health care. I needed ten minutes, no more, but her secretary kept phoning and postponing, phoning and postponing, until it was seven o'clock before I got in to see her. She was at her desk, two aides waiting for her signature, her assistant on the phone. Her damn husband in the corner with his overcoat in his lap. Right away he snaps, 'You can have two minutes with her. Not a minute more. We're already late for dinner.' And I blew up. I couldn't stop myself. I said, 'Look. I am going to be here until midnight, if I'm lucky, and I'll be ordering pizza, so don't accuse me of wasting your wife's time.' That shut him up. The ass. He sat there like a lamb while I went over my outline with Kathleen."

I waited for her to laugh at this overreaction too, or explain the office psychology involved. The husband sounded obnoxious, but hardly criminal. "You said that to him?"

She chewed and swallowed. "No. But I wanted to. God,

did I want to. He really burned me." She gave herself a derisive snort. "What did I tell you, Ralph? An institutional liar.
I've been telling myself the should-have-said version so much
that I've begun to believe it. But you need the ballast of bullshit to hold your own here. The bullshit has entered my
soul."

"Sounds like you need a vacation," I said worriedly.

"Except I've become such a workaholic that I'd go to
pieces without the routine to hold me together. I'd lie in bed
and never get up. Instead, I lie in restaurants."

Nancy's attitude toward the truth was always stricter than
mine. I did not feel superior over getting the real story. And I
did not think she'd lost her soul. She was in the thick of it
and I wasn't. I didn't feel like a child in her presence, but I
somehow felt shorter. When we finished dinner and got up to
go, I was surprised to rediscover I was taller than Nancy.

"I should tell you," I said when we were back on the
street. "I admire what you're doing. The world seems so out
there to me. Sealed up in itself. More black-box technology.
But you work inside the box. I respect you for that."

She shook her head. "Uh-uh, Ralph. It's nothing but
boxes within boxes, all the way in. I'm in just deep enough to
forget private life. Which is why I need to spend time with
you."

"Who's nothing but private life?"

She laughed. "It's a dirty job. But somebody has to do it."

3

Back at the apartment, I made a pot of tea and Nancy changed into a calico nightshirt. We sat facing each other on her sofa.

"City of bald heads," I said, pointing out the Capitol.

"Then you should feel right at home," she teased. "Except I have to say, I see it as a big white breast." She smiled and blew at her tea. She seemed relaxed, as if she'd unloaded a demon or two at dinner. "So how are you these days?" she asked.

"Fine. I've been oddly content this fall."

"Love and work?" There was a tiny note of skepticism.

"I have the bookstore. I have my friends." I squeezed her knee through her nightshirt.

"I don't know, Ralph. If it were me, I'd find those weak substitutes. You're not seeing anyone?"

"I'm having a quiet time right now."

"Not even your annual office romance?"

I laughed. "Those were in the spring. And I can't do that anymore since they promoted me. Just as well. The new kids are too young and insipid to interest me."

"You haven't been involved with anyone since Alberto first went into the hospital."

"Bert was never a boyfriend."

"You know what I mean."

I did. "No. My quiet has nothing to do with that."

"But it must be affecting you. One person after another. It never ends, does it?"

"You get used to it," I said. "I know how awful that sounds, but it doesn't upset me anymore. It's awful that you get used to it, but you do." This was one of the few places where Nancy couldn't understand me. But I didn't know how to talk about hospitals or death without sounding like I was either in denial or indulging in melodrama.

"You're not still stuck on that activist, are you?"

"Nick? God no. Nick was three years ago." I groaned with embarrassment. "I know him much too well now. And I'm tight with Peter, far tighter than I ever was with Nick."

"How is Peter?"

"Fine. His spirits are good. His T cells are up."

"And he knows about you and Nick?"

"Oh yeah. He even teases me about it. In front of Nick when he wants to annoy him." Nick didn't introduce me to Peter until our fling was ending, his friendly method of declaring it over.

"Sounds too complicated for me."

"It might look that way from outside. But just another scene of gay life. No worse than what you and I went through."

"It's different when you're younger. I have complications of my own right now, and they're no fun at all." She shifted into a tighter position in her corner of the sofa.

"You and Melissa?"

"Oh no. Not Melissa." She glumly looked out the window. "I left out a big piece of story at dinner, Ralph. I'm in love."

"Oh?" She made it sound like murder.

"With Kathleen."

I blinked. "Your boss?"

"Yup. Senator Freeman."

I took a deep breath. I winced, not just at Nancy but at myself for not understanding sooner. Her anger with the husband suddenly made sense.

"Stupid, isn't it?" she muttered.

"And dangerous, right?"

"I'll say."

"But she's married. She has kids."

"Yup."

And she was a United States senator. A vista of dangers opened in my mind. I became worried for Nancy, fearful. "Does she feel the same about you?"

"No. Of course not. She doesn't even know."

It took me a moment to factor that. "You're not sleeping with her?"

"God no! Are you kidding?"

Now I could smile, just a little. "So it's an infatuation?"

"Yes! An infatuation. A crush. A sentimental crush that's turned into an obsession. It's eating at me. Because I can't act on it. And it spills over in all kinds of stupid resentments and blowups around the office. I hate her husband."

"I got that."

"I get jealous of anyone who works close to her. I feel hurt whenever someone else gets an assignment or invited on a trip. And I can't let any of it show. Not a whimper, not a peep. I hold it all in and haven't told a soul. You're the first."

"But she's your boss. How can anyone be in love with their boss?"

"She's a remarkable woman."

"But you see her every day. You see her at her worst."

"I love differently than you, Ralph. Familiarity doesn't kill it for me. I love them that much deeper." She gave me a desperate, pleading look. "Keep going. Please. I want you to talk me out of this."

"It never works like that."

"I know. But I have to hear it said aloud, so I can tell if I'm crazy or not."

"Well, she's in her late fifties, right?" I'd seen her photo but could not remember how she looked. "It's like falling in love with your mother."

"She's nothing like my mother. Thank God. She plays up her age for the camera. She's sharp and lively and physical. Tough but graceful. Like a cowgirl crossed with a swan."

"Does she show any interest in you?"

"No. Not in the least. She's not encouraging it or using it to get more work out of me. It's all me. Like an anxiety attack I've projected on her. But it's making me a nervous wreck."

"Can you quit your job?"

"I've considered it. But I can't leave. Not yet. Only I don't know if it's the work I can't leave or Kathleen."

"There's always the Tim-and-Nina solution."

"Oh God."

"Just kidding."

She tried to smile. "It should be funny, shouldn't it? And nothing's going to happen. Absolutely nothing. It will pass. Unless I have a nervous breakdown, it will pass. Only then where will I be? What if love turns to hate and I can't work with her anymore?"

"Then you can quit this job and find another."

"Will anyone want me?"

"Come off it, Nancy. You're a good speechwriter. You've said so yourself. Every time she's quoted in the news, it's a phrase you coined. People must know that."

But she did not want compliments. "What really worries me is, whatever happens, I'll go into a black depression. Like I did after Annie broke up with me."

"You were depressed, but you weren't comatose. Or if you were, it was only by your standards."

"But I need to be excited. All the time or I feel like I'm dead."

Nancy called herself a manic depressive, but the depression expressed itself mainly in her fear of it. Nancy depressed looked like many people running at normal speed.

We circled over the same ground—love and work, impossible love, love as a symptom of something else—for the next hour without coming to any new conclusions, although Nancy became less fretful, more resigned, even witty.

"I have this horror of seeing a photo from our college yearbook in *The National Enquirer*," she said. "Under a headline like 'Lesbo Vampires on Capitol Hill.' "

"Or 'A Queer and Present Danger.' "

She laughed long and hard at that. And then she yawned.

"Sorry. Didn't know I was so tired. We can continue this later, can't we?"

She offered me the choice of the sofa or sleeping with her. "You should like the new bed. It's queen-sized."

"Ha ha," I said, but accepted.

Poor Nancy, I thought while I brushed my teeth, although I couldn't help feeling envy as well as sympathy for her. Other people's troubles are always more dramatic than one's own. She was in an exciting place of heartbreak and scandal here. Could love scandalize anyone nowadays?

When I came out of the bathroom, Nancy was on the far side of the bed, hands behind her head. "I don't believe it, Eck, but I feel calmer now than I have in weeks."

"Good. Maybe talking helped after all." I climbed into bed.

"Do you have any plans for tomorrow?" she asked. "Do you want to meet for lunch?"

I did. I wanted to see where Nancy worked, the scene of the crime, so to speak. We agreed to meet at her office in the Hart Building at noon. I hugged her good night.

"It's so good to have you here," she said, and kissed me.

"Likewise." I kissed her.

We scooted back to our pillows and she turned off the light.

We'd shared a bed many times, but it still carried a faint erotic charge, an echo of that first bed many years ago.

Nancy and I met on our school literary magazine, but did not connect until we fell in love—with different halves of a young married couple. I fell for the husband, Nancy for the wife.

It's hard to say what made Tim and Nina so symmetrically lovable. They weren't beautiful, only cute. Small and faintly androgynous, like children, they were seniors, but their marriage suggested two kids playing house. They were tickled to be married. They seemed to know something the rest of us didn't. College is supposed to be sexual Eden, but everyone in my circle was cramped with fear and embarrassment, even straight people, even those who regularly got laid. Everyone except Tim and Nina. They radiated a careless physical bliss. Alone with me, Tim let that bliss shine into my eyes like a secret he wanted to share. He rarely talked about sex, but spoke often about Bloomsbury. Tim said he and Nina read aloud from Virginia Woolf's diaries every night in bed, which sounded like heaven to me, that two people could be naked together—they must sleep nude—and still read.

I was a junior that year, a stuffy, shaggy, bearded boy who believed his intellect was his sole likable trait. Nancy was a stumpy girl from New Jersey with wild hair and a nasty sense of humor. We lingered after meetings at the magazine to talk with Tim or Nina, secretly courting them, suspiciously eyeing each other, not yet knowing how much we had in common.

Nancy and I were alone in the office one afternoon, reading poetry submissions, when she went into a tirade about the deluge of love poems, the blather of love, the cliché of it—we were all afraid our emotions were trite and secondhand. "Being in love is such a bore," she spat.

I pompously declared that I enjoyed it as a sweet agitation of soul, even when it went nowhere.

"Yeah, I thought you thought that," she sneered. "Is that why you're so moony around Tim?"

Stunned that someone had noticed, breathless and grateful, I blurted out the truth. "Well, yes. I'm in love with him."

Her face fell open. She was shocked that I didn't deny it. And she stammered out what she felt about Nina.

It was both beautiful and terrifying. I'm still amazed we didn't scare each other off. We read no more poems that day, but confessed everything. Our homosexualities were still purely emotional. I'd been to bed twice with the opposite sex, but neither of us had slept with our own. Lust was very well for straight fornication, but we needed the myth of love for gay sex. And much as we enjoyed our infatuations with Tim and Nina, we did not want to do anything that might hurt their marriage.

"It's the modern equivalent of courtly love," I claimed. "The strongest emotion coupled with the strongest discipline."

"I wonder if they know. I hope not. Nina is so open and sweet. She can't guess the signals I'm getting."

We were such innocent vultures.

We continued to see Tim and Nina, together and separately, while we waited for love to run its course like a bad cold. Our constant talks in private guaranteed it wouldn't.

This shared folly seemed to go on forever, but lasted less than a month. Tim and Nina invited us to their house for dinner one night. Just us. They lived off campus, in a cinderblock cottage out by the truck stop. We timidly walked there together, afraid the occasion had a purpose: They were going to confront our feelings and demand that we stop.

As it turned out, they understood what was going on, yet didn't understand at all. After much noisy talk about Reagan, Marx and Bloomsbury over spaghetti, after a jug and a half of white wine and one of those prankish college games whose sole purpose is to get people to take off their clothes, Tim and Nina invited us to join them in bed.

And we did. And it was wonderful. For me at least. For several long, ecstatic minutes. I was naked in the dark with the impossible, stroking his birdlike chest. I didn't mind that we were crowded by two rounder, softer bodies necking beside us. Tim was shamelessly fascinated with my dick, toying with its spring and heft. When he actually went down on me for a few bold strokes, I was too thrilled to feel it, or care that he was holding Nina's hand. I could generously share him with the wife whose teacup breasts were covered by a frantic head of hair. The few times I glimpsed Nancy's face, her eyes were squeezed shut as if to stop herself from crying. Our bed was full of asses and elbows, but it was *our* bed now. Taking Tim in my own mouth, awed by the simplicity of holding a live thing on my tongue, I excitedly believed that we were going to be happy, all of us, an elaborate knot of bodies, conversation and love.

I was kissing him when Tim began to lose interest. He drew back to inspect my beard, chuckled and rolled away. The next thing I knew, he and Nina were all over each other, and Nancy was stranded with me. I took her in my arms and cuddled a forlorn breast, but we were not what either of us wanted. When Tim and Nina began to screw, she turned away and hid her body against mine on the twitching, jouncing bed. I was too hurt to enjoy watching, but I watched. And they were too close for their fuck to be beautiful. A flat rump like a peeled potato squirmed between a wobbling pair of raised legs. The squashed eye of a tit stared out. Tim rolled his head like a mad elephant, but Nina sleepily smiled at us, pleased to have two witnesses to their grand passion. They strained into a duet of barnyard noises so loud and exaggerated it sounded sarcastic.

Everyone lay still for a minute, then began to unplug and disentangle.

They invited us to sleep over. We said no, we should be going. Out in the living room, we couldn't look at each other while we sorted through the pile of clothes discarded during the game, both of us feeling unlovably large and fleshy. When I was dressed, I went back to the bedroom to say good night. Tim and Nina lay snuggled together in the musky sheets.

"Wow," said Tim. "We've never done anything like that. We wanted to explore our bisexual sides. Thank you."

"Thank *you*," I said.

"Where's Nancy?" asked Nina.

"I'm out here," she hollered. "Good night. Hope nobody has a hangover tomorrow." She refused to come back in.

We walked up the cold highway with our hands buried deep in our coat pockets, unable to speak for the longest time. Finally I said, "I'm sorry."

"I don't want to talk about it!"

"Don't get mad at me. I feel like shit too."

"Why did I go along with that?" she snarled. "I was drunk and stupid. I knew how it was going to end. For you it was just sex, but I was in love with her, really in love. And to have it reduced to—cheap thrills. We were their kinky fun for the month, nothing more."

"They're sick. Both of them. Sick and selfish. And they dragged us down to their gutter."

"Oh shut up. I don't want to talk about it."

And we didn't, for the next two years. We talked about everything else, but not that, not until after we left Chapel Hill and had been to bed with enough people, with and without love, for sex to stop being such an enormous, all-important deed.

"When I tell people that story now," I later confessed, "it comes off as funny. Even sexy. I can't get across how humiliating it was."

"But it was funny," Nancy insisted. "And I don't regret it. Not really. It sure cured me of Nina. And hey, we each got to see our best friend in the act. We have no secrets now, Eck."

And it was true. We had nothing to hide from each other. Our friendship stood on the cold bedrock of shared shame and honesty.

4

Nancy had already left for work when I woke up on Thursday morning. I took the Metro to the Mall and hiked the long, grassy brown desert toward the newscast backdrop of the Capitol, an image of power as deceptively solid as a billboard. It did not look hospitable to romance of any kind.

The Hart Building was in a flock of offices beyond the great facade. Entering the enormous atrium of a white marble layer cake, I stood in line at the metal detectors with a class of fourth-graders who were tickled to be treated as potential assassins. Up above, plate-glass doors to Senate office suites lined the third-floor balcony. A Pennsylvania state seal was bolted to the marble under Senator Freeman's removable nameplate. I asked for Nancy at the front desk, which was tended by two boys in suspenders who had the premature jadedness of Ivy League success. A closed-circuit television in the corner showed a chamber in session. Even in Congress you watch Congress on television.

I was wondering where Senator Freeman was today, when I caught the suspendered boy in pink slipping me a timid peek.

Nancy came out. "Hey, Ralph. Come on back. I'll show you my office." It was the official Nancy, without bounce or glee, brusque only in comparison to her usual manner.

I followed her through the carpeted warren to a cubicle with a word processor, cabinets and a poster of Helen Mirren in *Prime Suspect*. She didn't even get a window. I kept my disappointment in her status to myself.

"So how are you doing today?" I whispered.

"Fine," she said automatically. "Kathleen has asked if she can join us for lunch."

"Really?" Her nonchalance threw me. "Uh, did you want me to make other plans?"

"Not at all. I want you to meet her." She lowered her voice. "And even when we're alone, we're not alone. We'll probably talk shop, but you don't mind, do you?"

"No. It'll be an education. Lunch with a senator."

"You bet." She grabbed a notepad and led me back through the maze. I opened my ratty duffel coat to display the proper ski sweater underneath.

We entered a large office where a middle-aged woman in a pleated blouse and tweed skirt stood conferring with a secretary.

"Kathleen?" said Nancy. "We're ready when you are."

"Right with you."

That was Senator Freeman? Lean and handsome, with short, bangy auburn hair, Nancy's cowgirl-swan looked more like a favorite high school teacher, until she faced me. Her authority worked like beauty.

"You must be Ralph," she said, shaking my hand. "I hope you don't mind my horning in on your lunch." She had an insinuating growl that might be described as grandmotherly, if your grandmother was Georgia O'Keeffe.

She was not famous, but she was important. I became tongue-tied in the force field of her title. "Not at all, Senator."

"Please. Call me Kathleen. Buzz me if Maggie Williams calls back," she told the secretary; she took up a dainty tweed jacket and jerked it on as she went out the door. She faced straight ahead, assuming we followed right behind her. "And

you know Nancy from college? Her Emily Dickinson days?"
She quoted:

"Are you nobody? I'm nobody, too.
How awful to be somebody, as public as a frog,
To sing your name all day long, to an admiring bog."

"Hang in there," she told the boys at the front desk.

Out in the corridor, I looked for the woman with whom Nancy was smitten, but not too closely, for fear of giving her away.

"You work in a bookstore, Ralph? I envy you. When the world is too much with us, my husband and I talk about opening a bookshop. In a nice little resort town. I realize it's hard work, like any business, and when business is slow you worry about being in the red. Still—"

We came to a bank of elevators. A set of bronze doors marked "Senators Only" beeped; Nancy had to remind Senator Freeman that we could all take it when we were with her.

She continued to talk about bookstores and publishing while we rode down. We stepped on a subway shuttle so quick and silent that it barely registered, especially when my attention was so full of Senator Freeman. I was afraid to notice anything else.

A wide, oak-paneled corridor opened into a dining room with a salad bar in the center. We sat down around a white tablecloth.

"Labor and Human Resources at four o'clock," said Nancy.

"I guess I should smile at the old buzzard." Kathleen turned her handsome profile and beamed at a stuffed figure who responded with a noblesse oblige nod. "How's the soup today, Gladys?" she asked the waitress. "How's your son doing?"

I watched Nancy to see how her beloved's presence affected her, but she showed none of the electric alertness I remembered from our Tim and Nina days. When she caught me looking, she only smirked, proud to be sharing a U.S. senator with me.

"Nancy," declared Kathleen after we ordered. "I keep meaning to tell you what a fine job you did on the AMA speech. First-rate. Absolutely."

"Yes? Well good. Thank you. All in a day's work." The compliment caught her off guard.

"Or a night's work. Jack sends his apologies for speaking out of turn the other evening. He was too frazzled to see that you were frazzled too. He hopes you understand."

"Oh that," said Nancy, pretending to need a second to remember. "No problem."

" 'If looks could kill,' he said." Kathleen chuckled.

Nancy winced. "Oh God. Did it show? I'm sorry."

"Poor Jack. Playing househusband to a college president was bad enough. He still hasn't adjusted to Washington life."

"What does your husband do?" I asked.

"He's a lawyer. Criminal law. He has no patience with the glad-handing required by public interest."

A fellow in a green suit stopped by the table. "Senator. Excuse me. I just want to tell you how much I look forward to working with your staff on the bill to—"

He and the Senator chatted and smiled at each other for two minutes, and he left.

"Who the blazes was that?" Kathleen asked Nancy.

"I haven't a clue."

"No?"

And both women burst out laughing, sharing disbelief over the absurdity of this strange new world.

Kathleen touched Nancy's hand—not quite a touch but a light swat. "It's *good* to hear you laugh." She turned to me. "She's been so serious lately. Help her to relax while you're in town. Take her to the movies. Take her dancing."

"I couldn't get Nancy on a dance floor at gunpoint." I wondered if Kathleen thought I was a boyfriend.

But she added, "You don't happen to know any nice women in New York you could introduce to her?"

Nancy nervously smoothed the napkin in her lap.

I covered for her. "That's more trouble than it's worth. Going back and forth between cities. Amtrak love."

Kathleen laughed; she'd never heard the phrase before.

Nancy groaned. "Gimme a break, guys. I'm fine. Really." She pretended to be embarrassed by the attention, but was clearly pleased, even relieved.

The arrival of the food signaled the end of private matters. The Senator brought up her trip to Pittsburgh and a scheduled appearance on a local Sunday talk show, who would be watching, whether comments would be picked up by state newspapers or vanish in the air. I was impressed by the hundred media details Nancy had on tap, the names of radio and TV stations, journalists and editors. They forgot I was there except when they grumbled over a particularly nasty columnist in Pittsburgh and Nancy explained that he was as vicious as the cranks who wrote for *American Truths*. Then they talked about next week's convention of insurance brokers in Harrisburg. They remembered me again only when the waitress asked if anyone wanted dessert. They were above sweets, but insisted I try the ice cream.

I did not feel neglected or bored. I was too busy listening for hidden personal meanings. Nothing they discussed needed the social lubricant of lunch. I sensed that this meeting was really about something else, and that it had already happened. I waited to be alone with Nancy to ask if I was right.

Nancy and the Senator were pondering the phrase "It's the nation's health, stupid"—catchy or stale?—when the pompous old man from the corner stopped by.

"Hello, Kathleen. Just wanted to ask if you'd had a chance to read the rider on the Moynihan bill?"

I didn't recognize him, but his face had the slight thickness of too much television exposure. A bald assistant stood a few respectful feet behind him.

"I did, Ben. We should talk. You going back?"

"Don't let me take you away from your lunch."

"I'm finished here." She looked kindly at Nancy, then at me. "This has been a pleasure." She shook my hand as she

stood up. "Have a nice visit. And please. Show my best word-
smith some fun while you're in town. What I want to know,
Ben, is why the blazes—"

Nancy and I watched Senator Freeman go. Nancy turned
to me with a guilty lift of eyebrows.

"So. What do you think?" she asked.

"I like her. She seems personable. Down-to-earth."

"She's not. Not really. But people want that and she puts
on a convincing act."

"I was wondering how real that was," I admitted. "And
also about her ease over your . . . crush."

The shadows under Nancy's eyes crinkled in alarm. "She
doesn't know. She can't. No way." She looked over her
shoulder, but Senator Freeman was long gone.

"Wasn't that what this lunch was about? To let you know
that it's okay?" I was surprised Nancy hadn't even suspected.
"Your shop talk didn't sound so burning. Not to me anyway."

"It wasn't. But this lunch was to make amends for
Tuesday night and show I'm appreciated. That's all. She
hasn't a clue about what I was feeling. Let's go. I'll sign for
this."

I followed her out to the corridor.

"*Was* feeling?" I said. "Past tense?"

"Yup." She took a long breath through her nose, as if to
smell the idea. "I think. Because now I feel different. Perfectly fine. All she had to do was give me some attention and
I'm happy as a clam."

"It's not just a temporary fix?"

"I'll have to wait and see. But when I came in this
morning, even before she suggested lunch, my agitation
didn't feel like the L-word anymore. Not really. It was about
esteem and ego and insecurity. That's all."

"Sounds like the L-word to me," I gently joked.

She directed us away from the waiting area of the shuttle
into a long, futuristic tunnel. We walked inside a tiled mega-
phone and had to keep our voices low.

"But you felt she knew?" she whispered, worried.

"I assumed she must."

"You mean it showed in me?"

"No. And I was looking. But I assume women are more alert to those frequencies."

She laughed, relieved. "Oh no. They can be as oblivious as men. Especially when there're a million more pressing matters on their minds. All Kathleen knew was that I felt unappreciated. And she may have been right. It was all in my head, not my skin. Thank God. But you untangled all that for me last night."

"I didn't do anything except listen."

"Exactly. Without sneers or pity or making me feel like an idiot. Or making too big a deal of it either."

I was skeptical that love had been talked away so easily. And oddly disappointed, as if my purpose in coming here were suddenly gone.

We came out of the tunnel into a hall under the office buildings. Other people walked past us.

"To be continued," she said. "Any plans this afternoon?"

"Oh, I don't know. Go to the Smithsonian. See what's playing at the movies. Visit the zoo?"

No, I hadn't forgotten. I'd remembered the appointment when I woke up, although a meeting for coffee had seemed awfully trivial in the face of Nancy's drama.

"You poor guy," said Nancy. "I hope you're not as desperate as that."

"I'll be fine."

We came to the elevators under the Hart Building. The Senators Only elevator beeped for a new arrival.

Nancy cringed. "Oh God. I hate it when I run into an asshole and have to be friendly to them."

The bronze doors opened and out stepped a lone fortyish man with a square jaw and enormous shoulders, like a former football player who now sold cars or power tools on television.

"Afternoon, Senator."

"Good afternoon. Nancy? Am I correct?" His thick Southern accent made his smile seem courtly, even flirtatious.

"Very good, Senator Griffith. Most can't even remember the names of their own staffs."

"Well, I try. Have a nice day, Nancy." And he strolled off, quite pleased with himself.

"Non-asshole?" I asked.

"Who knows? First-term senator from Tennessee. Moderate Republican but we said that about Bush. The religious right is wooing him but nobody knows if he's in their pocket yet."

I rode up to Nancy's floor and we exchanged good-byes in the corridor.

"I don't know what time I'll get out tonight," she said. "You should plan on dinner without me. Unless you want to come back here and we'll order a pizza?"

"Any cute interns working late tonight?"

"Hmm, maybe." Then she laughed. "No, Ralph. If you hit on one of those puppies, I wouldn't be able to work around him with a straight face."

"Come on. I'm hardly irresistible."

"Just knowing you were considering it would make me see him in that light. You thinking of anyone in particular?"

"Naw," I said, thinking of the boy in the pink shirt. "Just being hypothetical. But sure, congressional pizza sounds good. Something different for my political education."

I promised to telephone later.

5

I **went** back down in the Metro, deeper than before. I needed an elevator to return to earth at the National Zoo.

I went feeling nothing except idle curiosity and a strange regret that the high drama of illicit love on Capitol Hill was already over. Lunch with two serious, responsible women left me with an itch to do something queer and frivolous. Coffee with an old closet case would have to suffice if Nancy didn't want me flirting with interns that evening.

The zoo looked deserted on an overcast afternoon. It was so cold that most of the animals had gone indoors; a lone rhinoceros stood in its pen like a forlorn leather sculpture leaking steam. I found the reptile house, an old brick building with ceramic toads and tortoises around its entrance. The interior was dark, the halls illuminated by the soft glow of sealed habitats. It was as still as a church, as hushed as cyberspace. The mildewed smell of sawdust suggested snake shit.

A sea turtle the size of a lawn mower floated in a murky glass wall. A man with snow white hair turned to stare at me. A little girl came over and rested her face against his leg. They resumed watching the turtle together.

I checked out faces as I walked in. Everyone seemed remotely possible, even the trench-coated Sikh who escorted two women in wool saris. I came to the python case, a roomy terrarium full of artificial sunlight, tropical plants and a set of coils like a mound of brightly painted tires. At the glass stood a solitary six-year-old boy with spooky eyes and solemnly folded arms. I wondered, just for a second, if a child had the computer skills to have faked me out.

Other people wandered through, tourists with strollers, the Sikh again. A Young Dad type walked up to the glass between me and the six-year-old. But it was only the boy's father, come to break the python's spell.

When *he* came in, he was so indifferent to reptiles that I knew instantly. He strolled through the hall with a hurried, slap-shoe walk, in black-rimmed glasses and down vest, a large, pink-cheeked fellow who looked my age—no, younger.

He saw me. Our eyes met. He looked away and kept walking, but halted at the other end of the case.

He rocked on his heels, put his hands in his pockets. He pinched a smile to himself and looked at the snake, giving me the chance to check him out. His round face made him seem chubby, or maybe that was only the down vest. He wore a sweatshirt underneath and his brown hair was in a bland straight-boy cut. I'd been so prepared for someone with no physical appeal, however, that he seemed thoroughly plausible.

"Mr. Thersites?" I said.

He stared at me, blankly. Then he broke into a grin of perfect white baby teeth. "Sergeant Rock, I presume?"

We laughed and shook hands. He had a rattly, back-of-the-throat chuckle like the shake of maracas, and long, thick fingers. We quickly looked each other over.

"My word. You are a real New York gay," he said, taking in my head. "Or do you prefer queer?"

"I prefer Ralph. And you're—?"

"Bill. My name's Bill. So. Did you in fact want to see the zoo? Or shall we go somewhere for coffee?"

"Coffee sounds good."

"Excellent. I'm parked out front. Shall we?"

His boyish face and voice gave his stuffy phrases a likably clunky playfulness.

"There's something I have to know from the start," I told him outside. "*Who* is Thersites?"

"Do you know Shakespeare?"

"I've heard of him."

"*Troilus and Cressida*? I bet you haven't read that one. Thersites is the truth teller of the play. Toyota has a car called the Cressida," he added. "Obviously named by people who never read the play. Because Cressida is a nut and slut who betrays the man who loves her. Not qualities one wants in a motor vehicle."

He unlocked the door of a pearl gray Lexus whose interior smelled like a box of new shoes.

"What do you do for a living, Bill?"

"I'm a writer."

He was too young to have earned the car with words, and I knew firsthand that "writer" was often a synonym for bum.

"What do you write?"

"Journalism. Freelance. What do you do?"

"I'm a shipping clerk in a bookstore."

"Truly? Maybe you'll be selling my book when it comes out."

"You've written a book?"

"A first book. Expanding an old article," he said dismissively, as if everyone wrote and published such things. "There's a fine coffee bar nearby. Or, if you like, I have an espresso machine. We could go back to my place." He smiled, a complex double smile, as if smiling at his own smile.

Yes? No? Why not?

"Espresso sounds good," I said casually.

"You mean at my place?" He could not believe his luck.

"Why not?" I said aloud. In New York I might not have looked at him twice. Tricking with strangers was not high on my menu and I hadn't been to bed with anyone in months. But being in another city with time on my hands opened my mind, extended my standards. His nerdy cheerfulness promised a quick yet friendly boff.

"For how long are you in D.C.?" he asked. "Do you get down often? How long have you lived in New York? Where are you from originally? You don't sound Southern, you realize."

He peppered me with questions that I answered truthfully while we drove a mile or so, past a Metro stop labeled Cleveland Park—I needed to know the closest public transportation—and swung into the parking lot of a tall, flinty twenties apartment building in a tangled net of bare trees.

The simple sensual act of walking from raw cold into a warm lobby was enough to chub me in my pants.

"Swank place," I said in the elevator. "What's the rent?"

"None of your business." He chuckled. "But I will tell you—it's a friend's apartment. His rent is very reasonable."

I'll bet, I thought, assuming it was a boyfriend's apartment, a boyfriend's car—and the boyfriend was away.

"Home," he said as he opened the door with his maraca laugh. We stepped into a dark, overheated apartment large enough to have a front hallway. "Take your wrap, sir?"

I waited until he hung my coat and his vest in the closet. Then I laid an arm across his shoulder and turned him toward me. I expected a flinch or a startled laugh, but his lips promptly opened to my kiss.

"Mmm? Mmm." He took me in his arms. He'd recently brushed his teeth. "You don't want espresso," he murmured.

We were all over each other. I was surprised to find he was slightly taller than I, and solid, a six-foot cherub in glasses. We stumbled deeper into the apartment and I noticed three televisions side by side, a printer and an open Powerbook. From software to underwear, I thought, my hand down the back of his pants. High tech, high touch. He had the most muscular lips and tongue.

"You're a good kisser," I muttered.

"Played trumpet," he croaked. "My high school band."

We were on a sofa, undoing buttons and sliding hands under clothes while our tongues squirreled in a tight, wet room of joined mouths. There was the porno ritual of undressing each other item by item as we necked, the slow unwrapping of gifts. We were down to white briefs—he was more acculturated than he seemed: Calvins—when he stood up to examine me. His baby face, vague and piglet-eyed without glasses, was misleading. He wasn't fat, but firmly upholstered in plush skin. His arms were thick and his waist narrow, with a neat trail of hair under a knotted belly button and a thick diagonal fold in his cotton.

I didn't break him into details until later. Sex is like classical music for me in that I never quite hear a piece the first time. I can only rehear it, not comprehending what's there until a second or third listening. Surprised at how much I'd enjoyed the first hearing, I reassembled him later, when I needed to know what made Bill O'Connor so damn enthralling.

"No tattoos?" he said, pleased with what he saw.

"Too permanent. And I'm too hairy."

"Hmm. But not *too* hairy."

He took my hand, pulled me to my feet and led me down the hall, as if to involve more of the apartment in his tryst. He turned on a lamp in the bedroom—it was getting dark outside—and we resumed making out on a very solid, king-sized bed, rubbing and rolling in our underpants. I postponed the electric moment of complete nakedness, often the high point for me of first encounters, not because their cocks proved disappointing but because getting the other guy bare turned out to be all I really wanted. Then he peeled me and I peeled him, and we did not disappear behind our dicks but became acquainted all over again.

The sex was not wild and frantic, but more like ballroom dancing, each of us taking turns, taking our time, enjoying our excitement yet remaining friendly around it. He took me in his mouth without fear. When I went down on him, I stroked his chest with my free hand. I could not touch enough of him. A body can be so three-dimensional with a hard-on. His was wide, almost double-barreled, his balls nearly flush underneath. The hair of his genitals, armpits and scalp was different grades of the same smooth corn silk.

He kept smiling at me and I couldn't help smiling back. So many men treat sex as work or theater, but this guy gleefully accepted it as something natural as eating.

Covering him from head to toe, holding his face and gently rocking our cocks, I broke off kissing just to see his smile again, a breathless, blissful grin. He ran a hand over my bristles—his fingers were in love with my skull—and said, "Can't remember—the last time—enjoyed this so much."

"You sure know how to enjoy yourself," I said admiringly.

There was no mention of condoms, no suggestion we fuck. I don't like fucking, even with someone I know; it is too deliberate and final. I prefer to exhaust the other variations. Sooner or later, one of you just wants to make the other come, although that wasn't happening here. Each time someone got close, he stopped the other and we touched something else. I was enjoying this too much to want to finish yet, there was no place I had to be, and nothing else I wanted to do with this fellow. He seemed to feel the same about me. We moved out of the routine arc of sex into a daze of flesh and hormones.

We were sitting up, our legs around each other's waist, his hand holding us together and slowly pumping, when he took his tongue from my mouth to whisper, "You have dinner plans?"

"Want to have dinner together?"

"Oh yeah."

It would mean calling Nancy and telling her I wouldn't be dropping by. She could guess why. It would leave me open to her teasing, but that seemed a small price for the chance to prolong this and maybe get to know this guy whose desires were such a perfect fit with mine. "Okay," I said.

And he threw his head back and grinned. His hand had tightened its grip and quickened its strokes and he was moaning behind clenched teeth. I did not want to end yet, but his frantic rise in pitch and the slickness against my cock were too strong. I let go, clutching him with my knees while we shamelessly groaned in each other's ear and squirted in his hand.

I fell back on the bed, gasping, my legs still wrapped around him. I clutched his soft foot and pressed the sole against my face like a telephone. I did not want to break contact. It was only sex; but sex for its own sake, with no consequences, no future, out-of-town sex with somebody else's boyfriend, had been thoroughly satisfying.

He reappeared overhead, straddling me on extended arms, grinning. "Yow," he said, then flipped around and nested in my armpit.

I liked having him there. His eyes were closed, his mouth still flush. A tomcat smile stood out on his pale face as if he wore lipstick.

"Do this often?" I teased. "Take home roadkill from the information superhighway?"

A brown eye snapped open. "I am not roadkill." His indignation took me by surprise.

"Not you, silly. Me."

"You? Well, you shouldn't put yourself down either." He seemed to have lost his sense of humor with his orgasm.

"All I meant was you know how to enjoy yourself with someone you just met."

"I usually don't. Do this or enjoy it." He smiled and laid a leg across my middle to make clear that he enjoyed me, and to keep my body beside him.

But I was content to stay, glad that he wasn't the type who promptly wipes off and gets dressed. It took practice to be so comfortable with tricking. I assumed he was being modest about his experience.

"How old are you?" I asked.

"Twenty-eight. And you?"

"Thirty-four. Like I said on the chatline."

"I said I wouldn't read that. I didn't. So. Did we surprise each other, Sergeant Rock?"

"Oh yeah." I didn't tell him what I'd expected. If he couldn't laugh at my roadkill crack, he wouldn't be amused to hear what I had pictured.

"Do you have a lover?" he asked. The old-fashioned word.

"Nope." As gently as possible, not wanting to make him guilty, I said, "But you do?"

"No."

"Really?"

"No!" He was offended I didn't believe him.

"Sorry. Just thought that's why you had such a big bed."

"It was here when I moved in. Almost everything belongs to the friend who owns it. He stays here when he's in town, but he has his own room."

"A gay friend or a straight friend?"

"Straight. And married. Why does it matter?"

"Just curious." I wanted him to be attached or kept, to explain his apartment and car. Otherwise, I'd been picked up by a very successful younger man, and I really was roadkill.

"Everything has to be gay or straight with you New York types," he grumbled, stroking the rill of bone by my temple.

While our voices said one thing, our bodies said something else. We remained curled against each other, too content to climb out of this warm bath of shared skin.

"Why do you do this to your head?" he asked.

"I like the look. The feel. Saves money on haircuts."

"It's not for the politics?"

"Oh, it's like any haircut. It might have social meaning at first, but then it becomes just a haircut."

I enjoy talking in bed with strangers. Often they just want to sleep or go home or I am too disappointed to want to loiter myself. But when the mood is right, I love the inside-out intimacy of learning about the vertical life of a body that I've already known horizontally.

"How long have you been out?" I asked.

"Depends on how you define out."

I wasn't alarmed; it's always a tricky question. "When did you start having sex with guys?"

"Oh, seventeen."

"Really? You have the jump on me."

"How old were you?"

"Depends on what counts as the first time."

"Your first time in bed with a man."

"Twenty-one. Only his wife and another woman were in bed with us."

"Truly?" he said, making a face.

I told him the story, the comic version, which I hadn't repeated since my days when all postcoital talk seemed to be about first times. I gave no names.

He listened with growing concern for my shame, and distress that women were present. "I hope you didn't have sex with *them.*"

I assured him I hadn't, although that disappointed some men.

"What an awful couple," he muttered. "What kind of wife can do that with her husband? Both those women sound awful."

His righteous disgust amused me. After all, I'd been appalled myself at the time. "But I was just as bad. Tim and Nina's only crime was that they didn't know how serious Nancy and I were. My only regret is that I was too stupidly romantic to enjoy it as the goof it was."

"No. You couldn't help yourself. You were in love. And women are wired differently from men. For a woman to do that, a married woman especially, a moral defect is present."

I didn't know what to say to that. He must not have known many women. "So how did it happen for you?"

"Oh—" He drew close again and stroked the hairs on my arm. "I had a paper route. I saved up my money. And hired a hustler."

"At seventeen?"

"Uh-huh." His grin was back. "My parents went off to an aunt's funeral one weekend. I couldn't go because of my paper route. That night I dialed a number I'd found in a gay newspaper and asked for a call boy."

"Where was this?"

"Baltimore."

"They have call boys in Baltimore?"

"They have them everywhere," he said, surprised at my

naïveté. "But he drove out to the house, saw I was just a kid and, well—we had fun all night long. We didn't get a wink of sleep. He even helped me deliver my papers the next morning. And he only charged his basic house-call rate."

"How old was he?"

"Twenty-five, twenty-six."

"You could've charged him." I hid my unease over his cold practicality, and my envy, wondering which of us had been more bourgeois, me for thinking sex needed love or him for reducing it to cash. "But he was nice?"

"Very." He stroked my arm as if comparing me to his hustler.

I noticed a clock by the telephone. It was after seven. We'd been together for three hours, most of it naked.

"You still serious about dinner?"

"Of course."

"Then I better call the friend I'm staying with. Tell her not to expect me."

I got up and went out to the living room and my clothes. Passing a mirror in the hall, I paused to see if I was as hot and beautiful as I'd felt during sex. No, I was the same ropy, slightly hairy rectangle crowned with a bare lightbulb. Fishing Nancy's number from my jeans, I considered getting dressed before calling her, but I wanted to shower before we went to eat. The apartment was warm, an old steam-heated cave with high ceilings and thick walls. I noticed the three televisions again in the darkness. I stopped to inspect a bookcase, hoping we had something in common besides lust. The only novel was by Tom Clancy. The rest was political nonfiction, memoirs and journalism, with nothing remotely gay except a recent biography of Eleanor Roosevelt.

When I returned to the light, Bill lay on the white ice floe of the bed with one knee raised, his other leg laid across it, smiling to himself, the triangle of legs framing his fuzzy core. There was nothing beautiful about his nudity either, but his face remained cute. I sat with my back to him to use the phone.

It was a direct line. Nancy answered after a single ring.

"Hi, it's me," I said.

"Was just thinking about you." She sounded quite chipper. "So you coming over?"

"Not tonight. Do you mind? I ran into an old friend and he asked me to have dinner with him."

Silence. "How old a friend?"

"Old enough."

"You know what I mean." She snorted amiably. "So should I expect you home later or do you want to call here tomorrow?"

It wasn't as if this were a common occurrence when I visited Nancy. "I'll be back tonight. It's just dinner."

"You don't have to apologize. It was only going to be pizza. Although one of the Harvard boys did ask about my bald friend."

I laughed—a large bare foot was stroking my back. "You just want to make me feel bad for standing you up."

"He did ask. Honest. I don't know the depth of his interest. I always assumed he was neuter. But he did ask."

"I'll come by the office tomorrow night. I promise." I grabbed the pesky foot and held it in my lap.

"He won't be here tomorrow night."

"But you will. I'll see you later."

I hung up guiltily, unsure why I felt guilty. I found Bill watching me with his double smile, that smile behind a smile. His foot was smooth, with no calluses or corns, the suburban foot of a man with a car. He wiggled his toes in my hand.

"*Would* you like to spend the night?" he asked.

"I can't. I promised my friend I'd meet her later." But I lay back down beside him. After being away for ten minutes, I'd forgotten how good his body felt. He still had the fresh smutty smell of an ailanthus tree in full bud.

"Where does your friend work?" he asked.

"The Hart Building."

"Oh. She works for a senator?"

"Uh-huh. Freeman."

"Hmm." A note of contempt.

"You don't like Senator Freeman?"

He opened his mouth, then shut it and snuggled against me. "Let's not talk about *that.*"

I put my arm around him, but I was curious now, suspicious. "What do you write for, Bill? Newspapers? Magazines?"

"Whoever will have me. Although recently I've been too busy finishing my book to write for anyone. But I've appeared in the op-ed pages of the *Wall Street Journal.* Twice."

"Then you write about business?"

"Politics."

I approached warily, fearing the worst. "Who's your steadiest customer?"

"The *Washington Times.* Although my best work goes to *American Truths.*"

"So you're"— I almost said right-wing but caught myself—"conservative."

"I don't label my point of view. Although the liberal press isn't interested in what I want to talk about."

Only a right-winger would talk like that. Yet I felt no twinge of shock or nausea. Holding him against me, I found my beliefs suspended, my righteousness gone. I stroked the cool mound of his bottom. "What do you think of Pat Robertson?"

"A bigot. He and the rest of the religious right. A gay man would have to be an idiot to support them."

At least he considered himself gay. "But you don't have problems with other conservatives?"

"There're all kinds of Republicans, just as there're all kinds of gay people. Despite how things look from New York."

So I'd tricked with a young Republican, a journalist. And it changed him. He no longer seemed like a friendly, horny kid but older, colder, slightly smug, even as his chin nuzzled my chest.

"I remember when I first started going to bars," I began. "I went home with this guy. We were already in bed and he suddenly said, 'Excuse me. But I have to ask before we continue. What are your politics?' "

Bill laughed, his breath tickling my chest hair. "What did you tell him?"

"The truth. That I was sort of a leftist liberal with socialist pretentions. Which was fine. He just didn't want to have sex with a neo-Nazi."

His face jerked up. He looked stung. "You think I'm a Nazi?"

"No, no," I quickly said. "Just something I remembered. And how funny his timing was." I drew him against me to assure us both that I didn't really think he was the enemy.

"It is funny," he said. "And stupid." He thought for a moment. "Once my book is published," he muttered, "I won't be able to meet guys like you. It'll be the end of my anonymity."

The happy, groundless fear of the first-time author. "What's your book about?"

"Washington under the Clintons."

"An attack?"

"An objective appraisal."

I doubted that. "But you have a publisher?"

"Yes!" Again he sounded hurt; his skin was not only soft but thin. "Crown. It's due out in April. I'm finished except for correcting the galleys. Which is how I'll spend next month."

"Congratulations. They're a good house." Maybe his book actually was an objective appraisal.

"Thanks," he sniffed. "Sorry to be so touchy. My humor and other people's don't always mesh. Which is why I have things like 'laugh' and 'pun intended' on the function keys of my Powerbook. But you can't do that in person without sounding autistic."

He changed again, from a smug ideologue to a sweetly insecure nerd.

"Well, I know *American Truths* only by its reputation. I've never looked at it."

"You should. It has a wide range of opinion. Some good people write for it."

I slipped a hand between his legs. "Do the editors know about you?"

"Two or three. The ones I respect."

"And they're not nervous? Knowing what readers would think if they knew who they were reading?"

"My private life is my own affair." He glanced down at our tangled legs and my very intimate hand.

"Do you write about gay issues?"

"No. Not my domain."

"So you've never said anything against gay rights or gays in the military or any of that?"

"Never. And I wouldn't."

I knew how ludicrous I sounded, talking politics while I cupped his balls and petted his penis with my thumb. But I needed to address my unease, even if it meant talking myself off this fence, out of this bed, although my body wanted to stay.

"What does your family think?" I asked.

He clung to me more tightly, as if my questions might shake him off. "They're proud of my success."

"What do you think about the rest of you?"

"Hmm," he irritably murmured, and stretched up to silence me with his mouth.

I thought it was only a tactical kiss, but gave in to it, rejoining him in our slippery room of tongue and teeth. When he softly ballooned and snapped to attention in my hand, I went with that too. I hadn't come twice in the same go since I was his age, and with a man I'd been pursuing for weeks. I assumed it would be only Bill this round, but I was never going to see him again; I wanted to watch him pop one last time.

He was grinning again, forgetting our words, grateful for this bonus. And he was so appreciative of me, so delighted with my shoulders, ass and mouth, that I became hard too. Even then it was a willed lust, all nerves and friction, but I began to excite myself with the idea that anyone who enjoyed sex so much was not beyond hope, that I could bring this Republican to his senses. One more orgasm just might save him. It was pure fantasy, yet I wanted to believe it long enough to wring out my own farewell burst of joy.

6

"**I don't** get it. I just don't get it," Nick declared, but he was being rhetorical. Nick Rosi always got it. "How can the *Times* call itself liberal and use this lead for a news story?" He read a damning sentence about Clinton and an old real estate deal.

"We are most critical of those most like us?" I offered over my section of the paper.

"No," he said. "It goes back to the fact that their liberalism is all for show. An illusion of choice. They're as reactionary as the other fucks."

Peter sat with us, a tall, long-faced Picasso of the Blue Period quietly chewing toast while he skimmed Arts and Leisure.

"So why not read the *Post* or *News* instead?" I said. "At least we know where they're coming from."

"Because we need to know the current language of hypocrisy."

"And the *Times* has full-page underwear ads," Peter added.

It was Sunday and I was back in New York, eating breakfast with Nick and Peter in the glassed-in porch of a coffee shop on Cooper Square before Peter and I walked to work. Sheets of yesterday's paper tumbled and scraped in the concrete desert outside, as grim in winter as a square in East Berlin. At the entrance to St. Mark's Place across the way, the old four-story cartoon of a boho face with an eye patch and cigarette pouted on the blackboard-like side of a building.

Nick was in his mood, his all-knowing petulance. Short and dark, with a clone mustache of another era, he had a groomed, corporate look even on weekends in sweatshirt and jeans. Nick was a stockbroker who'd stepped down to be the office manager of a small accounting firm in order to have more time for activist work. His cool, professional certainty had once seemed magnetic to me when he stood to speak at ACT UP meetings, his anger full of purpose and hope. Now that ACT UP was dead—although he was furious if anyone said so except himself—his anger came out in machine-gun bursts that were not intended to persuade, only give him a righteous place to stand. I was no longer afraid to disagree with Nick.

"It's a game to all of them," he declared. "The *Times* is worse because they make it respectable. Entertain the populace with fake conflicts. Bread and circuses, without the bread. Every group gets its shot of fame, and you damn well better make yours count, because people get bored. They tricked us into wasting our shot with that gays-in-the-military shit. God knows what we have to do to get another chance."

"But the *Times* has changed," I insisted. "And for the better. This, for example." I read aloud from the obituary of a dancer. " 'He died of AIDS-related pneumonia, said his mother.' *His mother.* Remember when we had to decode it, when nobody called it what it was?"

"So what?" said Nick. "The silence is over and hasn't changed a damn thing except to make death respectable."

"I think it has," I claimed. "Just not as much as we hoped."

Peter wearily folded up the arts pages. "All I know is that death is boring. It's no fun anymore."

I glanced nervously at Nick. "Was it ever fun?" I asked.

Peter arched his eyebrows, surprised himself by what he'd said. "It didn't feel like it at the time," he admitted. "But now, in comparison, it was certainly new and exciting. The emotions it touched were new and exciting. So dramatic."

"Now it skips over emotion," I said.

He nodded. "And eats right into your soul."

"Will you two cut this morbid crap," snapped Nick.

Peter frowned. "What's morbid? Just the facts of life."

"It's maudlin. It's defeatist." Nick shifted in his chair. He swatted the front page with the back of his hand. "What gets me is how the military and now this Whitewater shit have been used to divert interest from issues—"

While Nick went off on a new tirade, Peter gave me a resigned, knowing look. "Right back," he said, and got up to visit the toilet.

Nick waited until he was around the corner. "It's not good when he gets like that. You shouldn't encourage him."

"When he gets like what? He was just talking about how it feels these days. I feel it too."

"That kind of talk is maudlin and decadent."

I attempted a disarming smile—confrontation did not come easily to me. "You remind me of my father, Nick. Whenever my grandmother talked about death, my grandfather's or her own, he always jumped in and changed the subject. He hated hearing any talk of dying. She had to wait until he was gone and she could talk with my mother or me."

"Peter's not an old lady with one foot in the grave."

"But if he wants to talk about it, why not let him?"

"Because it leads to self-pity."

"He seemed perfectly cool. And what's wrong with a little self-pity now and then?"

"You don't know him the way I do. If Peter begins to feel sorry for himself, it's the beginning of the end."

I didn't believe that. This policy of silence was about Nick, not Peter. His anger had been doubled, even tripled by fears for his lover, yet he'd lost his faith in the political uses of anger. He kept all his other emotions tightly reined in.

But couples are like foreign countries: You behave by

their rules whenever you visit. Peter returned and I obeyed Nick, resuming my account of Nancy's tales of gay Washington, playing up the accomplishments, playing down her frustration. "Looks like D.C. is the new center of gay politics," I said. "New York is becoming a backwater."

Nick twisted his mustache at me, taking the observation as a deliberate jab, which was how I intended it.

I did not dislike Nick. I was no longer infatuated, but I was still fond of him. I just needed to rebel against his authority now and then.

When it was time to go, Nick stood up to fuss with the wrap of Peter's long, tasseled scarf. "You sure you don't want to take a cab? Awfully windy today."

"I feel up for a brisk walk."

Nick kissed Peter on the lips, nodded good-bye to me, and sat down to renew his private war with the *Times*.

Broadway was a ghost canyon of empty sidewalks and closed storefronts at this hour. A harsh burn of smoke drifted from a pretzel cart being set up on the corner.

"That must be hard," I told Peter as we walked. "Nick never wanting you to talk about it. Even indirectly."

"Not really. Because I usually don't want to talk about it either."

I took the hint and didn't press. Peter marched with his head held high, his mouth pursed over the effort to feel healthy and unconcerned. Illness is like a clock whose ticking you don't hear until someone mentions it. It ticked very loudly now, but I knew we should enjoy the peace while it lasted. My one consolation was knowing that I would not be primary caregiver this time around.

"Gloomy Sunday," I said. "Maybe it'll keep the crowds down."

"So. You do anything else in D.C. besides jaw with Good Queen Wenceslas?"

"Oh, this and that."

"Yeeesss?" Peter purred. Here was something he wanted to talk about.

"Okay. I met Thersites."

"And?"

I shrugged. "Did him."

"Oooooh." A lewd smile split his face. "And?"

"Nothing to tell."

"Like hell. Who is he? What did he look like? Young, old, fat, thin?"

I had wanted to keep Bill a secret, a private mistake, but I needed to tell someone, and Peter was so eager to hear.

"He's twenty-eight."

"Nice ripe age. I thought he'd be older."

"But—" I took a deep breath. "You can't tell anyone this. Not a soul."

"That's no fun."

"Seriously. You can't tell Nick. Promise me that." I'd learned the hard way that couples were not one person except when their separateness was an absolute necessity.

"Why? Is it going to make him envious?" he scoffed.

"It might make him think less of me."

"Yeah?" He was obscenely interested now. "Okay. I promise. Not a word. To Nick or anyone else."

"All right." I had to build up to it. "I met him at the zoo. We went back to his place. We boffed. And then he told me he was a journalist. Who writes for *American Truths*."

"The right-wing rag that called Anita Hill a nympho?"

"Yup. We have met the enemy," I said. "And sucked his dick."

Peter laughed. "I hope he sucked yours."

"Oh yeah. Royally. A liberal-hating Republican who works with the homophobes. And it hurts to admit, but he was the most fun I've had in a long, long time."

"Doesn't surprise me. Selfishness can be a virtue in bed. Some of the best sex I ever had was with greedy pigs: executives and army officers and happily married men."

Knowing what Nick was like in bed, I was not surprised to hear Peter say that.

"He was greedy, but so was I," I admitted. "Only our greeds clicked."

"And he was a gorgeous blond preppy?"

"No. Irish-looking. Fleshy. Not conventionally attractive. But cute. I found him cute."

"Quick and dirty in the sack, I bet. But when it was over, he turned Catholic on you."

"No. He was hot but leisurely. Good kisser. And very affectionate afterward."

"Doesn't sound like the Irish closet cases I've known."

"No. He's a puzzle. He claimed he wasn't in the closet, but he must be to write for those people. He doesn't hang together."

"But he was hung?"

I frowned. "I don't care about that."

"Uh-huh. So when you seeing him again?"

"I'm not. We swapped phone numbers and addresses, but I trashed his. Just a one-afternoon stand."

"Why, if he was such hot sex?"

"Once you're a philosopher, twice you're a Republican. Or thrice maybe. We did it a couple of times."

"Ah youth," he said, without envy or resentment.

When Peter and I first bonded, after his suspicion and my guilt had been replaced by the discovery that we had more in common than Nick and I ever did—a love of good novels, bad movies and playing the fool now and then, things Nick never stooped to—I was shy over sharing my sex life with Peter, afraid to rub his face in what he no longer got. It turned out, however, that vicarious lust was what he wanted now, either from my present or his past. Any other kind was too complicated.

He shook his head at me. "Why be so damn scrupulous? It's not like you sucked off Rush Limbaugh. Just a little reporter, for God's sake. If it was me, I'd be back on that train next weekend. Political integrity be damned."

"You just think you would. And I'm hardly Mr. Integrity. But I can't go to bed with someone a second time without going to bed with the whole person. Their job and family and politics and favorite books."

"Jesus, Ralph. No wonder you're single."

We arrived at the bookstore and I had to shift into a

more responsible, adult persona. I was the acting manager on
Sundays. While I turned on lights, turned up the thermostat
and opened the safe, the staff trooped in, a pack of sulky
twenty-somethings, including Alec, my basement assistant, a
pasty straight boy with pierced nose and eyebrows and a
failed beard that suggested a toddler who'd crawled under
a bed with jam on his chin.

"This is a first, Alec. Never known you to be on time."

"Was already in the neighborhood," he said sheepishly.

Then I noticed that he was with Erica, a new employee,
and they had the self-conscious cool of two people who *may*
have spent the night together—I seemed keenly alert to
everyone else's love life this morning.

Peter took his post at the telephone desk in the back. It
was a slow morning, but we didn't talk again until my lunch
break, when he found me reading at my desk in the basement.

"Giving up the Victorians for the Elizabethans?" he
asked.

"Never read this one." I showed him the paperback of
Troilus and Cressida that I'd found upstairs. "You know me," I
said. "A promiscuous range of intellectual interests."

I hadn't really lied to Peter. I still intended to toss Bill's
number. When I returned to Nancy's apartment Thursday
night, all lust and curiosity about Bill had been safely flushed
from my system. The next afternoon I sat in on a hearing of
the Senate Banking Committee, where Nancy played shadow
to Senator Freeman in a sluggish theater piece performed to
a nearly empty house. That night I ate pizza with Nancy and
an aide—although not the boy in the pink shirt—while she
fiddled with the final wording of the Pittsburgh speech,
reading and rereading it aloud to me. We spent Saturday
wandering from café to café, continuing our examination of
love and work. She was certain now that her crush had been
only a case of spilt job anxiety, that the talking cure had
ended it. Nancy asked about my adventure, but she assumed
such encounters were a simple matter of penises. She shook
her head over how little I'd learned about a guy I said I'd met

at Lambda Rising Bookstore. Not until I was riding the train home that night did I think about Bill again, amusing myself with a regret that I hadn't swung by his apartment for one last throw after saying good-bye to Nancy.

There was no trace of his affectionate body in an oddly nasty play by Shakespeare, a cynical riff on characters from the *Iliad*. Thersites turned out to be an ugly clown kicked around by Ajax, Ulysses and Achilles; the last was clearly homosexual, but all were shits. Thersites was a truth teller of a sort, but a very narrow sort, pathologically obsessed with other people's lechery. I couldn't tell if Bill was simply a bad reader or more self-mocking than he seemed in person. I needed his function keys to tell me "(joke)" and "(gentle laughter)."

"Hey, Sergeant Rock."

"How was DC?"

"Do anything or one special?"

The Monday night gang in Gayworld wanted the dirt. I remained coy and Shanghai Lily did not give me away. Nobody had much news, but I stayed on the chatline for two hours on the chance that Thersites might drop in and I could cross-examine him on Shakespeare. He didn't, which was just as well. There was no word from him in my E-mail either.

We had a staff meeting Tuesday to discuss the Christmas schedule. Thanksgiving was two days off, marking the start of six-day workweeks, overtime and an escalating madness that left no room for thought. I took perverse pleasure in this time of year, all conscious life suspended for five weeks in a kind of blue-collar Zen.

I did not think about Bill all day until I stopped by my local newsstand after work and saw *American Truths* in the rack. With a glossy black cover and fastidious columns of print broken by collages of diced photos, it looked respectable enough. Bill had nothing in this issue, but was listed in the staff box: William O'Connor, Jr. The newsstand had only three copies—this *was* the East Village. I bought one, just to have something to read while I ate my Chinese takeout, with a blush similar to what I'd felt when I purchased my first skin magazine.

Initially, it seemed only slightly worse than *The Village Voice*, as glib and self-congratulatory, frequently damning the same people the *Voice* damned, yet for entirely different reasons and with fewer facts. But while it was difficult to tell what the *Truths* writers were for, it quickly became clear what they were against: Clinton, liberals, the media, feminists, black guiltmongers, environmentalists and gay activists—which suggested inactivists might be tolerated, which perhaps left room for Bill.

The magazine was not excitingly evil, merely slippery and tedious. Nevertheless, I left it on the floor by my futon while I masturbated, needing to test its effect on the sensory snapshots in my head: plush skin, a double-barreled cock, an open smile. Bill was good porn, nothing else. Feeling more foolish than usual after a wank, I pulled up my gym shorts, threw his magazine in the trash and went back to Trollope.

There were two huge shipments from wholesalers on Wednesday. Alec and I spent the morning playing stevedore, loading and unloading solid boxes of books in the wheelos that we sent up and down on the freight elevator in the sidewalk. Alec, usually so resentful and listless, enjoyed the butch game of heavy manual labor as much as I did. We heaved and yoed, swaggered and scratched. The last wheelo sank below the pavement, the iron doors closed shut. I went back inside, high on muscular exertion and covered with sweat. Peter called me over to the phone desk.

"We need your signature, dear," he said with a leer.

A delivery man in a bow tie thrust a clipboard at me. I saw a large foil-wrapped bundle on the counter.

"I didn't order anything," I said.

Peter laughed. "You don't order flowers, dummy. You're sent them."

I wiped a hand on my sweatshirt and nervously signed my name. I timidly peeled the foil back an inch. Yes, flowers. Garish red roses.

"They won't bite," said Peter. "Here." He lifted the glass

vase they were in so I could pull the foil off. "Who're they from? There's a card. Read the card. Hasn't anyone ever sent you flowers?"

"Never." I opened a small white square of cardboard. "Shit. They're from Thersites."

"Ah. *Him.*"

The card said simply: "I won't be in New York until after New Year. I sent these so you might remember me. Warmly, Bill."

"What the hell am I supposed to do with flowers?" I grumbled.

"Take them home. Take them down to your desk. They're roses. You don't have to do a thing with them."

"Do you want them?"

"No. They were sent to you."

"Would you like a couple?" I needed to share my complicity.

"They're yours, Ralph. Enjoy them. Or throw them out. They're meaningless to anyone else. They're a show of his affection for you."

"I guess. How much do you think this cost?"

"Forty, fifty dollars." Peter grinned and shook his head. "Second time must have been a lulu."

I gingerly carried the cylinder of trembling stalks down-stairs, annoyed with Bill, strangely humiliated by his gift. I set the gratuitous flowers on my desk. The thorny, lobster green stems were magnified by glass and water; the unfurled knots of red velvet nodded overhead. They looked surreal beside the yellowed UPS rate chart Scotch-taped to the wall. I imag-ined keeping them there for their absurdity.

"Somebody sent *you* flowers?" said Alec.

"What of it?"

"No, it's kind of, uh, sweet."

"But corny," I said. "Very corny."

"Hey. Kitsch can be fun. So long as you know it's kitsch."

"This is definitely kitsch," I agreed.

And the worst kitsch was me. Because I had to admit that I was touched someone liked me so much that he'd sent roses. I never dreamed I could be so cheap. Love's most banal signifier, yet I was as giddily unnerved as a boy in junior high receiving a valentine from another boy. It wasn't as if I'd never been loved. I had, for weeks and months at a time. Just not so conventionally, or from such an inappropriate source.

All right, I thought. Let's see where this goes. January was a long way off. There was no telling where our heads or pricks would be by then. I sent a card that afternoon— "Thanks for the flowers. I'll certainly remember you"— tucked inside a copy of *Cures* by Martin Duberman. I wanted Bill to know who and what I was, daring him to remain interested. I almost sent him *The Epistemology of the Closet*, yet that seemed much too blunt, and I'd been unable to read more than fifty pages of it myself.

7

Temperatures plunged after Thanksgiving; the world froze. Newspapers, radio and television agreed that the winter was the coldest since the Great Depression. There was snow in December. Peter came to work every day by cab. The locusts of Christmas swarmed, then vanished with the New Year; the store became a cold tomb of books. I spent my evenings at home, drinking hot tea and burrowing through Palliser novels. The streets of the East Village, a moonscape of white and black glass, were deserted by nine each night. The homeless disappeared into shelters and the forgotten corners of train stations. The fluorescent lights of the subway platforms froze gray in their tubes.

At a time when the sun seemed to have died, the thought of a warm body in a warm bed became a beautiful necessity.

"So how have you been?"

"Good. Excellent, in fact. And yourself?"

"I can't complain."

I'd arrived at his room at noon. It was now three and our nudities were still tangled under the blankets. Even his

expensive hotel could not produce enough heat in this ice
age for guests to remain uncovered after afternoon trysts. We
had said little more than hello when Bill opened the door
and our grins merged. His body was as excited and grabby as
mine, although I was also driven by a fear that talk might
dilute biology.

"And you're free all night?" he asked again.

"I left tonight wide open."

"I have this brief meeting in the lobby at five. But afterward I'm all yours."

"Great," I said, and meant it. I needed to see who Bill
was, out of bed and outside my head. We'd spoken only a few
times by E-mail in December, cramped postcard notes, and
once by phone. He called to thank me for my gift, unthreat-
ened by it, but conversation was awkward without our bodies
to explain what we wanted from each other. His telephone
voice was clipped and formal, as if he'd learned it off FM
radio. He grew more distracted the longer we spoke. When I
asked if someone else was in the apartment, he apologized
for being preoccupied with his galley proofs. "I can give
myself to only one occupation at a time," he explained. That
was fine with me. He was not the most important fact in my
life either.

"So what did you think of the Duberman?" I now asked.

"I've been too busy to read it. But I will."

"Your own book?"

"Done. My editor is very excited. He took me around the
offices yesterday and introduced me as someone special."

"Is that why you're so happy today?"

"One reason." A soft sole caressed my calf.

We spoke comfortably now about the most trivial
things, an amiable noise accompanying the real dialogue of
shared skin.

"Did you have a good Christmas?" he asked.

"Working retail burns the romance out of the holidays.
But the store had a good Christmas."

"Should that matter to you?"

"It's my job. I don't want them to go out of business."

"Someone with your brains could do better than retail."

I enjoyed hearing him say that, though he knew little of my brains or much else about me.

I'd come uptown eager to see Bill again, first to learn if the sex was as good as I remembered, then to discover what, if anything, existed on the other side of sex. I'd been right about his smooth skin and avid kissing, but wrong about other things. His face looked neither round nor cherubic but indescribably Billish, open and affectionate, with chestnut brown eyes I didn't remember from our first meeting. His cock no longer felt shotgunlike in my hand; the familiarity of touch had rubbed away its edges. There was a disquieting moment when he broke off to whisper, "You're negative, aren't you? I want you to come in my mouth," and I was thrown that he hadn't already figured that out, that we didn't play by the same rules.

"Did you see your family?" he asked.

"No. I only get two days off and they're down in Raleigh."

"Your mother wasn't hurt that you weren't there?"

"She understands. And both my brothers and their families were down, so it's not like Uncle Ralph was missed. I'm a fly in Dad's eggnog anyway. He enjoys the holidays more when I'm not there to suggest father *doesn't* know best." I rolled my eyes and sighed. I actually found my father's nervous silences comic and forgivable. I'd outgrown any need for his approval.

"Well, I spent Christmas with my family," said Bill. "They're in Baltimore and I see them every other weekend. But my mother makes Christmas a special treat. She's an angel. I'm all my parents have, you see. My mother's always been wise and supportive, but recently I've made my father respect me too. He disliked journalism before I went into it."

I nodded indifferently. We were engaged in the gentle blasphemy of using family for postcoital conversation, a way of taming them, only family clearly meant more to Bill. I've never understood gay men who need to define themselves as sons after they've left home. Nancy thought I was "amiably alienated" from my own family, and maybe I was, but there is no dignity in grown-ups loving, or hating, their parents too much.

"But you poor guy," he said. "You spent Christmas alone."

"No. With friends. We went to a movie and had our Christmas orphans dinner afterward."

"Your Senate friend didn't visit while Congress was out?"

"No. She had to go to the Virgin Islands on business."

"One of those federal junkets disguised as work?"

"No, this was work. A so-called health conference held by the insurance industry."

"She went with Senator Freeman?"

"No. All by her lonesome. And she hates hotels, so it wasn't her idea of a vacation."

No longer listening, he laid his head on my chest and wrapped his arms snugly around my waist.

Having pulled a doubleheader our first time, we patiently waited for our bodies to recharge so we could do it again. This was about sex, I told myself, just sex. I felt pleasantly stupid with sex. Yet there was affection too, a fondness that began as lust but lingered afterward.

" 'He eats nothing but doves,' " I said, " 'and that breeds hot blood, and hot blood begets hot thoughts, and hot thoughts beget hot deeds, and hot deeds is love.' "

"Huh?"

"Troilus and Cressida."

He looked suspicious. "You read it?"

"Right after we met," I admitted. "You put yourself down by calling yourself Thersites, you know."

"How do you mean?"

"He's kind of a clown. Isn't he?"

"Not at all. He's the one honest man in the entire play."

The telephone rang before I could explain. On the second ring Bill pulled free to crawl across the bed, as wide as his bed in Washington. It was as though we'd never left that first bed.

"Hello? Jeb, hello! Quite well, thank you. I very much look forward to seeing you at five."

His FM voice with its absurdly precise enunciation was back. Up on all threes and out of the blankets, he contradicted the voice with his ass, a flattened white peach with a pink pawprint of toothmarks lingering on its left cheek.

"Now? Of course, yes. I understand. Only—um. Could you give me ten minutes? I just returned from the hotel gym and haven't changed. Very good then. The Oak Bar. Ten minutes."

He hung up and swung out of bed.

"Drat. My five o'clock is downstairs and can only fit me in now. Drat drat drat." He stumbled around the room, picking up my underpants, then his own before saying, "I better wash off. Sorry." He hurried into the bathroom. "Open my Powerbook and turn it on," he called out. "There's a date I need."

His bossy command took me by surprise, but I spotted his laptop on the Empire-style desk by the window and automatically threw back the covers. The cold air slapped me awake. We were at the Plaza Hotel, something else I kept forgetting. I walked barefoot through a lush carpet and saw the trees and snow of Central Park in a fog of silk curtains. "Who did you say is paying for this room?"

"My publisher. They said I could have whatever I wanted on this trip. I wanted to feel like F. Scott Fitzgerald."

"They must love your book." Knowing how miserly most publishing houses were, I wondered if someone else provided this perk. I seemed to be one more luxury item on a visit to New York.

I popped open his computer, its anonymous gray lid personalized with a little air force decal from an airplane model. After much hunting and fumbling, I found the switch and flicked it on.

There was a chiming of coat hangers around the corner as Bill quickly dressed.

"What file do you need?" My finger played with the mouse, a buried ball rolling like a testicle.

"I'll get it."

"Who's this guy you're seeing?"

"A political consultant but more. A one-man think tank. A very helpful, useful fellow. A good friend, in fact."

Bill returned to the room in gray wool slacks, blue suit jacket and a candy-striped shirt without a tie. He caged his eyes with his black-wired glasses and the look was complete: a pampered, casual, Republican look.

"You must be freezing," he scolded. "Get back in bed."

I did but the covers were not as warmly narcotic as before.

He bent over the desk and diddled the keyboard. "Right!" he told his screen. "Shoes. Where're my shoes?" He saw the loafers by the bed and came over. He thrust his crisply combed head in my face. "Can you smell us in my hair?"

I smelled only scented gel. "You're safe," I said, a barb in my voice.

He grinned obliviously. "You won't go away?" he teased, as if that were unimaginable. He leaned in for a quick kiss.

I kissed back hard and tried to throw an arm around his neck, suddenly annoyed with him and wanting to spoil his appointment. He ducked away, laughing.

"Business before pleasure. This will take thirty minutes. Maybe less. I promise." He stepped backward, blushing and beaming, sincere in his regret to leave me like this.

The door clicked shut and I was alone. Stranded in an enormous bed in an expensive room in a once distinguished, now gaudy hotel. What the hell was I doing here?

I grimaced and snorted at myself. I could still feel guilt, but the weight amused me, even excited me, as if I were cheating on a lover. I had no lover, but I did have my political principles. Cheating on those was as exciting as cheating on a boyfriend. But what were my principles? A distrust of wealth. A fear of Republicans. A desperate, Godot-like faith in the Democrats. All seemed irrelevant to a few hours of fun with a horny young journalist. I was not afraid for my virtue. I was the older man and could hold my own. And shifting the guilt, adding to the thrill, was the idea that Bill cheated on his principles by sleeping with me.

I regretted that I hadn't sucked a lurid hickey on his neck, so his important visitor might know what he'd interrupted on a wintry Saturday afternoon. What were they discussing downstairs anyway? Money or politics or public relations, which passed for politics after the age of Reagan.

I grew restless lounging in the warm corruption of soft sheets and heavy blankets. I got up and pulled my scratchy ski sweater over the gummed hair of my stomach. The Powerbook remained open on the desk, its screen full of electrified mother-of-pearl. I parked my bare ass in the chair to look at it.

Bill had left a calendar file open. "February 24: Flight 2734 to Miami 2:35 pm.—AFC Conference, Omni Hotel." I scrolled back up, wondering if there'd be diary entries on days already past. No, it was all appointments and upcoming events: "February 19: Dr. Leavis, tooth cleaning." "February 5: Mama's birthday." "January 15: Plaza Hotel, Ralph E. noon, Jeb 5 pm." Did I require an initial because he had another Ralph in his life?

I made a quick dissolve into the main catalog, wondering if there was anything about me here. I found no listing for "ralph" or "eckhart" or "tricks." There was a string of "regiment1," "regiment2," on up to "regiment5," and a file labeled "thersites." Maybe there? I went in. It was just a page with his pseudonym, codes and basic instructions on how to use a chatline.

The laptop was so explorable that I was tempted to peek at "regiment"—notes for his book?—but I suddenly felt ashamed over rifling in his digital drawers. I quickly closed down, feeling first virtuous, then glad that I'd found nothing to spoil my visit, whether stale prose or bad ideology.

I went to my coat and fished *The Eustace Diamonds* from the pocket. I climbed back into bed to read, but my eyes slid off the page into my thoughts. Why didn't I either confront Bill's politics or ignore them? What kind of game was I playing with myself? What did I want from him? What did I

fear? This was more complicated than sex, wasn't it? I tried
out the idea that I was falling in love, yet that seemed too
ridiculous. I lowered my face to his pillow, but Bill was like
any good aroma, that of an orange, for example, which you
can smell only so long before your olfactory nerves are satu-
rated and the nose goes blank.

I returned to Trollope and was actually following Lucy
Greystock's conniving when I heard the key. The door
opened and shut softly around the corner. Bill did not come
into the room. The fluorescent light in the bathroom sputtered on. I heard him pee and flush. I waited a minute, then
got out of bed and stepped to the door. Had he forgotten I
was here?

He stood in the pink quartz bathroom, a solemn young
man studying his faces in the triple mirrors around the sink.

"How was your meeting?"

He jumped, slapping a hand to his chest before he
turned and saw me. "Oh God. You startled me."

"You forget you had a guest?" I was annoyed, even hurt
that my presence could take him by surprise.

"No, I just—I thought you were asleep. I needed a
minute to change modes after—" He frowned at me. "The
meeting went fine. Much news and useful information.
Although I was slightly distracted." He tried to smile, but he
still seemed distracted, blinking at a man who was rudely
nude from the waist down. "I wanted you to be asleep," he
complained. "So I could slip back into bed and we'd never
know I was gone."

"Sorry to disappoint you." His air of annoyance annoyed
me. I was full of petty, inexplicable irritation. I didn't know
what to do with my aggravation except step up and embrace
him from behind.

"No. Wait. Oh." He fearfully watched the mirror as I ran
my tongue in a blushing gutter of ear.

"Where's your head now?" I whispered.

He relaxed against me and I instantly felt better. I
peeled off my sweater to rub against his wool and buttons
while we kissed. I kept us turned toward the mirrors so he

had to see who we were: two men necking, one of us raw, the other in a hypocrisy of nice Republican clothes. The mirrors replicated and extended us in long chambered curves. My nose kept knocking his glasses so I took them off and set them on the sink, forgetting how blind he was. He couldn't see us when I steered him to his knees, but I watched, enjoying the classic image of a naked thug arching his back and dimpling his ass while he was serviced by a well-dressed superior. Then I looked down and saw Bill, his eyes trustingly closed, his mouth open and vulnerable. I tenderly pulled him up, away from the obscene mirrors and back to bed.

We went down to the East Village for dinner, at Bill's request. He wanted to see my neighborhood, he said, wanted to know my life. His curiosity pleased me, although he was alarmed when I suggested we take the subway. He had an out-of-towner's horror of the underground and insisted we catch a cab.

Not until we got out at East Eleventh Street did I think about running into people I knew, but nobody idly strolled the icy sidewalks, and it wasn't like Bill had a swastika on his forehead. He wore a presentably collegiate sweater and jeans under his new parka. I decided to risk the Ukrainian Polish restaurant I frequented with friends, a bright, high-ceilinged place full of cabbage steam, young artist types and solitary diners who scribbled poetry while they ate. It suggested a working-class bohemia with roots in the thirties, a Hart Crane–Jack Kerouac New York that was more wish than reality nowadays, but I needed it after the Plaza.

We found a table by a plate-glass window zigzagged with ice crystals. Bill took in the noise and grubby faces and the Russian primitive mural with a polite smile. "But the food's good?"

"Very. And cheap."

"I wanted this to be my treat."

"I don't want you spending money on me. But thank you."

He looked miffed. I couldn't let him buy me, but I

didn't want to insult him either. I gently explained what items on the menu were good. When he ordered, he adopted the bossy tone of a businessman who feared that strangers would get second best.

It was odd seeing Bill in my terrain. His face looked thicker, an opaque mask of baby fat. All that remained from our hours in bed were the brown pupils peeking between fat eyelids. We'd spent more time together naked than clothed. I could not decide if nudity was the reality or another disguise. We needed to talk when we were dressed and vertical. I needed to know how deep his interest in me went, if he was playing a game similar to mine.

"You like me, don't you?" I said.

He laughed as if I'd made a silly joke. "It's possible."

"Why?"

"Why not? Why do you like *me*?" He made it sound as childish as "Why is the sky blue?"

"I don't know," I said bluntly. "I thoroughly enjoy being in bed with you."

He frowned as if I'd said something dirty.

"And you're a good kisser. And—" I was surprised by how quickly I ran through his attractions. "You're happy. You're cheerful. Maybe that's it. Everybody else I know is bitter or melancholy. It's nice to be with someone who enjoys his life."

"I can be very cheerful," he admitted. "Especially now."

Me? I hoped not. "Your book?" I said.

"That's part of it. The most recent episode of how far I've come." He warmed to the subject of himself. "You met me at the right time, Ralph. If you had met me in college, you would've found a very different fellow. Miserable and neurotic. A Gloomy Gus who hated everyone, himself included. A great big *nerd*"—he had to spit the word to get it out—"whom the cool gay guys never noticed. I was afraid to want anything, as if I didn't have the right."

"Not even sex? The paperboy's hustler?" I reminded him.

He chuckled and lowered his eyes. "I went through a, um, latency period in college. Stupid Catholic guilt. But nothing succeeds like success. I needed accomplishment, something to stand upon before I could be myself. I found it as a journalist and it unlocked me. Ambition isn't a bad thing, Ralph. It gives one purpose, makes life an adventure. It's exciting to want things and go out and get them. Fame and riches," he said with a sheepish grin. "And the company of attractive men."

He made his success sound so healthy and liberating that I wished I could celebrate it with him.

"I've looked at *American Truths*," I said.

"You've read me?" His eyes widened.

"Not yet. Recent issues with nothing of yours." Why hadn't I read him? It would've been easy enough to find back issues at the library. "I still don't understand how you, as a gay man, can write for those people."

He kept his smile. "Their bark is worse than their bite. They're an intelligent, well-educated bunch."

I had to break through the courtesy even if it ended my fun. "But the magazine is written by and for straight white men. Everyone else is the enemy."

"That's not true. Which writers did you read?"

"It wasn't one in particular. It's the general tone, the assumptions under the tone."

"I don't agree with everything they print." He was not nearly as defensive as he'd been two months ago. "They're not antigay."

"No?"

"Critical," he admitted. "But not of all gay people. Just a certain element."

"What if I'm a member of that element?"

Not even that fazed him. "Then you skip those articles. I do. I write for *Truths* because the editors let me write what I want to write. I'm an investigative reporter. My beat is corruption. The only axe I grind is the truth."

"Republican or Democrat corruption?"

"Both."

"Whose corruption is your book about?"

"The Democrats. Because they're the ones in power. Surely you don't think the Clintons are paragons of virtue?"

"No. But they're the best hope we've had in the past twelve years." I fell into his habit of referring to Clinton as if his wife were president too.

"Wait until you read my book," he said.

"When can I? Are there bound galleys?"

"Not yet. They're treating them like gold when they are available. They don't want too many people seeing it before pub. I don't even know if I'll get one."

"All right. I can wait and read it when everyone else does." The truth was I dreaded reading his book, not just for its politics but for the fact that it would be journalism, gray and dreary, acceptable for newspapers but numbing in book form. I wondered if I'd be able to finish it.

Our food arrived. Bill did not condescend to his cutlet and potato pancakes but ate with obvious enjoyment. There was nothing fussy about his table manners.

"Ralph? What are these questions really about?"

It took me a moment to understand what he meant. "I want to know who you are."

"Why?" He was grinning again.

"I like to know who I've been—kissing."

"My book and the Clintons have nothing to do with us."

Was there an us? Did he take my questions as a declaration of love? "They have something to do with you. I'd like to know more about you."

"This is a real New York conversation, isn't it?" He shook his head and laughed. "What do you want to do with *your* life?"

"Pardon?"

"What are your ambitions?"

I was surprised to have myself made the subject.

"I know so little about *you*," he explained. "I'm curious too. What do you want from life?"

I shrugged. "Just to live. To be happy."

"To what purpose?"

"No purpose."

"You've never had ambitions for success or fame?"

"I once wanted to be famous as a poet," I confessed. "Which is a tiny fame. Like wanting to be famous as a champion bowler."

He gave my joke the brief maraca laugh it deserved.

"But I was too literal to be a good poet. Too prosaic. My poetry was all self-conscious knots and secondhand phrases. I got no pleasure in writing it, so I put it aside. Maybe I'll go back to it one day, when I have more faith in my own words."

"What did you replace it with?"

"Life itself. Friendship. Love now and then. Sex," I quickly added. "Books. I get more pleasure reading than I ever got from writing." I heard how trifling that sounded. "They say poetry makes nothing happen. So maybe I'm still a poet."

"And doing good? You once told me you liked to do good."

I must have said that in one of my more righteous moments. I did not feel righteous tonight. "Oh, now and then. When the opportunity presents itself. Like last year. A man I worked with at the bookstore became sick, and I took care of him. I didn't do much," I explained. "There wasn't much I could do. Except visit him in the hospital, help with the home care and paperwork, contact his family. Arrange the funeral."

Bill looked uncomfortable, even embarrassed. "He was a good friend?"

"Not really. Alberto was good company when other people were around, but we were never close. Until he became sick. A snippy young queen from Indiana. Nastily funny when he had an audience, but with nothing to fall back on when he was alone. A difficult person to be with when he was ill."

"Then why did you do it?"

"Because he had nobody else. When he first went into the hospital, I found I was the only person visiting him. No lover, no friends. I did it as much for me as for him," I insisted. "First for the experience. Lovers of friends had died, and acquaintances and neighbors, always at a distance. And out of duty: I thought it was time I did *more*. I felt quite virtuous during his first stay, very pleased with myself walking to the hospital each day. But that wore off by the second stay, then the third. I continued because I'd committed myself, and because I felt I'd be all paid up when it was over."

"Paid for what?"

It was hard to explain, it seemed such a natural, human need. "I don't know. My friend Peter says one can't feel guilty for living. And I don't. But I did feel I'd had it easy and owed people something and could balance the account with Alberto. It didn't work that way. It was a humbling experience, a lesson in helplessness. I did what I could, and it wasn't much."

"Well, I think it was admirable," said Bill. "Noble."

"It wasn't noble. Just one of those things you do because *not* doing it makes you feel worse." I hadn't intended to say so much about Alberto. Bill should know that I was more than sex and politics, but I was unsure what the story said about me or what he might make of it. He gave me a sad, quizzical look of admiration, but he remained uncomfortable, intimidated by what I'd done. He seemed so innocent, so young.

"You have no goals now?" he asked. "Nothing solid? For example, don't you want a boyfriend?"

"I've had boyfriends," I said, surprised by the new topic.

"But a real one. Someone with whom you'd want to spend the rest of your life."

He shyly stepped past death to sniff out my intentions about *him*. We resumed playing poker with our hearts.

"I've had too many boyfriends to think like that anymore. I know myself too well." I decided to be blunt. "I should tell you, Bill, I'm not boyfriend material."

"I wasn't thinking that," he said with a laugh. "I enjoy being with you. But I don't think of you like that. You flatter yourself," he added, without nastiness, only his serene housecat smile.

"And I enjoy being with you," I told him. "Today."

There, we'd said it—we'd both declared a lack of romantic motives. We smiled at each other and resumed eating. I believed him and was relieved. This could get messy if one of us was more serious than the other.

"Would you like to come with me to Miami next month?"

He proposed it as idly as a trip to Coney Island.

I laughed. "You've heard how I live. I can't afford to zip down to Florida. But thank you just the same."

"I'll take care of it. Or rather, the people who're flying me will pay. I've been invited to a conference. To promote my book. I'm allowed to bring a spouse. Or a personal assistant."

"You're serious?"

"Truly."

"What kind of conference?"

"A Republican thing," he admitted blithely. "But I only have to make one appearance. The rest of the weekend is mine."

"Who's paying for it?"

"The conference. Hence the 'personal assistant' euphemism. There's no such thing as 'spousal equivalent' in the GOP."

"Won't that make you complicitous in political corruption?" I said to mark time before I refused his invitation.

"Just an airplane ticket. And when in Rome . . ."

"It's tempting," I said. "Very. But—" I frowned. I sighed. "Oh hell. Why not?"

"You will?" he said. "You want to?"

I did, and I understood my pride well enough to realize that if I said no I would later say yes. I should save myself the loss of face that would come of changing my mind.

"Be nice to go somewhere warm," I said. "I've never been to Miami. And it'd be nice to see you again. When would this be?"

"Last weekend in February. They'll fly you out of D.C. or Baltimore, not New York, but that won't be a problem, will it? I have to make a phone call or two, but I can't imagine them refusing."

"If they do, no problem." The possibility that this might not happen made it easier to accept. I enjoyed the joke of the

Republicans bankrolling a weekend of sodomy, but didn't share it with Bill.

"We should probably pay and go," I said. "There's people waiting for this table. Can I take you to a real New York gay bar? My favorite bar is a few blocks over." Since he was showing me his world, I should show him more of mine, although it was too early for any of my crowd to be at Wonderbar.

"I don't like bars."

"You don't go to any in D.C.?"

"Never."

"Then how do you meet guys?"

"There're other ways." He aimed his grin at me.

"So how many men have you had sex with?"

He laughed uncomfortably. "What a question! I've never sat down and tallied it, if you must know."

I'd counted mine but, since he didn't ask, I didn't volunteer the number. "We pay up front," I said as I stood and put on my coat.

I was halfway to the register before I noticed, among the bundled people thawing inside the door, the dark eyes and wet mustache of Nick Rosi. He was already watching us. He lifted a black-gloved hand and smirked knowingly at the baby-faced boy at my heels.

"Nick, hi! What brings you to this end of town? Cold night like this?" I said more loudly than necessary.

"Maura and I wanted to compare notes before our committee meeting next week. You remember Ralph?" he asked the stocky redheaded woman beside him, Maura Morris, who sometimes wrote for the *Voice*. She wiped her fogged glasses with a big knit mitten.

"Right. Haven't seen you lately at meetings, Ralph."

"Sorry. Time and work and other things." I did not want to get into that conversation.

Nick was checking out Bill, half a head taller than he was.

"This is Bill," I explained. "My friend Nick. His friend Maura." I left off their last names on the slight chance that one of them might have heard of the other.

Nick and Bill scanned each other as they shook hands, Bill wary, Nick amused. Maura looked bored, as if a dog-loving friend had stopped to fuss over a spaniel on the street.

"You live in New York?" Nick asked while I hurriedly paid.

"Washington," Bill said in his stuffiest voice. "I'm up for the weekend on business."

"Spic-and-span D.C.," Nick scoffed. "This must be like the lower depths for you."

"It's different," Bill snootily declared.

"Uh-huh. Well. Have a nice visit." Nick decided this boy was not worth his time. "Maura and I were talking attrition, Ralph. We could really use someone who knows the ropes on our committee. Couldn't we, Maura?"

This was for her benefit; Nick no longer pressured me when we were alone.

"Definitely," said Maura. "Too many alpha wolves and not enough betas. And most of the alphas have walked."

"I wasn't good for much except stuffing envelopes," I said.

"Stuffing envelopes is good," said Nick. "Not as much fun as stuffing other things, but necessary." He grinned lewdly.

"Got to go," I said. "I'll think about it." I put a hand at Bill's back to send him out.

"So we shouldn't expect you at breakfast tomorrow?"

"Probably not. But I'll see Peter at work. Good night."

I followed Bill outside into a gust of arctic air and dumb remorse. Who cared if two contradictory pieces of my life had just met and stared straight through each other? So what if I spent a weekend in Miami while my friends froze?

Bill stepped away from me, pulling up his hood and turning his back to the wind.

"I live around the corner," I told him. "I'd invite you up, but the place is a mess."

"Cold," he said. "Why don't we go back to the hotel? You are coming back, aren't you?"

"Of course." Had I said something wrong?

"I thought you might change your mind after seeing your pals," he said haughtily.

"Don't be silly. They have nothing to do with—us."

"I didn't like them. I could tell they didn't like me."

"But they don't even know you." Thank God.

"The way that guy looked at me. Like I was an insect."

"Nick looks at everyone like that. He looks at me like that." Which was true, but I wondered if Bill had picked up on something I missed. Did Nick know who Bill was? No, he would've torn into him if he had.

I went to the curb to flag down a cab that skated to a halt. I held the door open and Bill climbed in. He sat stiffly while I gave directions to the driver. My kicking and poking at his magazine didn't threaten Bill, but a nasty look from Nick Rosi was enough to send him into a sulk.

"New Yorkers," I claimed. "We're not as polite as people in other cities."

"Is he an old boyfriend?"

"Nick? Oh no. Not Nick. We know each other from ACT UP. His lover works with me at the bookstore."

"I see." Bill took my hand and held it in his lap. He thumbed my knuckles through the glove. "Sorry. I don't know why I reacted to him like that. Except I hate it when people look down their nose at me. I know you have this other life that has nothing to do with me. I certainly have mine."

"Which I'll get to see in Miami," I said.

He clutched my hand tightly, reassured to remember that. "I'm not going to inflict them on you. We'll have better things to do than hobnob with politicos and blue-haired ladies."

By the time we walked through the white dazzle and red carpets of the lobby at the Plaza, Bill had regained his smooth cheerfulness, although I was still confused by his hatred of Nick and my feeling that I'd been disloyal to someone, either Nick or Bill, I wasn't sure which.

It was early, but I proposed we get ready for bed. We brushed our teeth, then undressed on opposite sides of the mattress, nonchalantly stripping to our underwear, then stripping off that as well. Sex had become as automatic for us as breathing. When we met again under the covers, however, I placed my hand against his chest and looked into his eyes for a moment. I liked him again. I was glad to have his body back. If this Bill ever flowed into the Bill of the vertical world then our affair would be more real, but also disruptive, even dangerous. We resumed kissing and nothing else mattered to me except seeing his face go blank with bliss one more time.

Afterward, we turned out the light and fitted ourselves together. It often takes a night or two for my body to grow accustomed enough to another person for me to sleep comfortably. Bill promptly dozed off, holding my arm across his chest like a teddy bear. I quickly joined him.

I woke only once that night, when he began to twitch and moan in his sleep, like a dog dreaming of punishment. I rubbed his chest and drew him to my side, and we sank back down into oblivion.

8

"**Who's the** real enemy? We cannot forget our real enemy. Not Jesse Helms. Not that two-faced coward in the White House. Not the turncoat Log Cabin queers of the Republican Party. No, our most powerful, scurrilous foe in the war against AIDS is—John Cardinal O'Connor!"

The drumroll of names by the speaker, a young woman with the short speckled hair of a baby chick, prepared us for a fresh new villain, not that tired old bogeyman in skirts. There were enough ex-Catholics in the audience, however, for the claps to outweigh the yawns. In the aisle seat beside me, Nick seethed like an ulcer.

This was my first ACT UP meeting in over a year. Numbers had been dropping when I dropped out. They no longer needed the Cooper Union auditorium in my neighborhood for the weekly general meeting but had moved back to their first home, the assembly room of the Community Center in the West Village. Even here, under the white tin ceiling and cast-iron columns as thin as birthday candles, half the folding chairs were empty.

Meetings were once as exhilarating as the trial by sansculottes in *A Tale of Two Cities*—if you were a sansculotte—their energy almost compensating for the hours required to reach the simplest decision. Now people actually took turns to talk, not because they were more disciplined but because they had less to say. Gone were the speakers who hoped to piggyback this cause with campaigns against racism, sexism and class. The humpy beauties no longer came either; there were few licorice black leather jackets tonight and no sixty-dollar haircuts. Despite their torn jeans and earrings, the two white boys facilitating tonight's meeting suggested a pair of student-council presidents. When they opened with the ritual announcement that police or FBI agents were required by law to identify themselves, Nick had grumbled, "As if such people would waste their time here."

Nick had pressed me hard this week about joining him tonight. It was already February and I was definitely going to Miami. I attended the meeting thinking that it might be good for me, like going to church. I listened piously, sheepishly, but my chief emotion was nostalgia for the old illusion that sitting through long-winded debates and occasionally being hauled off in plastic handcuffs were all that was needed to set things right.

"I am disgusted that the Education Committee can propose we sit and reason with that bastard. About getting safe-sex instruction into their hospitals? He's not going to meet with us. Even if he did, he's not going to listen. And if he did listen, it'd mean kissing the devil's anus."

"If, if, if," muttered Nick.

I couldn't understand why he'd been so insistent on my coming tonight, unless he wanted me to see firsthand what made him so frustrated and ill-tempered. Concentrating on committee work, even Nick often skipped general meetings. Peter had never attended. "I don't do politics but I will do food," he'd said, and he'd worked briefly in the God's Love kitchen when his health was good.

The facilitator in Weimar granny glasses called for a

vote. Should the Education Committee approach the cardinal's office? When a show of hands showed no clear majority, the proposal was returned to committee for further discussion.

"Next, Daniel Carp has asked to speak about the midterm elections in November. Okay, Dan. You have five minutes."

Carp, a pudgy fellow with shaggy hair, spoke loudly and to the point: The Democrats didn't give AIDS squat but they took our votes for granted. It was time we broke their complacency by threatening to boycott the election. Without the gay vote, the Democrats would lose their shirts.

That snapped the audience to life. A dozen hands flew up when the floor opened to discussion. An older man accused Carp of proposing political suicide. A young woman supported suicide, declaring that only when the Republicans got what they wanted would people wake up and go socialist.

"I don't believe this shit!"

Nick's voice tore into my ear as he jumped to his feet.

"I've been sitting here listening! And it's nothing but—yack yack yack yack yack!" he shouted.

"Someone still has the floor, Nick. If you'll sit down and raise your hand—"

"Fuck the floor!" Nick strode up the aisle. "I don't believe you people. You fuss over the same nothing solutions you fussed with a year ago. And you know what I say?" He faced the room. "Just do it!"

"Do what?" someone called out.

"*Anything!* If we have to kiss ass, let's kiss ass. If we have to kick it, let's kick it. Why not meet with Cardinal Turd? You won't get the time of day from him, but it's something. And go ahead, threaten the Democrats with a boycott. Maybe you'll find a candidate dumb enough to think we control some votes. But I have to say that idea is one more piece of passive-aggressive horseshit! All our actions are inactions! Our biggest threat is to do nothing!"

He stood up there, a mustached Victorian boxer in a

turtleneck, raking the crowd with glinting eyes. He loudly snorted his nose clear of tears. He was crying.

"*No*, I'm not rational tonight. I can't afford to be rational anymore. You people would rather be right than effective. You'd rather do nothing than the wrong thing. But I have a lover, Peter. Who has been my life for fifteen years. Many of you've met him. Some of you know him. Unless something radically changes, he's going to be dead in a year or so. All right. Some of you are as sick and even sicker. To be blunt, I don't care about you. Not in the way I care about him. But caring makes me crazy enough to try *anything*."

He spoke more wildly than I'd ever heard him before, without detachment. He couldn't discuss death with Peter but talked about it now with a hundred acquaintances and strangers. His fury, like a public nervous breakdown, shamed me for fretting over my own petty matters.

"All right then. Let's be pure. Political suicide? That'll show them. Let's let the Republicans win. Let them get what they want. The cities gone to hell and health care down the toilet. Hey, why don't we go all the way and work for the Republicans? Only that would mean getting our hands dirty, wouldn't it? But this way, when it's all in ruins, we can feel good about ourselves. Because we will've been pure. But Peter'll be dead. And we will have let him die. Do you think I want to sacrifice my lover so that you assholes can feel moral?"

"So what do *you* think we should do?" somebody shouted.

"I don't know!" He glared at the man. "I don't know," he repeated. "We need a stick of dynamite up the country's ass. But you're not the people to do it! I've been wasting my time with you. And I say fuck you!"

He stormed up the aisle. He didn't look at me as he snatched his coat off his chair and headed for the door.

I jumped up and followed, coming into the lobby as he charged through the front door. When I got out to the frigid street, I expected to find him halfway down the block. But no, he stood at the curb, bent over, hands on his hips like a man who'd run a hundred-yard dash.

"Nick? You okay?" I timidly touched him.

"Yeah. Oh yeah." He was catching his plumed breath.

"What set you off in there? I've never seen you like that." Only then did it hit me. "Did Peter get bad news today?"

"No. Peter's the same. The same fucking same." He faced me, the damp streaks on his cheeks already freezing white. "So did I make my point? Do you think I got through?"

"Through to—?"

"Go back in. Listen and tell me what they're saying."

"Sure," I said. "If that's what you want."

"I'll wait for you out of the wind."

I crept back inside and stood at the entrance to the assembly room while the truth finished sinking in: Nick's breakdown had been deliberate, a rhetorical stunt similar to what Larry Kramer used to pull, but more raw, less transparent, less expected.

"Order! Quiet! Shush!" cried the facilitator in granny glasses. "The man is upset and we understand why. If anyone wants to respond, we'll discuss it under new business. But we have not yet finished with Dan Carp's proposal. . . ."

I listened for five minutes, as disgusted by their retreat into procedure as Nick was, but without losing my unease over Nick's use of Peter.

I went back out to the street and found him huddled in a doorway. "You did nothing," I told him. "They've gone back to discussing the boycott."

"Shit! Won't anything knock those people off their butts?" He kicked the building.

"What did you hope to get?"

"Something. Shake the fuckers up. They just go round and round, like they had all the time in the world."

"But that's why you wanted me here tonight? So you could have a friendly observer for your performance?"

He glared at me. "That wasn't an act. You think I was faking emotion in there?"

"No. I assume it was real. I just can't get over that you could use Peter to make your point."

He bared his teeth at me in a scornful grin. "You think I was playing the sick-boyfriend card? That I don't really care about Peter?" he sneered. "I care about him so much I'll use anything, even soppy talk of love for him."

I didn't know how to answer. He already had words for what I'd been thinking. He was right, but I didn't feel I was completely wrong.

He looked at the front door. "Shit. Can't go back in now without looking like a drama queen. Might as well go home. You going or staying?"

"I'll walk with you."

I had no business being surprised by Nick's calculation or lack of guilt. His freedom from doubt had once been enormously attractive. A hairy man with a hairy ass, he did not split hairs.

He didn't attempt to justify himself as we walked down Seventh Avenue, but jumped ahead to the real issues. "Tragedy has become cozy," he declared. "Everyone accepts it. What's maddening is that I don't know what to do either. We need something new to shock people awake."

"Literal sticks of dynamite?"

He thought I was serious. "No. Terrorism would make it look like *we* were the problem. But something to get AIDS back on the front page and force people to feel it again. Not another celebrity victim. They've seen that. But a desperate act. Like the Buddhist monks who torched themselves in Vietnam. Only that's just victim writ large."

"So you're not planning to show up outside the White House with a can of gasoline?"

"Not me. But if the right person stepped forward, someone who was good copy, I'd call the networks and be there with the matches." He gave me a disdainful, damning look. "If a tree falls in the forest and there's no TV camera present, does it make a sound? Don't waste your ends-don't-justify-the-means tone on me, Ralph. There's more to life than old books and new love affairs."

"I'm not judging," I claimed. "Just sharing doubts. I don't know anything anymore. And it's been ages since my last affair."

"Yeah?"

"Uh, yeah," I said uncomfortably. Had Peter told him?

"That guy last month?" Nick shook his head—I kept forgetting he'd met Bill. "Washington twinkie. Cute in their twenties, pudgy in their thirties, fat old men by the time they're forty."

"He was only a trick. Someone I met in a bar that night."

"Too bad. I figured it was romance distracting you lately. Which is at least a pleasant way of doing nothing."

I relaxed. He didn't know and didn't care. "I remember when you weren't above an occasional affair yourself."

"It was fun to let off steam. When we had steam to spare. I never let it distract me from the work at hand."

"No, you didn't."

We stood by the canopy and ice-candied shrubs outside their apartment building, an oversized redbrick tower off Seventh Avenue. Nick looked at me, remembering something, although not necessarily what I remembered. "Good night, Ralph."

"Give my love to Peter." We parted without embrace or handshake. Nick was not a touchy-huggy guy in clothes.

His faults did not make Bill look virtuous, but they changed the equation, made my affair less criminal. Walking home in the cold, I tried to sort out my sympathy and unease, respect and disapproval, collating the Nick I knew now with the capable, intimidating figure whom I'd courted three and a half years ago.

I'd noticed Nick Rosi at the first meetings I attended. An intense, self-possessed man of few words, his remarks carried more weight than the showboating of others. Even his silence had authority. He was handsome, but what attracted me was his cool air of knowing something the rest of us didn't.

Nick didn't notice me until the mammoth protest at City Hall that April. Two thousand chanting people circled the muddy green park while hundreds of cops stood by and troops of mounted police guarded the approaches to Brooklyn Bridge; a helicopter played a prolonged organ chord overhead. A friend and I had taken civil-disobedience training with Nick's squad, but Jonathan could not get off work that day. Alone in the crowd, I felt like an outsider, too old to be one of the led, too shy and tongue-tied to ever lead. I wanted to get inside the thing. I hung close to Nick, vaguely hoping for a chance to help him.

He blew his whistle. We ducked under the barricade and into the street. We sat chanting while police and television crews gathered along the curb, Nick stepping over us in his gray Wall Street suit, our cheerleader and scoutmaster. As the beeping paddy wagons backed around us and the police prepared to charge, he was still standing. "I've saved you a place," I called up to him. He saw me, looked around, saw nobody else to sit with and squeezed in with me. He called out a final command. We all went flat on the cold asphalt, the budding trees leaping against the sky at a startling new angle, and Nick Rosi lay beside me. "We got to stop meeting like this," I said. He turned his face into mine—as if we were already in bed. Mistaking my excitement for fear, he grabbed my hand and gave it a squeeze. I startled us both by lifting his hand and kissing the black-bristled knuckles.

All at once, the cops rushed the carpet of bodies. There was a chorus of disco whistles and a string of cries like the delighted shrieks at a horror movie—we called our government fascist yet trusted our police. I had no difficulty in playing cool for Nick's eyes. When they hoisted me off the pavement, it was like being lifted by a gentle blue surf of history.

We were rushed into separate paddy wagons and different jails and I didn't see Nick again until the next meeting. He sought *me* out to ask how I'd been treated. He'd learned my name. I flirtatiously asked if he'd been strip-searched. He asked where I lived. I seemed like a bright guy and could we talk at my place? "I'd like that," I replied, although I'd heard he was attached.

The affair lasted two months. Meetings were an aphro-
disiac for Nick, and I lived within a five-minute walk of Cooper
Union. He went home with me almost every Monday night,
sharing his analysis of who said what as we climbed the stairs,
listening to my comments while we undressed, resuming discussion when he knelt in my bathtub and sponged off at
the spigot—a wet head after a shower would announce too
brazenly why he was late. He and his lover had an understanding, he said, which included the agreement to be discreet. Peter later confirmed this. When Nick began to include
occasional complaints about Peter in our talks, I wondered if
he was signaling something more serious for us. But no, Nick
assumed he and Peter were for life, even before Peter got sick.
He could criticize his other half without ever feeling that he
injured their shared reality.

Three and a half years ago, I was a younger, more
hopeful, careless person. I got inside the thing, only to find
that there was no inside. The excitement of making politics
erotic and sex political now seemed as foreign as my love of
theory in college. My sexiest memory was from our first night,
when a cool, capable authority figure suddenly lay before me
in nothing but a frayed body stocking of curly black hair, giddily grinning as I plucked his green plaid boxer shorts off his
feet. Then he swallowed his grin, shook his head and said,
"God but you're sweet. Maybe too damn sweet for this world."

A few months after the affair ended and Nick had introduced me to Peter, I was on a chartered bus coming back
from an action at Burroughs Wellcome when I overheard two
expensive haircuts badmouthing Nick Rosi for being such a
control freak, especially in the sack. I was not jealous, only
indignant for Nick's sake, and alarmed that we sansculottes
could judge our leaders by how they performed sans pants.

I spoke on the phone with Nancy a few nights after
Nick's public eruption, told her something about it, then was
talking about the store when she abruptly asked, "Ralph, are
you mad at me?"

"No." I laughed nervously. "Should I be?"

"I don't think so. It's just that you've seemed slightly distant since your visit here. I was wondering if I unloaded too much of my shit and didn't pay enough attention to yours."

I assured her that I had no shit and was fine. "Hey, if I ever get mad at you, you'll know."

9

New snow covered the streets the morning I caught a train in New York to catch the plane in Baltimore. New Jersey was a stark sketch of black factories in white marshes, white smoke against white skies. When my flight lifted off over Maryland, I saw frozen rivers and white rime around Chesapeake Bay, an arteriosclerosis of ice. Miles to the west, Washington was a faint vapor over a rough patch of earth. I sat in a window seat with another Palliser novel in my lap, *Phineas Redux*, which I'd begun on the train but didn't even open now.

It was Friday. Bill had flown down Thursday. We were flying back together on Sunday. This was a new and worldly experience for me, to be brought a thousand miles for a weekend with a lover. And we were lovers, even if neither of us was in love.

Nevertheless, the future tense of travel and mild vertigo of being airborne fed a giddiness in my chest, a keen anticipation, a weightlessness like love. Or was it only lust? What did it matter so long as I enjoyed myself?

I had no romantic illusions. I'd learned years ago that love could be temporary and still be love. I enjoyed falling in love yet knew not to trust it. It began as an elation of pure possibility, a wishful thinking so strong that it dissolved the other person. It was like falling in love with light and air, which could be fun until the dream broke in the soft fact of another ego. Two or three times in my life, the fact of the other person had been there from the start. He seemed more real than I was and *I* dissolved in possibility. There'd been traces of that with Nick, although I'd been drawn at the time not just to Nick but to the life he represented.

I didn't really believe that I was in love with Bill. Today, however, in a steady march of sunlit clouds high above the Carolinas, I wondered again if he was in love with me, something I never wished except when I thought I could return it.

Even requited, such love would be foolish, messy and brief. Unless it changed Bill's politics. That fantasy was back, larger than before, giving value to lust, turning sex with a Republican from a self-betrayal to a good deed, a moral rescue. Bill went against his best interests by seeing me. Maybe he wanted to be changed.

But what if love changed *me*? Could it rearrange and corrupt *my* identity? Oddly enough, that scenario wasn't frightening, but produced a nasty thrill. As if I were bored with who I was and enjoyed the impossible notion of becoming someone new.

Idle notions, transitory thoughts, ideas you entertain only in transit. Such plot twists seemed no more binding of me than those in the fat paperback in my lap. I amused myself with my own private novel, playing with abstract emotions, treating them as make-believe, forgetting that love often begins as just another story you tell yourself in private.

The plane began its descent and I stopped playing at love to fasten my seat belt. Terra cotta rooftops, quill-like palm trees and a green baize golf course raced beneath the wing, their colors a shock after months of monochrome.

The long carpeted corridor from the gate was full of tanned old people in cheerful prints and plaids. I was a child of winter with my superfluous duffel coat under my arm.

I saw him before he saw me. He sat against a tubbed

orange tree outside the metal detectors, in khakis and polo shirt, his skin so pale that he stood out like a white crow. His eyes were lowered, lost in thought. Who would he be this time?

He looked up and blinked in his glasses, as if asking himself a similar question about me. His body responded before his face, pitching forward a split second before a grin appeared.

"Welcome to Miami." He held out one hand, then the other.

I embraced him. His hesitance warned me against kissing him, but he smelled so good, like hotel linen, that I sneaked a kiss on his neck.

He gently broke the embrace. "Can I carry something? I rented a car. It's parked out front. It's good to see you."

I gave him my coat and followed, wondering why I felt slightly disappointed, what else I had hoped to feel.

"It's good to see you," he repeated. "I was afraid you might change your mind at the last minute."

"Oh no. I wasn't going to miss this for the world. The chance to see you again, in a whole new setting."

"Good. Very good. I am so glad you came, Ralph."

Catching his little notes of protest, I tried to joke them away. "I assume we both will this weekend. Many times."

His smile was uneasy, his laugh as tight as the warning chirp of his Powerbook. He wanted me to want more than sex? He was bored with the affair? Was I reading too much into every detail?

Outdoors in the covered walkway to the car park, the air was not just warm but tactile, fluffy handfuls of vacant space.

"We're not staying at the convention hotel," he said as he unlocked the door on my side of the car. "But in South Beach. It's nicer. I'll keep you away from the big bad Republicans."

"But I want to see big bad Republicans. I want to hear your presentation and catch some of this conference." It was my political justification for coming. I was here for knowledge. Know thy enemy, I told myself, which might not include Bill.

He was too busy navigating the car to answer immediately. "I'd rather you didn't, Ralph. Firstly, I'm nervous enough without knowing that you're in the audience. And secondly, this conference is more, uh, conservative than I expected. You wouldn't like it. I'm not sure I like it."

Maybe I hadn't been fooling myself; maybe he did want to be changed. "So what does AFC stand for?"

"American Family Coalition."

"That's the Christian right, right?"

"Oh yes. The right right. Most definitely." He glanced at me. "How did you know?"

"You mean you didn't?" I hadn't heard of them, but "family" was always the giveaway.

"No. I meant how did you know this was the AFC?"

"You told me, didn't you?" He hadn't. I knew it from reading his Powerbook.

"I thought I was careful not to. Because, to be frank, I was afraid you wouldn't come."

But I was already on the slippery slope; I could slide into the far right with no additional guilt. I was pleased that Bill respected my beliefs enough to want to keep this from me.

"That's where I'll be tomorrow," he said when we were on the highway, pointing out downtown Miami, a Sunbelt skyline like a bar graph. "I have a presentation in the morning. A panel in the afternoon. But I'm all yours tonight and tomorrow night and all day Sunday before we fly back. So you don't need to make yourself unwelcome on the chance that we might have time for lunch. Or so you can see me make an ass of myself. If they even let you in."

"It's closed to the public?"

He shrugged. "You're not registered. They might think you're a potential troublemaker with that haircut."

I hadn't considered that when I took the electric razor to my head this morning. Considering it now, I saw another reason for Bill's request. "Will you get in trouble if you're seen with someone who looks like me?"

"No. Probably not. Oh I don't know," he declared,

offended by the idea. "I hadn't thought that. If I truly thought that, would I have wanted you here?"

"No, I guess not," I admitted.

We started across a causeway over the turquoise bay that would lie between us and the righteous Christians, between Bill in bed and Bill at a podium. He *had* taken a risk in bringing me to Miami. I decided not to press the issue, to be patient.

The causeway ended in a whitewashed resort town against a low horizon. We drove down an oceanside street lined with small beveled hotels the color of sea taffy. The first few were delightful, but the eye quickly wearied of Art Deco; it was the planet of retired decorators. Bill parked in a side street by a squat reptilian palm tree like a prehistoric bird. A school of muscle boys in sunglasses flew past on Rollerblades as we walked around to the front of the hotel. The end of the day was balmy, the air sensual, but Bill's body English, the stiffness of spine and shoulders, suggested he was not sensually at home today.

Up in his room, I dumped my bag in the corner, glanced at yet another king-sized bed, then went to the window to look at the ocean. The beach was wide and rumpled, the Atlantic a dark blue as the afternoon sky turned a powdery, dusky blue.

"Nice, isn't it?" said Bill while he hung up my coat. "There's a big Jacuzzi in the bathroom. Which I haven't used yet. We can help ourselves to snacks and beverages in the little fridge. Would you care for a beverage?"

I asked for seltzer. He busied himself with ice and glasses while I looked down at people on the street, feeling not like a lover but an inconvenient guest.

He came up behind me and set the glasses on a table. He pressed against my back and wrapped his arms around my chest.

"Oh, but it's good to have you here," he said, with a sadness that finally gave the phrase weight.

I turned and kissed his mouth, at the window where anyone could see us. I was relieved to be kissing him again.

He nibbled timidly. "I should warn you," he whispered. "I'm distracted about tomorrow. I don't know how in the mood I'll be."

"Do you want to wait until later?" I offered insincerely, rubbing the seat of his pants.

"No, I want to now. But you should know, I might seem different."

"I can work with that."

And he was different. It made me different. We hurried through the neck-and-strip phase to get to the heart of the matter; there were no breathless smiles over the first thrill of skin-deep nudity. We twisted, rubbed and pressed in an attempt to squeeze ourselves back into our skin. The warm breeze blowing through our middles brought the sounds of traffic and pedestrians into the room. Anyone watching us might think this was the same ballroom dance of sex as before, but inside the act it felt different, deeper, hungrier.

I was doing him with my mouth, hand and finger—he hadn't wanted me there before—when he gripped the back of my neck and breathlessly said, "I want you—to fuck me."

"I didn't bring condoms."

"Buy some. Tomorrow. Will you?"

"Yeah," I said, not wanting to argue, wanting only to return to the inside-out shapes in my face: the bared throat of his erection, the balls against my palm, the buried "mouse" rolling under my fingertip.

The shoulders of his cock swelled; his sphincter swallowed. I uncorked him and he came. His inhaled cries sounded like sobs. "Don't stop, don't stop!" he pleaded after he finished and I was rubbing him raw.

But even orgasm failed to calm him. He went straight at me again, frantically clutching and sucking, then pumping with his fist. "Gently, gently," I whispered. I pulled him to my side and buried my nose in his hair. I released a long, deep sigh of relief, caught my breath, and smiled.

Bill slowly sat up, looking at my torso, unsure what else to do with me. He frowned at the puddle around my navel.

He abruptly bent down and rubbed his grimace in the spill, angrily smearing closed lips and eyelids in me. I grabbed his head to stop him.

"Are you okay?" I asked.

"I'm fine. I'm excellent. It's good to have you here."

"Good to be here," I said worriedly. I brushed the hair off his damp forehead and wiped his face with the sheet.

He did not want to snuggle and talk, but jumped up, insisting we try the heart-shaped Jacuzzi. He made the water as hot as we could stand. He turned on the tanning light and the wainscotted closet glowed like a toaster oven. We sat side by side in twin ventricles of swirling heat that came up to our nipples, feeling nothing when our knees touched. With his eyes closed and head tilted back, Bill finally relaxed, the water burning away whatever it was that sex hadn't.

"Feel better?" I asked.

"Much," he claimed.

"What's bothering you?"

"Nothing. I feel fine."

"Do you feel bad about bringing me here?"

"No. I'm glad to have you here."

But I persisted. "Then do you feel strange about being with me tonight, and getting thrown to the Christians tomorrow?"

"I'm not being *thrown* to them," he grumbled. "I support them. Most of the time. They have nothing to do with you, Ralph. You have nothing to do with them." An eye peeked and closed. "Like I said, if I'm preoccupied, it's stage fright. I've never appeared in public. I'm worried I'll make an ass of myself."

No, it was more than that. He didn't understand his own guilty dissonance. "What do you have to do?"

"Read from my book. Take questions from the audience."

"Then you have nothing to fear. They'll love anything bad you say about Clinton." I couldn't believe I said that. "What's the worst that can happen?"

"They'll laugh at me. It's what I fear most in life. That people will laugh at me."

"There're worse things than being laughed at."

"Not for me."

I wasn't surprised. Bill's undeveloped sense of humor left him deaf to other people's irony, and unprotected with jokes at his expense.

"I have a theory," I said. "About people revealing their true character by what they fear."

"That doesn't define me," Bill muttered. "Everyone's afraid of being laughed at."

"But different people have different key fears. I've got one friend who's terrified of being depressed. Another who's afraid of being ineffectual. Another who's afraid of—" I was going to say death, but everyone feared death, and I didn't know how often Peter thought about it.

"What fear defines you?" Bill said.

"I don't know. Maybe hurting people. Deliberately or by accident. Physically or emotionally."

"Yeah?" He lifted his head to stare at me.

And it did sound ridiculous when said aloud, sentimental and self-congratulatory. "Okay. The theory works only when somebody else names your fear. We can't name our own. We only name what we *like* to think is our defining fear."

Bill closed his eyes and leaned back. "You don't have to worry about hurting my feelings. Just be patient until I get through tomorrow. I'll be myself again tomorrow night."

"Well, you're not bad company in the meantime," I claimed.

Patches of blue and pink neon spilled from the open fronts of bars and restaurants along the ocean. The colored shadows of potted palms were cast on a young crowd jostling up and down the sidewalk: European tourists, American models, beautiful women in high-heeled sandals, handsome men with butts like the jacked-up rears of hot rods, and us.

Out on the street, Bill became more himself again—only what was his true self? He made his old cheerfulness flow in talk about Miami and the movies we'd seen over the past month. He remained distracted behind his smiles, yet I patiently accepted that, much to my surprise. I'd come down here with fantasies and fears about the drama of love, only to find myself content with friendly courtesy.

We ate dinner in a sidewalk café. When I reached over to take a bit of the chicken tarragon salad that Bill said was so delicious, he stiffened, as if I'd just groped him in public, then was guilty over his distress. When we went for a walk on the dark, surfless, deserted beach, he held my hand for a minute, until his fingers grew sweaty and we both let go.

"Do you like your shadow?" he asked. "I hate mine. My shadow looks like a cello."

I did not laugh, but assured him his shadow was fine. We tried identifying constellations and returned to the hotel.

After brushing his teeth, Bill announced, "Do you mind if we just sleep tonight? I'm not in a frisky mood."

I'd expected that. "No problem. It's you being in the mood that puts me in the mood."

He had pajamas and actually wore them, full-length cotton with blue stripes. He frowned when I shucked my briefs to climb in nude, but sat up so I could slip an arm around him. He turned off the light and laid his head on my shoulder as before, holding my teddy bear arm across his chest.

"I feel like I'm in bed with my father," I muttered.

"Don't say that! What an awful thing to say."

"Your pajamas," I explained. "Can you sleep like this?"

"We'll see. If I end up on the other side, don't be offended."

"I won't." I took strange pride over sharing a bed with Bill without lust, pleased to discover that I didn't need to anesthetize myself with sex to be with him. I assumed my satisfaction would wear off and I'd have to roll away to go to sleep. But very quickly, the hours of travel, the change of season and all my chameleon thinking caught up with me. The ocean air dissolved the street noise and the body beside me.

I strolled into an overheated hall full of gaslight and

men in ink black frock coats. The men held gloves and
stovepipe hats at their sides while they discussed a new bill
in Parliament. I was thrilled to eavesdrop in the corridors
of power, until I realized that I wasn't dressed for the occasion. I was naked. I panicked, cupped my hands over my pri-
vates. I considered snatching hats to cover myself fore and aft
so I could get to the cloakroom where I seemed to have left
my clothes. But then I understood: Nobody noticed me. I was
invisible. These proper English gentlemen looked straight
through me. Or did they only pretend to look through me?
A naked queer was too incongruous to be acknowledged in
a scene from Trollope. Whether my invisibility was real or a
social fiction, I decided to take advantage of it. I wandered
freely among their important conversations, regretting only
that I had no pockets where I could put my hands. A young,
beardless fellow with black-rimmed glasses suddenly stared at
me; he turned away, blushing.

"Wake up! Get up! They're here!"

Hands jerked my shoulders. He shouted in my ear.

"Get dressed. Get some clothes on. Please. We can't let
them see you like this."

"Who?" I bolted up and wildly looked around, seeing a
hotel room in Miami Beach, recognizing the frightened man
in my bed.

"Please, please," he pleaded. "I know they've seen us,
but—if I can make them understand. If I can explain."

"There's nobody here. You were dreaming, Bill. Just us."

I put my arm around him, but he threw it off.

"Yes? What? We're somewhere else?" He stared at me,
shoved my shoulder and found it was real. "Oh God." He fell
back on his pillow. "Only a dream. A nightmare. Jesus. The
door's locked?"

"It's locked. But there's nobody out there." Yet I
couldn't shake the idea that the hall was full of frock-coated
politicians from my own dream. "Who did you think was in
the room?"

He lay there catching his breath. "What a stupid dream.

Nobody particular. Truly. Nobody at all. Just people." And almost instantly, he was asleep again.

I remained propped on an elbow, watching his face subside into peace, wondering who his enemies were, wanting to know what I could do to protect him.

We were up early the next morning. I worked to put Bill at ease while he got dressed, assuring him he'd do fine, even helping him with his tie. My support was sincere, but with an ulterior motive. I waited until I walked him out to his car before trying again.

"I promise not to go to your presentation. But I'd really like to see some of this. Can't I drop by? If you run into me and can't say hello, I'll understand."

"No, Ralph. If there's any chance I might see you, I'll be tense all day. Promise you won't. Please. Hang out on the beach. Enjoy yourself."

"All right. If that's what you want. I brought a fat book."

He looked quite adult in his blue suit, burgundy suspenders and striped tie, although his briefcase bulged like a school bookbag. "Good luck," I told him. "They'll love you. See you at four." Unable to kiss him on the street, I reached under his jacket and gave his suspender a hard snap. Then I went inside and asked at the desk where one could catch a bus to the mainland.

* * *

Shaggy palms lined the boulevard in downtown Miami outside a concrete fortress the color of a wasp nest. "Welcome American Family," declared the marquee of the Omni Hotel and Convention Center.

They trooped into the hotel's street entrance, middle-aged and elderly couples, everyone eager, chatty and clean. Packed with a dozen in the elevator, I was overcome by an aroma of fresh ironing.

There were hundreds more upstairs in the echoing gray lobby of the convention hall. I was glad they were so many; it decreased my chances of running into Bill. I regretted lying to him, but I did need to see this. I would tell him I'd been here, later, when no harm came of my visit. He should be flattered. I hid my blatant head with the baseball cap that I never wore in New York. Turned forward, the cap signified only a love of sport. I wore a plaid shirt and tweed jacket, which made me look like a liberal academic, but it was the best I could manage. I feared I stood out like a Communist flag, yet nobody asked to see my pass, nobody gave me a dirty look. I was back in last night's dream of invisibility, until a faintly butch grandmother thrust a pamphlet in my hand—"Death, Taxes and Eternal Life"—and stuck a button in my lapel— "Jesus Does Not Vote Democrat"—presumably less sacrilegious than claiming he voted Republican. "I'm supposed to ask for a dollar donation," she drawled. "But I'm too full of glory today."

Everyone was beaming, everyone looked friendly. I did not expect *Triumph of the Will*, but this was more neighborly than I'd anticipated, like our shopping mall back home on a Sunday afternoon, people dropping by after church, others coming in from the golf course. The chief differences were the scarcity of black faces and the complete absence of children. Well, you couldn't expose the kids to what might be discussed at something called the American Family Coalition. I wanted to see absurdities, but knew that toxic pastels and an occasional Wookie hairdo were not the enemy. The handful of twenty-somethings had a too-good-to-be-true possessed look, yet the elderly majority seemed perfectly human.

Finding a red, white and blue brochure for the conference in the trash, I hunted through the listings to see where Bill was. "11:00 A.M. The Okeechobee Room. 'Everything You Wanted to Know About Bill and Hillary. And Were Not Afraid to Ask.' William O'Connor of *American Truths* reads from his forthcoming exposé of the Clinton administration, *The Regiment of Women*."

That was the title? Another Shakespeare allusion? In other circumstances, I'd assume it was feminist, but here it worried me. The presentation began in ten minutes. Could I risk exposure by looking in? The Okeechobee Room sounded too small for me to sit in a corner unnoticed. Perhaps I could stand outside the door.

The conference rooms were on the mezzanine. Riding up the escalator with a column of churchgoers, I turned to watch the pastel mob through the gauze stripes of an American flag hung from the ceiling. I turned around as the next floor came into view—just in time to see Bill.

He stood in profile against jungle wallpaper, twenty feet away, talking to a man in a gray suit. I stood paralyzed on the escalator that carried me toward them, staring at Bill, his fat briefcase in both arms, his head respectfully bowed to a short, thick, fiftyish fellow with a chin beard.

I saw them for three seconds, so intensely that they registered like a snapshot. Then I jerked my cap over my eyes, stepped off the escalator, quickly turned and jumped on the escalator going down. The motor of the stairs hummed in my knees. My heart pounded so hard that I feared I wouldn't hear him call out my name. I reached the main floor and stepped away, catching my breath and looking up at the balcony to see if he came to the parapet to look for me. He didn't. He hadn't seen me. I was safe.

I began to laugh at my slapstick escape and fright. What was I afraid of? I just didn't want to spook Bill before his talk, even if I disapproved of what he said. Knowing he'd be occupied for the next hour, I felt free to stay and explore.

Nothing was happening in the ballroom auditorium. A lone woman dozed in the acres of peach plush chairs. The brochure listed a plenary session for noon: "Meet the Leaders of Tomorrow." I saw a rest room in the back and suddenly needed to pee. I opened the door on the sound of a choir singing "Rock of Ages." Two men stood at the marble sink with a tape recorder; the thin, sandy man in khaki and wire rims was praying.

"Excuse me." I started to back out on what seemed a very intimate act.

"No. Please," said the nonpraying man, gesturing toward the toilets in the rear.

I nodded and hurried past as the comforter laid his hand on the sandy man's head.

"Let the Spirit be with Claude in his time of need. Let his words persuade the multitudes. We beseech thee, Lord. . . ."

Peeing was difficult with that going on outside my stall. I flushed before I realized it might sound disrespectful. When I came out, they were still serenely at it. Such solid, old-fashioned faith seemed oddly heroic in these glitzy trappings.

Know thy enemy, know thy enemy, I repeated to myself, my mantra for the weekend. I was a fly on the wall of a realm that people like Nick and Maura Morris knew only by hearsay.

I wandered into a hall lined with booths selling books, bumper stickers and T-shirts: *Get Rich While You Sleep,* "Heil Hillary" and, in Coca-Cola lettering, "Jesus Christ: He's the Real Thing." Raised as an Episcopalian, the easiest religion in the world to shed, I could still be amazed by the sacrilege of believers. The one stone I noticed being thrown at my kind was on a video playing in the *700 Club* booth, the voice of Pat Robertson declaring, "We must turn back Bill Clinton's socialist agenda," over an image of two men holding hands.

A display of real books caught my eye, titles by John Henry Newman and other Brits on the table of a Catholic publisher. I took up an edition of prose by Gerard Manley Hopkins that I'd never seen before. The right at least pretended to read good literature. A balding man in bifocals was perusing *Everlasting Man* by G. K. Chesterton. He glanced over, noticing my book while I noticed his.

"Ah, Hopkins!" he said in a warm, husky voice. "Hopkins is great. You like Hopkins?"

"I know his poetry, but not his prose." I also knew the poet-priest was said to be gay, but didn't think this the time or place to mention that.

"You know Chesterton?" the man asked eagerly. "You should. Great prose, strong feeling." He thrust the book on me, as if expecting me to read it then and there. "Unafraid of intellect. Intellect is not the enemy. Frank Calabrese," he said, holding out a pale, leopard-spotted hand.

"Ralph Eckhart," I replied. He had a gentle handshake.

"You down from Lejeune, Ralph? I thought at first you might be at the Citadel, but you're too old to be a cadet. When you get to be my age, all young men are youths."

So that was why my shaved head didn't alarm anyone. Context was all, and in their context I must be in the military. "Yes, sir. Lejeune," I mumbled, opening his book.

"Quite a gathering of the tribe, this. You down alone or with family, Ralph?"

"Alone." He stood quite close to me, closer than straight men usually stand to strangers. Was this courtly gentleman trying to pick me up?

"Chesterton was great pals with Hilaire Belloc, you know. They went for hikes in the country, stopping at pubs and inns along the way. Theirs was a hearty, sensual religion."

This was perfect: I was being hit on among the Christians, and over G. K. Chesterton.

"Irene!" he called out. "C'mere. I've met someone else."

A woman with tight gray hair and the solidity of a stuffed chair glided over. "Hello?" she said uncertainly.

"Ralph here is a serviceman who *reads*. He knows Hopkins. I'm selling him on Chesterton."

She had fretful eyes and a falcon-beak nose. She smiled weakly. "Don't mind my husband. He has so few people in Kenosha to talk books to that he can come on a little strong."

"I wasn't coming on strong. Was I, Ralph?"

"Uh no. Not at all." I was ashamed of thinking what I'd thought. There must be closet cases here, but most of these people were what they seemed. Among their kind, they could talk to strangers without secret motives.

Irene tugged at her watch. "Shouldn't we be getting to the auditorium? If we want a seat for the noon thing."

"All righty," said Frank. "You coming, Ralph? Would you like to sit with us?"

"Thank you. Yes. That'd be nice." Know thy enemy, I thought, although Frank and Irene seemed too innocent to count as foe. But if I were in there with someone, I'd be less visible to Bill.

We settled in the center of a back row. Surrounded again by that uniform smell of fresh-baked clothes, I wondered if Republicans all used the same brand of spray starch.

"Yup. No Robertson or Falwell," said Frank, reading his brochure. "Someone was telling me they were asked not to come."

"Fine by me," said Irene. "I don't trust those Protestant evangelicals. They have no one to answer to but themselves."

"Open mind," Frank chided. "Open mind."

The gray screen over the stage snapped on like a television, magnifying the head and shoulders of the man at the podium. Even those in the front rows craned their necks up, more accustomed to public figures on TV than in person. A smooth-faced boy in pinstripes—he looked all of fourteen—the speaker had the easy voice and manners of a game show host. A bar on the screen identified him as Ren Whitaker.

He opened the session by declaring that politicians were what was wrong with Washington, but there were exceptions and we were going to meet them. He introduced a congressman from Georgia as if he were a special treat. A white-haired man like a dyspeptic Phil Donahue stepped up and declared that the American family was besieged on all fronts: crime, drugs, sex, taxes and attacks on religion. It was time government worked with the family, not against it. Liberals held the White House, but the Republicans were going to sweep Congress in the midterm elections this fall and render the president helpless.

"That's right, that's right," Frank agreed, talking back as if he were watching TV in his living room.

To the left of the stage, four or five television cameras nodded on and off according to the cameramen's whims.

I braced myself for vicious words, but there were no sneers at welfare mothers or AIDS spending or gays in the military. Hate was confined to smirky jokes about liberalism and the Clintons. The rest was bromides about family virtue and Republican success, yet the audience basked in the speech as if it were a warm fire.

The politicians who followed, a half dozen smoothly coiffed talking heads, kept their remarks as short and general as contestants at a beauty pageant. A familiar, square-jawed face appeared, Senator Mike Griffith, whom I'd seen at the Capitol elevators with Nancy. His speech was totally noncommittal. "It's an honor to be with you this weekend. I've enjoyed talking to some very wonderful people. Thank you for inviting me."

A startlingly raw face popped onto the screen, a sunburn with sandy hair and wire rims. It was the man I'd seen praying in the rest room. No name appeared with him. The men in suits upstage went into a panic of whispers and pointed fingers.

"My name is Claude Raymond," he declared loudly, not trusting the mike; the loudspeakers brayed with feedback. "Our so-called friends in the Republican Party did not want me to speak today. And no wonder. Because the party that claims to be our friend is a party of compromise and mendacity. What does it gain a man to lose his soul for the kingdom of earth?"

A stage manager in a headset came out from the wings to signal the control booth. Whitaker, the boy emcee, hurried over and gestured that everything was fine.

"You who know me can guess what I intend to say. Which is that this party is a home for sodomites and baby killers!"

Somebody shouted, "Amen!" The crowd began to ripple and shift uncomfortably. Nobody booed.

"Yes, sodomites and baby killers. In league with each

other in their unholy war against the unborn. And we are
among those who can compromise with such people. Let our
so-called friends prove their belief by purging their ranks. Let
them clean their own house before making cause with ours."

He glared at Whitaker, who stood a few feet away, nodding as if granting him permission to speak. They looked surreal up there, the rawboned face in the big screen, the small
yet controlling figure to the side.

All the television cameras were on, straining forward like
cows at a trough. A young woman hurried up the aisle, arms
folded angrily across her chest.

"They only want your votes," Raymond continued. "So
that they can achieve a program that deals naught with the
Kingdom of Heaven. What does God care for capital gains?
How does the national deficit compare to our country's
deficit of righteousness? We spend billions on overseas war,
but not one cent to stop the massacre of innocents at home."

There was applause, Frank and Irene clapping with the
others. "Good," said Frank. "Time someone said that."

Even Whitaker applauded as he approached the podium.

"That is what I came here to tell you today," Raymond
declared, satisfied by the response. "Know that you are
dealing with murderers. Do not trade righteousness for a por-
tion of bloodstained pottage. I leave you to your consciences
and your love of Jesus Christ. The unborn dead are all in
heaven. But those who do nothing will burn in hell."

I expected a tussle at the podium, but Raymond only
sniffed at Whitaker and marched past him off the stage.
Whitaker stepped up, still smiling. In the magnifying glass of
the screen, his smile looked less convincing. His audience was
now two and even three audiences: the shouting supporters
of Raymond, the polite clappers like Frank and Irene, and
the uneasily silent.

"God's house has many mansions," Whitaker declared.
"And so do we. We can make room for all causes, so long as
we keep our common cause in view. And just as Protestant,
Catholic and Greek Orthodox alike share a belief in one
Jesus Christ—and all Christians share a belief in one God

with our Jewish brethren," he remembered to add, "so do those of us with other goals all believe in the value and safety of the American family."

Despite appearances, this conference was as full of factions as any ACT UP meeting. I wondered about the amount of cynicism behind Whitaker's damage control. Which was reality and which the mask here: Whitaker and his smiling pols or the angry Raymond?

Whitaker made a closing statement about knowing who our friends were come November and declared the session over.

"Politicians," chuckled Frank as he stood and stretched. "Can't live with them, can't live without them. You got to admire that pro-life man though. Real conviction is a beautiful thing."

It was, which worried me. Purity was always more electric than compromise. "So the Republicans have to clean house before you'll cast your lot with them?"

"Ohhh," Frank hemmed. "Be nice if they took tougher stands on the moral issues. But they're still the best game in town."

"Something else I didn't get," I said, playing dumb to learn more. "What do homosexuals have to do with abortion? Getting pregnant is one thing they don't have to worry about."

"It's simple," said Frank, all too happy to explain. "People like that can't have children. They resent those who can. So they do everything in their power to trick normal women into aborting their babies."

I couldn't believe such a nice, personable man could believe anything so vile and idiotic. I didn't know how to respond, which made me angry, and anger carried me too far. "You should know that you've been sitting with one of those people."

"Oh?" said Frank. "You have a girlfriend who—?" He was too embarrassed to say it. "I'm so sorry. That must have been very painful for you. For both of you."

"Hmm?" went Irene, a whimper of distress that we even talked about this.

"No. The other category." Now *I* became embarrassed. "I'm gay."

"Ah!" he said, relieved, as if it were a lesser evil. Irene flinched and turned away, but Frank remained concerned. "That must be painful for you too. Being a marine and Catholic. But so long as you keep your nose clean, trust in the Church and read good books, you'll be able to overcome it."

"But I don't want to overcome it. It's who I am."

Even that didn't make a dent. "You might think so now, son. But you'll come around when you meet the right girl. We were going to get a bite to eat. Would you like to join us?"

Irene stared at him in alarm.

I stared with her. Was my sexuality so trivial to him? "Thank you, no. I should be getting back to my hotel."

"Certainly." He didn't press; the invitation was only a courtesy. "Nice meeting you, Ralph." He bravely shook my hand. "Enjoy the conference. And don't forget: G. K. Chesterton. A wonderful writer."

Irene refused to look at me as Frank took her arm. She whispered something as they strolled off; Frank responded with a sorrowful, worldly shrug.

I felt like a fool for firing that pistol in their faces. I should have at least brought the talk back to abortion. Did they really think gays were so malicious and pregnant women so passive? I was sorry I hadn't educated Frank about "sodomites." He was so cushioned with courtesy that to argue would have been like punching feathers, but I should have handled myself better. Too late now. Feeling very useless and stupid, and remembering Bill was still about, I had to get out of here.

I returned to the corridor of merchandise, recalling a back entrance that way. I noticed a booth for *American Truths* up ahead. Issues of the magazine were hung on the wall, a rogue's gallery of caricature liberals. I slowed my steps, then halted.

On the table stood a three-foot-high placard: "Coming

in April. The Truth the Liberal Press Does Not Want You to Know. *The Regiment of Women* by William O'Connor." On the placard were book dummies with glossy brown jackets, three of them staggered on little ledges to form a milk chocolate angel.

I pulled at a wing. It was taped to the cardboard but peeled off easily. It was not a dummy but bound galleys, the thing itself. I read the back. " 'There is a specter haunting American politics, the specter of feminists in government.' With a clear, objective, satirical eye, veteran journalist William O'Connor explores the effect of women in power as illustrated by the careers of Hillary Rodham Clinton and her friends. . . . Challenging, even shocking, certain to incite controversy and meaningful debate . . ."

I nervously opened it. The book was dedicated to his mother. The title was explained by the epigraph, which wasn't Shakespeare after all:

Weak, frail, impatient, feeble and foolish creatures.
—John Knox, 1558, *First Blast of the Trumpet Against the Monstrous Regiment of Women*

It was supposed to be funny, only who would be laughing?

"Excuse me?" I asked the attendant, a young woman in a frilly blouse. "Are these for sale?"

"Sorry, sir. No. They're not real books. Only for display." She frowned at what I'd done to her display. "You can look. But please return it to its exact spot when you're done."

I nodded and resumed reading.

The introduction began with the "specter of feminism" line, followed by promises of what the book would reveal about a powerful network of feminists in Washington. The contents page listed such chapters as "The Smoke-Filled Powder Room," "The Fall of a Quota Queen" and "Girls Just Want to Have Fun." When I opened at random, however, all I found was dull journalese about who knew whom in an alphabet soup of federal agencies.

But I couldn't concentrate knowing that this was Bill's

magazine and he might drop by. When the attendant began a
sales pitch to a possible subscriber, I slowly turned away while
I continued to read, and slipped the galleys under my coat. I
swung back around and tapped a remaining copy as if I'd just
returned it. "Thanks," I said, and walked away.

It could not be as bad as it looked, I told myself, hurrying downstairs into a level of shops under the hotel, shifting
the book from armpit to coat pocket. It was a critique of
Hillary Clinton, that was all, *packaged* as a sneering attack on
women in politics. You can't judge a book by its cover or
epigraph.

I didn't believe that for a minute. Nevertheless, passing a
pharmacy in the underground mall, I went in to buy the condoms that Bill wanted, as if to make amends for what I was
feeling, not yet able to blame him for his book. A cashier with
a cropped red beard studied me as he set a pack of Trojans
and tube of K-Y on the counter. "Not a teensy bit hypocritical,
are we? Honey?"

"What? Oh." *He* was gay. And I was still tagged with the
Jesus button. I frowned and pried it off. "Not me. Just visiting.
A tourist in the city of God."

"Hey. No skin off my ass if you shoot yourself in the
foot," he said. "But don't make it shitty for the rest of us."

I didn't have a good answer for that either. I hurried
out, nervously batting the weight in my coat pocket.

Riding the minibus back to South Beach, I kept opening
and closing the book, reading a sentence or two, then
shoving it back in my pocket, afraid to read more. Not until
I'd returned to the hotel and lay on our bed could I start at
the beginning.

It quickly became clear that it really was an ugly book. I
was not surprised. That was what disturbed me most: I wasn't
surprised. As if I'd known all along Bill's book would be
poison. And it was not just mean-spirited but dull, the prose
gray and pompous, the facts trivial. The first chapter, "Blond
Ambition," was a potted bio of Hillary Clinton where the simplest details—she won countless prizes in high school in

Illinois—were presented as sinister. Special attention was given to remarks that ran with her photo in the senior yearbook. "Most likely to succeed. And succeed and succeed. Unless Bob Dylan or Boone's Farm get her first." This proved that she was already a radical adept at passing as a Goody Two-shoes. As if it weren't a joke.

I felt like I was reading a report by an extraterrestrial: Familiar objects were presented with weird proportions and alien meaning. Whole passages made no sense unless you already shared the beliefs behind them. Bill expressed his meaning most clearly when he tried to deny it in a footnote: "15. This is not to suggest that women in politics are inherently ludicrous or that their feeling of inferiority makes them less flexible than men. History is full of admirable public women: Margaret Thatcher, Coretta King and Barbara Bush. Yet there is no denying that while difficult for a man to retain his humanity in political life, it is impossible for a woman to retain her femininity."

I would've snorted and shaken my head if I'd read that in Trollope. But Trollope died over a hundred years ago, and I hadn't swallowed gallons of his spit. This was Bill talking. These were his words, his thoughts, the real man behind the kisses.

I was wading through a chapter on Hillary's friend, Lani Guinier, "the Quota Queen," when keys jingled outside the door. I quickly stuffed the book between the mattress and box springs.

"Hey hey!" Bill crowed as he came in. "It's over! It's finished! I'm free!" He waltzed around the bed and tossed his briefcase in a chair. He had an exuberant, goofy grin.

"How did it go?"

"I was a hit!" he cried. He leaped on the bed, laughing and bouncing on all fours—I was afraid he'd dislodge the book. "People there knew who I was! Who've been reading me all along! They kept saying how amazed they were I was so young. That I sounded wiser than my years."

"Sorry I missed it."

"I shouldn't have told you not to come. I was afraid of

making an ass of myself in front of you. But they loved me! There were even people who think my book might make me famous."

I tried to smile. "What do they like about it?"

"That I told the truth. That I didn't pull punches. That I said the very things they'd suspected all along."

Seeing him crouched at my feet in his coat and dangling tie, I could feel nothing for Bill except cold courtesy. I had an inexplicable fear of being angry with him.

He rolled off the bed and pulled at his tie. "Care to join me in the Jacuzzi? Then we can go out and celebrate."

"Sure." I remained seated against the headboard, watching him remove his suit, wanting to think his suit had written the book and he might become likable again once he was out of it.

"I am so glad it's over. And I was good. You were right, Ralph. They were on my side. Did you have a good day? You don't look like you got much sun."

"Got out a little. It was too bright to read on the beach."

He returned in underwear and glasses and sat on the bed. He was already diagonal in his briefs. "Aren't you going to undress?" He gave my kneecap a squeeze.

"In a minute."

There was a worried pinch to his eyes as he stretched out beside me. I assumed it was my coolness that worried him, until he said, "Oh. There's been a change of plans for tomorrow. We're invited to go sailing by a friend of mine. With a senator. My friend wants to talk to this senator and needs me as his crew. And chaperon," he added with a laugh. "This senator's afraid people will think they're up to no good if they're out there alone. New man. Skittish. I told my friend I had a pal down visiting, but he said, 'Bring him along, bring him along. The more the merrier.' I'm sorry. Do you mind?"

"Not at all. Sounds interesting. Sailing."

"It means we won't be able to spend the day alone." He was surprised that I gave in so easily.

"No problem. We have tonight." Even that seemed too

long to be alone with someone who could write such rot. "You think I'm butch enough to pass for straight?"

He frowned. "Don't be silly. We just have to be discreet."

"Does your friend know about me?"

Bill shrugged. "He knows about me. He'll figure it out."

That caught me off guard. "Who is this guy?"

"Jeb Weiss. A lobbyist and consultant. He's done me a thousand favors. Which is why I couldn't tell him no."

"He's the man you met at the Plaza, right?"

"That's right." He was pleased I remembered. "He arranged this weekend for me, so the least I could do was say yes. But you really don't mind?" His bare toes plucked at my sock.

"Not at all." I did not respond to his signal that he wanted to play.

"I'm sorry about last night." He finally picked up on my distance, but attributed it to the sex.

"Last night was fine."

"I wanted to enjoy being with you. I tried. I really did."

"You seemed to enjoy it," I reminded him.

"My body did. But the rest of me was elsewhere."

"Your body was enough." I slid my hand into the fly of his briefs. His erection did nothing for me. I popped it out. Just a dick, a turkey neck with a flared cap too small for its shaft.

He lay there watching. "Miss me?" he asked.

I closed my eyes and kissed his mouth, accepting the challenge of making love without affection or even lust. I was afraid I wouldn't get hard, but my cock responded when he shinnied my pants off. We went into our nude routines and I was the erratic, unpredictable one, straining to connect.

"Should you—be doing that?" he sighed, after my tongue had been in the seam and buttonhole under his balls long enough for him to discover how good it could feel.

"No." I pressed his legs back and probed deeper in the gamy sweat.

"Oh my," he moaned. "Only—I could never do it to you."

"No? No?" I let his legs drop. "You wanna bet?" I scrambled up and squatted on his face, daring him to taste me.

He pushed me up, pleading, "You're suffocating me."

I furiously kissed his mouth, forcing him to taste a tongue that had been in his ass. "Still want me to fuck you?"

"That's okay."

"You wanted to last night. I got condoms while I was out."

"I was feeling strange last night. I've never been—no, Ralph. I'm enjoying you too much to spoil it."

He couldn't sense the anger in my moves?

"I can't believe you've never been fucked. You've got such an all-feeling asshole."

"Don't talk like that. Talk nicely."

"All right. You have a sensuous anus. I want to get in it."

He looked in my eyes. "Okay," he said. "I should. With you."

I got out of bed, broke open the condoms and uncapped the tube. The daylight made this more deliberate and dirty.

He lay on his stomach while I prepared him, "Ooh, cold," he giggled nervously. "Like I'm at the doctor."

I was nervous too, afraid a fuck would end the last bond I had with him. The latex turned my cock into an albino mugger.

His butt was raised by a pillow, his palms on the sheet.

"Go ahead. Hmm? Okay. Gently. Ow. Ow! *No!* Stop! Pull out, pull out! I can't—"

But I continued in, using my knees and one hand to keep him pinned, refusing to listen to his pleas. Until I was in him up to my balls and he was breathless with pain.

"Relax," I commanded. "Don't fight it." I was buried in tightness. And buried beneath us was the book that had hit me with the truth about Bill and how any love I'd had for him was built on self-deception.

He closed his eyes and breathed deeply, trying to inhale more space into his ass.

"Like it?" I said.

"No, it aches. Can't we do something else?"

"I want to come like this."

"Then just do it! Quickly."

I snuggled in. "Oh yeah, baby. You feel so good." I hated it when people talked to me like that during sex. "If only your Christians could see you now," I purred. "Mr. William O'Connor."

He didn't seem to hear. His face was clenched tight.

His lack of response fed my anger. I dug my hands in his hair. I spread his legs with my knees. I burrowed, rocked and stabbed. But when I let go, all fury and coldness vanished with the familiar, intimate beautiful jolts.

Before the last twitch, I was kissing his neck and face, whispering, "Sorry, sorry. Are you all right? Did I hurt you?" Because now that desire was satisfied, I was frightened by how badly I'd wanted to hurt him.

"I'm okay," he said. "Okay." He wiggled and found we were still joined. "You scared me. When you wouldn't listen. But after that—I trust you. I don't enjoy it. But I didn't have to."

Of course I hadn't hurt him, but I remained guilty, and guilt made me tender.

I eased out and flushed the white spleen in the bathroom. We resumed and it was solely Bill this time. He required attention to get worked up again, but I could be generous, knowing that tonight would be our last night. I silently declared us over. After I returned to New York and finished his book and became myself once more, I knew I'd never want to see him again.

We checked out when we left to go sailing the next morning. Our flight wasn't until six, but we didn't know how long we'd be on the water. Bill's book was buried safely inside my bag.

"And your friend Weiss knows you're gay?" I repeated on the ride over.

"That's right."

"Is he gay?"

"God no. Happily straight. A family man with three girls."

"He a Christian?"

"Nope. A real Texas Jewboy. As he likes to put it."

"But he has no problem with you being queer?"

"He considers it a totally private matter, no worse than alcoholism."

"How very liberal of him."

"Uh, Ralph. Promise me you won't be a professional homosexual today. Okay?"

"Sure. I'll be like you. An amateur."

He laughed as if it were a harmless jest—yesterday's

triumph had made him invulnerable—yet there was no real bitterness in my quips. Knowing we were finished, I felt very loose and careless with Bill this morning, and able to suppress all bad feeling for the sake of a close-up look at some Republican movers. Bill was sharing a lovely farewell gift with me.

We parked by a small marina on the Biscayne Bay side of the island, where a grove of masts gently rocked and rang their halyards like wind chimes. Miami fretted the horizon across the water. We found the boat at the end of the dock, a white twenty-five-foot sloop with "Born Free II" on the stern. The skipper, a leathery blond with an old face, an athletic body and a ponytail, stood on top of the cabin, unwrapping the boom while listening to a stout man in a gray suit on deck. It was the same stout man in the same gray suit whom I'd seen with Bill at the conference.

"Billy! Good morning!" the stout man called out. "Come aboard. Come aboard." His golden voice had a tinge of Texas. "This is Sam, the owner of this fine craft. You're Ralph," he told me. "The chum who Billy flew down for the weekend. Jeb Weiss," he announced when we shook hands. "Sorry if I spoiled you all's plans, but we'll have fun. Sun and water. Sun and water."

I wondered what else he knew besides my name and sexuality, but there was nothing else to know, was there?

Bill beamed, proudly showing me off like a trophy. He was instantly familiar with Weiss. "This your yachting outfit, Jeb?"

Weiss chuckled. "Forgot to bring my play clothes. Consider yourselves lucky. You wouldn't want to see my knobby knees."

His double-breasted suit and Windsor-knotted rep tie added to his comic look. Short and heavy, with a high forehead and salt-and-pepper chin beard, he suggested a love child of Napoleon and Burl Ives. His feet were surprisingly dainty, the ankles in thin blue socks like silk stockings.

"I think we're set. We've laid in plenty of Dr Pepper, which I hear is Mike's beverage of choice. I've asked Sam to stick to the bay. We don't want our guest getting seasick. All we need is our guest. And unless I'm mistaken, that's him yonder. Ahoy!" he shouted.

A tall man in a yellow windbreaker came out of the parking lot: the squared face and broad shoulders of Senator Mike Griffith. Won't Nancy be surprised, I thought, if I ever tell her about this weekend. He was accompanied by what looked like a teenage son.

"Will you look at who he's brought," said Weiss. "Our old friend Ren Whitaker. Mike's cagier than I thought."

In a rugby shirt and festive shorts, without his suit or podium, Whitaker looked more boyish than ever. He came down the dock with a preppy strut and Ultra Brite grin. The Senator had the bland geniality of a man doing a chore, but Whitaker was slyly tickled to be here.

"Oh God," groaned Bill. "We're stuck on a boat with *him*?"

"Relax, Billy. Ren can be perfectly pleasant when there's no other born-agains around. Having him along might make it easier to show Griffith who we are. Wouldn't hurt for us to spend time with Ren either. Mike!" he sang out. "Come aboard, come aboard. So glad you could make it. You found a friend, I see?"

"Hope you don't mind," said the Senator, climbing into the boat. "You know Ren Whitaker, don't you?" His half smile was more knowing than he pretended.

"We're good buddies," said Weiss. "Say hey, Ren."

"Morning, Jeb," the boy chirped, his voice perkier here than in public. "Ran into Mike at breakfast. He told me where he was headed. Sounded like fun, so I invited myself along."

"Afraid we were going to tell stories behind your back?" Weiss joshed.

The boy only laughed. "Nothing to tell, is there?"

"The more the merrier," said Weiss, and introduced the rest of us. "Billy's going to be a household word when his book comes out this spring, Mike. At least inside the Beltway. And his friend, Ralph. Who is not in politics but is a real person."

I wondered if Griffith might find my face familiar, but he

saw a hundred new faces a day. Whitaker shook my hand with a hard little grip and a suspicious glance at Bill. He and Bill greeted each other like estranged sibs at a family reunion; Whitaker did the better job of feigning friendliness. With his button nose and Sunday school haircut stiff with hairspray, he looked like he'd been specially designed to be hugged by grandmothers and pedophiles.

"If you're ready to shove off," said Sam, "I need one of you gentlemen to give a hand."

I volunteered, hoping Bill would join me and I could ask about Whitaker. He remained with the others, as if afraid leaving them would mean a loss of face.

Sam started the engine, I cast off the bow line and pushed us from the dock. We motored out into the water, a ship of fools on a day cruise. I doubted that I'd witness anything so obvious as money changing hands, but I hoped to learn something.

When I got back to the deck, Weiss was still on his feet, making a great show of inhaling the salt air. Whitaker and Senator Mike had parked themselves on the bench in the stern to watch the marina slide past. Bill sat self-importantly at a right angle to them, keeping an ear cocked in their direction. The engine was too loud for anyone to speak without shouting.

"Isn't this the life!" said Weiss.

"God is good!" said Whitaker.

When we were past the jetty, Sam sent me forward again to crank up the mainsail. I'd been demoted to crew, but didn't mind. Work gave me purpose. I furiously turned the winch and a shadow slowly climbed overhead. The sail thudded and buckled, then snapped taut and lifted the boat out of the water. We began to fly. Wind was alligatoring the blue-green bay, where other wings moved with a soothing running-in-place stillness, their masts and hulls tilted over the water at beautifully tense angles.

I received a brusque, comradely nod from Sam when I returned: the companionable silence of real men. If he only knew. Everything blew in one direction. Weiss's necktie slipped out and streamed from his neck. Only Whitaker's hair remained in place.

When the motor was shut off, the Republicans came out of their William F. Buckley reveries to chat. Weiss asked Whitaker about his kids.

"Couldn't be better. We have another on the way."

"Numero four, right? Karen must have her hands full. Have you met Karen yet, Mike? She's a doll."

I'd noticed the wedding ring on the boy's finger, but was startled to hear he was a multiple father.

I sat across from Bill, who kept his arms folded, looking miffed that Weiss gave so much attention to Whitaker. The Christian wasn't my type, but he was pretty. Even with that haircut, he would not look out of place at Wonderbar.

Their rivalry was about rank, not sex, of course, but old habits of seeing are hard to break. We were all men and, except for Weiss, not unattractive. I'd lived too long in New York: The scene suggested the setup for the obligatory orgy in a porn movie. I was amused to find myself checking out the slim thighs and basket of the spokesman for the Christian right.

When Bill finally looked at me, I stuck my index and middle fingers obscenely in my mouth, wanting to slap him out of his pompous pose. He frowned at me and tightly shook his head.

Weiss plumped down beside me, facing Senator Mike. "Feeling better, Mike? About being down here, I mean. Less negative than you feared. Am I right?"

Senator Mike shrugged. "For the most part. Until yesterday when Claude Raymond got up to speak."

Weiss smiled. "Good old Claude. We keep our distance from him, you realize."

"Your people sure loved him," said Mike, smiling too.

"Not everyone," Weiss insisted. "A faction."

"Sounded like everyone from where I was sitting."

"Ren," said Weiss. "I meant to compliment you on how well you handled that yesterday."

Whitaker rolled his eyes. "I did what I could. Once

Claude was up there, nothing I could do except let him say his piece. Or we'd have had half the conference walking out."

"Not half," Weiss claimed. "A few people. Not many."

I thought half was closer to the mark, but couldn't say so without letting Bill know I'd been there.

"Didn't I warn you?" Weiss chuckled. "You should've had someone tailing that boy to shy him away from the cameras."

"We did. Only he vanished a half hour before the session."

Into the men's room, where I had seen him.

"Now be honest with me," said Senator Mike, a wink in his tone. "You're telling the truth when you say that man's appearance wasn't planned? Not at all 'accidentally on purpose'?"

"Lord, no," said Whitaker. "You saw the networks last night. Sodomites and baby killers. That's the sound bite they chose to represent us. Not what we wanted."

"Just be glad it was a Saturday," said Weiss. "When nobody watches the news."

"Well, my wife watches," said Senator Mike. "It's the image she has of this conference. She did not want me coming, you know. She thinks the AFC is out to create a Baptist police state."

They all laughed, even Senator Mike.

"Is she the only one who thinks that?" asked Weiss. "You're among friends. You don't have to use her as your mouthpiece."

"No, I know better than that. But I listen to Martha. I have to. I live with her. And she's right every now and then."

I was fascinated by these maneuvers disguised as banter, but Bill looked bored. For a journalist he was awfully incurious.

"What do your wives say about your politics?" asked Mike.

"Karen backs me a hundred percent," said Whitaker.

"Mine couldn't care less," Weiss snorted. "So long as she gets a new car every year."

Senator Mike glanced at me and Bill, passed us over and

said, "Well, Martha is a skeptic. She's no feminist. I better make that clear. But she has friends who're feminists, friends who've had abortions, friends who're gay. She's of the 'mind your own business' school of government. She hates scape-goating. I'll have a hard time telling her I have no qualms about the AFC."

Bill shook his head and smirked. "So who wears the pants in your house?" he said scornfully. "You or your wife?"

Senator Mike flinched, then regained his smile, recog-nizing this was only a pup imitating the bigger dogs.

I couldn't understand why Bill jumped in, except Sena-tor Mike had lumped gays with feminists. Bill shared his smirk with the others, expecting them to laugh with him.

"Who wears the pants in your house, Billy?" said Whitaker.

Bill lifted his chin in the air. "I'm single," he sniffed.

"Ah. Then nobody wears pants at all," Whitaker quipped.

Bill indignantly puffed himself up, his face turning red. He sank back, glaring at Whitaker.

Weiss ignored their exchange. "Let's cut to the chase, Mike. You must agree with Martha some or you wouldn't bring her up. But this conference was about love, not hate. A veritable love feast. No fire and brimstone. And no Pats. Buchanan *or* Robertson. That wasn't just window dressing. Because we learned our lesson in ninety-two. People don't like hating other people. Oh, they hate them plenty in pri-vate, but get uncomfortable when their hate's made public. They don't like holier-than-thou-ness. Ren will back me on this. The coalition is pro-family without being anti-others. We don't have to go after feminists or anyone else to give our-selves a warm hug. Sure, you need bad guys to hold a move-ment together. But hey, we got Clinton in the White House." He laughed loudly. "Which has been a gift from heaven. People can hate someone in office without feeling that they're hating flesh and blood. And, by proxy, hate everyone and -thing he stands for, and still feel good about themselves. We didn't know it at the time, but Bubba and Hillary are the best thing that could've happened to us."

For a moment, I thought Weiss had been carried away by

his golden voice and said more than he intended. But no, it was what he wanted Senator Mike to hear. When I looked at Bill to see what he made of this rhetoric of sublimated hate, he sat with his head lowered, still stewing over Whitaker's supersubtle put-down.

"But when Clinton is out and the AFC is in?" said Senator Mike. "Will you stay nice? Or will we be hearing from the Claude Raymonds and Pat Robertsons again?"

"Ask me no questions and I'll tell you no lies," said Weiss, exchanging a look with Whitaker. "We don't even know if the AFC will be in business by then. Do we, Ren?"

"But we're committed to this new approach," said Whitaker. "It's not just an end run around the liberal media. And we'll be in operation long after Clinton is gone, if I have a say in it."

Weiss chuckled. "Ren is new to the game. But I'm an old whore. I think only in the short term. It's not like we're asking you to marry us, Mike. Just sleep with us for as long as it feels good. You know why a dog licks his dick? Because he can."

Before anyone could figure out what he meant by that, Weiss called out, "How about some music, Skipper? That's a tape deck by the helm, isn't it?"

"Affirmative. Any requests?" Sam asked over his shoulder.

"No rap music," said Whitaker. "And no gospel."

"What do you have?" Senator Mike got up to look at the tapes shelved under the instrument panel. "Any Grateful Dead?"

"Hey, a man who speaks my language," said Sam. He found a tape and popped it in. The speakers inside the cabin began to drive us through the water with the steady beat of "Truckin'."

"That's more like it," said Weiss. "We were getting too serious. Invited you out today, Mike, only so we could get better acquainted. Anybody hungry? Thirsty? I got soda, beer, sandwiches from Wolfie's." He glanced at the brooding Bill, but thought better of asking him and went to the cooler himself, handing out the drinks, wrapped sandwiches and napkins.

I was not yet ready to drop politics. A useful yet safe question had come to me. "Something I still don't understand," I said. "Why do Republicans hate Hillary Clinton so much?"

They all laughed, Bill joining with a thin, deliberate snicker while he warily watched me.

"No more than the rest of the country," said Weiss. "She's been a gift to us from the start."

"The lady could take paint off a barn just by looking at it," said Whitaker.

"Even Martha grumbles over Hillary," said Senator Mike.

"You haven't gotten the skinny from Billy here?" asked Weiss. "After all, he wrote the book."

"We haven't talked about his book."

"No?" That surprised Weiss. "You're in for a treat. Go for it, Billy. Give us your spiel. You should've seen the crowd at his presentation yesterday, Mike. They loved him."

Basking in the sudden attention, Bill smiled and sat up again. "She's a bitch," he said proudly. "So says anyone who's ever worked with her. Pushy, cold and humorless. Nobody elected her, but she carries on like they did." He had to know I'd disagree, but he wasn't speaking to me. "And there are things people suspect but that my book proves. Her marriage is a fraud. She doesn't love her husband and never did. She uses him as a front for her own ambition."

"How do you know that?" I said.

His smile broadened. "The evidence speaks for itself."

"What? You hid under their bed?" I faked a friendly laugh. "And what does their marriage have to do with their politics? It's a totally private matter. Isn't it?"

Bill didn't recognize his own phrase. "No, it's about character. Hers and his."

Before I could press him, Whitaker launched into the joke about Hillary and the high school sweetheart who'd become a wino. I'd first heard it from Nancy, but the joke had another meaning in this crowd. Bill's maraca laugh joined the chorus. He was happily one of them now.

He barely knew that I was here. I didn't care. This wasn't the place to attempt a serious conversation about sexism and hypocrisy anyway. I resumed my invisibility and ate my sandwich while Weiss shifted the talk into real estate and possessions.

"I hear you got yourself a Lexus, Mike."

Senator Mike shook his head. "You've made quite a study of me, Jeb." He lifted his can of Dr Pepper as further evidence.

"Small town. You hear things. Great car, isn't it? I own two. One in Houston and one for D.C. Billy takes care of the D.C. car when I'm at home. Still no problems, Billy?"

"Runs like a dream," he replied.

The boat lurched over the rocky wake of a cabin cruiser.

I stared at Bill. I chewed and swallowed. I said, "You keep an apartment in Washington, Jeb?"

"That's right. Out in Cleveland Park," he replied, assuming I already knew. "You and your wife still looking at weekend getaways out in Frederick, Mike?"

Bill was too busy wiping mustard off his chin to understand what I'd just learned. Jeb Weiss was "the friend." He owned the car that Bill drove, the fancy apartment where Bill lived. I'd forgotten such a man existed. Jeb Weiss was not just a useful contact, but an extremely important, necessary figure.

"If your wife is into horses," he was telling Senator Mike, "I should put you in touch with . . ."

Bill had kept his importance a secret from me. Why?

Ego? He wanted me to think he'd done it all alone?

Or were they lovers? That would be perfect, I thought, final proof of Bill's low worth. He was not his own man but a closeted politico's kept boy.

Yet much as I wanted to believe that, I couldn't. Bill said Weiss was a family man, but family men sometimes dabbled. And he said Weiss compared homosexuality to alcoholism, but maybe he drank too. No, the only justification for my disbelief was Weiss's perfect ease around me. A homely older man was not going to be so relaxed in the company of his boyfriend's trick.

I was not jealous myself. You cannot be jealous of something you've already rejected. If my pride was hurt, it was only over my failure to suspect any kind of sugar daddy in Bill's life, political or otherwise. I should be pleased to gain complete knowledge of this rat's nest before I said good-bye to it.

Bill nodded at me, smirking with a mouthful of sandwich, expecting me to share his happiness.

Just then, a catamaran hissed across our stern, a quartet of young women on board shouting and whistling at us. When we turned to look, they bent over in unison, dropped their sweatpants and flashed four white asses.

"Did you see that?" sputtered Whitaker. "That was gross!"

Senator Mike was laughing. "We can't let them get away with that," he said. "Skipper, Skipper. Can you come around? Can we pass them? We got to give as good as we got."

"Yeah yeah," cried Whitaker. "Let's moon them back!"

"Right you are, gentlemen," said Sam, and he spun the wheel, unfazed. "Watch your heads."

"Ho ho. You boys aren't serious," said Weiss.

"Come on. Are we men or are we mice?" cried Senator Mike, on his feet and undoing his belt, the man who listened to his wife now chortling like an adolescent. "All butts to port."

Bill stood up with them. Our boat was faster than the catamaran and we were gaining on his side. "Come on, Jeb. We're waiting for you. You too, Ralph."

"Not enough room," I said. And there wasn't after Weiss shuffled over, shaking his head while he fumbled with the buckle under his double-breasted jacket. He did not stand by Bill but next to Senator Mike.

"Oh ladies! Ladies!" hollered Whitaker.

But I could not sit by priggishly when four Republicans faced me and bowed. Before I knew what I was doing, I'd jumped up too, turned and yanked down my shorts.

There was a blast of air across damp skin, and shrieks from across the water.

"Hey! Don't moon *us!*" Whitaker shouted at my rear.

"Sorry," I said as we all straightened up, zipping and grinning. "Bad aim."

Fifty yards behind us, the girls jeered. All they had seen was a united battery of male cracks, with nothing to set off the intentions of one ass from the others.

12

It was over. The prolonged sigh of turbines and cabin pressure expressed my state of mind perfectly. A few hours of air and train travel would put my error safely in the past. It seemed a minor detail that half of what was over still sat beside me.

"Wild, weird, wondrous weekend," said Bill. "Many highs. One big low, but many highs."

He sank back, luxuriating in accomplishment, his cheeks and nose marzipan pink from his day in the sun.

Down in the darkness, the lights of a Florida city formed a neat grid of magnified microchips and printed circuits, as if the entire country were a computer.

"What was the low?" I asked indifferently.

"On the boat!" he said, shocked I didn't know. "When Whitaker put us down in front of everyone. For being gay," he whispered, though the aisle seat was empty.

"When did he do that?"

"His crack about you and me being girls."

"All I remember is something about nobody wearing pants when one's a bachelor."

"You didn't catch what he meant? He never comes right out and says it. But he knows. He's always full of little sneers and insinuations around me."

"You're not being paranoid?"

"I know how his mind works. Slick little twit. Jeb kisses up to him only in case Robertson crashes and the twit takes charge. Jeb likes to keep his bases covered."

"What's going to happen to Pat Robertson?"

"Nothing probably. Jeb thinks he might lose credibility if his crackpot theories get more cracked. Conspiracy stuff. Banks and Freemasonry, I forget the details. Not important."

Bill was too self-absorbed to notice many things. Driving out to the airport, I'd asked him what had been accomplished today, what seeds Weiss and Whitaker were planting with Senator Mike. Bill didn't know or care. To him it had been a blur of guy talk broken only by praise of his book. No wonder he was a lousy journalist. And to think that on the flight down two days ago, I had toyed with the notion of being in love with this man.

Now seemed a good time to announce that we were finished, but I couldn't. I didn't have the energy, the public privacy of an airplane was the wrong place for a scene, and I was in Bill's physical orbit again, our faces pillow-close. We spoke softly the way we had in bed. I had to wait until I was home and could write him a cool, firm, logical letter.

"Jeb Weiss sure seems to love you," I said.

"Oh yeah. Jeb's believed in me from the start. You couldn't guess how much he's done for me. I owe my life to Jeb."

"You never mentioned that it was his apartment you live in."

He didn't even blink. "No, it's *my* apartment. I rent it from Jeb. He stays there when he's in town, but it's my apartment. I told you that."

"You said you had that arrangement with someone. But not that it was Weiss."

"Well, you didn't know who he was until this weekend, so I guess I saw no point in mentioning it."

"Anything else you haven't mentioned?"

He looked at me blankly.

I wanted to know only so I could close the door on Bill with no unanswered questions. To make it easier to answer, I put the question in the past tense. "Was there ever anything personal between you?"

"Like arguments?"

"Like sex."

"With *Jeb*?" His open mouth pinched his nostrils shut. "He's old enough to be my father. And fat! You saw how fat he is."

"He was never interested in you that way?"

"No! He's straight." He began to laugh. "Is that the only reason you can imagine someone like him being interested in me?" He treated it as a hilarious impossibility.

"Why else wouldn't you tell me about him?"

"Because I didn't think it was important. Was that why you looked cranky on the boat? You were jealous?"

"I don't care what was between you and Weiss. I just like to know what's going on."

A more perceptive man would've picked up on what that implied about us, but not Bill. "Everything is sex to you. Do you ever think about anything except sex?"

"Maybe not," I muttered. "I can be stupid with sex."

He nudged my leg, thinking I was stupid with it now.

"So it's a professional relationship?" I asked.

"We're friends too. Jeb's been like a father to me. Well, not a father but a big brother."

"Did he help with this book?"

"He helped to get it published. He didn't help write it, if that's what you mean. Every word is mine."

I was sorry to hear that—but would it have changed anything if Bill were only the front for a ghost?

"I don't know, Bill. The whole idea of your book bothers me. Why write an entire book about their marriage?"

"That's just part of it. You'll see when you read it."

I didn't tell him that I was halfway through it for fear that my deceit would put me on the defensive.

"If you don't like Clinton's politics, attack his politics," I said. "Not his marriage."

"It's a character issue. The personal is political."

I was startled to hear that phrase from him. "Or just gossip," I said. "How would you like it if someone attacked your book by attacking your personal life?"

"I'm not a public official. And there's nothing wrong with *my* life."

"No?"

"Nothing wrong with being gay," he said.

"Did you mention it at your presentation?"

"Of course not. What do you expect me to say? 'I'll be reading from the chapter about the Clintons at home, and by the way, I'm a homosexual.' "

"How would they have responded?"

He shook his head. "You still think gay Republican is an oxymoron, don't you, Ralph? That conservatives are narrow-minded bigots. But Jeb was perfectly nice to you on the boat today."

"If they're so accepting, why did you feel humiliated by Whitaker?"

"Oh that. That's just him. Strictly personal. He uses it against me. He knows I can't call him on it, especially when other people are present. I wasn't humiliated. I was angry." But the sulk had returned to his face; he curled his mouth while he thought it through. "It's not easy being gay and conservative," he said righteously. "I get slings and arrows from the Whitakers, and dumped on by my own community. So-called. But I refuse to sacrifice my sexual identity for the sake of my political beliefs. Or vice versa. You think I should come out, don't you? Tell everyone I'm gay?"

No, I only wanted to confront Bill with his hypocrisy.

"Well, I can't! If it were just me, that'd be one thing. But I have other people to consider. There's my family for one."

"They don't know?"

"We don't talk about it, but they know. They're a different generation. It would hurt them if people knew their son was 'that way.' And there's Jeb. Who's done so much for me. We've talked about it. *He* brought it up. He's said maybe I can play that card when the time's right, but not yet. Which makes sense to me. Maybe after my book is out and I've made a name for myself. When conservatives hear that the author of *Regiment of Women* is gay, they'll think, 'Hey, homosexuals aren't all radical crazies but can be smart and right-thinking and just like us.' My example will make them more accepting."

"I'm sure it'll be greatly appreciated." I wanted Bill to stay in his closet. We already had Roy Cohn and J. Edgar Hoover. We didn't need William O'Connor.

"I can't stand it when radical types claim anyone not like them is a self-hating homosexual. Because I'm not."

"No, Bill. I think you love yourself very, very much."

He had talked himself into such a determined mood of self-love that all my sarcasms shot unnoticed over his head.

It was not yet nine when we landed in Baltimore and I put on the dead weight of my duffel coat again. Winter was a shock, the night dank and frigid, all light frozen from the black air as we hurried out to Jeb Weiss's cold, smug Lexus.

Bill was to drop me at the Amtrak station downtown, where I could catch the next train to New York. "My folks are on the way," he announced when we were on the highway. "I promised I'd say hi when I got back. Do you mind if we stop by before I take you to the station? There's a train every hour."

"Do you want me to wait in the car?" I said snidely.

He remained tone-deaf to my gibes. "No, I want them to meet you. But I'm only telling them you're a friend. Okay?"

"Oh, why not?" I enjoyed the irony of learning still more about Bill before I ended us. The owl of wisdom flies only at twilight.

We descended from the interstate into a region of shopping centers and subdivisions, one of those sixties boom suburbs that grew shabby instead of solid with age, a lower-middle-class world of disappointment and too much television. I was not being snobbish. I'd grown up in an identical setting outside Raleigh.

"That used to be my father's service station," said Bill, pointing out a white cube on the corner that housed a video store.

"He was a mechanic?"

"No. A businessman. Just not a very good one. He bought it right after he got out of the air force. Now he's the assistant manager of a Giant supermarket."

"What does your mother do?"

"She's a housewife. My parents believe the man should be the breadwinner in a real family."

We pulled into the driveway of a cramped split-level with a short, treeless front lawn. All the curtains were drawn except for a pair open on a tasteful, uninhabited living-room suite, like the window display of a furniture store.

"This is where your hustler made his house call?"

"Who? Oh. That." He spoke as if I'd mentioned something painful when I only intended small talk. "Yes."

Opening the car door, he checked his hair in the rearview mirror and took a shopping bag from the backseat. I followed him up the front walk. He rang the bell as if he were company.

A pinprick of light blinked in the peephole. Locks and chains clattered inside. The door was jerked open by a small, fiftyish woman with pale brown bangs and lipstick.

"Billy! You're back! How did it go? Did you have a good time? Come in, hon. You must be freezing."

Then she saw me and stiffened.

"Mom, this is my friend Ralph."

She couldn't look at me. "You should've called and said you were bringing company, William Junior. I'm a sight."

"No, Mom. You look great."

She wore earrings as well as lipstick with her slacks and blouse, even though it was after nine on a Sunday night.

"Pleased to meet you, Mrs. O'Connor."

She relaxed slightly when she discovered I was polite. I forgot the effect my shaved head sometimes had on strangers. "Let me take your coats. Come into the living room and I'll fix something warm to drink. Really, hon. You should've called."

"We can't stay, Mom. I have to get Ralph to his train. I just wanted you to know I was back. And give you these." He reached into the shopping bag for a box of chocolates.

"You shouldn't have," she said. "How nice."

"Is Dad home?"

"Oh Bill?" she softly called. "Billy's here. With a friend. Come up and say hello."

"Billy who?" Feet thudded up a short flight of steps around the corner. Bill's father strode into the front hall. I would've known it was Bill's father anywhere. The familiar lips and nose were stranded on a heavy face with horn rims and thinning hair. His eyes were gray instead of brown, so he looked like an old, padded Bill suit worn by a stranger. He was as tall as his son, with a beefy, muscular handshake.

"Bill O'Connor," he declared. "Big Bill." He was fiercely buddy-buddy once I introduced myself. "Real chrome dome you got there, Ralph. Must get cold this time of year. You use car wax or floor wax up there?"

He was an Irish Catholic good ole boy. He did not sound as Southern as his wife, so it was hard to tell what was the South and what was Irish in his noise; he combined the worst of both masculinities. One of the few things my own father and I shared was a distrust of blowhards.

Mrs. O'Connor looked worried again, then shut down and let her husband take over. Big Bill seemed too busy making a loud impression to suspect anything about the man with his son.

"What're we doing out here, woman? You should be making these boys at home."

"We can't stay, Dad. Just wanted you to know that I was a hit in Miami. And give you these." Bill reached into his bag and took out a box of cigars.

"Havanas. Real ones?" Big Bill did not thank him, but skeptically read the lid. "Huh. Your thing went well, you say?"

"Very. Jeb thinks that I might even do a few talk shows when the book comes out."

"Hear that, Helen? We might have a TV star in the family. Just don't let it go to your head, boy. Don't think it makes you better than the rest of us." He swatted his son's shoulder.

"No fear of that, Dad." Bill swatted him back. "I'll still put my pants on the same way as everyone else."

Watching their overdone father-and-son act, I almost felt sorry for Bill. I looked at Mrs. O'Connor, expecting her to share a knowing glance with me, but she stood there with her ceramic smile and a slight tremble of earrings, as timid as a sparrow. I decided her nervousness was not over me as her son's "friend," but as simply a stranger in her house. And this was the woman to whom Bill dedicated his book, as if she were his measure of all women?

We made our good-byes, Mr. O'Connor giving me another bear-paw handshake, Mrs. O'Connor regretting that we couldn't stay for cocoa. A few minutes later, Bill and I were in the car again, headed for the interstate.

"So. What did you think?" he asked.

"They seemed nice enough." What else could I say? Your father couldn't care less about your success and your mother's had a lobotomy? Other people's parents are rarely as interesting as their grown children think.

"You see now why it's so hard for me to come out?"

"Uh, no." Had that been the purpose of this visit?

"The salt of the earth, my folks. Private and unworldly. Innocent. It would hurt them to think that their neighbors knew the truth about their son."

"And they know you're gay, even your father?"

"They know. Oh yeah." He snorted over that. "Don't let my old man's bluffing fool you. He's a sentimental fool. And emotional. Too emotional for his own good. Which makes him a lousy businessman. Just a big kid at heart. But I love him."

He couldn't hide his condescension. The distance between father and son was mutual, even if Bill didn't want to admit it. "Do you know what time's the next train?" I asked.

"Ralph? Do you really have to go back tonight? Wouldn't

you rather come home with me and catch a train in the morning?"

"Sorry. I have to be at the bookstore at nine."

"Can't you call in sick? Please. I don't feel like spending tonight alone. Especially after seeing my folks."

He now used his parents for pity, but I resisted. "I can't do that to the people I work with. I'd leave them shorthanded."

He sighed through his nose. "I won't beg. Just an idea."

We drove downtown in silence. I worried about what to say if he asked when we'd see each other again. He didn't. Maybe he was waiting for me to ask him.

He did not pull into the illuminated portico of the station entrance but stopped the car in the shadows fifty yards away.

"I'll let you off here," he said, the engine still running. "Was a great weekend. Wasn't it?"

"I won't forget it. Thanks."

"Thanks for coming. Many times," he said with a smirk.

I was still undoing my seat belt when he leaned over and took my head in both hands. Despite everything I knew, his kiss was electric, naked, as if his heart were in my mouth. I could resist the sexual pull only by keeping my eyes open and watching his lids twitch in the panes of eyeglass between us.

"No?" he said when he let me breathe again, grinning confidently.

"Sorry." I jerked open the door and dragged my bag from the backseat. "We'll talk. You'll hear from me, don't worry."

"I never thought that," he laughed. "I was only worried about tonight. Your loss," he said cheerfully. "Good night."

"Good-bye." I swung the solid, clockwork door shut. I palmed a farewell to the hunched silhouette in a tinted window before I hurried into the station.

Solitude felt like wisdom. The northbound train pulled in ten minutes later, crowded with other relieved travelers returning from weekends with lovers or family. I found a seat beside a napping girl with a marketing textbook on her tray. I relaxed, closed my eyes and thought about nothing. The warm tube of light swayed through the darkness. I had no regrets about not going home with Bill, until we passed Wilmington.

I couldn't help it. One last time, one more orgasm. Sex had become a bad habit. It would not have been the mindless lark of before, yet bad sex tonight might make my kiss-off letter easier to write. There was no affection in my need, only hormones and resentment. By what right had he enjoyed me so much? I was angry with him for turning out to be so unlovable. Pictured nude, Bill now seemed to have been nothing but a smiley face with a hard-on.

I got up and took the bound galleys from my bag in the rack, needing to remind myself why I could never sleep with him again.

But his book was not as awful as I remembered. Dull, yes, tediously smug, but it no longer shocked me. Its antifeminist line seemed lazy, passionless and secondhand. Now and then, an argument was almost persuasive. The charge that feminism had ruined public education, once full of brilliant women barred from other careers, actually forced me to stop and think before I saw what was wrong with the assumption that women but not men should sacrifice their lives for the next generation.

I seemed to have an infinite capacity for being shocked, then digesting those shocks so I could see Bill again. Is that what my cool reading meant? I wasn't going to break off with him?

The chapter about the Clintons' marriage did not surprise me after the exchange on the boat. It focused on his infidelities, but blamed her for failing to provide "the intimate attentions any successful man requires." The last sentence read: "One cannot help but wonder why the First Lady seems incapable of showing more love for a man as handsome and virile, albeit overweight, as her husband."

The next chapter, "Girls Just Want to Have Fun," began: "It's a truth universally acknowledged that smart, independent women are attracted to other smart, independent women. The venerable tradition of the Washington lesbian . . ."

He was calling Hillary a dyke? I was shocked again. I wondered what his proof would be, what the libel lawyers said. But there was no mention of Hillary in what followed, only a discussion of Eleanor Roosevelt with footnotes citing a biography by a lesbian scholar, followed by tales of other "New Deal sisters," a woman in the Carter administration and a lengthy account of the recent confirmation hearings of the assistant secretary of HUD. His accusation of Hillary was pure innuendo, planted in the reader's mind yet never addressed.

As before, the denials of his footnotes were more honest than the text:

"12. This is not to suggest anything inherently wrong about lesbians in public office, whether elected or appointed, especially when they are in a loving, monogamous couple, as Achtenberg clearly is. Difficulties arise only in relationships that spill from private into public life, creating alliances and influences whose true nature is hidden from voters. One recently elected senator, a married mother with children, is known to have increased her support for such feminist measures as child care and federally funded abortion since she became the lover of her openly lesbian speechwriter. What the senator does on the side is a matter for her and her husband, of course, but any undue influence expressed between perfumed sheets should concern her peers and constituency."

I reread the footnote. I read it a third time. I stared out the window. There was nothing to see except darkness and my blurred, tilted reflection.

My first clear thought was: Nancy fibbed. She and Senator Freemen *were* lovers. But then I remembered who wrote this and realized it was a lie. A tremendous lie. About my best friend. Made public by a man I'd been humping. He didn't name names, only how many lesbian speechwriters were there who worked for women senators? I had to warn Nancy. A rumor like this could do terrible damage. Couldn't it?

And the next thought struck: Bill had gotten this from me. Had I mentioned Nancy's crush during our first meeting before I knew who he was? What had I told him that night? I couldn't recall. I knew I'd mentioned a friend who worked for Senator Freeman, so Bill knew that I knew her yet had said nothing.

The little shit. Poor Nancy. Criminally stupid me. When I remembered that these were "uncorrected proofs," and Bill hadn't corrected his galleys when we first met, it seemed too good to be true. He'd gotten this dirt somewhere else. Yet the feeling that *I'd* done something wrong remained stuck like a bone in my throat. That knot of culpability seemed to be the one thing that blocked my desire to kill the arrogant little bastard.

13

"Nancy. It's Ralph. Sorry to be calling so late but this is important. Are you there? I've come across something you should know. I don't know how major it is, but we need to talk. Give me a call. Tonight when you get in, no matter how late. Or tomorrow, except this might not be something you can discuss at work."

I phoned as soon as I got home. It was after midnight and I hoped Nancy would pick up, but was relieved when she didn't. I needed time to think this through, only thinking about it alone made the danger more elastic and imaginary, like a ghost story spun by a bad conscience. I did not fall asleep until three. The telephone never rang. A cold wind rattled the loose panes of my window all night long.

I took the galleys with me to the store the next day. Nobody even knew Bill existed except Peter. He arrived fifteen minutes after I did, stiffly bundled like a mummy when he trudged down the stairs. I followed him into the locker room. He'd hung up his coat and was unreeling his scarf.

"Cyberslut is back!" he laughed. "How was Anita Bryant country?"

"Can you look at something? Look and tell me what you think." I held up the generic gray galleys; I'd trashed the glossy brown jacket at home.

"And good morning to you," he snorted. "What is it?"

"A book that Thersites wrote. I want to know if I'm crazy or if something is as awful as it looks."

"Jesus, Ralph. It's only a book. You take the printed word much too seriously. So what's his big sin against literature?"

I opened at the dog-ear. "Just read the footnote. Tell me what you think."

"You have fun in sunny Florida?"

"No. Read."

His long face relaxed into a weary pout as his eyes twitched through the words.

"So monogamous dykes are A-okay," he muttered. "How nice."

"Keep going."

When he finished, he wrinkled his nose in mild disgust. "Smarmy. I've seen worse. But a gay man wrote this?"

"It's Nancy."

"*Your* Nancy? Oh my God." He dipped his face back into the pages. "And she's sleeping with her boss?"

"She isn't. But when this comes out next month, people will figure it's her and Senator Freeman and think they're lovers."

"Lesbo *Back Street*. Poor Queen Wenceslas. How embarrassing."

"Worse than embarrassing. It could hurt her with Freeman and the people they work with."

"But they're not lovers? You're sure?"

"Yes."

"No stolen kisses at the water fountain? No late-night muff-diving in the cloakroom?"

"No!"

"Then nobody will get hurt. She and her senator might even get a good laugh."

"You think?" I hadn't considered that.

"They're grown-ups. They must get this high school con-
fidential stuff all the time."

He said it idly, carelessly, yet his nonchalance was
enough to reduce my panic.

He flipped through pages. "This is the guy you're
seeing? What did you say to him?"

"I haven't said anything yet."

"He didn't give you this?"

"I swiped it. He doesn't know I have a copy."

Peter began to chuckle.

"What's so funny?"

"You, dear. This." He shut the book and returned it.
"The whole thing's a hoot. Don't you think?"

"No. I don't."

He gave me a lopsided, pitying smile. "Just trashy gossip
in another book about politics. Why do you want to make it
into *Tosca*? You need to believe that you're part of some big
drama?"

"I don't want *any* drama in my life. I can't believe I've
been going to bed with the kind of asshole who could write
this kind of sleaze. Not just about Nancy but other people
too."

"Love, oh careless love."

"I was never in love with him."

"You must have loved something if you could ignore his
calling until now."

"I was horny and stupid. You're the one who told me not
to let politics get in the way of a good lay, remember."

"Gee. Too bad I didn't get *my* nuts licked since it was my
fault." He was losing patience with my belated virtue.

"That's not what I meant. Okay. I knew I was playing in
shit. I just had no idea it was so deep."

"So you're not seeing him again?"

I glared at Peter in disbelief. "You think I'm that flakey?
I've damned him here"—I pointed at my head. "All that
remains is to tell him, which I intend to do tonight."

"Good. If he makes you unhappy." Peter closed his eyes
and sighed. "Sorry if I'm not taking your crisis in the proper

spirit, Ralph. But love affairs just don't seem all that tragic to me anymore. Only fun, then messy and absurd."

"Which is why you're such a good ear," I claimed, wondering how our conversation had become a quarrel, and if I should trust his judgment after all.

To: thersites @ br.caton.md.
From: sgtrock @ gw.ny.ny.
Bill,

When I returned to the store after our weekend in Miami, an advance copy of your book fell into my hands. I just finished reading it and I have to say: I am appalled. It's not the politics that disturb me, although that's the wrong word for this stew of gossip, innuendo and sexism. There are no ideas here, only prejudice and insult. I was shocked by your mindless slinging of mud. What I found absolutely unforgivable, however, was the footnote on page 175, where you accuse a U.S. senator of having an affair with her speechwriter.

You and I both know that this is Senator Freeman and my friend Nancy. I happen to know that they are not lovers and never were. You have opened yourself to a libel suit. Worse, your lie hurts a close friend of mine, someone who's never harmed you or anyone else. And you do it in a footnote, slamming her as carelessly as a man slapping a mosquito. I wonder how many others you anonymously harm that I didn't notice because I don't know them. You knew that I knew Nancy, yet said nothing to warn me or explain or apologize for what you were doing.

You would have to be blind not to realize that I've had second, third and fourth thoughts about us ever since we met. It was over our political differences yet I now see that your politics are symptoms of deeper faults: opportunism, thoughtlessness and self-absorption. I should be grateful to you for showing in cold print how morally blind you are, and what an ass I've been. I have been sleeping with the enemy—"sleeping" is the operative word. Thank you for waking me up.

I don't know what you have to say for yourself or if I want to hear it. Right now, I never want to speak to you again. I have never been so angry with anyone in my life. I cannot picture you tonight without wanting to punch your face in. That sounds like cheap cliché but it's exactly what I feel.

Ralph Eckhart

I'd intended to remain cool and objective so that my charges wouldn't seem merely personal. When I began to write, however, I found my anger flooding up in blunt sentences and raw words. If it had been a letter instead of E-mail, I might have reread and revised it. Instead I hit Send. The screen blinked while a black hole copied me. I held my breath, as if I expected the telephone to ring or the world to blow up.

14

The phone didn't ring until two days later, when I stood at the receiving table sorting through invoices with Alec.

"Someone up here to see you," Peter announced.

"Right there," I replied, too distracted to ask who.

"Doodly doodly do-do-doo," he said, and hung up.

I was tempted to call back, but didn't. "Wonder what this is about," I told Alec as I unrolled and buttoned my sleeves. I climbed the stairs toward the fake civility of Mozart on tape.

Nobody waited for me at Peter's window. I looked in at Peter. On the phone with a customer, he lifted his eyebrows and aimed his finger like a pistol toward Fiction.

Standing with the padded shoulder of an open trench coat squashed against a shelf, a hard briefcase propped beside her running shoes, Nancy suspiciously examined a copy of *Can You Forgive Her?*

I was overjoyed that it was her and not Bill, for a second. I cautiously approached. "Nancy?"

"Eck!" She broke into a grin and embraced me. Her coat was cold, her cheeks warm. She'd been by the store many times, but seeing her here today was as startling as a visit from the police.

"What're you doing in town? You got my message?"

"Oh yeah. Sorry I didn't call back. But I knew I was coming up for a bigwig lunch today. I thought I'd have time to visit, but the lunch thing dragged on and on."

"I don't get off until seven. You free for dinner?"

"Sorry. Kathleen and I are catching the five o'clock shuttle. I only have an hour."

"The Senator's with you?" I worriedly scanned the browsers scattered among the blond woodwork and wallpaper of book spines.

"Nyah. She wanted to go to Saks, if you can believe that. I took a cab down to see if you were free for coffee. I should've called?" She sensed my unease and thought it was only her timing.

"Not at all. I can take my break early. Let me get my coat."

"We can hang out in the basement, if that's better for you."

"No, no. Let's get out of here. Right back."

Peter produced a sort of shrug with one hand when I walked by, as if wearing a hand puppet who signaled that I had no cause for worry.

I took my coat from my locker and loaded a pocket with the bound galleys. I'd left the book here to avoid rereading and brooding on it at home.

The afternoon was cold but bright. West of the tall buildings and dense shadows along Broadway, the ice patches melted and glittered in the sun. I expected Nancy to drop her cheerful facade once we were outdoors, but she didn't.

"Lunch at the Harvard Club," she grumbled. "Miles of smiles and I'm the worst. My ego-petter goes on automatic pilot. I hate these in-and-out visits. I see just enough of New York to get a taste, then it's back to the hamster wheel."

Her confidence and energy made me feel that Peter must be right. The bomb in my pocket would only give her a good laugh.

"So how are you?" she asked. "You seem distracted."

"Didn't you get my message?"

"Oh yeah. You said you had some dirt?"

"It's more than dirt."

"Ralph? Oh." Concern filled her eyes. "Are you okay? I'm sorry. I thought it was only news about someone else."

"No, I'm fine. Quite fine," I said. "It's about you."

"Me?" She laughed, relieved and only slightly nervous. "Who's been bad-mouthing me now?"

"We should go somewhere where we can sit. You want coffee?"

"I don't need coffee. What is it, Ralph? Just tell me."

"Here. Let's sit in the sun." I led us to the wide sill of what had been the loading dock of a warehouse and was now the front of a pasta restaurant.

"Enough with the buildup," she said, jerking her coat taut and sitting beside me. "Out with it. You're getting me paranoid. Just tell me what you heard and who said it."

"It's not what someone said but what they wrote." I unsheathed the galleys from my pocket and set them on the briefcase she held across her lap.

"William O'Connor," she groaned. "*That* asshole."

"You know him?"

"God yeah. An old fart who writes for *American Truths*. So he's written a book. Whoop-de-do. *The Regiment of Women?* Ha! I can just bet what this is about."

"You know about this book?"

"No, but I know about him. Last year he wrote a slimy piece about Hillary Clinton that *almost* called her a lesbian."

"He does that here," I said, amazed that he'd pulled it before and Nancy knew and I hadn't guessed. But that meant she'd be prepared for what I was about to show her. "What you should see is on page one seventy-five. The footnote."

"He's famous for his footnotes. William 'Footnote in His Mouth' O'Connor," she sneered as she shuffled pages. "Twelve?"

"That's the one."

I shyly turned away while she read, as if she were

changing her clothes. Watching the backlit, steam-spouting pedestrians briskly file past, I waited for the defiant, scornful yelp that would show no harm had been done.

Her silence held. I turned to look.

Her straight cut nails were spread flat on both pages. Her face was full of pale sun, her eyes shut.

"Oh shit," she whispered. "Shit. I can't—" Her voice was reduced to a breath. She opened her eyes to read again, but the printed words hadn't changed.

"It's not true," I said. "Is it? It isn't. Right?"

She turned to me. The dark crinkles under her eyes italicized a wide empty stare.

"No," she murmured. "No. But that doesn't—" Her voice began to return as she flipped to the front of the book. "Is this out? Who's publishing it? Some pissant right-wing press?"

"No, a major house. It's listed for April, so it'll be in stores in a couple of weeks. Then I was right to be worried? It can do damage?"

"I don't know. Maybe. Right now the damage is—shit! It's so—shit, Ralph." Her enormous eyes covered me like headlights. "Here was this thing in my head, this private, personal thing. And to see it in print, where the whole world can see it! Where Kathleen can see it and know the whole world is looking. It's like I've been stripped in public!"

I laid an arm around her shoulder, wanting to provide cover. Her body had contracted to a tight tremble. My touch only helped her to focus her anger.

"Where the hell did he get this? Somebody in the office? Somebody in another senator's office?" she snarled. "Or did he make it up? Hey, Freeman's got a dyke speechwriter and we know how they can't help themselves around straight women. Fat old bastard. What gives him the right to smear Kathleen like this?"

"You've never met him?" I withdrew my arm.

"I know his type from his Hillary article. A bitter, middle-aged oaf with a couple of divorces. One of those losers who hang out in bars telling people what's wrong with America."

"At least he doesn't name names," I said.

"But everyone will know. Even you knew, and you're on Mars." Her anger was like buckshot; a stray pellet struck me. "If he named names, maybe I could stop this. Threaten them with a lawsuit. Only that would still mean telling Kathleen, because a threat from me doesn't mean shit. But he doesn't name us, so it doesn't matter, does it?"

"Shouldn't you show it to Kathleen?"

"I guess. Only—" She squeezed her eyes shut.

"How will she react?"

"I don't know," she said in a baby voice. "She won't be comfortable around me anymore. She might ask me to resign. Oh shit. Whatever happens, it'll change everything between us."

"Nancy. You're not still in love with her?"

Her lips pulled taut against her teeth. "Maybe I am, maybe I'm not. What difference does it make? I want her respect and trust, but after this"—she shook the book—"she's going to be paranoid as hell, for good reason."

"It's a stupid book, Nancy. From beginning to end. Nobody's going to take it seriously."

"You don't know Washington."

"Maybe it'll come and go without anyone hearing about it."

"No way. And I'll know it's out there and be waiting for it to drop. Damnit, Ralph! Why did you hit me like this? Couldn't you warn me that you were about to dump a ton of bricks?"

"I warned you. I left a message on your machine."

"How was I to know it was anything real? You're off on Mars with your little friends. You don't know anything of value."

I knew her anger wasn't about me, but that hit hard and I lost my temper. "Goddamnit, Nancy! Don't blame the fucking messenger. I wanted to help you."

"How else do you expect me to react? Be happy? Grateful?"

"I didn't expect to be called an idiot!"

"It's just a show to you, Ralph, a silly show on the news. Beltway Bozos. This bastard shits on us and you proudly bring me his turd. You think it's just a joke, but I'm in it to my neck."

"I know it's shit. That's why I'm showing you! I don't know where the bastard got it, but he didn't get it from me!"

She stared.

I bit my lips together.

"You know this ass?" she said.

I was so stunned by my slip that I didn't know what to say. My silence finished giving me away.

"Oh God, Ralph. You got this book from *him?*"

"Okay," I said. "Okay. Look. I didn't know who he was at first. He's not an old fart. He's in his late twenties. And gay."

"This misogynistic puke is gay?" Her eyes grew wide again. "And *you* slept with him?"

I nodded.

"When?"

"Last weekend."

Her eyes remained locked with mine.

"Then back in January. And in November. That's when it began. When I was visiting you." Once I started, I couldn't stop unloading facts into her stony look.

"You went to bed with this sleaze?"

"I don't believe it myself."

Her gaze darted down, a corner of her mouth knotted in a bitter smile. "Wow. You'll fuck anything. If it has a pretty face and penis, you'll hop right in bed with it."

"Nancy, I didn't know who he was."

"Don't you have any brains? Are you nothing but dick? You can hump a right-wing shoveler of shit like he was just another dumb gay boy?" She suddenly caged her mouth with her fingers. "Oh my God. He got this from you? You oh-so-casually mentioned that your friend in the Senate was hot for her boss."

"No! I told you. He didn't get it from me! I may be on Mars but I'm not a complete idiot. He'd already finished his book when we met. I don't go around telling strangers that my best friend's in love with a married senator. Believe me, Nancy."

"Why should I? You weren't even going to tell me how you got this excrement."

"If he got the story from me, wouldn't he have said this speechwriter only had a crush?"

"I don't know. Would he? You know him better than I do."

"When I read his book, I realized I didn't know him at all."

"And I'm feeling like I don't know *you*, Ralph. After all these years. Whether he got this from you or not. You could have sex with this worm? And not just once but repeatedly. Were you in love with him?" she sneered, twisting the phrase like a knife.

"It was only sex. Stupid, mindless sex."

"Jesus, Ralph. Didn't you have a clue?"

"I did and I didn't. I've ended it. As soon as I read his book, I ended it."

"Better late than never, huh?"

We sat there glaring at each other, breathing cold, dead air while pedestrians paraded past, politely averting their faces from what looked like any street squabble between lovers.

"I have to get to the airport," said Nancy. "God, how am I going to sit with Kathleen on the flight back knowing what I know?" She thrust the book at me.

"You don't want it?"

"And do what with it?"

"Show it to her. So you can prepare her. Wouldn't you rather choose the time and place when she first sees it?"

"Great. I get to throw the shit in the fan myself." But she opened her briefcase and tossed the book in. She wiped her hand against her coat and stood up. "Where can I catch a cab?"

"Let's go back to Broadway."

She started off in a clipped, hard, professional gait. I had to step quickly to catch up.

"Nancy, I fucked up. I'm sorry. But this had nothing to do with us. It was bad luck I tricked with a guy who smears you in a book. It might have been good luck if there was something we could do to stop it."

"Ralph, I am so furious with you right now that I can't think straight. I won't say another word in case I say something I can't unsay. I need time to sort this out."

"But you will, won't you? And you'll call me?"

She turned away and raised a hand.

A cab pulled over. I stepped off the curb and opened the door for her. I held on to it when she tried to pull it shut.

"I'm sorry," I told her again. "I love you."

"I'm sorry too, because I don't love *you* right now. That you could get involved with someone like that makes me feel like you just punched me in the stomach, whether you meant to or not."

"It was dumb lust and had nothing to do with you, damnit!"

She shook her head. "We'll continue this later, Ralph. Just let me go." She yanked the door, I released and it slammed shut.

Watching the cab ease into the traffic, I waited for her to look back or raise a hand, something. She gave me nothing.

I returned to the store kicking myself for spilling the entire pile of bricks when I'd intended to hand her only a few bricks she could use. So she saw me not as an equal but a fool from Mars. I seemed to have blurted out the truth about me and Bill to get even with her. It was *her* fault that I'd made a bad situation worse.

But I was only trying out other emotions in a vain attempt to wiggle off the hook. Because I knew in my bones that I deserved her contempt. I remained afraid for Nancy, worried over the damage the book might do, yet I couldn't help feeling someone had just died: the decent if occasionally foolish fellow I thought myself to be, at least in her eyes.

I gave Peter a shorthand account of the fiasco after work. He offered sympathy, although not in a manner to put my mind at ease. "Lesbians," he muttered. "They take sex *so* seriously. I'm sorry she didn't get a laugh out of it. But she's a tough cookie. She'll be okay."

When I got home that night, there was no message from Nancy on my machine. I stretched out on my futon and tried reading, but Trollope too had died on me since Miami. I turned on TV for the ten o'clock news, wanting to feed my black mood with a murder in Queens or fire in the Bronx. I can measure the depth of my depressions by the hours of news I watch in the evening.

The telephone rang and I jumped up to answer. "Yes?" I said to show that I'd been expecting her call.

"Let me begin by saying that I was more than a little ticked off by your letter."

I almost didn't recognize him. His tone was so unexpected, neither apologetic nor furious but dryly jocular. "Bill?"

"I had no idea that woman was a friend of yours. We hadn't met when I wrote that, remember. I'm sorry. But that's no reason for you to say the nasty things you said about me and my book."

He spoke as if it were a minor misunderstanding that would amuse us both once he cleared it up. I had difficulty connecting the man I despised with this friendly, reasonable voice.

"You told a lie about my best friend," I said calmly. "A lie that can hurt her with the people she works for."

He responded with an impatient sigh. "It's not going to hurt anybody. How did you get a copy of my book anyway? Nobody's supposed to see it until pub. Those are uncorrected proofs, you know. Full of things I've fixed."

"You mean—" There was a flash of hope, a lifting of the weight in my chest. "You cut the stuff about Nancy?"

He hesitated. "I can't remember. It's one sentence among thousands. I may have changed something."

He obviously hadn't. How could I hope for anything from Bill?

"So even after you knew that I knew her," I said, "you didn't take it out?"

"I couldn't. It would've spoiled the point I was making. As for being sued, lawyers have vetted the book. I don't name names. Gossip columns run blind items all the time. And how do you know it isn't true?"

"Because she told me."

"You believe everything she tells you?"

"Yes."

Another exasperated sigh. "Then why are you so worried? It's politics, Ralph. Where people say untrue things about each other all the time. You have no reason to be upset. God, I never dreamed you were so kneejerk p.c. Why're *you* playing feminist? You're a man. What's feminism got to do with you?"

I was baffled to hear my reaction dismissed as cliché. "It's not feminism. It's fairness. It's honesty. Hearing you talk about your book, I thought it'd at least be serious. I wouldn't agree with it but I'd have to argue with its ideas. But there're no ideas in it. You don't criticize the beliefs of Hillary and others. You trash them for being women and call them dykes. You don't see anything wrong about a gay man calling the First Lady lesbian?"

"Why are you so concerned about my book, Ralph? It's got my name on it, not yours. Your friend has you pussy-whipped."

I remained detached from my anger. I am so full of self-doubt that I usually bend to the other person's tone, and did so even now. It had been easier for me to lose my temper with Nancy, whom I loved, than with Bill, but then anger is so intimate.

"Nancy was in New York today," I said. "I saw her. I showed her the footnote. And I gave her your bound galleys."

Silence. "You shouldn't have done that, Ralph."

"And I told her how I know you."

Long silence. "What? Is she going to 'out' me? Is that what you're saying?"

"No." Neither Nancy nor I had even considered it.

"What would that accomplish? I just want you to know that she's already hurt by your book. It's not just politics to her. She blasted me for knowing you. Even if your footnote doesn't screw her job, it's going to take her a long time to trust me again."

"So it's my fault? You told on me to get even? Look, the three rules of politics are: You scratch my back and I'll scratch yours; smart rats desert a sinking ship; and, if you can't stand the heat, stay out of the kitchen."

He was covering his confusion with adult noise, but his panic scrambled his voice and logic.

"They can't stop my book, you know. Who is this girl to you anyway? Just a friend. A female friend. But I was in love with you. My book doesn't matter to you at all. You're just tired of me and want to break off and this way you can feel righteous about pulling the plug."

"What?" It was like dropping through a trapdoor into a different conversation. "What're you talking about? You loved me? When did you love me?"

"Why do you think I brought you to Miami? Why do you think I risked taking you out on that boat? I'm still in love with you or I wouldn't be calling after your hurtful letter." He swallowed loudly. "I've been waiting for an apology for what you wrote. But you only throw more fuel on the fire. I should have seen this coming. You were acting very odd when we said good-bye on Sunday. And to think that I never felt so close with another man as I did with you, Ralph. You enjoyed me. Admit it. We had great sex."

"I've been to bed with enough men not to confuse that with love." I remained baffled over how the argument had gotten here.

"Uh-uh. Bodies don't lie. Mine didn't lie and neither did yours. I can't believe you'd trash love for the sake of a twat."

I felt that I was talking to a lunatic. I was afraid to lose my temper. "Bill," I said calmly. "Do you realize how insane you sound?"

"I'm saner than you. I know what I want and you don't.

You're too concerned with what your friends think for you to commit yourself to anything. You are emotionally impaired."

"You've written an ugly book that smears a friend. And you say it's *my* problem with intimacy? I think you're nuts."

"Me? What about you?" His voice grew higher, shriller. "Have you heard me say anything about wanting to beat *your* face in? I couldn't believe it when I read that coming from a man I loved. I gave you the benefit of the doubt because you were upset for your friend. But you're sick, you're dangerous."

"It was hyperbole, it was to make a point."

"What a moron I've been. I cannot believe that I've spent the past three months being in love with a psychopath."

I was finding my own thoughts twisted in a fun-house mirror. "The feeling is mutual," I said. "Only neither of us was ever in love, so drop that line of crap and get real."

"That's all love is to you. Crap. You'll regret this. Years from now, when you're a lonely nobody still slinging books and I've become someone important, with a syndicated column or my own TV show, you're going to think, I could've shared that. I could've been part of his life. But you blew it."

I wanted to laugh, but made only a soundless shudder. "Uh-uh, Bill. I'll just smile and shake my head over the fact that I ever got mixed up with someone like you. But your book's going to die the quick, silent death it deserves. Although I doubt even that will slap you awake."

We'd reached the point in any telephone argument where you wait for the other person to hang up, but won't yourself because it will be a confession of weakness.

"And that's all you have to say?" said Bill. "That you hope my book dies?"

"Yeah. Because you don't get it, so why waste my breath?"

"Well, screw you, it won't die. Good-bye and good riddance."

"Good-bye, Bill."

Yet neither of us hung up. He breathed static in my ear. Then his breath stopped. "Good-bye," he repeated. Click.

And the cordless receiver went dead in my hand. I settled it into its slot in the answering machine, jiggling and scooting it around until the little light showed that the contacts had reconnected.

I fell on my bed, full of the exhaustion that follows anger, without having had any of the pleasure of ripping into someone. I'd expected to argue politics and moral principles and found myself instead stuck in an emotional tar baby. But I'd finally ended my idiocy. "My work here is done," I muttered sarcastically. All that remained was Nancy. I hoped no harm would come to her and I could do something to prove myself worthy again. We'd been angry at each other before, and it wasn't always my fault. I trusted that the bedrock of friendship remained in one piece under the bad feeling. And yet—

I had been in love, hadn't I? It was tangled with so many extenuating emotions that I couldn't call it love until now, when it was finished. I'd had a last glimpse of it in that blink of hope when I thought Bill might have changed the footnote. But he didn't care enough about me to do even that much. My love wasn't so much love of Bill as love for the surprise that someone like that could love me. I would not deny what Bill claimed to feel, even though his love was a blind, solipsistic thing that had nothing to do with me.

Pity. I'd been loved and in love before and knew I would fall again. Tonight, however, I found myself utterly unlovable.

15

But it wasn't over. Only Bill was over. His book remained.

Nancy called me the next night. "I didn't show it to Kathleen. I've decided to sit tight and play dumb until it hits. If my nerves hold out. Just back off, Ralph. This is my problem, not yours. I'll handle it my way. I know I had no business blowing up at you, but you were guilty by association. And you can't deny you associated. That's my gut, not my head, but it's going to take time for my gut to forget."

When I phoned her a few nights later, she asked me not to call for a while. Our talks only fed her anxiety about Kathleen and her anger with me. "I'll call *you* when I'm ready to talk."

It was never out of my thoughts over the next two weeks, yet, unable to discuss it with anyone, the threat became oddly normal, slipping to the back of things like an unpaid bill.

Until one afternoon, I cut into a box with my utility knife, pried open the cardboard and there, in the Styrofoam peanuts, was William O'Connor. His glossy brown jacket, as startling as a face, had multiplied in the dark; ten books crowded the box like square, flat toadstools. I nervously took

one out. There was no photo on the flap; the publishers kept
their author's youth a secret. The back carried blurbs from
Rush Limbaugh, Oliver North and his sibling rival, Ren
Whitaker. I flipped to page 175. It was still there, the same
exact words, in granite now that thousands of copies were
being unpacked all over the country.

I considered hiding the box under the table, unprocessed,
only what would that accomplish? Just another book, I told
myself, more slabs of foliated wood pulp. I stacked them on the
table, checked them off on the packing slip, stamped the backs
with price codes and set them in a cart to be taken up with the
other new titles. They squatted there for an hour until Robert,
who handled "New and Noteworthy," casually wheeled them
away. I hoped that they'd be digested in the forest of print
upstairs, not to reappear until we returned them unsold for
credit.

I wanted to call Nancy that night and say, "They're
here," but I stuck to her request.

Books exist in their own parallel universe, a slow, quiet
termite realm. *Regiment* sat unnoticed and unsold on a low
shelf facing the cash register that first week. Ray Kerrison in
the *New York Post* devoted half of his column to "a scathing
picture of harpy politics that justifies our worst nightmares."
But people who read the *Post* don't read books, or at least
don't buy them from us. I wouldn't have seen the column if
Peter, who was addicted to Page Six, hadn't spotted it.

But there was one other *Post* reader at the store. I
entered the staff lounge the next morning to find Alec sitting
cheek to cheek with Erica over an open copy of *Regiment of
Women.*

"Listen to this," said Erica. "It gets worse." She read out a
passage about the political effects of PMS.

"Disgusting," said Alec. "Downright gynophobic." He'd
become something of a feminist since he and Erica became a
couple. "You seen this, Ralph?"

"What is it?"

"This alleged book," snarled Erica, handing it to me.

"Misogynistic propaganda. The *Post* loves it, so you know it's evil. I can't believe we're selling it."

"We should show Elaine," said Alec. "She wouldn't have ordered it if she knew what it was."

I thumbed pages, pretending to see them for the first time. "You can talk to her," I said. "Although I doubt she'll send it back. She refuses to play censor."

"What if you talk to her, Ralph?" said Alec. "You know how to get around Elaine."

"Well, um, I haven't read it and we get bad books all the time." But I wanted us to carry it so I could watch its progress, although that made me feel weak and complicitous.

"No, no," Erica insisted. "I should do it. Woman to woman. I can make her see what insulting filth this is."

So Erica spoke to her and, as could be predicted, only irritated Elaine into giving her standard speech about freedom of the press and letting the buyer decide. Her one concession was that we wouldn't display the book in our windows.

That *Regiment of Women* gave right-thinking people such a wonderful opportunity to be righteous was the first indication it would not quietly die.

The next week, Anthony Lewis on the *Times* op-ed page denounced it as "a frat house bull session posing as journalism."

A few days later, Christopher Lehmann-Haupt reviewed it on the *Times* book page and, as if to spite his colleague, actually gave it a good review. Without saying what they were, he referred to allegations about Hillary Clinton as "speculative mischief."

The newsweeklies reviewed it the following Monday, then the *Voice* attacked it—in two different columns. And suddenly, in the insidious way of books, *Regiment of Women* seemed to be everywhere. I could not drop into my newsstand without a fresh reference to it leaping from a magazine cover or contents page. I was looking but hadn't expected it to be so blatant. The brown jacket intimately leered at me from the windows of other stores, not like a book I already owned, but one I'd written myself.

It briefly broke from its parallel universe into the news when, during a press conference on her health plan, the First Lady was asked to comment on a new book about her. With a cold glare and mechanical laugh, she said, "That would be like me asking if you still beat your wife, Brit. Next question."

Through it all, Bill himself was weirdly invisible. There were repeated mentions of someone named William O'Connor, treated even by his critics as a serious journalist, a sane adult who knew what he was doing. The affectionate body in a bed and frantic voice on a phone disappeared in clouds of print.

Hillary Clinton's press conference was on Friday, the first week of April. The following Wednesday, late at night, Nancy finally called me.

"You were wrong, Ralph. It didn't disappear."

"I know. But it's not selling," I said, grabbing at that silver lining. "Not here anyway."

"Well, New York," she mumbled. "What does New York know?" She sounded exhausted, beaten, a mood that worried me far more than her anger. I heard a collapse of ice cubes in a glass. "I can't get on the Metro without seeing people with their noses stuck up that book's ass."

"Has it been getting much press down there?"

"Does the pope shit in the woods? The papers have been full of it since Hillary's press conference, all tarted up with ethical thumb-sucking about journalism and privacy."

"I haven't seen any mention of the footnote. Not one. They talk only about the Clintons."

"People on the Hill have seen it. They know who it's about."

"What do they say?"

"Not a damn thing. But I can feel fingers pointing me out. The whispering that stops when I enter a room."

"Has Kathleen said anything?"

"Not yet. But it's coming. At first, whenever she was

cool or curt with me, I thought, She's seen it. Then an hour later she'd smile or joke and I thought, She hasn't. But this week, she started avoiding me. Meetings I usually attend with her? She takes one of the guys instead. But tomorrow—she's taking me to lunch tomorrow. Not here at the Capitol but out. Where we can talk in private. Which can mean only one thing."

Another pause, another echo of glass and ice.

"She's a smart woman, Nance. She's not going to let loose talk scare her into firing you."

"No, she *is* a smart woman. And smart women cut their losses. For political or personal reasons. Oh shit, Ralph." Her voice tightened, fighting tears. "I didn't know her respect meant so much to me. If she dumps me, who will I be? Nobody. Nothing. I'll just want to curl up and sleep for a hundred years."

She'd spoken the same way when she broke up with Annie. "What're you drinking, Nancy?"

"Screwdrivers. Appropriate for somebody who's been screwed."

She rarely drank, and never alone.

"Do you want me to come down this weekend?"

"And do what? Hold my hand? Say you're sorry for the umpteenth time? I'm not calling for help, Eck. I'm calling only because you're the one person on the planet I can discuss this with. But talking to you only reminds me that a person did this to me, and you know him."

I audibly winced.

"All right. I'm not being fair," she admitted. "But this thing in my gut has overwhelmed me, no matter what I tell myself. You and it and everything else. I feel so alone. There's nobody I can talk to or trust anymore."

"Well, I'm grateful you called to let me know what was happening."

"I didn't call for you, Ralph. I called only so I could hear myself talk and find out if I'm as crazy as I feel. Do I sound crazy to you?"

"You sound depressed. And a little drunk."

"I am depressed. But I'm not going to throw myself out a window anytime soon."

"I didn't think you would."

"But do you know what stops me from considering something like that? It might hurt Kathleen. Not personally, but it might hurt her reputation. Is that sick or what?"

I was too taken aback to know what to say except, "Don't drink anymore tonight, Nancy. It's only making you feel worse."

"No worse than talking about it makes me feel. I better get off before I say something even more stupid."

"Can I call tomorrow night and find out how the lunch went?"

"Why? You need to feel like you're in the loop?"

Again I felt slapped. "I'm your friend. I want to know what's happening."

"Oh all right. Call me. Although I can't promise I'll be more coherent than I am tonight."

"Good luck," I said. "Good night."

I hung up, more irritated than worried for Nancy. Her suffering was so superior, and irritation made a good defense against my fears for her.

The next day at work, Thursday, Peter came up to me in the men's room with a wicked grin. "Do you know your boyfriend's on *Nightline* tonight?"

"Shh." I checked the stalls for feet. *"Nightline?"* I whispered. "You're kidding. The whole show?"

"No, it's about journalism and ethics. But they announced on the radio this morning that *he* was one of the guests. You want to come over and watch with me?"

"In front of Nick? No way."

"Nick leaves for a medical conference in Boston this afternoon. He won't be back until Saturday. Come over. I've rented a couple of bad movies. We can order in food, watch a flick, then see your old trick get his fifteen minutes. Don't look at me like that."

"Like what?"

"Like I'm not taking this in the proper spirit. Would you rather I bitch and moan over what a terrible thing you did by knowing this person?"

"No, I bitch and moan plenty on my own." It was difficult to tell what was callous and what was good sense in Peter. "I'd rather nobody I cared about even see what this guy looks like."

"Well, I'm watching, with or without you. Wouldn't you like to be there to point out his good features?"

"Oh. Why not? Yeah. Maybe sharing the experience will undo the weirdness of seeing the jerk go national."

So instead of worrying about how Nancy's lunch went, I spent the day wondering what Peter might think and I might feel when we watched Bill on television.

We took a cab to Seventh Avenue after work, at Peter's request, and entered the building that with its tiers and pent-houses stood over the West Village like a redbrick ziggurat. Their one-bedroom co-op, purchased during Nick's years in high finance, was not a penthouse, but it had a terrace. The living room was big enough for their lemon tree to sit indoors during the cold months without turning the room into a jungle. The furniture was simple yet expensive, the television in an altar of honey-colored wood. Framed posters of off-Broadway and regional productions hung on the walls; Peter had played Peachum in both *The Threepenny Opera* and *The Beggar's Opera*.

Tossing my coat in their bedroom, I saw again the car-tons of medical supplies stacked against the wall, the IV stand like a medical gibbet in the corner. On the night table by Nick's side of the bed was a copy of the *New England Journal of Medicine*; on Peter's side, *The Wind in the Willows*.

"You don't have to do your drip tonight?" I asked when I returned to the living room.

"I'm off the IV for now. I'd love to get rid of that crap but don't know what my doctor will be pushing next month. Do you want Chinese or pizza?"

While Peter phoned our order, I looked again at the photos on the bookcase. Their long history was a touching, challenging mystery to me tonight. I picked up a snapshot in Lucite—Nick and Peter preserved as young clones in lumberjack shirts, Peter with a blond mustache that echoed Nick's black one. Peter appeared at my shoulder.

"They say lovers grow to resemble each other," he said. "Like people and their dogs. But not us. We grow more different."

"And you've been together, what, fifteen years?"

Peter rolled his eyes and groaned. He disliked having people count their years, hearing not envy but condescension, as if their longevity betrayed a lack of imagination.

"I just don't know how you do it."

"Habit, guilt and duty," he muttered.

"And love," I added.

"Oh sure. But you need the others as glue." He made a face. "I'm not the easiest person to live with either, you know."

I followed him into their shiny kitchen, where he poured himself a glass of juice.

"I know it's not easy," I said. "But I do envy you having each other."

"Like hell you do. You're a romantic lover. Nick and I are domestic lovers. The world is divided between those who want to live in couples and those who prefer quick hits of lightning. I don't think any less of you because you're single."

"I wasn't criticizing." How could he think I was in a position to judge anyone? "Just impressed by your ability to stay together. Especially when you're so different."

"Oh yes. The frivolous and the serious. The self-centered and the selfless."

"But you complete each other. It's good to be frivolous now and then. And you're not self-centered."

"Oh but I am. Now more than ever. I have to be. While Nick remains a man of principles. All thumbs with the personal, so he gives his love institutionally. Other boyfriends bring you soup. Mine goes to meetings. But Nicky doesn't know how to fuss or hand-hold, so this works out for the best."

These occasional grumbles were part of his normal gestalt with Nick. Each of us was at the center of his or her own story; I did not expect Peter to forget his story for the sake of mine.

"I didn't ask you over tonight to talk about Nick," he said. "Let's talk bad movies. What shall it be? *Madame X* or *Mothra?*"

The pizza arrived, Peter served it up on atomic-colored Fiestaware, and we settled on their wide, soft leather sofa to watch Japanese sci-fi. Peter enthused over the dada qualities of the poor dubbing and cheap special effects while I watched the digital clock in the VCR. I hadn't talked to Nancy today, but there would be time to call from my apartment after *Nightline.*

The movie was not yet over when Peter took it out to put in a blank cassette. "I'll tape this for you."

"What makes you think I want to save it?"

"For posterity."

"His posterior was his only good point," I grumbled.

The portentous theme music came on, a sliced spaceship of letters floated forward, and the giant moth flapping over Tokyo was replaced by the winglike ears of Ted Koppel.

"We have learned to say that the personal is political. But have the media gone too far? Are we in journalism engaged in real character issues or only tabloid excess? How much private life are men and women in public office required to share with us? These are the questions we hope to explore later in the broadcast with our guests, Ellen Goodman, syndicated columnist, and William O'Connor, author of a controversial new book about women in Washington. But first, a special commentary from our correspondent, Jeff Greenfield."

Introduced with old clips of Gennifer Flowers accusing and the Clintons denying, Greenfield delivered an instant history of sex and politics. There was stock footage of Franklin and Eleanor, JFK and LBJ—the good old days—followed by Gary Hart and a repeat of Hillary's unconvincing laugh at her news conference—examples of the New Honesty.

"Why are they all Democrats?" said Peter. "Republicans must have no sex drive. Except for yours."

"Joining us now in our Washington studios are Ellen Goodman and the author of the book cited by Mrs. Clinton—"

I didn't recognize him at first. He sat stiffly in the blue-gray ether, blinking behind his glasses like a marmoset appearing on a talk show.

"Him!" cried Peter. "You made yourself miserable over him?"

No, there was nothing appealing about Bill on TV. The studio lighting washed out his color and fattened his moon face. He looked shiny and stuffed, packed with more of the success that had begun in Miami. Only his skittish brown eyes suggested he was ever warm-blooded.

"He's better naked," I claimed.

But Goodman too looked like acrylic, the exactness of video giving too much definition to her lipstick and sienna hair. She spoke first, talking about the political uses of gossip and her concern that the phrase "The personal is political" had been taken from feminists to justify a new kind of mudslinging.

She and Bill were not with Koppel but on a screen within the screen, in another part of the studio, a separate room, just as Peter and I and the rest of the country were in our own rooms, the whole world a vast honeycomb of glass.

"What Ellen neglects to mention is that liberals have been slinging this kind of mud ever since . . ."

Bill used his pompous FM voice, yet it was enough to turn his moon face into a logo of dead love.

"We've had double standards for liberals and conservatives, men and women. What I do in *Regiment of Women*, Ted, is simply bring the same standard . . ."

As with any talking head, I stopped listening and studied his hair, his necktie, the stark absurdity of human ears. Yet I'd licked those very ears. He was a hole in the screen, an empty space that I filled with regret, shame and, yes, nostalgia.

"No," said Goodman. "The report of a rumor about President Bush in an alternative newspaper, which I won't repeat, or jokes about him on a late-night comedy show are not the same thing as calling someone a bad wife and claiming it's hard news."

"He looks like a pig," said Peter. "A paranoid little pig. Look at his eyes."

And it was true. When Bill spoke, he seemed at ease, yet when the camera caught him while Goodman or Koppel was talking, his eyes hardened with distrust.

I impatiently waited for Goodman to cut through the generalities and attack what was foul and stupid in Bill's book, only she couldn't report innuendoes without spreading them. It was like watching a fight between boxers in straitjackets.

"Yack yack yack yack yack," said Peter during the commercial. "What a load of windbaggage."

"You think I was a jerk for going to bed with him?"

"Not my type. But I don't understand the attraction of three-quarters of the men my friends find hot. Whatever blows your hair back. But you said he was a good kisser?"

"Yeah."

"I can see it. Oral. Although he looks like he'd have an easier time kissing doughnuts than guys."

When Koppel returned, his implacable brow had a faintly anxious crimp. Something had been said during the break. Bill looked cockier than ever, Goodman more edgy. Koppel said, "Ms. Goodman, I believe there was a new point you wanted to bring up?"

She cleared her throat. "I feel I have no choice. I did not want to get into the specifics of Mr. O'Connor's book tonight. But, because he continues to mention it, I fear viewers might get the impression that *Regiment of Women* is a serious work of journalism. It isn't. It's nothing but rumors. All smoke and no fire. A tired male fantasy about women in power."

Bill happily snorted. "One can tell an opponent is cornered, Ellen, when they resort to an ad hominem attack. And where there's smoke there's fire." He was proud of his retort.

"There's a fire, but not the one you claim, *Bill*," she said, rebelling against his TV intimacy. "All I see behind your

"I must say on Ms. Goodman's behalf," said Koppel, "that I don't think that's what she was implying."

"Well, we all know the little games used by the liberal media to get their enemy." He remained insanely pleased with himself. "But my book speaks for itself. And people who want the truth about Hillary and her kind will know better than to let you besmirch the man who brought them that truth."

"I am sure they won't," Koppel said kindly, the bizarre exchange producing little more than a slight rearrangement of his brow. He pressed a finger to his ear. "Ah. It seems we have run out of time. I regret that I cannot ask either of you for closing statements. But Mr. O'Connor, Ms. Goodman, thank you for joining us. Tomorrow night our guest will be Secretary of State Warren Christopher and we will discuss Bosnia and . . ."

Lady Glencora Palliser, the Duchess of Omnium, could not have dispatched a social embarrassment more adeptly.

"My God!" crowed Peter. "Do you believe that? Do you fucking believe that?" He fell back on the sofa, gasping and laughing. We'd been drawn to the edge of our seats during the scene.

"To receive a transcript of tonight's broadcast," began the announcer, and I realized that hundreds of thousands of people had seen that, Nancy and Kathleen among them.

"He's out of his mind," said Peter.

"I knew he was nuts," I said, "but I never dreamed—"

"A gay man has to be schizophrenic to work for the right. But he can kiss that career good-bye. Can't you just see it? All over the country, Republicans going yuck?"

"And flushing his book down the toilet," I laughed.

"Happy now?"

"Oh yeah." I was elated by the sheer surprise of it, but under that was something more solid: the feeling that the problem had solved itself. The revelation that the author of *Regiment of Women* was not just gay but as mad as a hatter would save Nancy's relationship with Kathleen.

"Uh, it didn't make him attractive again?" said Peter.

"Are you kidding? He's more screwed up than I ever dreamed. He calls a bunch of women dykes, then claims he's a victim?"

"A creep. A real creep." Peter got up. "I'm sorry. This is too good not to share. I'll just take a minute."

I followed him into the bedroom, where he sat at his desk and turned on his computer.

"You're not going to mention you know someone who knew him?" I worriedly asked.

"Hey, Shanghai Lily is the soul of discretion. And this dish is so good that I don't need you to make it tasty."

He clicked his mouse into another show already in progress, the box filling with handles that raced from their televisions as quickly as Peter had. I never knew *Nightline* had such a gay following.

"What an asshole."

"A real maroon."

"Just what we need. Another hypocrite homo."

"I thought he was kind of cute. Duh."

"You would. You find George F. Will humpy." Peter spoke the sentence as he typed it.

I watched for another minute before I stepped away to take my coat off the bed.

"Don't go," said Peter. "Tomorrow's Friday, remember? I'll be off in two shakes. I don't mean to be rude."

"No, I should get home and call Nancy. Share the good news." I kissed him good night and went out to the door, hearing the castanet clicking of his keyboard behind me. I could not stop grinning over the gorgeous comedy of William O'Connor's self-destruction.

It was half past midnight but I only got Nancy's machine. "Did you see it? He shot himself in the foot on *Nightline*. Nobody can take his book seriously now. Nancy? Are you there? How did your meeting with Kathleen go? Look, no matter what was said, it's not too late to undo. Right? Please pick up. I don't mean to be a pest, but this is good news. Isn't blanket attack on women in politics, an *ad feminem* attack if you will, is your own confusions and difficulties. Women cannot win in your book. If they date more than one man in their life, they're tramps. If their marriages look good, their husbands must be wimps. And if they're single, well, they can only be lesbians. One can't help concluding that you don't like women very much. You clearly don't know many. You seem to have a problem relating in any way to the opposite sex."

Bill's lips turned pale. His hard eyes glared at her. I'd seen that same insulted look in beds and restaurants.

When his silence lasted an infinity of seconds, Koppel said with deep concern, "I feel we should give you a chance to reply to that, Mr. O'Connor. We can cut to our affiliates while you gather your thoughts."

"No. Not necessary," said Bill. "I can answer that—that below-the-belt blow. It's exactly what I mean by the liberal media's double standard. Let me say right off that my criticisms of Hillary Clinton have nothing to do with my being gay."

My head jerked forward. He actually said that?

"I'm shocked a reputable journalist thinks she can humiliate me on national television. You can't. Because I'm not ashamed of being gay, and it does not kill the truth of my book."

The studio confusedly cut to Goodman staring, then back to Bill, then to a medium shot of them both while Goodman twisted around to glance off-camera in disbelief.

Peter and I turned to each other with our mouths wide open.

Goodman quickly recovered. "I hadn't stopped to think that you might be gay. In fact, until I saw how young you were, Mr. O'Connor, I assumed you'd been through a bad divorce. But that's neither here nor there. Whatever your sexual orientation, *you* have a problem with women."

Bill recovered too, a look of triumph replacing his hurt and anger. "You 'out' me in public and can't be honest about it? Dirty pool, Ellen. I'm ashamed of you."

it? Call when you get this message. Please. No matter how late."

I told myself not to worry. Nancy often turned off the volume of her machine when she didn't want to talk. I was much too happy to take seriously the possibility that her meeting with Senator Freeman had gone badly.

Still chuckling to myself, I fell asleep with an ease I hadn't experienced in weeks. It was over. Everything would be fine. I dropped into a dream of London and a street of bookstores full of new paperback editions of old novels I wanted to reread.

A telephone beeped. I grabbed it in my sleep.

"Hello?"

"Did you watch? Did you see me?"

I floated in warm darkness. "Bill?"

"Now I'm your equal. I did it for you."

I was not awake enough to be surprised that a voice from television now spoke to me. He seemed to be calling from somewhere inside my head.

"What did you do for me?"

"I came out. Nationally. It was a brave thing to do, but I did it. Uh, don't you watch *Nightline*?"

"No." I resisted letting him know, but only for a second. "But I did tonight. And I saw you self-destruct."

"It wasn't self-destruction. It was my moment of truth. And I did it for you. To prove that I'm not a coward or hypocrite."

"Bill. That was the least of my problems with you. Out or in, I don't care. And you didn't do it for me. You didn't even do it for yourself. I saw what happened. You thought you were being outed, which you weren't. You jumped at the chance to make yourself the injured party, the holy victim. What does your good buddy Jeb Weiss have to say?"

"I haven't talked to him yet. I don't care what he thinks. I care only what you think."

"Well, I think you made an ass of yourself. You showed the world that you're a paranoid twit."

"Okay. Okay. You say that but you don't really believe it.

You're envious. But success has made me magnanimous. I'm every bit as good as you are now. I am."

I was amazed that my damning words passed straight through him. He continued to speak softly, gently.

"I'm coming to New York, next week. For my book. I want to see you again."

"Bill? Don't you understand? I don't want to see you. Ever. Seeing you on TV tonight was bad enough, but I knew not to take a punch at the set."

"Do you know what I'm doing while we're talking?"

And I understood why his voice remained low and preoccupied.

"Here. Listen." He moved the receiver toward a brushing noise like a dog scratching at a door to be let in.

My skin crawled, but I did not hang up.

"I'm naked on my bed, pretending you're beside me," he said, as if afraid I hadn't figured it out.

"What? It's a turn-on to be called an idiot?"

"I know you don't mean it. I want to hear your voice."

It was like being told I was nobody, nothing. Anger poured through my head and muscles.

"You're dead, Bill. Your right-wing buddies are going to drop you like a stone. The chatline tonight was full of gay men who can't wait to piss on your grave."

"Keep talking. Hmm. I have your finger in my bottom."

I remembered a corner of flesh, the tight ring and soft core. "No. If it was me it'd be something that hurt."

"Uh-uh. You want your penis in there. Your tongue."

I was all nerves and no body. I didn't even touch myself to see if I had a body.

"Oh yeah. Getting there. Keep talking." His breathing thickened. "See me when I'm in New York, Ralph. You want to."

"Don't you get it, Bill!"

An overture of grunts indicated he'd soon be deaf. My thumb found the button on the phone.

"You're dead! I could kill you right now. I'm so angry. Only you're already dead, so why should I bother! You have

no soul, no brains. You mean nothing to me and I don't
care—"

But I suddenly heard myself snarling in the flat air of the
room. My thumb had pressed the button to kill the first
insulting sound of his joy. I pressed again, but there was only
the hum of electrons, a prolonged buzz of infinity.

I hung up. I was glad I'd accidentally cut him off. I
turned off my machine in case he called back for a postcoital
chat. But he continued to linger in the dark, as if somewhere
in my room. He couldn't seriously believe his televised breakdown had set things straight. No, he'd called only to let me
know that I was nothing to him now but jerk-off fodder.

Why had he called and not Nancy? Why was it that whenever I needed to hear from her, I heard from that bastard
instead?

Was she all right? Anger made my body hum like a
tuning fork, but my agitated thoughts suddenly swarmed
around Nancy. Without happiness to protect me, I became
full of concern and worry for her.

Was Bill's network suicide too late? Was that why she
didn't call? Had Kathleen broken her heart? I pictured Nancy
drinking herself sick while her phone rang and the dome of
the Capitol peered in at her window. *I'm not going to jump out
a window anytime soon.*

I hated imagining such a thing, but I carried the scene
to its trashy, melodramatic conclusion, needing to assure
myself that I was being ridiculous before I could get back to
sleep.

16

That should have been the end of it, but Friday was my day off; I had too much time to think. I woke up worried about Nancy, as if after a bad dream. I remembered Bill's call, knew it hadn't been a dream, but all thought and emotion gathered around Nancy.

I waited until ten and phoned her office. The receptionist said she was out for the day.

"Out sick? Did she call this morning or yesterday?" If she called this morning, then she should be all right.

"All I can say is that Ms. Wenceslas won't be in."

I phoned her machine again and ordered her to pick up. "You have me worried. If you don't call me back, I have no choice but to come down there and see if you're all right."

I grew more certain that something awful was happening. Poets are the antennas of the race, and I was a poet only to myself, but even neurotics can pick up danger signals inaudible to others. Waiting for a call, able to do nothing except sit and wait, my fear spun tales. Kathleen had ordered Nancy to clear her desk. She wandered the city in a daze. She'd drunk herself unconscious at home. Or she lay sober yet catatonic in bed, with no thought in her head except hatred for the man she had once considered her best friend. When I didn't deliver on my threat to come see her, she would write me off forever.

My slow, corrosive panic did not subside until that afternoon, when I was already on the train to Washington.

Only then, trapped in a crowded passenger car racing through New Jersey, committed to the long trip south, did I calm down enough to recognize the neurotic foolishness of my fears. What had I gotten myself so worked up about? Even at the best of times, Nancy didn't return calls. What did I hope to prove to myself with this gratuitous mission of mercy? I almost got off in Trenton to catch a train back to New York, but decided to finish this and let Nancy see that I cared about her so much I could behave like a lunatic.

My concern had been so genuine that I'd brought nothing to read. Relaxing into my foolishness, I could only watch the scenery, look at other passengers and give in to the erotic woolgathering of train travel. Six weeks ago, I had ridden this same route to Baltimore with simple expectations of sex and a nervous hope of love. Even today the sweep of fields and bridges had the three-dimensional depth of bodies in a bed.

No, I told myself. I was not going to see Bill. Not in Washington. Not next week in New York. Never. If this journey had an unconscious demon, it was a bad conscience, not vestigial lust for an old mistake.

I came up in Dupont Circle shortly after six, in twilit clouds of flowering trees. I felt like a vagrant arriving at Nancy's building without luggage. The doorman said Ms. Wenceslas was out. When I claimed that she was expecting me, he said she should be back sometime tonight, she had not left town.

I sat on the lobby sofa, prepared to wait all night if necessary with nothing to occupy me except my thoughts. I was afraid to go around the corner and buy a magazine for fear a pay phone might tempt me. My waiting began to feel less symbolic and more justified. What if I'd been right? Was Nancy okay? Now that I was here, what could I do for her? Call the police? Call the hospitals? I stewed in penitential helplessness.

Each time the door opened and someone climbed the short flight of stairs to the lobby, I hoped it would be her. It never was. I studied the elaborate mosaic floor and walls; I watched the doorman repeatedly disappear into a closet, where he presumably kept either cigarettes or a bottle.

I was alone in the lobby when the door opened again. Two flattened wings of frazzled hair mounted the steps, and a face with Edward Gorey eyes. She gazed forlornly in my direction, then stopped, squinting at me as if I were a migraine.

17

"And how was she?"

"Fine. Just fine. Unhappy but coping. And furious when she came in from spending the day at a Cineplex to find *me* parked in her lobby."

Peter shook his head. "So you went down there for nothing?"

"Not quite for nothing. Her anger got her out of her funk. She was livid I'd come down. She attacked me for treating her as a good deed to purge my guilty conscience. I wanted to catch the next train back, but then she accused me of playing martyr, so I had to spend the night. We talked some, like we always talk, but I felt very, very stupid."

"You're such a guilt queen, Ralph. A regular Boy Scout of guilt. And you're not even Jewish."

"I just hate the idea of friends being angry at me. It made me go off the deep end."

The sun was out Sunday morning, the unidentified trees across Cooper Square in dirty blooms of shredded tissue paper. Spring remained cold, but vendors were already setting out old clothes and magazines on the sidewalk. Nick had stopped off to get the Sunday paper; Peter and I had a few minutes alone in the coffee shop.

"What happened with her job?"

"Nothing for now. Kathleen is sympathetic but pragmatic. She told Nancy she wouldn't let her go, for fear it suggested something *was* going on. She asked her to stay on for three months, then they'll see where things stand. In the meantime—"

Nick came in with the bulky newspaper under his arm.

"Hey, Nick. How was Boston?"

"Don't ask," he grumbled as he took a seat.

Peter took the paper from him. "Seems like I was the only one who stayed put this weekend," he said idly.

"Where did you go?" Nick asked me.

"Nowhere. Well, the Cloisters," I quickly added. "Which is like going to Canada."

The waitress brought our food—we'd ordered for Nick. Peter opened the paper while his lover blasted the conference.

"Two days of doctors telling us in state-of-the-art language that they still don't know shit. And Boston. God I hate Boston. Old hippies and Harvard, with nothing in between."

"Oh my God," said Peter.

"Who now?" I asked.

He always went straight to the obituary page. His lantern jaw drew his closed mouth into a bud. He gingerly folded the section in half and passed it to me.

I saw the age first, which was how we read obits, looking for numbers under sixty. There was no photo. I saw the figure beside Peter's thumb—"28"—before I saw the name: "William O'Connor, Author . . ."

"What is it?" said Nick.

My eyes raced through the first paragraphs:

William O'Connor Jr., a journalist whose work appeared in the *Wall Street Journal*, the *Washington Times* and *American Truths*, and whose controversial best-selling book, *The Regiment of Women*, was published this month, died in his home on Friday. He was 28.

According to Detective Larry Polk of the District of Columbia police, he was the victim of a homicide apparently committed in the course of a burglary.

"Oh *that*," said Nick. "You didn't hear about that?"

Peter laid a hand on my arm, then caught himself. "It's just— Small world. Ralph and I saw this guy on *Nightline* only the other night. Huh," he went, pretending it was just another oddity in the news.

"Was in the *Post* yesterday afternoon," said Nick. "Leave it to the *Times* to bury it in the obits."

I heard every word, but their voices came to me from miles away. Bill was dead? This was Bill, right?

"They think a hustler did it," said Nick. "Convenient hustler, if you ask me. I missed his tantrum on *Nightline*, but I certainly heard about it."

Someone I knew had been murdered. Yet I could not let Nick know that I knew him. It was a trivial consideration, but it forced me to show nothing while I tried to identify what I was feeling, if I felt anything.

Peter watched me, waiting for a signal that he could tell Nick the full story. He suddenly asked, "You think somebody had him killed?"

"The timing is too good to be accidental," said Nick. "But it's too good to be deliberate either. I can't imagine any right-wingers thinking they had to clean house by killing a journalist. I mean, a journalist? Why bother? Something wrong, Ralph? You look like you've been hit with a two-by-four."

Looking up, I found Nick watching me with a puzzled smile.

"I don't know," I said. "Somebody I saw on television. I don't know why it should bother me. Just another death." I took a bite of potatoes but my mouth was bone-dry.

"Oh God. Another damn article on Whitewater," said Peter.

It took me a moment to understand that he was diverting Nick so that I could think in peace. But all I thought

was: Words. Print. People accuse me of treating the printed
word as the ultimate reality. Yet here in print was news about
someone I knew, and it was as unbelievable as a bad novel.
Unable to talk in front of Nick, my mind went blank while the
enormous fact worked through my chest and spine.

Then Peter said good-bye to Nick and we started
walking. Neither of us spoke until we turned the corner.

"You poor baby," he said. "I'm sorry."

I said nothing, then, "Why sorry? He was no friend of
mine. I hate him, remember."

"Which must make it weirder. Unfinished business."

I thought about that. "It does. But the weirdest part is
how I felt something awful was happening this weekend.
Which was why I went down."

"You never saw him while you were there. Right?"

"No. I was with Nancy the whole time." Then the
meaning of his question caught up with me. "You wonder if *I*
killed him?"

"No. I never thought that. Not you, Ralph."

Someone had done a deed that I should have done? The
thought passed as quickly as a blink.

"You're sure you don't want to tell Nick?" said Peter.

"Why? What could he do?"

"He might be able to make more sense of it. I know
murder only from movies, but it does look strange."

"I know only—it's all strange. He's dead? I can't believe
it. It's so sudden. So—" I flipped my hand in the air.

"Out of nowhere," said Peter. "I forgot what it's like.
Old-fashioned car wrecks and drownings. But it's not just
another death. You were wrong about that back there. It's a
murder, which feels, I don't know, more human? Man-made.
Meaningful." He grimaced at his words. "New and exciting. I
know that sounds callous, Ralph, but I never met him. He's
not real to me."

But death had changed any reality Bill ever had for me.

We arrived at the store and I had to play manager. Going
through my routines with a broken reality in my head was like

being stoned. The good weather brought in more customers than usual for a Sunday morning. His book still sat on its bottom shelf, a stack of little brown grave markers.

My numbness released a few isolated thoughts, sentences that hung like fixed stars in my daze. He had it coming to him. Whoever did it had freed me from him. But I hated the killer more cleanly than I had ever hated him.

At lunch I went up the street to a newsstand that sold out-of-town papers. The *Washington Post* had the story on the front of their City section. I found a doorway where I could sit and learn a few facts and give shape to this rumor of death.

On Saturday morning, J. D. Weiss of Houston arrived at the apartment he kept in Washington and found it had been robbed. He discovered his tenant's body in O'Connor's bedroom. The absence of any signs of forcible entry, and the body's "state of undress," suggested to the police that O'Connor had been killed and robbed by someone he'd brought home the night before. Weiss was quoted as saying, "He was gay, but new to that lifestyle and too trusting. He liked tough, dangerous men. A gifted young talent, his death is a sad loss to journalism."

I read the article several times. There was one sentence I read only once. "Cause of death, according to the coroner's report, was asphyxiation resulting from head injuries."

When I returned to the store, I went to the back window and showed the article to Peter. "Oh God," he said when he finished reading. "He was beaten to death? How awful."

I nodded. "But Weiss says he was into rough trade. He wasn't. He was white-bread through and through. Weiss is either talking off the top of his head or lying."

"You think this guy Weiss did it?"

I remembered him on the boat, such a personable, jolly, short man. "No. But maybe he hired someone."

"Would they go that far? Just because he came out?"

"I don't know." What made sense in a movie didn't translate to life, but something was wrong with this story, something off.

"You going to tell the police what you know?"

"I don't know much."

"It might make you feel better."

That was an odd way to put it, but Peter was right. I had to do something to make this real. I stepped into his cubbyhole to use his phone, needing him to see me make the call in order to make that real too.

I got an operator, then a woman in homicide, and finally Detective Larry Polk's voice mail.

"My name is Ralph Eckhart. I live in New York City. I have some information regarding the murder of William O'Connor. I don't know how useful it is. But I can be reached at . . ." I gave my work and home numbers, and hung up, feeling more blank than ever.

"There," said Peter. "Nothing else we can do. You okay?"

I told him I was fine and went back to work.

My lack of strong, hard emotion did not alarm me. I knew firsthand the different ways grief can express itself. There'd been immediate tears over my downstairs neighbor, Martin, my first death since the grandmothers and aunts of childhood. The death of Eric Thomas, long after our hot-and-cold affair, had been like a kick in my chest. By the time Alberto died, however, after a year in and out of hospitals, months of home care, and two weeks of listening to his sandpaper breaths and the soft seethe of an oxygen line while I watched him gutter, fade and drown, I was so relieved by the end of his suffering and my helplessness that I felt no pain, no sorrow. Not until a month later when I unpacked his Mac and thought, Damn you, Bert, leaving me this when you know I hate machines. My old, tender exasperation with him gave way to a convulsion of sobs.

But I'd never hated those people. And murder was a different kind of death. Peter was right. This did mean more. Death was not yet private or metaphysical but unfinished, criminal, human.

Polk did not call me at work or that evening at home. Nor did Nancy. She had to have heard about Bill, but she never phoned. I refused to call her. I couldn't after what she'd said to me on Friday night. "This has nothing to do with you, Ralph. It's my crisis. Why do you insist on sharing it? Stay out of it. You want a crisis in your life, get your own. But don't feel you have to make me part of yours."

18

"Mr. Ralph Eckhart, please."

"Speaking."

The call came Monday morning at the store.

"Robert Loveless. Federal Bureau of Investigation. I'm calling in regards to William O'Connor. You knew him?"

"Yes. This is about his murder?"

"*Yes.*" The brusque voice turned friendly when he found that I expected his call. "We'd like to talk with you. Hear what you can tell us about O'Connor's life and friends."

"Definitely. Where would you like to meet?"

"I could come uptown and see you at work. Or, if you prefer, you might drop by my office at Federal Plaza."

The idea of the FBI visiting the store made me uneasy. "I'd rather come to you. Except I don't get off until six."

"There's no rush. Whatever's most convenient."

He told me the floor and said to give his name to the receptionist. "We appreciate you taking the time to come in, Mr. Eckhart. It makes our job that much easier."

I hung up with nothing worse than a case of butterflies over a blind date. As with any blind date, I doubted anything would come of this. After my neurotic rescue mission I had no faith in my actions, yet was relieved to do something with my—I still couldn't call it grief. It remained a numb state of disbelief.

The Federal Plaza Building was off Foley Square, downtown near City Hall, a tall, white, concrete box perforated like a cheese grater. The mammoth courthouse with its blackened Roman facade and endless stairs crouched across the street. Riding up in the elevator, I felt improperly dressed in my duffel coat, as if this were only a job interview. My strongest emotion was dry curiosity, a grim satisfaction over this chance to peer inside an institution that none of my crowd knew firsthand. I doubted the value of the knowledge I brought, but hoped to learn more about Bill's death. I still believed in knowledge for its own sake.

The elevator opened into bare fluorescent space. There were no chairs or plants, only a white marble floor and beige walls. The bureau seal hung between a thick glass window like a ticket booth and a simple wood-veneered door. I asked the man in the window for Agent Loveless, stepped back and waited, remembering again some lines from a Delmore Schwartz poem about love not being just and justice being loveless.

The door buzzed and was opened from inside by a man with a mustache and shark gray suit.

"Mr. Eckhart?" He gave me a quick, cold, judging look. "Come in. Agent Loveless is expecting you."

And it finally poured into me, the natural fear elicited by any police station. I stepped through the suddenly important door into a warren of chin-high cubicles. Most of the desks were empty, the computer terminals swimming with silent schools of screensavers. Following the crinkled gray shoulders down a mute, carpeted hall, I told myself that I had no business being afraid. My guilt was moral, not criminal.

We entered a narrow room. A blond man in pink shirt-sleeves rose behind his desk. "Bob Lovelace," he said, leaning forward with a sunny smile and firm handshake. "Thanks for coming down. You've met Pruitt, I see. I've asked him to sit in on this. We often work in pairs, you know. Like Jehovah's Witnesses. Take a seat, Ralph. Would you like coffee? Soda? Spring water? No? Fine, this shouldn't take long."

Lovelace—I'd misheard his name—was not what one expected in an FBI agent, but sociable, easy, even humorous. He had a freckled complexion, an attractive pastel tie and french cuffs. When he scanned my face and body, I had to wonder about him, until I saw the photo of a woman and two little girls on the shelf behind his desk. The reflex of glances had a different meaning here.

He set a tape recorder not much bigger than a cigarette pack on his desk, with the lid open. "In case we need a statement later. Until then, we won't tape anything."

"Fine," I said.

Pruitt stood stiffly against the wall to my right. A cipher with a half-inch of mustache across his upper lip, *he* fit the stereotype, his glumness making him seem older than Lovelace. It took a moment for the authority of both men to wear off enough for me to see that they were roughly my age.

"The case has been turned over to the FBI?" I asked.

Lovelace was glancing at notes hidden in a drawer. "Not really. We're just helping out for now. Gathering data."

"You got my name from the police in D.C.?"

"You've spoken with the Metropolitan PD?"

"I called them but nobody's talked with me yet."

"Really? Well, no need to worry about that." He closed the drawer, leaned forward on his starched cuffs and smiled again. His transparent ice blue eyes, like well-sucked hard candies, gazed into me. "So. What do you have for us, Ralph?"

"Not much. Except that I don't think this story that Bill O'Connor was killed by rough trade is convincing."

"It certainly isn't. We agree with you there."

"For one thing, it's such a cliché. And for another, Bill wasn't into anything like that."

"Anything like what?"

"Going home with someone rough or dangerous."

"How do you know that?"

"Because—I had an affair with him."

"For how long?"

Lovelace showed no surprise or distaste; Pruitt watched from the side with a bored expression. I was surprised that neither man took notes.

"It began in November, ended in February. So four months. But we saw each other only four times. Or no, three times." I had counted our nights in Miami twice.

"When did you last see Bill?"

"In February. In Miami."

"What were you doing in Miami?"

"He brought me down as his guest. He was there for a Republican conference."

"How would you describe yourself? His friend, boy-friend, lover, what?"

I wanted to say "trick," but a straight man might not understand, and it wasn't the full truth. "It was a romance that almost happened but didn't."

"So it was just sex?"

Maybe he did understand. "That's how it turned out. Yeah."

Pruitt heaved himself off the wall. "Right back," he grumbled. "Anybody want anything?"

"You sure you don't want something to drink, Ralph?"

"I'm fine, thanks."

Lovelace nodded at him and Pruitt pulled the door shut.

"Don't mind Pruitt," Lovelace assured me. "Nebraska kind of guy. Gets uncomfortable around certain topics."

I preferred being alone with Lovelace anyway.

"Do you think of yourself as gay, Ralph?"

"Gay? Yes." I shrugged, surprised by the question.

"Did Bill ever give you anything? Gifts? Favors?"

"He arranged for my ticket to Miami."

"Did he ever give you money?"

"Money? No. He didn't pay me to sleep with him, if that's what you mean." I finally laughed. "I'm not a hustler.

I'm assistant manager at a bookstore. I saw him because I enjoyed seeing him, and because I thought it might lead to something. He sent me flowers once. That's all."

"Just trying to get a clearer picture of your relationship. How did you meet?"

"In Gayworld. A computer chatline."

"What is that exactly?"

"Like a phone sex line, only on computer. Gay Internet. People use it mostly to chat. About books and movies. And only sometimes to meet. For sex."

"And that was in November?"

"Right. I was going to D.C. He suggested we get together, and we did."

"Why did it end?"

"He wrote a book I didn't like. You know about his book?"

"Controversial?"

"Not just that but ugly. Nasty. I got an advance copy and read it. I hated the politics but worse than that was the way he trashed women." I did not need to mention Nancy.

"Do you consider yourself political?"

"No. Not really."

"Do you belong to any political organizations?"

"I was with ACT UP for a while, but dropped out a year ago. No, Bill's book just made me see that his politics were a symptom of deeper flaws. So I ended the relationship."

"Badly? Amicably?"

"Badly. All by E-mail and phone and we were angry with each other. But he couldn't get it through his head it was over." I felt funny saying so much about *us*. "But that has nothing to do with why I think this killer trick business is fishy."

"Okay then. What can you tell me there?"

"Only that Bill wasn't into sleaze or hustlers. He'd never casually pick up the kind of man who'd rob or kill him."

"I don't know, Ralph. Your description of how you met sounds awfully casual to me."

"Maybe," I admitted. "Except we talked on the computer first. And we met at the zoo." I rolled my eyes and tried to laugh again, but humor sank like lead here. "Anybody with a computer can't be too dangerous."

"Did he like to get rough in bed?"

"Bill? No. He was very white-bread."

"Meaning?"

How does one talk about sex with the FBI? "He liked to kiss. He liked to hug. He was—affectionate."

"Active or passive?"

"We weren't into anal sex, if that's what you're asking."

"Why not?"

He didn't need to know each and every act we performed. "Because we weren't into it. And because of AIDS."

"Oh right," he said, as if he'd forgotten that. "So if he wasn't into rough trade, who do you think killed him?"

"I don't really know except—" I took the plunge. "He came out on *Nightline* the night before. It may be coincidence, but there are people who wouldn't want it known that their new star was gay."

"People like Jeb Weiss?"

"That's right." They already knew about Weiss? "He insisted Bill stay in the closet. Weiss was courting the Christian right. When Bill came out the other night, it would've hurt Weiss with the Christians. And so he could have had Bill murdered. Maybe hired someone to do it."

"What would he gain by that?"

I became more tentative. "Well, he'd get rid of an embarrassment. And making it look like it was done by a gay man, he could turn Bill into an asset. A martyr to that lifestyle. A dead sinner is easier to take than a live one."

"Possible," said Lovelace, leaning back to consider it. "But ruthless. Do you really think it's plausible?"

"No," I admitted. "But more plausible than his being killed by a trick."

"You don't think Weiss could've done it in the heat of the moment? Out of anger? Then faked the robbery to protect himself?"

"Maybe." I hid my excitement; he not only took my suspicions seriously but improved them, made them more solid.

"You've met Weiss?" he asked.

"Briefly. When I was in Miami."

"Do you know if Weiss was in D.C. the night of the murder?"

"No. I spoke to Bill Thursday night, after *Nightline.* But he hadn't spoken to Weiss yet, so I don't know if he was there."

"You called him from New York?"

"No. He called me. In New York." Should I say that I went down to see Nancy? No. It would confuse matters and I needed to leave Nancy out of this.

"Did he sound at all worried or frightened?"

"No. He sounded thoroughly pleased with himself."

"But you were in New York all weekend?"

"Uh-huh." An unreserved train, there would be no record of my trip. Only Nancy knew I was down there.

"Do you know a man named Renfield Whitaker?"

"Yes. He's one of the Christian right people Weiss was courting. He's involved in this?"

"His name came up. You met him?"

"In Miami. When I met Weiss. We all went sailing one morning with Senator—" I couldn't remember his name.

"Griffith?"

"Yes!" He already knew more about this than I'd ever guessed. "Do you think they're all involved?"

"Just considering possibilities. Assembling a cast of characters. What would you say, Ralph, if I told you Jeb Weiss says he can prove that he was in Houston on Friday night?"

"He can? Then maybe he didn't do it in the heat of the moment. Maybe he hired someone after all."

"True. Only this did not look professional." He picked up the phone and punched a button. "Tell Pruitt we need him back here. Sorry," he said. "You were saying. Thursday. Bill called you. Why?"

"He thought coming out on television made everything all right. He wanted to see me again."

"And what did you say?"

"That he was still a shit and I never wanted to see him."

"Harsh words. Could he have gotten so upset he'd go out the next night and pick up just anybody for sex? Maybe rough sex?"

"Maybe. Only you have to be angry with yourself to do something like that. He was too in love with himself for that."

The door opened and Pruitt returned, carrying a folder.

"Here we go," said Lovelace. "Look at these, Ralph. Tell me what you think."

Pruitt slapped the folder on the desk.

I opened it: a sheaf of gray photos on glossy computer paper. The first showed a pale figure against a dark ground. The resolution was sharp, but angle and perspective were skewed; it took a moment to make out a man in underpants sprawled on his stomach. Fleshy back and mussed hair. The brand name printed on the waistband. The face was wrenched away from the camera, but the next photo showed the body from the other side. The face was distorted by a shadow, no, a bruise. The lips were pale with white lip gloss, the eyes slightly parted. Under the bed behind him, a wadded sock lay on the carpet.

I knew that these were police photos of the crime, yet only slowly recognized Bill in the abstract patterns.

I closed my eyes and tried to swallow the knot in my throat.

Pruitt stood over my shoulder. "Why so pale, Eckhart? Can't be the first time you've seen your pal like this."

But because I had seen this, his undressed body an emblem of everything likable about Bill, his murder turned from a disturbing idea into a brutal physical fact.

But that wasn't what Pruitt meant, was it?

A chair squeaked as Lovelace tilted back, dryly watching my response. I craned my neck up and around and saw Pruitt overhead, glaring down at me, so close that I noticed a tiny razor nick between his nose and mustache.

"See what I mean?" said Lovelace, still pretending we

were merely speculating together. "Not professional. This was done out of anger. He choked to death after being beaten unconscious."

I looked around for a window. A window would assure me that I was in a real place, but the walls were solid, the room sealed.

"Why did you do it?" demanded the voice above my head.

"I didn't." I was amazed by how calm I sounded. "If I did, would I have come down to tell you what I know?"

"Would you?" Pruitt snapped. "We don't know how you think, Eckhart. Maybe you came down to throw us off track. Maybe you killed O'Connor to set up Weiss. So you could punish O'Connor, ruin Weiss and help the gay cause, all at once."

"That's ridiculous."

"It's no more ridiculous than what you just accused Weiss of doing. How could you come up with something so cockamamie unless you thought it for yourself?"

Pruitt took over. He knew everything I had said. He must have been listening outside the door the entire time.

"Look. Look at this," he barked in my ear, spreading the photos on the desk, a half dozen dead boys, a massacre of Bills. "You proud of that? That's what you wanted. That's what you went down there to do."

He jabbed a finger at a close-up of the face, lids open, Bill's eyes dry and flat, as if air had been let out of them.

"No, I can't believe that of Ralph here," Lovelace gently disagreed. "He's not someone who'd kill in cold blood. But maybe he had to go to bed with Bill one last time. Ralph got angry and the sex got nasty and the next thing you knew, he was dead. Is that how it happened, Ralph?"

It was as though he'd crawled around inside my imagination. I almost said, "Maybe," but caught myself and said, "I didn't kill him. I didn't have sex with him. I didn't even see him."

I knew that they were playing good cop/bad cop. I was amazed by how clearly I understood what was happening. I remained keenly aware, eerily detached, even as fear raced through my nerves.

"Don't look at us!" snapped Pruitt. "The answer isn't on our faces. Look at the pictures. You proud of that?"

My body tensed, expecting to be hit. I told myself I was in an office with bookcases and a family photo and there could be no violence—we'd break something—but my body didn't believe me.

You think irony can protect you. An ironic clearing remained in my head, a quiet place where I thought: This is ridiculous. I didn't kill him, but I'll need a lawyer. How will I pay for a lawyer?

"Shouldn't I have a lawyer?"

"Not at all," Lovelace assured me. "You need a lawyer only if we charge you. We haven't charged you with a thing, Ralph. We're just chatting. You can leave any time you like."

"I can just get up and walk out?"

"That's right. Only this will still be hanging over your head. So we might as well clear it up tonight. Right?"

But the closed room seemed detached from the world, with nothing at all outside the shut door.

"You've told us everything you know?" Lovelace continued in his reasonable manner, working to put me at ease again. "You're not covering for someone?"

"No, I didn't know anything about this murder until I saw the obituary in the *Times*."

"You mean today?"

"No. Sunday."

"The *Times* didn't run an obituary on Sunday."

"It did. I saw it." They were trying to confuse me. I refused to be confused. "That's why I called the police yesterday."

"We know nothing about you calling the police," said Lovelace.

"Isn't that where you got my name?"

Pruitt jumped back in. "You didn't go to D.C. with the intention of settling a score with O'Connor?"

"No."

"What would you say if I told you someone saw you at the airport on Friday?"

"I'd say they were lying."

"So you didn't go down there?"

They didn't know, did they? "No."

"Did you go to work on Friday?"

"No. I have Fridays off."

"What did you do Friday night?" asked Lovelace.

"I stayed home and read."

"What did you read?"

"Trollope."

"What was the title?"

Did he know Trollope or was he bluffing there too? "*Phineas Redux.* One of the Palliser novels."

"Ralph, Ralph, Ralph." Lovelace shook his head as if it were the wrong answer. "Let's start over. From the beginning. How did you and O'Connor meet?"

We went over the story again, with the same questions and new questions, blunt accusation from Pruitt, requests for more details from Lovelace, a bombardment of threat and trivia.

"How many times did you have sex?"

"I don't remember."

"You said four times."

"What do you mean by sex? How many nights we spent together? How many times we did it?"

"Tell us both."

To count orgasms over photos of Bill's corpse made my own body feel queasily absent. Whenever I closed the folder, Pruitt opened it again.

"Why do you hate Christians, Ralph? Are you an ex-Catholic? You're not Jewish, are you?"

"No. I'm ex-Episcopalian. And I don't hate Christians. I don't trust right-wing fundamentalists, that's all."

"Might interest you, Ralph, that Pruitt here is a born-again Christian."

Pruitt remained stone-faced, but his animosity gained a personality; he no longer seemed purely legal.

"I don't hate Christians," I repeated.

"What happened to the stuff you stole to make it look like a robbery?" Pruitt barked.

"I didn't steal anything. Look, I don't even have a car. How could I've carried off a television and whatever else was taken?"

"How did you know they stole the TV?"

"I'm guessing. What else would a thief take?"

"Is that why the cops found almost everything in a nearby Dumpster? You couldn't lug it on the Metro? But you kept his laptop, right? So nobody would see your letters. Bet you didn't know that O'Connor made hard copies of his correspondence."

"We have a transcript of your Thursday night phone call, Ralph," said Lovelace. "O'Connor taped his calls, you know."

"He did?" I tried to remember what I'd said. "Yeah. I was angry with him. But not angry enough to kill him." Had Bill really taped his calls? Was that why I was a suspect?

I could no longer guess what they knew, what they didn't and what was wholly imaginary. The truth behind their questions became frighteningly amorphous. Whatever I said could be turned against me. In my schizophrenic confusion of certainty and fear, I clung to two beliefs, one true, the other false. First, that I hadn't killed Bill; second, that I hadn't gone to Washington. It seemed such an arbitrary, unnecessary lie, yet I stuck to it, initially not to involve Nancy, then for fear that if I admitted one lie, everything I'd said would look false.

They took turns with me, usually in the room together, but, after the first hour, one of them would step out. They did things out there with telephones, faxes and invisible superiors, a black-box technology of threat. Everything outside the room was part of a great black box. Alone with me, Pruitt remained loud and aggressive, his charges wilder without

Lovelace present, as if he knew fewer facts than his partner. Lovelace alone grew gentler, more intimate.

"You can be frank with me, Ralph," he whispered when Pruitt was out. "I know what it's like. Gay, straight, whatever. Love can make you crazy. You were in love with Bill and hurt when he didn't love you back."

"No. I was never in love with him. If anyone loved anybody, he loved me. If you can call his kind of solipsism love."

"Then that must have infuriated you. When someone like that could love someone like you. The worst insult imaginable."

"Some. But it's nice to feel lovable. Even by the wrong person. When I broke off with Bill, I felt unlovable. But when I feel unlovable, I want to hurt myself, not other people."

I couldn't believe I was saying this to the FBI. I'd never been in therapy but this was how I imagined it, a fine-tooth combing of guilt and motive and free association, a dissolving of self to get at the truth. But this therapist had courts and prisons behind him.

When we'd been through everything three or four times, Lovelace and Pruitt left the room together. I took a deep breath of solitude. I'd been sitting perfectly still, outwardly calm; I suddenly discovered how clenched my body was, every muscle tensed against panic. My heart continued to race. In the abrupt quiet, I could think again, only all I thought was, A lawyer. How am I going to pay for a lawyer? The idea that I could go to prison for murder remained too preposterous to be taken seriously. I could imagine only the days, maybe weeks of my life that would be consumed by a grotesque misunderstanding.

The grim photos remained on the desk. Looking at them now, I briefly wished that I *had* killed Bill, because then my denials would sound less pleading, more defiant and proud.

I seemed to think and feel everything, yet could think or feel nothing clearly.

The door opened. They entered together, Lovelace with a broad smile, Pruitt looking darkly disappointed. I dared to think: They were only testing me, and I passed.

"You didn't do it," Lovelace declared.

My heart lifted; I was so relieved that I said, "Thank you."

"But"—he sustained his smile—"I just spoke to the police in D.C., Ralph. I really think you should go talk to them."

"Why? I already told you what I know."

"They want to hear it from the horse's mouth. We can fly you down tonight as a material witness and have you back by morning. Probably. You're not under arrest, you understand."

My heart froze. My nerves instantly knew. "But if I say no? You'll arrest me and fly me down anyway?"

"I didn't say that. Did I say that, John?"

"No," Pruitt grunted.

I didn't understand their fancy footwork. All I knew was that, whatever they called it, they still had me. Suddenly, as if my moment of hope had lifted me just high enough to crash with the next blow, my resistance fell and broke, softly, like that silent movie clip of an early airplane with too many wings collapsing upon itself. "Okay," I said. "Okay." I paused to see how that felt. "I'll go. Right now?"

"We'll swing by your apartment first so you can pick up anything you need. We have to go there anyway when they send the search warrant over, which should be momentarily. The search is purely routine, you understand. To enable us to clear this up more quickly. You can let us in and we won't damage the locks. We should finish up there before you go with Pruitt to the airport."

"Me?" said Pruitt. "I thought you were flying him down."

"I need to input whatever we turn up, John. You can fly down and fly back, and that's the end of it, okay?"

"I don't—" Pruitt glared at Lovelace, then at me. He turned on his heel and left the room.

"Excuse me," said Lovelace, and he followed Pruitt.

I sat numbly in the chair, thinking: I am under arrest. No matter what they called it, I was caught in a soft machine of legal fiction and unknown evidence. But the knowledge didn't terrify me. I took strange satisfaction in giving in to it, as if I'd been pointlessly fighting a natural need to sleep, or a fuck that I'd reluctantly agreed to but was taking forever. I was no longer my own person, and the loss wasn't painful, but easeful, narcotic, soothing.

19

Lovelace sat beside me on the short ride uptown, Pruitt up front with the driver. The shadowy sidewalks and motley storefronts of the East Village looked foreign and diminished in the windows of their unmarked sedan. My own building appeared flat and generic when we pulled up outside, as if seen through the eyes of a stranger. I continued to experience my loss of will as a new yet simpler identity.

The habitual five flights of stairs became long and steep with Lovelace and Pruitt trudging behind me. I unlocked the door and turned on the overhead light I rarely used, the naked bulb making the room so tall and gaunt.

They did not charge in and rifle through my things, but shyly stepped around, just looking. Neither man mentioned the shelves of books, unmade futon and peeling paint.

"Here we go," said Lovelace, going to the Mac on my desk. "We'd rather not take your computer, Ralph, but if you give me any passwords, I can copy it all on disk."

"It's open files," I said. "Help yourself."

He drew a floppy from his inside coat pocket, next to the

shoulder holster he'd strapped on when we left Federal Plaza. There was nothing in the Mac except letters and old poems.

I found the overnight bag and put in my underwear, toilet kit and electric shaver. What else does one need in jail? Would I actually go to jail? Remembering court, I added a clean shirt and my Sunday necktie. I picked up the Trollope that I hadn't looked at since returning from Miami. "See. *Phineas Redux*," I said, showing Lovelace before I tossed it in.

He didn't care. He stood at my keyboard, clicking in codes that made the machine chirp and whir. Pruitt wandered the room, inspecting my television, VCR and answering machine, running a finger through the films of dust. He opened my closet and groped in the folded clothes on the top shelf.

"Can I call someone I work with? Let him know I might not be in tomorrow?"

"Call anyone you like," said Lovelace. "It's your home."

That was a lie. I hoped I'd get Peter's machine and wouldn't have to talk. My easy surrender suddenly embarrassed me.

"Hello?"

"*Nick*. Hi. Um, it's Ralph." I didn't expect to get Nick. "Just calling to tell Peter I might not be in tomorrow and could he tell Elaine—just tell her I called in sick."

"What's wrong, Ralph?"

But Nick would know, if anyone knew, what I should do. I took a deep breath. "I'm with two FBI agents. They're taking me to Washington tonight. To be questioned by the police. In connection with the William O'Connor murder."

He did not gasp or cry, "Oh my God!" but quietly said, "You, Ralph? Why you?"

"I—they—I—we—" I didn't know where to begin.

"Just stay cool. Be calm." I didn't know I'd sounded so panicked. "Where are you?" He became quick and pragmatic.

"I'm home, getting my bag while they search the apartment."

"Do they have a search warrant?"

"Yes."

"Are you under arrest?"

"No. Not yet."

"Are you a suspect or merely a witness?"

"I'm a material witness, right?" I asked Lovelace.

"You freely offered yourself as a material witness," he repeated without looking up from the keyboard.

Nick heard him. "What're the names of the agents?"

I told him.

He was writing everything down. "Let me speak to them."

"My friend wants to talk to you."

"He your lawyer?" said Lovelace. "I can't talk to anyone except your lawyer."

"They won't talk to you, Nick."

"Shit. Okay. Let me think. You can't pull out now without getting in deeper. Go ahead to Washington. When you get there, call this number. You have a pencil?"

He gave me a name and number that I wrote on a deposit slip from my wallet.

"I'll call Brian and tell him to expect to hear from you. Once you're down there, tell the police you'll cooperate but you won't talk without your lawyer present."

"I've already told them a lot, Nick."

"Don't worry. If you told them anything that made you a suspect, you'd be under arrest. Don't panic. Stay cool. You have nothing to fear, but this might take time."

"Was I an idiot to agree to go down? Have I fucked myself?"

"No. I don't think so. I'm sure I would've done the same."

Lovelace was booting down my computer. He tapped at his watch. "We better get a move on if you men want to catch the nine o'clock shuttle."

"I got to go, Nick."

"I'll be in touch through Brian. And don't worry. Everything will turn out fine. You won't get hurt. I promise."

"No? Okay. Good-bye, Nick. Thanks."

Any relief I gained from his words, however, vanished as soon as I hung up. It wasn't in Nick's power to promise me a thing. We were both in the dark, but Nick was on one side of the cage while I was already on the other.

Pruitt sat with the driver again on the ride to La Guardia. I sat in the back with my bag and the unlocked doors. After the first three traffic lights I stopped thinking about jumping out. Alone with me in the terminal, Pruitt spoke only to hurry us toward our gate. His role of "bad cop" over, he showed no anger, only irritation over being seen with me.

I assumed we'd fly on a small government plane, but we boarded a commercial flight and sat in business class, surrounded by men in suits.

"I guess you want me by the window," I said.

"You're free to sit wherever you like. You don't even have to get on this plane if you don't want to."

"Right," I scoffed, and cornered myself at the window.

He buckled himself beside me. A drone in a suit escorting a scruffily dressed fellow with a cropped scalp, our relationship could not have been more obvious if I were handcuffed to him. Imagining handcuffs between us, I had an inexplicable urge to hold Pruitt's hand. I blocked the urge by stuffing my fingers between my legs.

"Cold," I claimed.

"For your own protection, I strongly suggest that you say nothing pertaining to your case."

"I didn't say a thing."

"I'm warning you now."

I turned to the window. Lights floated back as we taxied out until all that remained in the layered glass was my blurred double face. When we took off, vaguely familiar cities of scrambled circuitry tilted beneath me.

"Never liked flying," I said. "I don't know why. Except that it messes up time and space in my head."

Pruitt said nothing, but I didn't expect a reply. Needing to talk, feeling reckless and obstinate, I decided to say aloud whatever came into my head.

"Last time I flew was coming back from Miami. With Bill. The deceased. Ironic, huh? And I remember telling myself I'd never see him again. I was right, only I don't think I fully believed it at the time. I don't believe this is happening. This is too unreal for me to believe. I don't fucking believe I'm doing this. I keep thinking variations of that, as if this were something I could believe or not believe, like religion."

Pruitt took the in-flight magazine from the seat pocket.

"You really born-again, Pruitt? Or did Lovelace make that up too, just to spook me?"

"My religion is of no concern to you *or* Agent Lovelace." He crossed his inside leg over his outside leg, as if to protect himself.

"You married, Pruitt?" I saw the ring on his knuckle. "Yeah. You have that I-know-what's-real-I'm-a-husband-and-father look. But we homos don't, you know. We make ourselves up as we go along. We're fictional. Postmodern."

I was making this up, wanting only to get under my captor's skin with idle chatter. I didn't look at Pruitt but addressed my clutched knees and the velvet seat back.

"Some of us are more plausible than others. Like Bill. He didn't have a clue. A Republican homo. A homo who worked for the homo-haters. A straight-identified fag who hated women. Like that made him as good as straight. Only I don't know if Bill really hated women. Or was he just parroting his buddies? When you come right down to it, I never knew much about the bastard. Except that he was hot to succeed. And he was fun in bed. And his silly Calvin Kleins." I snorted over my incongruous recall of underwear. "He pretended to be so damn unique. But he was a secret clone in his pants. What a deluded case. But did he deserve to die? No. If stupidity's a crime, we all deserve to be killed. But so violently?"

The police photos swam into my mind's eye, like the images of young pigs after the bristles were scalded off at hog killings on my grandfather's farm. Lard white flesh. A closed fist like a cleft hoof. I saw the flat, half-open eyes again. No longer distracted by the need to deny I'd done it, the cruelty of his murder struck deep inside me.

"Why? Nobody deserves to die like that. Was he in pain? Did he know he was going to die? I hope not. I hope they hit him from behind and knocked him cold. He'd just undressed and was all excited to go to bed with them, because I never met anybody who enjoyed sex as much as . . ."

And it flooded into my throat, a spastic, muscular grief. It seized my entire body. I clenched my teeth to stop the sobs. I squeezed my eyes shut, but the water spilled down my cheeks, a shudder of tears as humiliating as pissing in my pants.

When I could breathe again, raw and hollowed out, panting as though I'd nearly drowned, I turned to look at Pruitt.

He already faced me, his manicured mustache drawn down, his black pupils taking me in through tight hazel irises.

I defiantly wiped my eyes and nose with the butt of my hand. "You think I'm crying for myself," I sneered. "You think this is all self-pity. You think I did it, don't you?"

He cleared his throat. "Doesn't matter what I think." He frowned and turned away. "All I think is that you better be damn more careful about what you say if you want to stay out of jail."

"Isn't that where I'm going?"

He turned a page in his magazine. "No." The paper stuck to his finger. "Not to my knowledge."

But I knew better than to hope for anything else. I fell against my seat, scornful and exhausted, and sorry for poor, stupid Bill, who did not deserve such an awful death. My gloom was so black and heavy that I could not distinguish between grief for Bill and hopelessness for myself.

The plane docked. Everyone rose. Pruitt took my bag down and passed it to me. I stepped from the corridor of the plane into the sloping corridor of the ramp behind a pair of grumbling businessmen. Entering the lounge, I saw the two detectives before they saw me. One was black, the other white, both men stocky and impatient. Not until Pruitt came alongside me did they spot us and hurry into our path.

"Ralph Eckhart?" said the black man.

"Yes?"

"Metropolitan Police of the District of Columbia." He flashed a billfold at me. "We have a warrant for your arrest."

When I saw the white detective take out a pair of tarnished handcuffs, I set down my bag and offered my wrists.

He ignored them and jabbed his hands into my armpits. He spun me around, slapping my sides, then cuffed my hands at my back. The metal was colder and heavier than the handcuffs of my imagination.

"What the hell is this?" cried Pruitt. "You can't arrest this man. He came down here as a material witness."

"We were told different. He may have been a witness an hour ago, but now he's a suspect."

I was amazed that Pruitt acted surprised; I'd expected something like this all along, only not so soon.

"You can't just take him."

"Is he in FBI custody?"

"You know damn well he's not in custody or we wouldn't be traveling like this. Show me your warrant."

The black detective pulled out a fold of paper while the white detective chanted, "You have the right to remain silent with the understanding that anything you say may be used . . ."

People glanced our way and hurried past.

"I'm calling my office," Pruitt snapped. "Find out what the hell's going on here."

"Go ahead, Agent. But we got orders to get this man downtown ASAP. We're not going to stand around with our thumbs up our ass while you and your supers uncross your wires." The black detective grabbed my arm; the white detective picked up my bag.

"I got to find a phone," said Pruitt. "Go on, damn it. I'll catch up with you, damn it."

He ran ahead of us. We started walking. I held one hand in the other behind my back, an automatic reflex that disguised the handcuffs. The fingers clutching my arm relaxed, keeping up just enough pressure to steer me. People stopped noticing us. Flanked by two older men, I must have looked like a visiting cousin with a black in-law. So this is how a real arrest feels, I told myself, with cold metal instead of warm plastic around my wrists, and no friends being thrown into jail with me.

We walked past Pruitt at a bank of phones, grimacing in a receiver, his interrogation fury back.

He caught up with us again fifty yards farther on. "Out of my hands," he snarled. "He's all yours. But I think this business stinks and I'm going to say so in my report."

"No skin off our butt," said the black detective. "You got your people to answer to, we got ours."

Pruitt tried to look at me, but couldn't. Then he saw something up ahead. Just beyond the metal detectors stood a man with a television camera on his shoulder. A half dozen men and women waited with him.

"Damn it to hell," said Pruitt. "You brought the media? Is that what this is all about?"

The hand on my arm slowed me down. "Shit no. Nobody told us we were picking up press meat."

"Local cable," said his partner. "Not network."

The detective pushed at my arm again. "Oh screw it. Let's run the gauntlet and get out of here."

There was a single flicker of heat lightning, and I saw the other cameras. We swung to the right of the X-ray machines. A headlight on the TV camera snapped on and I had to turn away. We were surrounded by glare and shouts and waving hands.

"This the O'Connor case?" "This the killer, Detective?" "Where did you nab him?"

Somebody shook a tape recorder like a fist in my face.

"Ralph! Ralph! Did you do it, Ralph?"

I was stunned that the media knew my first name.

They followed us for ten yards, a compact storm of grins, cries and flashing cameras. All at once, they let us go. We rode down an escalator in silence, passersby glancing our way as if one of us might be famous.

Not until we were downstairs did I notice that Pruitt was gone. In the cool night air, I came to myself just long enough to miss him. Then a strong hand gripped my head and thrust me into the back of a police car.

20

The bright white mound of the Jefferson Memorial swung past the bridge over the Potomac, a fraud tonight, a bad joke for someone who sat twisted sideways with steel bracelets at his back. The entire city was a mocking cartoon, a sarcasm of public parks and monuments. Even the police building, a coffered brick facade in a campus full of illuminated fronts, looked glibly ironic.

I was plunged into a glare of strip lighting, mustard yellow cinder block, blue uniforms and beeping phones. A black man with a gashed forehead stood across the room, armless in torn sweats, one eye gummed shut with red jam; I stared at him as if at a mirror. Authority stopped having names and became simply black or white. The white detective unlocked his cuffs and gave me to a black cop in uniform. The black cop grabbed my hand, jammed the fingers in ink and then, with startling care, pressed them one by one in a grid, like an impatient father teaching a three-year-old how to tie his shoes. He sat me in a chair and lowered a bar with plastic numbers across my chest. A strobe light softly thumped in my eyes, then my ear.

Then another mustard yellow room, with the black detective again, who pointed at the pay phone on the wall and said, "I bet you want to call your lawyer."

I dialed the number that Nick had given me. I expected little and got less.

"Rosi had no business telling you to contact me. You need a criminal lawyer, not a civil rights attorney. It's one thing to bail out protestors, but a capital crime is a whole new ball game. I can't get down there tonight, but we'll have somebody for you tomorrow. If I can't find anyone, I *guess* I can handle it."

I sat at the detective's desk, told him I wouldn't talk without a lawyer, but I wouldn't have a lawyer until tomorrow. He had expected that. He rolled a form into a typewriter and took my name, birthday, HIV status and other pieces of my life.

"This is the first time anything like this ever happened to me," I said. "What now?"

"What do you think? We put you in jail. Don't worry. Your lawyer will know where to find you. You ain't going anywhere."

I was not afraid. Emotion shut down in me. I hadn't known how deeply my sense of reality depended on emotion until now, when every feeling was gone. Fear, hope, grief, anger, shame. I'd been detached from them all night, but now they disappeared. I didn't even have enough fear to wonder what would become of me. There was only this minute, the next, then the one after.

Another cinder-block corridor, a different cop, another black man in uniform who gripped my arm with one hand and carried my bag with the other. We seemed to be under-ground. We entered a large room with a long counter and a white cop in glasses.

"Why ya bringing a fresh turd at the end of my shift, Dalton? Can't you leave him in the tank until tomorrow?"

"Orders from upstairs, Sarge. Read it and weep."

The white cop frowned at the requisition chit. "Lucky for them we got room at the inn. Okay, bub. Empty your pockets. Valuables here. Strip to your shoes, socks and drawers. Clothes here."

While he groped inside my bag, I removed layers of myself and laid them on the counter. When I stood in my boots, squalidly half-naked before two cops, I coldly remembered our jokes at demonstrations about *wanting* to be strip-searched. The black cop remained off to the side. The white jailer set out my toothbrush—"Nothing you need except this"—then shoved my clothes and duffel coat into the bag, wrapped a strip of yellow tape around it and tossed the bag in a corner. He flopped a pair of orange coveralls on the counter. "What're you waiting for? Put 'em on. Lights out in fifteen minutes."

I stepped into the loose, short-sleeved garment that was like baggy hospital scrubs; the wiry seams bit into my skin. Taking my toothbrush and a roll of toilet paper in one hand, a change of sheets under my arm, I followed the jailer to a pneumatic steel door with a Plexiglas window, the honest version of that first, simple door at the FBI.

The door gasped open on a steady muttering. Not men but radios, two or three boom boxes playing rap. The songs echoed in the hard interior. A harsh smell of ammonia filled the humid passageway, stale cigarette smoke and the gamy ferment of unwashed bodies. The floor was slick with condensed breath. My passing produced no sneers or catcalls, only bored glances from deep within the enameled bars.

"Don't worry about your sweet A getting popped here," said the jailer. "We keep you bad boys apart until arraignment."

He stopped outside an empty cell. I stepped in. I stood there, in a six-by-eight-foot cement cube, looking at a shiny steel toilet, the metal shelf with a mattress pad folded up at one end. The door rolled shut at my back; I heard the clunk of the lock.

It was as though I'd been swallowed by the surface of the earth. And it was all surface, wasn't it? This was the reality underneath, a maze of cinder block and solitary cells. At least I was alone, but then I'd always been alone.

"Hey, skinhead," a voice shouted. "Throw me your cigs."

The cells were staggered and I couldn't see into the cell opposite. I had to step up to my bars before I saw a bleached palm making a gimme gesture across the way.

"Sorry. Don't smoke," I said, in the guilty tone I used with homeless people on the street.

The hand withdrew. A bloodshot eye appeared between the bars. "Sorry? You ain't sorry. White piece of shit. Must make you sick to be thrown in with niggers, skinhead." His lower teeth were solid metal, gold or brass, with two artificial fangs. "You just another shit-eating faggot. You skinheads think you're tough, but just a pack of Nazi Jew fags." He stepped away from the bars, having no further use for me.

I took a loud, self-conscious piss in the saucepan toilet. Unfolding the mattress on its shelf, I saw the pattern of stains covering the middle. Of course. There was nothing else for men to do here. The wall beside the bed had been scratched by a fork or thumbnail with crude pictures of vaginas, breasts and guns. I wished I'd asked to keep my book, not because I thought I could read, but having a smooth, literate object at hand might remind me who I was. I covered the mattress with a sheet and lay down without removing my boots. Now I'm living this minute, I thought, now the next. Eternity stretched out before me.

I had broken with gravity tonight and hurtled through time, only to come to a dead halt at the dead end of a jail cell. I thought everything would catch up with me and I'd understand what it meant. But I couldn't think in the racket of rap songs, a chant of bad moods that canceled each other out. I was canceled out. The music stopped when the lights were killed, but living voices called to each other. "Who you?" "Nobody you know." "You righteous?" "More righteous than you, homeboy." "Shut up, bitches. Save it for the suits." When the voices died out, there were more private sounds: moans and splashes and farts. Even the toughest thug waited for darkness to ease his bowels.

What was I doing here? I seemed to have wanted this. Why? To make Bill's death real? To punish myself? I seemed to be guilty of something. I wondered if maybe I had killed

Bill and it had slipped my mind, as so much had slipped from my mind. Anything seemed possible tonight, everything was a dream. Looking at my hands, however, the cuticles rimmed with fingerprint ink, I assured myself I couldn't have killed him or I would not be so stunned to find myself here.

Hatred began in the next hour. Not anger, but hatred, a cold fury with no clear object. I could blame myself for only so long, but found no other target smaller than the entire world. It resembled my last gasps of faith in college, when I was an atheist who still believed in God whenever I was caught in the rain. Chilled and wet, water stinging my eyes while I bicycled home from a class, I'd think angrily, Go ahead, spit on me, punish me, make me suffer, as if my misery were not bad luck and poor planning but directed personally at me by a hidden power. There was only me and the universe, me and not-me, me and *It*, an egotism of suffering that made God necessary again.

God tonight was a police station. God was a zoo. The night light outside the bars resembled the dim glow of the reptile house where Bill and I had met. Except I'd become one of the reptiles, a cold-blooded thing outside time. And Bill existed nowhere at all. Yet we remained connected, more tightly now than when he was alive, trapped under the glass of his death.

The It that put me here had murdered Bill. There was no other explanation. I wanted a They who could do that, but this required such a vast They—cops and jailer and detectives, Pruitt and Lovelace, the reporters at the airport—that my old suspicion about Jeb Weiss seemed naive and sentimental.

21

I didn't sleep that first night, so I never felt as if I woke up the next morning. The night leaked away in snores and groans, the flush of toilets and the constant fuming of one crack-raw voice cursing us all in a fever. Then the lights and music came back on and I was still here, in a cement box with a barred gate. Breakfast was wheeled into the lockup in covered trays like trays in a hospital. We ate in silence like dogs in a kennel.

"Jackson, Albert. You got counsel."

"Washington, Ahmed. You're going to the Roach Motel."

"Park your ass here, kid. Chill."

I saw the others only when they were taken out or brought in, quick glimpses of pumpkin orange coveralls and dark faces. All appeared younger than I, all were black. They were allowed to keep cigarettes and even boom boxes, but I'd been denied everything except my toothbrush. As punishment for being white? I longed to see another white inmate, not from fellow feeling but to prove to a trace of old identity that my fear of the others wasn't racist. I was not just physically but mentally afraid, frightened by what would become of my mind when I was thrown with them in the main jail, the Roach Motel. I fought my fear by hating them, their loud voices and angry music. Each time one was taken out to meet with a lawyer, I hated the white people who'd forgotten me: Brian the attorney, Nick in New York, even Agent Pruitt, who'd acted at the airport like he *wanted* to protect me. This was the city where Nancy lived, but only in name: I was in a different city, another dimension.

Time stood still, a time outside time, all present and no past or future. An hour that trickled out in seconds disappeared completely when it was over. I tried to kill time by reciting passages of poetry from memory: "Sailing to Byzantium," "Neither Out Far Nor In Deep" and "Lullaby." But the lines were full of holes, the remembered words so empty that I might've been chanting my multiplication tables.

"Eckhart, Ralph," shouted a guard in the eternity after lunch. I had a name again. "You got meeting with counsel."

He unlocked my gate. I was stunned to walk ten, then twenty yards, wobbling on sea legs down a long cinder-block corridor, into a low-ceilinged room cut in half by a counter with a foot-high divider down the center. The cop pointed to a short white man with a large, balding head and a blue suit with padded shoulders. He sat hunched over a legal pad at the far end, away from the only others there, an inmate and lawyer who glowered at each other like an estranged couple.

The man did not stand or offer his hand when I pulled out the chair across from him. He frowned at me while he quivered the pencil between his thumb and finger.

"Mr. Eckhart? Jack Freeman. Somebody else in the firm will be handling your case. I'm here just to get you out as quickly as possible."

"Brian Golden called you?"

"Golden? I know no Golden. No, my wife asked me to take care of this. A friend of yours works for her."

"Friend? You mean Nancy? You mean Senator Freeman?"

"Yeah, I'm Freeman's husband," he grunted.

Nancy had sent her boss's husband to rescue me? My emotions came back to life, first joy, then shame that Nancy even knew I was here.

"We don't have much time. Let's cut to the chase. You're being charged with the murder of William O'Connor. What did you say in your statement to the FBI?"

"Statement? What I told them when we talked?"

"No, your statement. Statement!" he barked. "What they put down on paper and had you sign."

"I never signed anything."

"You must've."

"I didn't."

"You're sure?"

"They interrogated me forever, but gave me nothing to sign." This was another interrogation; I would spend the rest of my life being interrogated.

"So they weren't holding out on me," he muttered. "So then. Square one. Where were you Friday, the night of the murder?"

"I was in Washington. With Nancy in fact." Nancy knew and I could mention her now.

"All night?"

"From seven that night to seven or eight the next morning."

"Is she willing to say so in writing?"

"She should. It's true."

"And you told the FBI that?"

"No. I told them I was home. In New York."

Freeman stared at me, his pencil quivering again. "Jesus Christ, man. Why?"

"I thought it'd make me a suspect. And I didn't want to involve Nancy."

"You didn't want to inconvenience a friend, so you lied to the FBI? Do you have any brains at all?" he snapped.

"Yeah, it was stupid," I snapped back. "I don't know why I did it." Had he read Bill's footnote about his wife? "I didn't think there was any way they'd know I'd come down."

"Airline tickets? Credit card receipts? What century you living in? You had a perfectly good alibi and trashed it."

"I took an unreserved train and paid cash."

"Well, somebody must've seen you and reported it. Or they picked you out from closed-circuit monitors in Union Station or the Metro. Whatever, they must've known you were lying or they wouldn't have gone to the trouble of shipping you down. Didn't the fact that it was the FBI tip you off that something was up?"

"They said they were just helping out."

"The feds don't just *help out.* I don't get why they were even involved. Looking for possible conspiracy? I can't get over that they never got a statement from you. You had no business letting them fly you down."

"I'm not a suspicious person. Nothing like this has ever happened to me."

"Well, it's sure as hell happening now, so let's get on with it. Anything else that might make you a suspect?"

"Only that I was fucking O'Connor. For four months." I no longer cared what words I used. "I hadn't seen him since February. But I wrote to him."

"What kind of letter?"

"E-mail. Angry."

"Did you threaten him? Say you were going to kill him?"

I hesitated. "I may have said I *felt* like killing him. And there were phone calls. Two of them. The FBI told me Bill taped his calls. I don't know if they were telling the truth or just out to confuse me. They got me very confused and rattled."

"Okay. Tell me about that."

I did and Freeman wrote it all down, their friendly, legal half lies, my naive gullibility.

He disdainfully shook his head. "You were a fool to go to them in the first place. You should have let them come to you."

"I'll know better next time." I was sarcastic, but his scorn also made me feel that I hadn't done this to myself after all. There actually was a *They* who had done it to me.

"All right," he said when we finished. "Arraignment isn't scheduled until tomorrow afternoon. I'll try to move it up. With a statement from Wenceslas, plus all the improper procedure and the way you fell between fed and D.C. jurisdiction, I'll ask that charges be dismissed. That's not likely, not with the case gone as far as it has. But we'll argue for dismissal every chance we get. And my wife has offered to cover your bail. I think she's making a big mistake getting that involved, but she insists. It won't hurt having a U.S. senator in your corner."

"That's good of her," I said, meaning it, yet unable to shake the sarcasm from my tone. I remembered something else I should mention. "I'm innocent, you know. I didn't do it."

"Fine," he said, as if that were of absolutely no importance.

A half hour later, in a room upstairs, Polk, the black detective, took my statement with Freeman wearily looking on. Freeman insisted I keep to the facts: what time I caught the train, what time I saw Nancy, what time I left.

"This isn't what you told the three-piecers," Polk grumbled.

"Doesn't matter what he told *them*," said Freeman. "You don't have a statement from them. Will they be at the arraignment?"

When I was returned to the cellblock, I'd been out just long enough to be able to smell and even taste the smoked sweat stench again. I was still in jail, but I'd regained my future tense; I could imagine getting out.

My second night lasted longer than the first. The shock had worn off, and a man howled and banged in his cell all night long, going crazy with withdrawal. Another man screamed at him to be quiet, until the others shouted at *him* to shut up and ignore the poor pipe-bitch. I fell in and out of sleep. Having a future closed the past and I didn't think once about Bill.

They came the next morning and handcuffed me again, clamping my wrists in front this time. They took me down a long corridor to an elevator with my neighbor, the boy with metal teeth. He was just a boy, fifteen or sixteen, softly padded with baby fat. His vampire fangs now suggested the toy teeth worn by kids at Halloween, except this child had an old, dead look in his jellied eyes.

Justice was arranged like a theme park here, police headquarters and courthouses in a single complex connected underground. Freeman waited for me upstairs. The courtroom was small, the proceedings quick and informal.

"The United States versus Ralph Eckhart," said the judge, a stern black woman with a paisley scarf in the collar of her robe. I learned later that all the D.C. courts were federal, but it was a shock to hear I had not just a state but the whole country against me.

Freeman, Polk and a fluffy-haired man from the prosecutor's office approached the bench and showed the judge various papers. There was nobody from the FBI. I stood behind them, watching the judge, wondering if she was part of the mysterious They who'd put me here. When she didn't look at me, I turned toward the rows of benches like church pews. Someone's girlfriend or sister sat up front—the vampire boy?—and a man in a sports coat who scribbled in a steno pad. Then I saw Nancy sitting in the back, her arms folded like she'd been dragged to church against her will. She tried to smile at me, but her lips stuck, her eyes remained pinched with fear. I saw myself in her eyes: pathetic and unshaven, a prisoner in highway safety orange.

"Improper procedure or not, Counselor, I cannot dismiss the charge. And no, I am not being swayed by the fact the arrest made the papers." They conferred a minute longer and she declared, "Bail is set at twenty-five thousand dollars. Next case."

The cop led me out. Freeman followed us to the elevator. Nancy remained in the courtroom.

"The judge didn't drop the charges," I said glumly.

"But she knows something smells or she wouldn't set bail so low and grant you permission to leave the District. Just sit tight. We should have you out soon enough."

"Freeman! Mr. Freeman!" The man with the steno pad raced down the hall. "You're defending the Eckhart case?"

"*No.* And there's no case, no story. So do everyone a big favor and go home."

The man turned his hungry grin to me; the elevator doors closed before he could speak.

I passed the next hour in my cell, and another hour. I became afraid that they'd changed their minds and I wouldn't get out today, which felt the same as never getting out. Then keys jingled in the passage. "Eckhart, Ralph. Move it. You made bail."

Out in the receiving room, a white man in a knit shirt and leather coat lounged against the counter. "You're Ralph Eckhart? I'm Sammy Greco. Your bail bondsman."

Half listening while he explained the rules, I got my bag from the cops and eagerly shucked off the coveralls to climb back into my soft, familiar clothes, desperate to become myself again.

Greco said I had to report to him by phone every Friday. He needed my passport. "I don't get that passport FedExed to me in two days, your ass goes back in the can. You forget to call me just once, you go back in the can. Your friends have bet a lot of money on you, Ralphie, so don't fuck with me or them. Sign this. And this." He gave me his card. "Treat my number like it was your family jewels. I make no exceptions, friend. All right. Get out of here. Your ride's waiting for you outside."

I found Freeman standing in the hallway.

"I'm parked out back," he said. "So we can avoid any press that I didn't give the slip by rescheduling the arraignment."

Walking with my warm, battered bag in my hand again, I waited to feel the joy of being restored to myself, yet the rough bite of coveralls still haunted my skin. I climbed the stairs toward a door with a small dirty window. I assumed it was raining outside—it had to be raining. The sunlight startled me. The sky was too bright, the day a hallucination.

Light glowed in the speckled sphere of a fruit tree by the parking lot, its fallen blossoms casting a pink shadow on the neon green grass.

Nancy waited on the sidewalk. When she embraced me, my body took a moment to understand it should hug back.

"Oh Ralph. I am sorry. I am so sorry."

I walked with my arm around her waist, pressing her against my hip, breathing the cool, sweet air, hoping touch and smell would give me back to myself. There was too much sky overhead.

When we got in the car, I sat up front with Freeman, Nancy in the back. She clutched and squeezed my shoulder from behind to assure us both that I'd come out in one piece. Trees and buildings spun dizzily around me.

"I'm finished with you," said Freeman as he drove. "Michael Diaz, an associate in the New York office, will take the case from here. You can regularly meet with him without having to travel. But I don't see this case getting past a grand jury. It's been a muck-up from the start. The FBI knew they didn't have any evidence but were too chickenshit to let you go once you were in custody. So they dumped the whole mess on D.C., where Unsworth, the prosecutor, is covering his ass by bringing charges. Diaz can get them on improper proce-dure, lack of evidence, violation of rights."

Listening to Freeman, I realized that this was far from over and any happiness I experienced now was only temporary.

"But damn it, Eckhart. How could you let them gull and con you like that? How could you let this go so far?"

"I was innocent and trusting," I said. "I'm not innocent anymore."

We pulled up outside Nancy's building. I asked when I could return to New York.

"Catch the next train if you like. You're a free man. Semifree until your next day in court. You can't leave the country, of course. And you need to let Greco know if you leave New York for any reason. One last word of advice. Let your hair grow. Look normal until this mess is settled."

"Okay. Well. Thank you," I said.

"Don't thank me. Thank my wife and your friend here."

Nancy and I got out and he drove off. I stood at the curb, looking up at the ornate climb of corniced windows against the clear blue sky. I was reluctant to go indoors, wary of interiors.

"How're you feeling?" Nancy asked.

"Better. Some." I winced at her question and my answer.

"Oh Ralph, I'm so sorry this happened to you. You of all people. I really am sorry."

"You keep saying sorry like it was something you did. You got me out. Nick said he'd protect me and he didn't do shit."

"But he did," she said. "He's been on the phone since yesterday. He called early Tuesday morning and told me you were with the FBI. Then I saw in the paper that you'd been arrested. I called Nick and I told Kathleen. She called her husband. We're behind you, Ralph. All of us."

That was something, I thought. Something. I mechanically followed her up the steps into the lobby. She stroked my arm in the cell-like elevator. A worried crimp remained in her face.

As she unlocked her door, the phone rang. She hurried inside and answered it.

"Yes? Just now. It went fine. Jack got him out. No, on bail. Twenty-five thousand. Yes, he's here. Just a minute." She held out the phone. "It's Kathleen. She needs to talk to you."

Something as commonplace as a molded plastic receiver felt very odd in my hand. "Hello?"

"Ralph? Kathleen Freeman here." Her clarinet burr was quick and to the point. "I don't have time for this nonsense, but I couldn't walk away in good conscience. I just want you to realize the degree to which I've stuck my neck out for you."

"I don't know how to thank you, Senator Freeman. But your bail money is safe. I want to see this through to the end."

"The money's nothing. If people find out I paid it, however, and my husband's firm is handling your case, they're going to think things. But I'm in a no-win situation. They'll think worse things if they hear I let you hang in the wind. All I ask of you, Ralph, is that you let the law take care of this. I can't tell you not to talk to the press but I ask that you keep it to a minimum. And say as little as possible about that idiotic book. Except in court, if it goes to court. I don't want you to perjure yourself. But the *Washington Times* would have a field day with a scenario where you killed that twit to avenge me and Nancy, and that's why I came to your aid. I'm helping you only so I can sleep at night, and because I gain nothing if I let you hang. Fair enough?"

"Fair enough," I said. "Thank you."

She was as indifferent to gratitude as her husband. "That's all I had to say. Give me back to Nancy."

I passed Nancy the receiver.

"Yes? Yes. I'm sure he does. Did you want me to come in? No, I don't think I'd be much good either. Thanks. I'd like some time with him. He's been through a trauma. See you tomorrow." She hung up and faced me.

"She sounds pissed," I said.

"We all are. Aren't you pissed?"

"Yeah. Only I don't know who to be pissed at." I tugged my shirt, feeling the ghost creep of jailhouse coveralls again. "I need to take a shower. I'm itchy with the funk of that place."

"You poor guy. Take a long, hot one. Then we can talk."

It felt good to undress and wash in private again. The jet of hot water was glorious, as if I hadn't bathed in months. I thought I could soap away the jail, but it had gotten under my skin, and Nancy's bathroom had no window. All the old rituals seemed thin and strange. I took out my electric shaver and, remembering what Freeman said, shaved only my face. The man in the mirror looked pale and alien, with sleepless raccoon circles under the squared cage of eyebrows.

When I dressed and came out, Nancy was on the sofa under the window, her shoes off, her feet folded up, gravely waiting.

"I made some tea," she began.

I took the hot mug and sat at the other end of the sofa, blew at the steam and sipped.

She watched me. "What you said downstairs about me saying sorry too often? You're right." She frowned. "Jack told me about your lie to the FBI. When he got my statement saying that you *were* here Friday night. Why didn't you tell them, Ralph?"

"I didn't want to involve you. I didn't think it important."

"Was it because of the things I said on Friday night?"

I cocked an ear at her, pretending I hadn't heard right.

"I'm sorry about blowing up at you. I know you meant well. But why didn't you tell them you were here? You weren't out to punish yourself or prove yourself or get back at me, were you?"

"That's crazy."

"I know it's crazy. But I can't understand why else you'd do it. Why did you give in to them? It was a crazy thing to do, Ralph. A masochistic thing. It scares me that you'd want to punish yourself like that. What were you out to prove?"

"Scares me too," I said. "But I didn't know. I did it out of ignorance, not masochism." I was annoyed she thought this was about her. There may have been a grain of her at the start, but it had grown much larger. "You've been angry at me before without my flipping out. I didn't get into that to punish myself or prove anything to you."

"Okay. Not me then. But I know you, Ralph." She balled her hands in her lap. "I'm sorry about . . . him. He was no friend of mine. I know you stopped liking him too. Still, it must've been hard hearing he'd been killed. Even before they accused you."

"It happened too fast for me to feel anything clearly." I irritably turned away from her, and noticed the front page on the stack of newspapers by the sofa.

"You've made yourself into a punching bag, Ralph. Over me or him or *something*. You frighten me. What's going on in your head?"

"I don't know!" I said. "But it's not just me. It's not just psychology. It's much bigger." I snatched up the newspaper.

"Oh that," she said. "You haven't seen that." She snorted. "You won't find your answer there."

It lay below the fold of the *Washington Times* front page, three columns wide: "AIDS Activist Arrested in Author Murder." There was a photo of an armless man with a lowered head, a flare of light on his gritty skull. He hurried through what looked like a mob of reporters, not just six or seven.

"Not a flattering angle," Nancy scoffed.

I finally understood why Freeman insisted we leave by a back entrance, and what the man with the steno pad had wanted, and what the cameras at the airport had meant. My punishment, self- or state-inflicted, wasn't private but an enormous public nudity.

"It's all so-and-so alleges and the police speculate," said Nancy. "With a quote from Nick."

The lead read: "The mysterious death of William O'Connor, controversial author of *The Regiment of Women*, took a dramatic turn yesterday with the arrest of a New York man active in gay politics. Ralph Eckhart, 34 . . .'"

There was a rehash of earlier reports about the murder, and a statement by Detective Polk that "Our sources indicate that Eckhart once provided sexual services to O'Connor." They cited my old arrest at City Hall, which was where they got "activist." Nicholas Rosi, identified as a spokesperson for ACT UP, told them, "I know Eckhart personally. He's a quiet, caring man. A lamb, he's incapable of murder. This charge is either a prejudiced mistake or a calculated frame-up."

I suffered a quiet chaos reading about this person who was and wasn't me: annoyance that I was misrepresented, even by Nick; relief that there was so little resemblance; unease over the crude thrill I took in seeing my name on a front page.

The quote from Nick appeared in the continuation

inside. Attached to the foot of the article was a single paragraph under the heading "Services for *Times* Contributor." A
memorial for William O'Connor was scheduled for Wednesday, 3 P.M., at St. Agatha's Church in Baltimore, followed by
burial in Catonsville Memorial Park.

"Satisfied?" said Nancy. She sighed and added, "Seeing
what they do to you in print makes what was done to me look
like small potatoes. They make you out to be a radical
whore."

"What day is this?"

"Wednesday."

I looked at my recently returned watch; it too seemed
altered by its hours in jail. I couldn't believe it was not yet one
o'clock. What had been a vague notion became a necessity.
"Can I borrow your car?"

"For what?" She glared down at the paper.

"I want to pay my last respects."

"You can't, Ralph. That's nuts. Why?"

"It's something I need to do right now." I resented
having to explain. The need was simply there, like a desire to
breathe, with no concern for how it struck others.

"You're not thinking straight. You just got out of jail.
How will his family feel if the accused murderer shows up?"

"I don't care about them. This is for me. Hey, I'm
an accused murderer. I don't have to care what anyone
feels." I said it for the sake of argument, but it was true. I
was freed from the opinions of other people. Could anyone think worse of me? "I'm fed up with just reading and
hearing and being accused of this. I want to say good-bye
to the poor bastard. I shared sexual services with him,
remember?"

"Send a card. Send flowers." She gritted her teeth.
"What? His murder absolves him and you love him again?"
she sneered. "Is that it?"

"What if I do? Why should it matter to you what I feel?" It
wasn't love, but it was something. "Do you feel insulted that I
can grieve for someone who wronged you?"

She stared at me, her lips drawn tight, her brow knotted, confused by the anger that poured from both of us.

"Okay," she said. "Okay, damn it. If it'll give you closure. But I don't trust you with my car in your state of mind. I'll drive. I want to be there and make sure you don't do anything even more cracked."

22

The shirt and tie that I'd packed for court were worn instead to a funeral. Baltimore was less than an hour away. Nancy asked about jail while she drove. I gave her a dry, cursory account, not wanting to use the experience as an excuse for my strange new temper and obstinacy. We worked to reconnect after our anger, but a nervous, uncertain distance remained.

We found St. Agatha's, a suburban Catholic chapel behind the highway of strip malls near Bill's home. A white hearse crowded the parking lot. The service had already begun. The urgency of my need subsided, and I agreed with Nancy that we couldn't go in. We parked across the street and sat in the car.

The long stillness was broken by the sob of a pipe organ. The front doors opened and six men squeezed through with a glossy black box. The sight threw me. Everyone else I knew had been cremated, but Bill was being buried whole. The pallbearers stopped to reposition their grip of the heavy coffin, and it made death real. Again. Was that why I needed to come? For yet another fix of death to get my bearings in the confusion of lawyers and newspapers? Other mourners followed, including Bill's parents. We were too far away to see the pallbearers' faces, but, among the young men who must have been cousins and friends from school, I recognized the squat shape of Jeb Weiss. The coffin disappeared into the hearse. Gaudy sprays of flowers were placed inside, and I remembered a gift of roses.

"Seen enough?" said Nancy.

"No. Let's go to the cemetery. Don't worry. I won't talk to anyone. I can pay my respects from a distance."

There was no cortege behind the hearse and limo. We followed a car with two pallbearers and their girlfriends to a new cemetery five miles away. A treeless slope beside a golf course, it was barely distinguishable from the fairway, the lawn looped with lanes, the memorial stones in isolated patches. We parked a hundred yards uphill from the burial marquee. The hearse and cars gathered below. I got out and wandered to the nearest markers, pretending to visit my own family plot. Nancy joined me.

"Nothing to see, Ralph. Just another stinking funeral."

"But at least there's one homo saying good-bye to him today."

I'd forgotten how formal and impersonal straight funerals can be. Generic organ music played on tape. I drifted down the hill to the next family of stones, then the next, bowing my head like a passerby paying his respects, clasping my hands exactly as I'd clasped them that morning in handcuffs.

Nancy caught up and wrapped her arm in mine, gently preventing me from going closer. We'd come down far enough to have a clear view under the marquee twenty yards away. The pallbearers had set the coffin in a bed of flowers, a black box like an idea of death, a geometry of death, Bill reduced to a piece of furniture. The priest in white smock and black skirt shook water from his fingers and delivered the last words. A trio of colored specks pursued their golf balls in the distance.

I noticed Ren Whitaker carefully tiptoeing behind the

mourners outside the tent. A pack of men in similar haircuts and glasses must all have been from *American Truths*. I saw Jeb Weiss again, his arm around Bill's mother at the coffin. She held her head straight, her gloved hands at her chest in a fist of prayer. Her pink suit and veiled hat suggested an ancient memory of Jackie Kennedy. Mrs. O'Connor's grief was genuine, yet she displayed it as carefully as she displayed her living room at night in its open curtains. Weiss supported and comforted her, although Big Bill looked like he was in more need of consoling. He stood behind them, his shoulders shaking, his horn-rimmed face twisted with crying, as overly emotional as his son once told me he was. I was stabbed by the sentimental regret that Bill would never know how deeply his father mourned him.

A motor whirred; the casket sank in the flowers. Good-bye, I thought, but it gave me no release, no conclusion. My timing was permanently off. I could cry on a plane in FBI custody but not at a funeral. I seemed to have come today in hopes of finishing with Bill before I went on with my other wars.

Weiss steered Mrs. O'Connor out of the tent into the sun, her face dry, stony, stunned. Passing around the ropes supporting the marquee, they walked toward us for a few paces, and Weiss saw me. He lowered his bushy eyebrows and lifted his indignant chin beard. His eyes burned a hole in me.

I politely nodded.

He tightened his frown, signaling I was not to come over. Bill's mother felt him staring and looked up. She gazed blankly for a moment, then sadly nodded and, before going the way Weiss turned her, *smiled*. She remembered me. She must not have known that the fellow her son had brought by the house one night was his accused murderer. Mr. O'Connor followed, too busy with horn-rims, handkerchief and tears to notice anything.

Nancy tugged at my arm. "Let's go. This is creeping me out."

But I remained there, shaken by a mother's oblivious smile. Then I noticed Ren Whitaker looking at us as he strutted toward the cars. His mouth came open. He didn't stop but changed course and swung toward us. "Excuse me! Excuse me!" he called out, although Nancy and I weren't going anywhere.

"Yes?" I played impassive and innocent.

He stood in front of us, looking me up and down. "Dear Lord. It really is you." He glanced back to see where the others were. "What're you doing here? You're supposed to be in jail."

"I posted bail this morning."

He righteously drew himself up. "Do you have no sense of decency? Haven't you brought enough pain to this family without coming here? Do you have to add insult to injury?"

"If *you* killed someone, would *you* go to their funeral?"

He gave me a startled, skeptical look. It was not just a rhetorical question, was it? He shook his head. "I just hope his family didn't see you. Because they're heartbroken. *Heartbroken.*" He stormed off, not toward the limo with Weiss and the O'Connors but toward his own car.

Nancy and I started up the hill. "Ren Whitaker knows you?" She sounded as if she'd been holding her breath. "Thank God he didn't know who I was. Lucky for me no Senate people came. But I should've known this thing would be lousy with cons and fundies."

I was still weighing the question I'd asked Whitaker. "Would the killer come to the funeral?" I asked her.

"Is that why you had to make an appearance?" she said scornfully. "To prove to those assholes you're innocent?"

"Not me. One of them."

Now it was her turn to stare. "No, Ralph. No. Forget it."

And it was such a cold, cruel twist: the real murderer giving sympathy to Bill's parents. Neither of us said anything until we got into the car.

"Look," said Nancy. "I don't like those people either. But I meet with them and know them and they're not gangsters. They're no more likely to kill in cold blood than we are. They kill with neglect or capital punishment, but they don't do it themselves."

"They could've hired someone"—my tired old solution.

She angrily started the engine and put it in gear. "Why? Because your pal came out?" she sneered.

"You're the one who thought her life would be ruined by a footnote."

"But I'd never kill for something like that. And neither would they. Jeb Weiss is a big game-player whose only concern is playing power broker and getting tax breaks for Texas billionaires. Ren Whitaker watches his ass so carefully he won't even admit he works for Pat Robertson, much less risk his future by arranging a killing. And the Republican Party is full of homos. Nobody cares, Ralph. Being gay is not the sin of sins, the be-all and end-all."

"Why're you defending them?"

"I'm not defending them! I'm defending you. Because if you start hurling charges, you're going to ruin your case and go to prison for sure. After seeing you dressed like a convict this morning, I can't bear the thought of that." She had to swallow a thickness in her voice. "You're paranoid. Which is understandable after what you've been through. But it's insane thinking and you have to let go of it."

"So who killed him?" I demanded.

"I don't know! All I know is you didn't. You were with me. Why not a pickup? Like the police first said. Another trick. Is that it? You hate to think he was fucking someone else?"

"I don't care who he was fucking. I just want to know who did it and stuck the crime on me."

Nancy was silent for a moment. "They don't have to be the same person. They don't even have to be connected. Circumstance and bad luck, and you put yourself right in the middle of it. Would that be too hard to accept?"

"No. It's too easy," I admitted. "It feels cowardly to call it bad luck, like I got caught in the rain."

"You want it to mean something, Ralph. You want it all tied up in a neat explanation. The chances of that are nil. Accept that or you're going to make yourself crazy."

"Maybe I am crazy. But maybe paranoia is wisdom here."

"No. Your paranoia is only shock and grief and God

knows what else. You saw them back there. Do you really
think one of them engineered the whole thing?"

I angrily turned away from her. "No. I don't."

Because I'd looked into the eyes of two men I wanted to
believe were responsible and had seen no guilt, nothing monstrous, only concern for the surviving family and shock with
my bad manners. The They that had seemed so plausible my
first night in jail became an It again in daylight when I
couldn't give the enemy a human face.

23

I returned to New York that evening. I wanted to get back to my life. The phantom machinery that had brought me here didn't care how I got home. I had to borrow money from Nancy for the train.

An accused murderer had two seats to himself in a crowded Amtrak car; my first person now carried a third-person singular wherever I went.

The New York subway was loud and shrill when I arrived, like a knife factory, as if I'd been away for months. Coming up the stairs of my building, I expected yellow police tape on my door, but the door was blank. The apartment seemed changed, however, as if robbed. Everything was here but with its familiarity stripped away by the FBI's visit. Strange voices filled my answering machine: reporters wanting to talk, a lawyer with an 800 number offering his services. The last voice sounded familiar: "Nick here. I just spoke to Nancy and heard the good news. You're probably still badly shaken, but don't despair. We're all behind you. You have many options. Call when you get in."

The accused murderer called nobody that night. He

opened his windows to air the strangeness from his room, then sat on a sill to assure himself that interiors and exteriors connected here. I looked out on the Gothic twists of ailanthus trees not yet in bud, the half-moon over the chimney pots and water tanks, the bright windows ranged up and down the alley with security bars that made each home look like a cell.

I went to work the next day, walking the long blocks I'd walked a thousand times. I entered the store with a casual, ironic lope, sarcastically pretending nothing had happened. Erica snapped to attention at the cash register; Robert and Lucy did a frightened double take across the room. People couldn't have been more startled if I'd returned from the dead.

Striding toward the back of the store, I saw Peter look up in his cubbyhole. He sat very still, his gaze softening as I approached. He jumped up, threw back the counter and came out. "Oh baby," he said and embraced the murderer.

Of course. Peter would understand. A murder charge was like illness. I held him for a moment, feeling the poke of the catheter in his chest, like a spigot in his heart.

"I was afraid we'd never see you again." He brushed his hand down my spine and patted my ass. "But here you are."

"I gather word is out."

"Oh yeah. You better believe it." He led me downstairs, as if I might have forgotten the way. "Look who's here," he announced.

"Hey hey!" Alec cried. "The man! Free at last. Free at last. Back from the room with stri-ped sunshine," he laughed.

"Back from the gulag," I said, trying to joke with him, surprised by his ability to find humor here, wondering at his sudden fondness for me.

"Saved you something," he said, reaching into his nook under the worktable. He proudly slapped down two *New York Posts*.

No wonder people knew. I was half of Tuesday's front page. The grim airport photo appeared beside the headline "Pundit Killer Nabbed." Death had promoted Bill; "pundit" had fewer letters than "journalist."

I never dreamed the story would reach New York. It was the same story as the one in the *Washington Times*, shortened, paragraphs reshuffled. I rated only a box on Wednesday's front page, but inside was a news feature titled "Strange Bedfellows."

"Your fifteen minutes," said Peter dryly.

"You got thirty seconds on CNN," chirped Alec. "I taped it if you'd like to see it."

The Wednesday piece included a college yearbook photo of Bill, wholesome and insipid, alongside a close-up of my airport photo, more sinister than ever when enlarged. "Eckhart: 'A queer and present danger,' " said the caption. The pun that was dumbly funny when Nancy and I coined it months ago had been recoined by Rush Limbaugh on the radio; the *Post* found it too clever not to repeat.

Again, what facts they cited were true—my City Hall arrest, my Southern origin, my blue-collar-sounding job—yet the absence of so many other facts—my English degree, for one—suggested an uneducated, redneck queer. There were more quotes from Nick, and even one from Alec. "Alec Stevenson, a co-worker at Left Bank Books, said Eckhart seemed normal enough. 'A serious worker whose only real interest outside his job was sex.' "

"I said '*books* and sex,' " Alec insisted. "Honest. And other stuff, but they didn't use it."

"What's in today's paper?"

"Just a teeny item about you being let out."

"Your fifteen minutes are up," Peter noted.

"So it's over? You're free?" said Alec.

I explained how I was only out on bail but that my lawyers hoped to get the charges dismissed.

"Great," said Alec. I couldn't tell if he was pleased I wouldn't go to prison or that it wasn't quite finished. He treated my fame as an exciting diversion, a harmless farce.

Peter leaned against the worktable on one elbow, his long hand drooped over the edge, looking concerned.

"They didn't interview *you*?" I said.

"They tried. But I told them to get lost."

I felt grateful for his simple no. "You still think murder is more human?"

He frowned guiltily. "But it is. For us jaded bystanders."

The office door at the rear of the basement suddenly opened. Elaine had heard us. "Ralph?" she said. "You're back?"

"That's what they tell me."

She offered awkward condolences, then asked me to step into her office. Peter made a face, wondering what this was about.

Elaine closed the door and became timid, respectful. "I just wanted to ask about your, um, future here."

I repeated what I'd told Peter and Alec. I suspected that she wanted to fire me, but, instead of my usual courtesy, I was nastily flippant. "You uncomfortable having a suspected murderer in shipping and receiving?"

"No, no, no. I *presume* you're innocent. I was just wondering if I should start looking for a replacement. And if reporters would still be coming by. If you don't mind, I'm making Robert acting manager on Sundays. The insurance company, you understand. Until this is wrapped up."

"Of course." I assured her I would not let a murder charge get in the way of my duties. I was amazingly indifferent to it all, my future here, my boss's fear of me, the absurdity of dealing with such things at a time like this.

When I came out, Peter was waiting with Alec.

"She said I could stay."

Peter rolled his eyes and laughed. "You never know. I better get back to my post. But we can talk at lunch." He petted my shoulder and went upstairs.

Alone with unopened boxes and a giddily admiring assistant, I struggled to remember what was important about my work here.

The phone rang. It was Nick. He welcomed me back, asked how I was and told me again not to despair.

"A lamb, huh?" I quoted his quote at him.

"I'm sorry, Ralph. About my bum advice that going

along was the best solution. I had no idea how deep you were in this."

"I didn't do it because of you. I'd already decided to do it." I disliked his presumption that this was all his doing.

"But we can turn this around," he said. "Can you meet after work? We need to keep the ball rolling while it has momentum."

"The key is to keep people talking. You have to stay in the public eye, Ralph. So they can't disappear your case."

"Homophobia," said Maura Morris. "It means silence too."

"You got coverage only because it was a slow news day," Nick added. "But people don't like reading about gays, even when they kill each other. The tabs have already dropped the story."

"If you were a woman, they'd run it forever," said Maura. "But fags don't sell papers."

"The *Times* never touched it. But Maura's pitched an article to the *Voice.*"

"And they want it," she said. "What with that misogynistic book, police homophobia and the sleeping-with-the-enemy angle, you're good copy."

We met in Nick and Peter's living room that night, sitting in a circle under the cozy pools of light on their ceiling. The curtains blew lightly at the door to the terrace; I'd asked that the door be cracked open. I sat low in an armchair, Maura on a stool to my left. Her red hair in a bowl cut so short it seemed to have been done with a saucer, she looked like a radical berry in wire-rims. Nick hunched forward on the edge of the sofa to my right, elbows on his knees. Peter was folded in the far corner of the sofa, saying little, watching his lover with admiration, even love. Here was Nick at his best: public, capable, decisive.

I was moved that Nick wanted to do so much, yet I already knew that this wasn't just about me.

"I propose a fund-raiser," he said. "To help with legal costs but also to get attention. Both for you, Ralph, and for everything your case represents. Because it's part of something much bigger. Media apathy, the right wing's war against gays and women, the demonization of AIDS activism. They don't know they've demonized a dead horse, but a story about a falsely accused man might flog that horse back to life."

"I was never much of an activist," I pointed out.

"But it's how they perceive you. And reality is nine parts perception here."

"You want to use the lamb," I said tartly.

He didn't take offense. "Yes. It begins with you, Ralph, but doesn't have to end there. You can be a cause celeb"—he didn't even attempt the French. "I don't know how far we can go, if we can break into big media, but it's worth pushing for all it's worth."

"There's a chance the charge will be dropped," I warned him.

"All the better. We get the benefits of a martyr and none of the blood."

"Baaa," went Peter, then frowned, unsure what the joke might mean here.

But the truth was I craved to be used. I wanted my anger, suspicion and helplessness to be harnessed to something large and impersonal.

"What about O'Connor?" I asked. "What if we include his name with mine. He's a victim with blood."

"No," said Nick. "His name will turn too many people off."

"You'll put women off," said Maura. "I doubt it'll get any Log Cabin types in our camp. If we wanted them."

"You don't want me even mentioning Bill?"

"You can say anything you like," said Nick. "But we can't put him front and center."

It made sense. And I could control our link, without feeling that I was handcuffed to a corpse. I wanted to be finished with Bill.

The doorman phoned from downstairs. "Send him up," said Nick. "Your lawyer."

Nick had suggested I invite Michael Diaz tonight. I hadn't met him myself yet. He'd sounded cold on the phone, unhappy with the idea of first meeting me with others present. He was having dinner in the neighborhood, however, and said he might drop by.

"Nick Rosi," said Nick at the door. "Thanks for coming."

He strolled into the room, a tall, thirty-something black man in a turtleneck sweater. He had a tight, close beard of black moss. He checked out the apartment and people, just as we were checking him out.

"You're Mr. Eckhart," he said and shook my hand. He had a large, soft hand, and guarded, heavy-lidded eyes. Latin American or Caribbean, there was no trace of family tree in his accent. After what I'd thought and felt in jail, it seemed fitting that I have a black defender.

"Have a seat, Mike. Can I offer you coffee, beer?"

"Thank you, no. I can only stay a minute." He took Nick's spot on the sofa. "What's going on here, Mr. Eckhart? Who are these people?"

"My friends. We're discussing strategy."

"That's my job. You should see me before you talk with anyone."

"Which was why we wanted you here," said Nick. "We're talking extralegal action." He described the proposed fundraiser, Maura's contacts at the *Voice*—although not that she wrote for them—and the need for publicity.

Diaz listened with his legs coolly crossed, a finger pressed over his lips. In contrast to the noisily confident Freeman, he seemed a quiet, careful, worried man.

"Interesting," he murmured when Nick finished. "However." He turned to me. "If you go public, Mr. Eckhart, you *might* embarrass the prosecution into dropping charges, if their case has no floor. On the other hand, if they think they have something, you risk forcing them to trial."

"But it's already public," said Nick. "The front page of the *Post*? They might be done with it but there're others. I didn't tell you yet, Ralph, but I got a call today from a writer with *American Truths*. He wanted to know about you, your sex life, politics, friends. I told him to shove it, but they're planning to run something. We can't let them call the shots."

"I'm not saying you can't do it," Diaz quickly added. "I just want to point out that it's not without risk."

"Have you spoken with Senator Freeman?" I asked. She wanted me to avoid the media; I wondered if she had influenced Diaz.

"No. I know she paid your bail but she's not paying my fee. I have no contact with her. It wouldn't be appropriate."

Nick jumped back in. "I don't trust the silence-is-golden approach. Ralph needs to be as loud and visible as possible."

"Nick has an agenda that goes beyond me," I said. "I'm part of a bigger cause." I wanted Diaz to know that I wasn't Nick's stooge either.

"You are," said Nick. "But your welfare is part of that cause. I wouldn't pursue this at your expense."

Peter got up and quietly left the room, stooping to make himself invisible.

"My job is to keep you out of jail," said Diaz. "Simply that. Maybe a publicity campaign will help, but stories in the news have a way of developing a life of their own that nobody can control. If you can even get them born."

"Exactly," said Nick. "Nothing may come of it, but it's worth a shot."

Diaz studied Nick, then Maura, then me. He let out a sigh and stood up. "Nothing further I can say at this point. I need to meet with you alone, Mr. Eckhart, and get a clearer idea what kind of case we have. I recommend that you hold off on the media. But the decision is yours. We'll set a meeting later this week. Good night all."

Nick escorted him out and returned.

"Legalistic wimp," sneered Maura. "I hate how the law turns men of color into hairsplitters. Some of the women too."

"He's only looking out for his client," argued Nick. "He might be right, Ralph. But if we take a wait-and-see on this, we lose media momentum. What do you think?"

The decision remained mine. I wondered if Peter had

left to protest the risk Nick wanted me to take. I remembered my vague obligation to Senator Freeman. An excuse to do nothing, I resented it, rebelled against it. The chance to use my personal situation for something larger made the risk attractive, necessary. "Let's do it," I said.

Nick didn't break into a triumphant grin, but accepted my choice with a grave nod. "This'll consume time, energy and emotion, you know. It's a commitment."

"I know." But I did not feel trapped in a bad decision. I felt strengthened by it, as if it were the right one. "I'm in."

"Good then. Very good." He continued to nod, then got down to business. He asked me to get him the names of the reporters on my answering machine, none of whom ever called back. Maura set a day for a first interview. They swapped the names of people who might prove useful.

"Ralph!" Peter shouted from the bedroom. "Come back here. You might want to see this."

Of course. It was the hour of the computer. Peter had walked out only because it was time to commune with his digital spooks.

I found him sitting at his monitor. He leaned back so I could read the lines racing up the top of the split white screen.

"He did it. You just know he did it."

"Lie with dogs, get up with fleas."

"He looked like those French women whose heads got shaved for sleeping with Nazis."

"Just what we need. A killer queer."

Sentences crowded in and scrolled up like the music roll in a player piano, judging me, condemning me, reinventing me.

Shanghai Lily attempted to mitigate their criticism. "I doubt we've gotten the full story, darlings. Put yourself in the poor boy's shoes."

Delayed responses to previous remarks continued— "Why do killer homos get all the attention?"—before someone replied, "No way, Shang. Did you see his eyes?"

"Not his shoes I want to be in. Sexy killer."

"I bet the right hired him and he's not even gay."

"Or Hillary hired him. What if Hillary had that guy killed for his book?"

There was no moral rage, no emotion at all. These weren't real judgments, just idle notions pulled out of thin air. "It's all make-believe," I said. "Why do they want to do that?"

"It's fun," said Peter. "They get to be clever and cynical. And righteous. Virtual virtue. They don't know the killer is their own Sergeant Rock."

"We're not telling them," I said. I wanted them to stew in their ignorance.

"Of course. But it'll die away in a day or two."

"Or get serious?" I offered.

"No. It'll fade once Nick and Maura and you give them facts and spoil their fantasies. Or they'll get tired of you. Like Tanya Harding, that Kennedy cousin and the rest of them."

"Fools' names and fools' faces," I muttered, such a quaint, old-fashioned sentiment. I gave up my anonymity by agreeing to Nick's campaign, but I'd already become what every twentieth-century person yearned to be, public property. I was neither thrilled nor disgusted. I took a cold, belligerent satisfaction in being changed into something so new and various.

That night when I walked home, however, nobody on the street looked twice at me. The figure in the public unconscious had not yet spilled into physical space.

24

My life now had purpose, meaning, an overload of meaning. I expected my days to be all being and no thinking. Yet the mind is frighteningly flexible. Given enough time, it can accept wars and plagues and even murder charges as everyday realities.

I had my first meeting with Diaz the following Monday in the firm's New York offices, downtown near Federal Plaza. It was hard to believe that my arrest had been only a week ago today. The waiting room looked impressive, all suede and mahogany, a host of brass nameplates on the door. Alone with me in his office, with a window with a partial view and a Yale law degree on the wall, in a tapered blue suit that he wore like a second skin, Diaz was as smooth and detached as he'd been the other night, poker-faced, although his manner suggested a brainier game, bridge or chess. His stillness was like the careful repose of a large man who doesn't want to frighten children.

He began by asking about my meeting with the FBI, to learn what their evidence might be. "Believe it or not, Mr. Eckhart, you know more about this case than anyone else."

He'd received a copy of the police file, an intimidating thickness of papers all bearing my name. The only relevant documents, he explained, were my statement, the crime report, my booking sheet and an illegible computer printout with my City Hall arrest. The crime report suggested no unidentified fingerprints, hairs or blood had been discovered at the scene. No murder weapon had been found either, although a trace of blood on the wall indicated that the decedent had hit it during a struggle. A list of stolen property included a Sony Trinitron television, the Powerbook, a CD player, assorted male jewelry from Jeb Weiss's room and, presumably to carry most of it, Weiss's Louis Vuitton suitcase. Nothing had been recovered. Lovelace and Pruitt had lied about that. I asked if we could get them on misleading me.

"That's the least of the procedural infirmities here. It sounds like they violated your rights repeatedly in this so-called chat. But we have only your word against theirs. Which is why they didn't tape the session."

He had told me to bring any correspondence with Bill, but there'd only been my E-mail epistle, which I had trashed after sending. Freeman would've called me a fool, but Diaz accepted the loss with a shrug. "Even if they recovered it from your system, computer letters are inadmissible in court. And they only copied it on disk. I don't understand why they didn't impound your machine, but it may have given them their lead. A taped phone conversation, however, if it exists, is another story. What did you say?"

I remembered all I could of our last exchange, starting with the fact that Bill was jerking off. Diaz blandly noted it in his legal pad. He asked if Bill was the sort who'd record us as a turn-on for later. Maybe, I said. I didn't know Bill anymore. I could remember nothing but murder metaphors from that night. My claim that hundreds of gay men couldn't wait to piss on his grave seemed especially damning now that I'd seen that grave. Worst of all was that I'd told him he was dead.

"Was it a threat?"

"No. I meant only that he was dead to me and I didn't

care what he did. But I—I accidentally cut myself off while I said it. I don't know if I made myself clear."

Diaz blandly wrote that down too, nodding as if it were a matter of small importance.

"When will we know if they actually have me on tape?"

"Not until they tell us. I assume they do. Unless there's something else you're holding back that makes you a suspect."

Next we went over the day and night of the crime: what time I caught the train, when I met Nancy, what contact we had with the outside world, if only shows watched on TV. He was sorry to hear the doorman hadn't seen me and Nancy go up to her apartment. "You didn't go out all evening? A bar or restaurant where someone may have seen you?" No, we'd only fussed and fumed with each other and didn't even turn on the news. Diaz lifted his upper lip to suck air through his teeth, his sole display of exasperation.

Finally, he asked for my history with Bill. I told him about Weiss and Miami, the book and *Nightline*, of course, but also odd bits that randomly came to me: an exchange in an East Village restaurant about ambition, Bill's confession that his greatest fear was to be thought ridiculous, the tale of the paperboy and the hustler. All pieces of Bill became only dry bones when retold in a search for evidence.

We were there for three hours, the light in the window turning from white to orange to blue, Diaz filling his pad with seismic scratch while I refilled a glass from the water jug on his desk. Then Diaz declared, "That's enough for tonight, Ralph." Sometime during the session, I'd become my first name. "We'll continue this at our next session. Next week?"

But I had my own questions to ask. First, how much would this cost? He was working pro bono, but it could still run from ten to twenty thousand dollars, he explained, depending on whether we went to trial. If we had to hire a private investigator, it could be much more. "But we'll find a suitable arrangement for payment. Don't worry about that yet. You have more pressing concerns."

"So what are the chances that this *will* go to trial?" The chief question.

"Hope for the best, expect the worst. I'll press for dismissal every step of the way. We need to see if they have enough evidence to get an indictment from a grand jury." He placed a finger across his lips, thought a moment and said, "I think we should count on going to trial."

"But I have a solid alibi. My friend Nancy."

"Which we can use only in court. And it's not as solid as it looks." He explained how a determined prosecutor would go after Nancy to prove she had cause to lie for me. "I'll have to meet with her sometime. For whatever reason, people in D.C. seem hot to pursue this, despite the weakness of their case."

I was not surprised. I'd grown beyond surprise. "Do you know if any of them are involved with the Christian right?"

He lifted a suspicious eyelid at that. "There's politics involved. There's always politics. But the chief political threat here is that this is a nondrug, nonblack, middle-class murder. They get to prove they're an equal-opportunity prosecutor."

"Is that why Freeman gave you my case? Your race?"

He ignored the distrust in my tone. "No. He gave it to me because I asked for it. It sounded . . . *interesting*." He calmly looked me in the eye. "The politics is for me to worry over, Ralph. You just need to help us build the best defense possible."

I sighed, nodded and stood up.

He remained seated. "Am I right in assuming that you decided to let your friends publicize your case?"

Neither of us had mentioned it yet. I told him I had.

"Fine. I just need to know. My objections the other night were more instinct than head. Hearing what we have, I don't think it can harm you. But the public domain can be terribly confusing for anyone new to it. You already have a full plate. In your position, I'd prefer to stay out of the limelight. But then I'm a rather retiring person myself."

Was there such a thing as a shy defense attorney?

"My advice is talk about your innocence, not other

people's guilt. Complex scenarios involving Christians and Republicans will only make you look paranoid and guilty. Leave the paranoid scenarios to me. If Weiss goes on the witness stand, I intend to suggest that he had reasons to frame you."

"*You* think Weiss was behind the murder?" If one person believed it, my dead belief might come back to life.

"Not at all," he said flatly. "But a good defense is about casting doubt in all directions. Which I intend to do. I *think* we can win in court."

He stood up, and I saw his height again—his size enabled him to be uncertain without losing authority. He walked me to the door, but didn't open it.

"A personal question, Ralph. Do you have any hopes of settling a score here?"

"No. All I want is an explanation."

His mouth tightened in the first approximation of a smile I'd seen on his face during the entire meeting. "That's no good either. I should warn you, you're going to come out of this more baffled than ever. Police files are full of pointless, unsolved murders. The best we can do is keep you out of jail. We know O'Connor used a hustler at least once. So a hustler or pickup is not impossible. If we go to trial, I'll use his history, blame a hypothetical trick, then suggest Weiss set you up."

We fought fiction not with truth but another fiction?

"When will we know when we're going to trial?"

"That's for the prosecution to decide. Once they get an indictment in grand jury, I'll start pressing for a court date. But this could go on for months. A year or longer. You're always waiting for the other shoe to drop. Except there are a hundred shoes. Good night."

Only when I was out on the street did I begin to worry about Diaz. Whatever you think of lawyers, you want your own to be a ruthless fire-breather. I missed Freeman's arrogance and condescension. Diaz treated me as an equal, showing me all his cards, including his doubt. He did not set my mind at ease.

"Is he a cousin?" Peter asked at work the next day.

"I don't know. Maybe." He'd seemed awfully knowledge-able and matter-of-fact about gay life. "What difference would it make?"

"None. I just wonder it about everyone I meet."

"That's the least of my concerns about him."

Nancy telephoned to see how I was holding up. I asked *her* about Diaz. "He's smart," I said. "Maybe too smart. Too careful and low-key."

"Jack says he could use more venom in court, but that he's a very smooth deal maker."

"He's smooth all right. If it goes to trial, would Jack step back in?"

"No. Jack feels they've done too much already. But it shouldn't go to trial, Ralph."

"Diaz thinks it will." I told her what he'd said. "He needs to meet with you and find out what kind of witness you'll make."

"Shit. I thought I was done with this! The whole thing was supposed to be over by now." She recovered from her alarm. "I'm sorry, Ralph. Of course I'll come up and meet with him. Whenever he needs to see me." She spoke with the air of someone making a dental appointment she hoped would prove unnecessary.

When I told her about the fund-raiser and possible article in the *Voice*, she was accusingly silent.

"Look," I said testily. "I can't just sit here and do nothing while this goes on. I won't mention you or Kathleen or the book. She doesn't own me just because she paid my bail."

"No. I understand. Do what you have to. You're certainly going to need the money. Still—" Her tongue clicked her teeth. "Kathleen didn't help just to shut you up, you know."

"That's nice to hear," I sneered.

I continued to snap at the people I loved and trusted. My crisis gave me the right to say what I pleased without regret.

Nick called to report that he was forming a defense com-mittee. He'd spoken to the reporters whose names I gave him, but all said the story was a one-day fluke, a dead fish. He discussed my upcoming interview with Maura. "She's going to want you to name names. Don't. Keep the enemy large and vague. It protects you and gives us a bigger target."

"I thought you and Maura were in this together."

"We are. But our agendas don't always match. For all her tough talk, she's a pushover for sentimental melodrama. You know, conspiracy and revolution."

Then *he* brought up Diaz, wondering if I might be happier with another attorney, someone less pin-striped and more media savvy. I declared full faith in Diaz. The thought of losing him made me realize how much I valued his detachment. His uncertainty was contagious, yet I trusted his impersonality. And working with two men who did not fully approve of each other should enable me to retain some control.

Maura came to my apartment Friday afternoon. She circled the room, describing the many books and minimal furniture to a black tape recorder in her hand. Setting the recorder between us on my kitchen table, she began her questions, the same questions I'd been asked by FBI agents, detectives and lawyers. I sat stiffly and answered tersely. She worked at being objective, biting her lip to keep her views to herself, but class and gender politics kept slipping out. Was Bill rich? Had he been to prep school? She was disappointed to hear that he wasn't blond or handsome.

"What was sex with him like?"

"I won't talk about that. I'll say only that he was a better person in bed than in print."

"Were you in love with him?"

"No."

"Not even a little?" She had a nasty wink in her voice.

I shook my head. Whatever I'd felt for him, it was too slippery to share with the public.

I expected condescension from Maura. After all, I was white and male and had slept with a known pig. Maura had always treated me as just another superfluous twink. Not even my time in jail impressed her. She pointed out how easy I'd had it, how I'd still be in jail if I were black—she never asked who paid my bail. She was so aggressively blasé that I had to wonder if she envied me for being charged with murder.

"Who do you think killed him?" she asked.

"I don't know. I really don't."

"You've lost many friends to AIDS, haven't you?"

"Yes?" The change of subject threw me.

"You were primary çaregiver to Alberto Lowry?"

She must've talked to Nick. I refused to use Bert to make myself look good. "I did no more for him than others have done for their friends."

She frowned. "Well, just visiting friends in the hospital upsets me too much. I give them one visit and that's it. Not that it does anyone any good," she added abruptly.

But too late. She'd revealed a flaw in her righteousness, a tender heart or weak stomach, yet something vulnerable.

"It must make you angry," she continued. "That our country lets so many of your friends die, then calls *you* a murderer."

"My country? Our government? Something. Maybe fate. I don't know." I resisted her effort to turn my It into such an easy They. "But anger is an overrated emotion. What I'm feeling now is too cold and deep to be called anger."

"Don't you find it odd? That of the hundreds of thousands of people who've died of AIDS, none has committed a political assassination?"

Nick was right. She had a very melodramatic imagination. "You're sorry I didn't kill him?"

"No. Just a question I ask myself. I haven't assassinated anyone either. But then we're both healthy, aren't we?"

A photographer came and took pictures, some in front of the bookcase, others at the window with security bars—the once and future inmate.

The article was scheduled for the first week in June, on the eve of the fund-raiser. It was still the end of April. Nick hoped the two events would create enough critical mass to interest the general media again. The mainstream had dropped me completely. There were belated mentions in the gay press, whose lead times were longer, but only summarizing what was in the wire services. A lull set in. Peter reported that all talk of me in Gayworld had been replaced by new rumors about Marky Mark. The sole indication that the crime's public life might not be over was that *Regiment of Women* continued to float at the bottom of the best-seller list.

One evening after work, I found a cream-colored envelope with a Maryland postmark in my mailbox. Inside the formal thank-you card, under the printed script expressing gratitude for my sympathy, a delicate hand had scribbled:

Thank you for coming to the service. It must have been difficult. I know my son was very fond of you. When you are next in Baltimore, I would so like to talk. There is much about his life I do not know. Sincerely, Helen O'Connor.

"His mother," I told Diaz when I showed him the card at our next meeting. "She doesn't have a clue. Or does she? 'It must have been difficult'? Is it a trick? Why would she want to talk to her son's killer?"

When I described her, a small, timid, conventional woman, Diaz decided the card was probably sincere. "She doesn't sound like someone who'd come after you with a .38. Still, it's inappropriate for you to see her or respond at this time."

But I didn't want to talk to Mrs. O'Connor. Her card annoyed me, like a criticism for no longer grieving about her son.

"But *you* went to the funeral?" said Diaz, pressing his finger over his lips again as if to stop a smile. "You're a surprising fellow, Ralph."

"Stupid?" I said fiercely.

"No. Just surprising. And possibly useful in court."

I remained a case in his eyes, just another prolonged

event in the cold brain of a lawyer. Which was for the best, I decided.

He kept Mrs. O'Connor's card both to prove that I'd attended the funeral and, if the prosecution called her as a witness, to impeach her credibility. "I might feel her out as a witness myself. You never know what's going to alarm the opposition."

We went over the details of my arrest again, looking for technicalities that made my arrest illegal. Diaz treated the trial as a hypothetical play that might or might not be performed at an undetermined date. Everything was scripted in advance, both sides sketching every possible scene and speech, outlines they later presented to each other, daring their collaborator to stage it. We fought fiction with fiction, but I grew accustomed to the cynicism and proud of my acceptance. It seemed so worldly, so tough.

I remained remarkably cool those first weeks. Sometimes when I woke up in the morning, an old self surfaced who wanted the whole business to have been nothing more than a bad dream. But I had a mind that bounced like a ball when it dropped. Compared to my vague old identity of sympathy and fret, my new toughness was a relief, a simpler, more concentrated self. I actively craved things: to be declared innocent, to do good and, despite Diaz's warning, to learn what had really happened. I was excited, but kept it buried deep with all my other emotions, like the panic of a tightrope walker who knows not to look down.

25

"Free Ralph Eckhart!" declared the mock-up of the poster, the implication I remained in jail reinforced by the arrest photo, so familiar now it was no longer a picture, but an ideogram, a trademark. The headline was in magnified typewriter face, the photo pasted at a jaunty angle. The text began:

> Ralph Eckhart. Friend. Neighbor. Member of ACT UP. Gay and proud. He could be you. On Monday night, April 18, he was arrested for the murder of a right-wing journalist, on no grounds except that he was a politically aware gay man who once knew the victim. Join us in our fight against homophobia when we . . .

"I'd cut the exclamation point," explained James, the designer, a gray-haired boy in a sweatshirt. "Too seventies."

"What if we drop the Ralph?" Nick suggested. " 'Free Eckhart.' Make people feel they already know who he is?"

"Still sounds like you're giving out free samples," quipped Peter.

"Why not drop my name altogether?" I proposed. "Just say 'Homophobia' or 'Framed'?"

"Too abstract," said Nick. "We need to keep it personal."

We stood beside an empty stage, James's portfolio on the apron, in an empty club called Tarantula in west Chelsea, the new center of gay nightlife after years in the East Village. It was a weeknight; the club didn't open until ten. All the lights were on, exposing the former warehouse behind the high-tech trappings, while two female electricians replaced bulbs. A multipaneled video monitor hung over the stage like the digitized eye of a fly.

Peter and I had come from the store to meet with Nick, James and the man organizing the fund-raiser, a professional party giver named Veronica, who was late. Maura didn't join us. A journalist again, she had to keep her distance from the campaign. James was nervous in my presence at first, then treated me as simply a problem in design.

Looking up from his poster to the giant fly eye overhead, I pictured myself as a human billboard. It gave me neither pleasure nor shame, only a calm, cheerless satisfaction. My suggestion that we remove my name had been more habit than a sincere grasp at privacy. I knew now that this campaign did not save me from helplessness but enlarged me into something huge and selfless, vulnerable to others. I wanted to lose myself in their demands.

Veronica arrived, an overaged club kid with a pumped body and, despite the hour, sunglasses. Only his name was drag. Nick introduced me.

"You! You? I was expecting Superqueer."

With an inch of hair, I looked like a thousand other men.

"You will not do, Eckhart. You will not do at all." He gave me a high, goofy giggle.

I knew his manic type and was not insulted. Nick maintained a friendly, businesslike tone, but he could still wince at "queer." He was uncomfortable with this campy schizophrenia.

Veronica was giddy and giggly one moment, deeply solemn the next. "An event to awaken the conscience of a community," he grandly declared. "With go-go boys and

Lypsinka? I doubt we can get RuPaul but do you know anyone who knows Lypsinka? Or if you want politics, Hitler's Daughter. This guy does a wonderful act in pigtails and lederhosen. Funny yet angry."

"You could call it, 'Eichmann in Las Vegas,' " Peter snorted.

Nick ignored him, Veronica didn't get it. Peter looked surprised when I silenced him with a frown.

"No, it needs a serious note," said Nick. "Music, yes, but I was thinking we ask an important political figure to speak."

"Do you want people to come or don't you?" said Veronica. "Okay, okay. We include someone serious, but we need fun too. Do you want to emcee?"

"Not me," said Nick. "I'm a terrible public speaker."

"Okay. A fun emcee. A serious guest speaker. How about . . ."

They discussed who could sell me. Fun figures were no problem, but it was hard coming up with someone who'd give weight to the program without being too heavy. Kramer, Stoddard, Vaid? Veronica groaned at each. Their public appeal had been burned up long ago. Nick grew uncomfortable playing this frivolous name game in front of me. When Veronica suggested we go to the club manager and hear his ideas, Nick told me that I didn't have to stay. Feeling embarrassed for Nick, I left with Peter.

"Poor old Nicky," Peter chuckled when we were out on the street. "The club scene. God, is he out of his element."

"He never guessed his campaign could be a comedy," I agreed.

"So, why aren't you laughing?"

He was right. I saw the absurdities but did not find them funny. " 'He who laughs has not yet heard the terrible news.' "

Peter knew the quote; I'd first heard it from him. "Brecht didn't know what he was talking about. A little humor keeps one sane and human. You can't let this turn you to stone, Ralph."

"I'm not stone. I've grown a tougher skin. Which I

needed. How else am I supposed to behave, up to my neck in this?"

"You need some distance between you and it. You looked so pious back there, so holy."

I gritted my teeth. "No matter what one does or feels, there's always somebody to tell you it's the wrong thing."

Peter said nothing for a moment, then, "Do you really believe that you'll go to prison, Ralph?"

"I don't know," I admitted. "I try not to think that far ahead."

"I know the very feeling. But then my odds are higher than yours, aren't they?"

A judicious slap, but a slap nevertheless. I wanted Peter to see his situation in mine, so that someone might understand. But it wasn't the same thing, was it?

My guilt kept my anger in check. "You don't play fair, Peter. You hate it when other people see you as a sick man. But you're quick to use it yourself whenever it serves you."

Peter sighed. "It's my illness. I should be able to use it as I please."

I couldn't argue with that. "Sorry," I said. "I have no business sniping at you."

He apologized in return by saying, "Don't take me so seriously, Ralph. What do I know? Nothing."

I didn't believe that, yet our crises put us in different spheres, worlds strangely at odds with each other.

We walked down a cross street tented with new foliage to Eighth Avenue. It was a mild May evening and the sidewalks were crowded with men in shirtsleeves and even shorts. Bandanas appeared to be replacing baseball caps as the headwear of choice.

"I have too much energy to go home yet," said Peter. "Let's go to a bar. I haven't been to a bar in ages. Might be your last chance to be Joe Blow in public before Nick finishes with you."

"You want to make me human?"

"I want both of us to take a brief vacation."

We went to Juice, where I hadn't been in months and

Peter had never visited, an old bar modernized and renamed to compete with the new industrial bars in the neighborhood. We perched on two stools; I ordered a beer and Peter challenged the bartender to make a sidecar. While old disco throbbed in the sound system, a video projector showed even older porn on a screen fixed like a window in the back wall. Skinny fellows with mustaches and dandelion hair unpeeled bell-bottoms on a blanket in the desert.

"I know, I know," said Peter as he watched. "To you it looks frumpy, but to me it's Proust."

But a few swigs of beer were enough to put me back into my body; I began to find their pastel humping sexy. The bar was cruisy for a weeknight. Guys glanced at me and turned away, smiling to themselves. Two boys in buzz cuts and T-shirts in a corner booth appeared to give me special attention.

Somebody passed through the curtain to the right of the screen. A moment later, a different man hurried out.

"Is that a back room?" said Peter.

"A safe one. You ought to visit. For old time's sake."

"Thanks but no thanks. Even if it's so dark they can't see how old I am, I'd only embarrass myself. Can't remember the last time I had a stiffy. No, wait. I had one two weeks ago. While reading *The New Yorker*. A long article about chaos theory. Not remotely erotic, but I suddenly noticed I was hard. And I just lay on the sofa thinking: Hey. I remember you."

I hadn't even masturbated since jail, but couldn't tell Peter that.

"Hello there! What're *you* doing out?"

I turned around. Ned Wing stood at the bar, grinning like a gargoyle, thinking I should be overjoyed to see him. I'd pursued Ned for a split second two years ago. High cheekbones, flirty black eyes and a crow's flap of silky hair, he'd seemed so open and available. He had only wanted me to want him. When I did, he told me I wasn't successful enough to be boyfriend material.

"Peter? This is Ned Wing. My friend, Peter."

Ned nodded and promptly ignored Peter. "Haven't seen you in ages. But hey. I've read about you."

Now I understood what tonight's glances were all about. The general public forgot, but acquaintances remembered, and acquaintances of acquaintances—a widening circle of rumor.

"This your incognito?" said Ned, an excuse to stroke my bristly hair. "You didn't escape, did you?"

"That's between me and my probation officer," I weakly joked. I enjoyed the graze of his fingers, the glimpse of collarbone in his shirt. His physical appeal annoyed me.

"I had no idea," he said. "I always thought you were Mr. Sweet. But it's the nice guys you have to watch out for. You still live in the East Village?"

"Yeah."

"I live in Chelsea but have a boyfriend now."

"Good for you."

"Yeah. Well." He shrugged. "I was going to check out the back, then mosey on home."

He'd been a prudish pricktease when I pursued him; married life apparently liberated a trash side. "Have fun," I said. "Maybe see you around."

He sidled backward with a blatantly telegraphic grin. He turned and his kiltlike baggies danced over twin globes with no trace of underpants. He disappeared through the curtain.

"A butt you could quote Shakespeare off of," said Peter. "It might be what you need."

"Like a hole in the head," I said, and drained my beer. "Hold this." I gave him my wallet. I trusted Ned but you never knew who else might grope you in the dark. A quick feel, a bit of tongue, I thought. Better late than never. I'd show Peter that I hadn't turned into a pious prig.

The narrow space behind the curtain was lit by a wash of light from the translucent screen set high in the wall. Two solitary figures hovered in a dark corner, but Ned stood up front in the blur of color like a milky glow of sun through animated stained glass. He grinned when I came over to him. With the music loudly pounding, we were in a movie where you didn't have to speak or even think. I touched his shoulder, his back. He wrapped his arms around me and kissed. This is what I need, I thought, a three-dimensional body and mouth. But Ned's body was slight and weightless, his mouth too shallow. His shorts slipped against a meaningless ass. When I wrestled him down to the bench built in the wall, straining to find something to excite me, he whispered, "Oh yeah, you *are* dangerous."

Below the water level of light, I got my hand up a leg of the baggy shorts, which seemed designed for back rooms. I found balls in mussed mink, then a stubby satin bone. Having a bare cock in my hand wasn't as golden as I'd expected.

The vultures came out of their corner to watch. The curtain blinked and another shadow joined them. Men often swarmed like bees around necking couples here, coming in to look and even touch. I assumed they'd touch Ned, but someone eased down behind me, peering around as if reading over my shoulder. His hand brushed my hip, then brushed deeper when I didn't push it away. He pressed against my back, a compact bull in a T-shirt. It was one of the buzz cuts who'd been checking me out at the bar, now undoing my belt, unzipping my fly. "Yay," he whispered when he pulled at the waistband and I sprang into the open air. Ned purred in my mouth, excited to share. When one of the kibitzers tried to squeeze in behind him, however, he blocked the man with his knee and shooed him away.

The hand I had up Ned's pants became the hand that clutched me, a mirror of sex, a genital Möbius strip, except Ned and the bull never touched each other, only me, their four hands feeling like a dozen. Suddenly I knew that they didn't want me but the rumor of me, the name in the newspaper, the accused murderer. Why else would Ned finally give in? What else could make a baby bull want to frig an older guy? I resented their fantasy, yet my body was so keyed up that even resentment became erotic. I bit at Ned's mouth with my lips; I broke off the kisses to bite his shoulder. But no matter how much I did, I remained the object under the mob of hands. With the woof side of old porn playing overhead, I felt I was being gently raped inside a TV set.

"Uh-uh, uh-uh." I let go of Ned to slow the bull's hand. It only beat harder. I could feel his grin at my ear. His other hand clutched a nipple through my shirt. I threw my head back and saw the cutouts watching, but I didn't care. I let go, loudly, angrily, too contemptuous to worry about what anyone thought of my moans and spurts.

When I finished, when there was nothing left to expose, the bull withdrew his hand, then himself. I glimpsed his proud smirk slipping out the curtain. The silhouettes returned to their corner—they didn't know who I was. Ned fished out a pack of Kleenex, dabbed his shorts, then passed a tissue to me. "You get no nooky in jail?" he whispered. "I'd just love to hear the real story, but I have to get home." He kissed my forehead and hurried out.

Abandoned on the bench, drained and half-open, I wiped off and stuffed myself back in. I was embarrassed over coming in public, and furious with my partners, alarmed by my disgust for them. These were the people Nick wanted to rally around me for the good of a greater cause?

Coming out into the bar, I timidly glanced at the screen, as if my mauling had been projected up there for all to see. I sensed the player piano roll from Gayworld scrolling through heads around the room. The bull in a T-shirt sat with his friend again, gloating in my direction when he showed his friend the fingers that'd done a front-page dick.

"So how did you make out?" asked Peter. "Never mind. You have that guilty why-did-I-bother look."

"It's not guilt, it's—" I sat on the stool and crossed my forearms over the sensation like a runny nose in my lap. "I got mauled in there."

"Lucky you."

I shook my head. "No, they were devouring something else. My notoriety. My criminal reputation."

"Hey. Whatever gets you laid."

There was no dignity in complaining about an orgasm, but that wasn't what disturbed me. "Nick's wrong, you know.

People don't want an innocent man. It's more fun to think I did it."

"I could've told you that," said Peter. "They need bad guys. Villains doing all the nasty stuff that they fear they might do themselves. A nice change from their own good gray lives." He produced a thin, satirical smile. "Why else would anyone give a hoot about total strangers?"

"Then Nick would get more use out of me if I were guilty."

"Nick doesn't always get it. He's old-fashioned that way. Good guys and bad guys." He shrugged. "I sometimes wonder how much of his greater-cause stuff is for real."

"Why wouldn't it be?"

"I don't know. I keep meaning to press him on what he hopes to get out of this. Why not do it just for you? You're in trouble. You don't feel you deserve his help?"

"I like to think we're helping each other."

"You learn to accept favors from anyone who offers. Whatever their reasons." He gave me a look that seemed half wisdom, half pity. "Nick's always had a soft spot for you."

He said it matter-of-factly, without a hint of jealousy, but I quickly insisted, "No. He would've done the same for anyone in my position."

"Would he? I wonder."

He took a sip of his sidecar and turned back to the video screen, supporting his chin in a long hand whose fingers came up to his temple. A new thought seemed to shut down the light in his eyes.

"Oh look," he suddenly said. "Sixty-nine. How nostalgic. We used to think sixty-nine the height of fairness. So democratic. So mutual."

26

"Ralph? Michael Diaz. The grand jury met yesterday. No surprise. They indicted you for first-degree murder. The DA just spoke to me. If you plead guilty to manslaughter, she can get you off with ten years. She said they had you up and down but all she could cite was a taped telephone conversation. So they have it. I've already filed a motion in limene."

Hearing a cool, deadpan voice on my answering machine, the tightrope walker looked down. Ten years? It was like seeing no safety net at all below me. I'd been told the grand jury would probably indict me, but the possibility they wouldn't had been like a tiny window that gave more light than I knew, until now when it was shut.

I promptly called Diaz. My panic surprised him. He said prosecutors always bluff at this point and he'd rejected the plea bargain. The motion in limene, a motion to eliminate, would remove the tape from evidence on the grounds that it only showed my state of mind when I spoke to Bill and would be prejudicial to a jury.

"You called the DA she?"

"Elizabeth Gaskins, yes." Unsworth, the fluffy-haired prosecutor at my arraignment, had turned the case over to her.

I disliked how the enemy changed faces. "And a woman," I said. "I'm being prosecuted by a woman for the murder of a man who wrote a book attacking career women."

"Oh I see. Yes," said Diaz. "Well, irony's such a stock-in-trade that I no longer take notice. I'm not sure what this means. If they gave it to her because it's become a low-profile case. Or because a female DA will make the prosecution look cleaner if questions of homophobia and sexism are raised."

"Look at this," Nick crowed when he and Peter came to breakfast Sunday morning. He slapped down a new issue of *American Truths.* "William O'Connor Remembered," whispered a triangle in the corner of the cover. I rapidly flipped through the magazine.

"No, no," said Nick. "The editor's note up front."

Under the photo of a mean smile in glasses, the editor began by mourning the death of his "good friend and colleague." He compared the murder to the "so-called Vincent Foster suicide," speculating that a liberal conspiracy would save Eckhart from indictment—he was wrong there. He went on to imply that reports of O'Connor's "lifestyle" were a media smear, trusting readers to forget the eruption on *Nightline.* "Even in death, my good friend remains a victim in a war of words and values."

"Don't you see?" said Nick. "We get a battle going between the left and right fringe presses, it'll snowball. The mainstream will have to pick it up."

"Good," I said. "Very good."

I found "William O'Connor Remembered," two facing pages of brief tributes and a photo of an ebullient, boyish Bill shaking hands with the corroded waxwork of Ronald Reagan. The remarks were formal nothings about how smart and promising Bill had been, a hint of envy in their terseness. Nobody said anything that made Bill more than a byline. The sole mention of his sexuality was in a paragraph from Ren Whitaker, who discussed his mysterious death. "One should not be surprised if it later comes out that homosexual activists arranged the murder to punish a member of the tribe who rejected their liberal, antifamily line."

"And people say *we're* paranoid," sneered Nick after I read the sentence aloud. He pressed on to other matters, asking if I'd given any thought to what I wanted to say at the fund-raiser, still three weeks away. "You don't have to make a big speech. Just a few words. You're an articulate guy. You might want to read a poem."

I expected a wisecrack from Peter over that, but he just sat there chewing. He looked tired this morning, sullen.

He remained sullen when we left together to walk to the store. I asked if something was wrong.

"Not a damn thing. Just leave me alone."

We hadn't talked since our visit to Juice. "What's eating you, Peter? Was it something I said the other night?"

"You?" he said. "God, it's always you, isn't it? You think you do it all, don't you?"

His anger took me completely by surprise. "No, I just—"

"Forget it." He quickly regained his temper. "I'm not angry with you. I'm just bored. Bored with the whole business. Aren't you bored with it?"

"I'm in the middle of it. I can't afford to be bored."

"Well, I'm a bystander. I can be bored. Eckhart in the morning, Eckhart in the evening, Eckhart at suppertime. I can't believe anything good will come of all this sound and fury."

"We don't know," I said. "But it's worth a shot."

"A shot in the dark," he grumbled. "Only who'll get hit? Forget it. I'm just overdosed on politics and too many meetings in our living room."

I wondered what had happened or been said over the weekend to spoil his infinite sense of humor. Was he jealous that I'd become the center of Nick's attention? My crisis created a sibling rivalry? No, Peter was too smart, and too jaded, to think that. Did his bad mood have anything to do with me at all? Maybe it was only fatigue from a new treatment.

I stopped worrying about it while I did my work. Robert

was the Sunday manager but constantly came to me with questions. The staff at the store had digested me by now, treating my arrest as one more ongoing story that was slightly more interesting than the usual in-house romances.

The anonymous calls did not begin until the new issue of *American Truths* appeared. Gay men, whether they thought good or ill of me, felt no burning need to hunt me down and share their opinions. Other people felt differently.

"Your kind's made our country a sick place to live."

"Jesus loves you but hates your sin. I don't mean murder."

"Is this Ralph Eckhart? If not, ignore this message. But I just want you to know that I read you like a book, Ralph Eckhart. You got AIDS and couldn't bear the thought of O'Connor living when you were dying and so you killed him. You ever show your diseased face here in Jackson, there's people here who'll cut you open from your breakfast to your asshole."

The vilest messages were all left on my machine. When they got me in person, they usually hemmed and hawed and sputtered something about God being tougher than the liberal courts. Most of the callers were men, but one young woman with ribbons in her voice called me scum for saying a cute guy like O'Connor was a faggot.

The calls didn't upset me. I was bitterly amused, even relieved to learn that I had real enemies out there, people whose fantasies were sincere and psychotic, unlike the notions entertained by my own "tribe." I received a dozen such calls before I got an unlisted number. It had not yet gone into effect when my phone rang early Saturday morning.

"Hello, dear."

I hesitated, suspecting a trick. "Mom?"

"Hadn't heard from you in ages. Just wanted to check in and see how you were doing."

She didn't know. Of course. Most people didn't know or care. I was amazed by how pleased I was to rediscover that.

"Fine," I said. "The same old same old. How are you?"

I had never considered telling my family. How did I begin now? It'd taken me years to come out to my parents. When the case went to trial, then I would tell my mother. What was the point of worrying her now? I gave her my new number, claiming the phone company had asked me to change it.

"You sound a bit down in the mouth. Everything okay?"

"Just a little tuckered out this week."

"You taking care of yourself? You been safe?" The one danger that she could imagine for me.

"Always," I said. I took refuge in the ritual of asking about my father, brothers, nieces and the family dogs, Peanut and Reddie, the homely facts of home that I usually discussed with fond yet condescending amusement. Today, however, such innocent, private life seemed profoundly beautiful to me.

"Ralph Eckhart?"

"Speaking."

"I'm calling to tell you something important."

I sat in the basement at the store. I feared my hecklers had learned where I worked and the calls would resume.

"Tell your lawyer to contact Detective Harry Williams of the Baltimore City Police Department. Ask him about his investigation of a series of gay-related robberies."

"Who is this?"

"Unimportant. Just pass that name to your attorney."

My body remembered before my head; the officious voice reminded me of an urge to hold a stranger's hand. "Is this Pruitt?" I said. "Agent Pruitt of the FBI?"

Silence, then, "Negative. Somebody else. Someone who wants to make amends for a gross injustice. Harry Williams. Baltimore City PD. You got that? That's all I'll say. It's all you need to know. Good luck." Click.

It had to be Pruitt. I was stunned by his concern, touched by it. Then I feared a trick, then I called Diaz.

"Interesting," he said when I finished, his favorite word. Neither good news nor bad could ruffle his cryptic calm. "I'll look into it. I don't know what we can do with it. It'll be useless if they've already arrested someone. A hypothetical killer does more for us than a two-bit felon. More important is knowing that this Pruitt might be sympathetic if we need him on the witness stand."

I was amazed the tip meant so little in the thicket of legal maybes. Diaz continued to assemble the cast for a play that kept changing its script. He'd heard nothing on his motion to eliminate and didn't expect to for another month.

"Wenceslas hasn't returned my call."

"She gets that way," I said. "I'll mention it next time I talk to her. She still doesn't believe there'll be a trial."

"Well, no hurry. I just want to get your ducks in a row."

Diaz had other cases besides mine, of course, and I was temporarily on the shelf. We communicated by phone, but I missed our meetings, his physical presence, the fact of his office. The world remained more out there than ever. You'd think murder would bring you into the center, yet everything continued to occur offstage, coming to me in conversations and phone calls. There were weeks when the chief event in the case was my Friday call-in to Greco, my bondsman, who didn't care what I did so long as I did it in New York.

In this long unreality, dreams should have been superfluous, yet my sleep was full of dreams. Most were only symbols of what was happening, discharges of the emotions that I couldn't quite feel when I was awake, such as the dream where I was in a cage with a rat the size of a lion. Armed with nothing but a broom, I desperately swung at its snout; its head broke off and rotting sawdust spilled out. I felt foolish for having been so terrified, and sorry for the rat. I dreamed of a Dickens courtroom, full of fog and gaslight, where I stood in a high witness stand like the prow of a ship, looking out on an audience of children, unsure if this were a trial or a play. When the wigged prosecutor asked for my favorite color, my mind went blank, I couldn't remember. I woke up gasping and had to remind myself that the trial was months away and Diaz said we'd carefully go over all of my words before I went on the stand.

But the strangest dreams were mundane ones indistinguishable from my waking life, information dreams of newspapers, radio broadcasts and telephone calls.

"Hello, Ralph? This is Hillary Clinton."

"Mrs. Clinton?"

"Yes." She sounded so sweet, so kind, so unlike her reputation. "I just want to thank you for killing the man who wrote that awful book about me."

I was overjoyed by her call; the First Lady would save me. Then I realized her mistake and said, "Thank you very much, Mrs. Clinton. Only you should know, I didn't kill Bill O'Connor."

"Do I have the wrong number? This isn't Ralph Eckhart?"

"It is. But I didn't kill anyone."

"Then who are you?"

"I am Eckhart."

"But you can't be. Because Eckhart killed O'Connor. If you didn't, you're someone else entirely. Who are you? Really?"

The dream was so convincing that even when I found myself tangled in blankets in the gray light of my apartment, I was furious with the real Hillary Clinton for refusing to help me, and hurt that the dream Hillary had insisted I was someone else. If only people knew who I was, I thought, they'd know I couldn't have killed Bill. But the reverse was also true: Only when I proved that I hadn't killed him could I be myself again.

My real phone rang shortly before midnight on a Wednesday.

"Quick. Hang up and plug into Gayworld. Now!"

"Peter? What is it?"

"Just do it. Before he disappears. Then tell me I'm crazy."

Peter had an extra line and could use his computer while on the phone. I didn't. I hung up, unplugged and plugged in. My screen lit up on words twitching over phosphor-coated glass.

"What you should read is Best Little Boy in the World."

"No. Closet case book. Read Dancer."

"Prehistoric. My first gay book was . . ."

I couldn't understand what Peter wanted me to see. The gang was eagerly advising a newbie on books to help him be gay.

Then the newbie replied:

Thersites: Thank you for your help.

It lurched off the screen just as I understood what I'd seen. I was about to hit the command that would list who was here tonight, when Shanghai Lily asked, "Thersites, darling. May I introduce Sergeant Rock. Or have you met?"

The others chimed in: "Hi, Sarge," "Long time no read," "Surfing elsewhere, Rock?"

"Hi," said Thersites.

It was him. His ghost. The ultimate ghost in the machine. My fingers fumbled out, "Don't you know me?"

Long pause. "Should I? (Gentle laughter.)"

My heart raced, my ears hummed. Did anyone else use stage directions? "I'm sure we met," I replied.

"It is possible."

"You don't remember my handle?"

"No."

His entries were delayed but short. Maybe the dead type badly.

"Perhaps you'd like to be alone," offered Shanghai Lily. Peter was thinking more clearly than I could.

"Can we go into a private room?" I suggested.

"Why not?" said Thersites.

I brought down a sidebar and entered our handles. An empty box filled the screen and remained empty.

"Are you with me?" I asked, afraid I'd lost him.

"All work and no play makes Jack a dull boy," he replied.

"Where are you?"

The long pause before his answer added to the eeriness. "With you."

"Where in physical space?"

"Nohwere and everhwere. (Hysterical laughter.)"

His nervous fingers made mistakes. But I'd seen photos of the corpse. I was charged with his murder. He *was* dead. But this had to be his Powerbook, still programmed with his handle and stage directions. I was talking with a dead man's machine.

"You are Thersites?" I asked.

"Correct."

"Then I met you F2F."

"Explain."

"Face-to-face."

"You think?"

"I know."

"What do you know?"

I took the question literally. "I know that you are dead."

No response.

Realizing that I'd gone too far, I went all the way. "You were murdered."

No response.

"Who are you?"

His handle flickered in the border of our box; he was gone.

I unplugged the jack, plugged in my phone and called Peter. He answered immediately.

"Is he back in the main room?" I asked.

"No. What happened?"

"I scared him off. Whoever he is."

"It's not him?"

"No. But someone using his machine. That's the only explanation."

"God, I thought I was hallucinating when his name popped up and he started asking Homo 101 questions. Sorry, but I didn't think to save anything until after I called you."

I cursed myself for saving none of our private talk either. It was too late now. The words had evaporated in electronic ether. "But we both saw it," I said. "His handle *was* there."

"Oh yeah. And I couldn't help thinking: It's all make-believe, there was no murder. He's still alive."

"But it wasn't him," I said. "It's somebody else."

"His killer?"

My stomach lurched. "No. No killer would be so stupid as to use his victim's handle. He sold Bill's machine? Or maybe it is the killer and he's too stupid to know he's giving himself away." After my glimpse of a dead-eyed child in jail, I should not expect cunning of killers. "I'll tell Diaz tomorrow and see what he makes of it."

"Let me ask Nick about it."

"What would Nick know?"

"I don't know. Nothing. Probably nothing," he said, suddenly fed up with the whole business again, despite his call.

I got off the phone, plugged back in and E-mailed the monitor. I doubted the chatline had been monitored tonight, but I reported that the handle of a man I knew to be deceased had appeared. Maybe they could tag and trace the call the next time he popped up.

When I was done, when there was nothing else to do, I sat at the computer catching my breath, my stomach fluttering, my nerves firing in all directions. Why couldn't Bill be alive? Why had I explained away his return so quickly? I'd been unable to enjoy even for a minute the illusion that Bill wasn't dead.

"*Very* interesting," said Diaz after I described the encounter. I waited for him to talk through his surprise to what had to be good news for us. But the reappearance of Thersites produced more questions than answers. It might be connected with the killer, he said, but could be dismissed as the computer equivalent of a crank call. He would request a log of telephone calls for that night, just as he'd requested records for Bill's phone from the night of the murder, but it was a complicated, time-consuming process. He told me to get the E-mail addresses of people who'd been in Gayworld last night, as possible witnesses.

"You're saying this means nothing?"

"Oh, it means something. But less in court than you'd imagine. Even if we connect it to the Baltimore robberies, bring in your witnesses *and* an expert who'll explain how chatlines work, all we can do is add more reasonable doubt."

He'd spoken with Detective Williams. Yes, there'd been a set of gay-related robberies in Baltimore, but only four and nothing to indicate the suspect had expanded his territory to Washington. Victims described a short, blond fellow in his twenties, an overly friendly white Southerner who called himself Tim, Jim or John and claimed to be in the navy or marines or just out. He'd beaten one man unconscious when the man resisted. Williams had not yet sent files with the full particulars, but he said the pickup took only money, never goods.

"What we get," said Diaz, "is a tool to challenge the competence of the police. Why didn't they look at a connection with the Baltimore robberies? Talking about that, and bringing up this appearance in cyberspace, we *might* make a few people on the jury think Tim-Jim-John did it."

But even I couldn't believe in the existence of anyone so ethereal and convenient. Diaz and I seemed to have invented him out of pure necessity.

27

Suddenly I was all over the street. A chorus of "Free Eckhart" cried from alley walls, derelict buildings and the sidings around construction sites, multiples of our poster slapped over the glossy crust of movie, music and underwear ads. I disappeared a few days later under a sleepy bodybuilder in boxer briefs, but reappeared over the weekend. Teams of strangers went out after midnight with buckets of paste and rolls of me.

Nick reported that the campaign was bringing dropouts and burnouts back to activism. I spent an evening with Nick and a half dozen volunteers at the apartment, folding and stamping flyers, a backstage extra in my own show. The others were flustered to meet me, surprised I wasn't in jail, disappointed by my reality, except for one earnest, overweight man who courted me with pitying eyes that made the smirky cool of people like Ned Wing seem preferable. Peter hid himself in the bedroom, reading.

I grew frustrated with how little there was for me to do. Nick worked to line up more interviews, but could get only the gay press. A man from *The Advocate* met with me over coffee. *The Washington Blade* questioned me by phone. The media apathy was especially aggravating now that I had something to say: The real murderer was still at large. We'd seen signs of him in a computer yet an innocent man remained stuck in legal tar.

The fund-raiser was scheduled for a Monday, a slow night for clubs, which was why we were able to use Tarantula. The *Voice* came out the preceding Wednesday, the newsstands displaying a whole new set of ads for us. I was the front page, a quarter of it anyway, sharing space with Bosnia and designer water. A washed-out color head shot showed me with new hair and a soulful or sulky frown—all in the eye of the beholder—against white bars. "Caregiver or Killer?" asked the headline. "Did This Man Murder the Author of *Regiment of Women?*"

The article itself was titled "Strange Bedfellows"—the press never tired of the phrase—with the subhead "Love and Death in a Time of Political Cholera."

"They met in cyberspace, made love in Washington, New York and Miami, and ended their affair on the six o'clock news. One could say that William O'Connor and Ralph Eckhart had a very nineties relationship."

Smart-ass yet better written than I'd expected, it began with the public version of the crime, then cut back and forth between me and Bill. I should have been inured to reading about myself, but the tabloids had given only a shadow of me, an empty cutout. Maura included pieces of flesh. I'd wanted to use her article to tell people who I really was. Despite everything I knew, I read it half hoping that she would tell me.

"Defense attorneys like to say that there's no such thing as an innocent defendant. Yet Eckhart appears to be innocent, in all meanings of the word.

"Currently free on bail, he spoke to me in his cramped East Village apartment. A North Carolinian with a slight, denatured drawl, Eckhart comes across as another gay wannabe who fled to the bright lights and freedom of the North. Despite the ethnic-sounding name, he has deep Southern roots. He is a strange mix of the cool and the uncool. This typical-seeming queer is an unashamed Anglophile. His bookcases are full of Dickens and Trollope. Friends call him an example of Tory Grunge"—Peter once said that as a joke—"which might explain how a politically aware yet half-committed gay man could fall for a Shakespeare-quoting mouthpiece for the far right.

"Eckhart does not apologize for the affair. 'He was a better person in bed than in print,' he said."

Her portrait of Bill was based solely on print. She quoted an op-ed piece he wrote attacking his own Generation X and another ripping into "victim chic." She called his book "a pathological whine of heterosexual male terror; or it seemed heterosexual." She described his appearance on *Nightline*. "He was not the dyspeptic middle-aged crank one expected but a bespectacled, baby-faced boy next door, if you live in Pat Buchanan's hood." When Ellen Goodman attacked his book, he "cleverly used his homosexuality to turn himself from basher into bashee." Maura assumed he'd been in complete control.

Despite the errors and constant sniping—the misogyny "prevalent among gay men" made them natural allies for the right—I continued to give her the benefit of the doubt, until her conclusion. She spoke at surprising length about the effect of AIDS on my life, from sex to ACT UP to what I'd done for Alberto.

He expects no praise for this. "I did no more than others have done for their friends."

Which is true enough. The gay male community is not one of warriors but of caregivers and mourners. White gay men continue to treat the epidemic as their own private tragedy, not recognizing how it affects women and people of color.

"What I feel is too deep and cold to be called anger," he said cryptically. "Anger is an overrated emotion."

Why isn't Eckhart angrier? He clearly resents

finding himself impaled in the jaws of prejudice. Under that, however, is an emotional and political autism. He seems split from what has happened to him. Or is he split from what he did?

Talking with Eckhart, I bought his story completely. I still do. Yet thinking about it afterward, suspicions set in, the feeling that half of this man was missing. Could thirteen years of epidemic, right-wing attack and the false hope of Clinton give gay men a split personality? Could it create a violent unconscious? Is it possible that Eckhart actually did kill O'Connor, out of personal guilt or political rage, then blocked it out completely?

I doubt it. Sadly enough, we are "a gentle, loving people." But it's a wonder that queer men and women aren't more desperate, schizophrenic or dangerous. Because then the world would have to pay attention.

"So what the hell's she saying at the end?" I demanded from Nick. "That I could have killed Bill? Or that I should have?"

"She just wants to leave some mystery. Don't worry. Few people are going to read it to the end. The important thing is we get them thinking about you."

I was angry but not surprised. Maura had turned her own discomfort with illness into a posture of toughness. It was the radical-politics version of the fantasies in Gayworld and Juice: Murder was more exciting than passive virtue.

Nick was right though. Nobody over thirty actually read the *Voice* anymore, although the cover alone had an effect. Older people in my building stopped to ask me about the case and wish me luck. Out on the street, strangers absentmindedly nodded, knowing they'd seen me somewhere, a friend of a friend or perhaps a waiter. Others did recognize me, but walked on, smiling to themselves. New Yorkers can spot a face from the news without needing to stop and speak to it; the sighting alone makes them feel in touch with the world.

"I hated it," said Nancy over the phone. "Really hated it. So glib and condescending."

"It could have been worse," I claimed. "But you see? I never told her about you. She didn't even find out who paid my bail."

"That was a relief, but no surprise. Journalists don't investigate anymore. They just write up their assumptions."

Still, she was pleased her secret was safe or she wouldn't have wanted to come to New York for the fund-raiser.

"I owe you, Ralph. It'll be almost as strange for me as for you, but I should be there. To smooth the cognitive dissonance."

Since she was coming to town, she agreed to meet with Diaz. "Let me get it over with," she grumbled. She would go to his office when her shuttle got in at noon, then come by my place afterward.

I took that Monday off. I woke up anxious, shaky, queasy, yet focused all my fears on whether anyone would even come tonight. I didn't worry for my sake but for Nick's and all the work he'd put into this. I stayed home that morning, looking for a poem to read tonight, something short and strong. Nothing seemed appropriate. Yeats and Auden were at their best when damning public life, hearts of stone and low, dishonest decades. I decided to be selfless with my moment and say simply, "Words fail me. Except thank you. It's good to know that I am not alone in this." For good or ill, I was not alone.

Diaz called after lunch. "I have good news and sticky news. They've agreed to hear our motion to eliminate. Which means we get to hear this tape and learn just how damaging it is. More important, I can confront the DA and see what else she's got. I hate to admit it, but your friend's artsy article expedited the process. The hearing's Wednesday morning, which isn't much notice but I can get down to D.C. if you can."

"Sure. That's not so sticky."

"That's not the sticky news. What's sticky is that I just met with Wenceslas. She's reluctant to appear in court."

"Why?"

"She wouldn't be explicit. She said only that things could come out that would hurt her, and possibly weaken our case."

"Nancy won't testify?"

"She didn't refuse. But I need to know exactly what might come out before I put her on the stand. You have to assure her that whatever she tells me will remain in strict confidence, whatever she's afraid of."

I already knew. It was that damn footnote, which I'd never mentioned to Diaz. I was annoyed that Nancy could still be frightened by an idle rumor with so much else at stake, but assumed I'd easily be able to put her fears about Diaz to rest.

I waited for Nancy to come to the apartment. When she hadn't shown up by three, I left a note on the door and walked to the West Village. She had a key. I had cabin fever. I needed some air and thought I should check in with Nick.

It was a fine June day outside, warm and sunny and green, Washington Square full of sunbathers, the sidewalks full of teenagers and street people, none of whom read the *Voice*.

Nick answered the door with papers in his hand, on his way out with a last-minute fax to the local media. I told him about the hearing.

"Great. Maybe the press will cover it."

"No, it's a closed hearing."

"Oh. But it'll be good for your case," he said, admitting that was important too. "I got to run. Peter's home if you want to hang out until I get back. How you doing? Excited about tonight?" He raced down the hall without waiting for an answer.

I walked through their apartment. The sliding glass door to the terrace was wide open; I saw Peter's long bony feet and big-jointed knees on a mat in the sun. I stepped heavily to let him know I was coming. The legs didn't move.

He lay on his back in a gray sleep mask and sky blue bikini briefs. His elongated hands, like a second pair of feet, were folded over his tummy, the one place where he could gain weight. His lips were parted, his sandy skin pinking. His birdcage chest rose and fell with its knot of gauze and tubing in the center. He looked heartbreakingly frail against the sea of tar-paper roofs and high-rise mesas beyond the parapet, a conical roof like a slate dunce cap directly across the street.

My first time on their terrace this year, I remembered last spring when Peter and I had sat out here together by their dwarf lemon tree, talking and daydreaming while a sunset turned the clouds into pure Maxfield Parrish, our pocket Eden lifted high above the grumble and bleat of traffic by the roar of something gloriously bombastic, a Strauss waltz or the auto-da-fé scene from *Don Carlo*, on the stereo inside. Those purposeless hours seemed like paradise lost now.

I rapped the plate glass behind me.

"What!" He jolted up, yanked down the mask with one hand and covered himself with the other, not his crotch but his catheter. He remained startled even when he saw who it was. "Damn it, Ralph. Give me heart failure, why don't you?" He grabbed a T-shirt and pulled it over his head. "What're you doing here?"

"Sorry. Nick let me in. You called in sick today?"

"No. I called in well. Wanted to lie in the sun and burn myself clean. So if you'll excuse me—" He adjusted the mask over his eyes and stretched out again, his T-shirt like a chemise.

"Isn't that bad for your immune system?"

"Fuck it. I wanted some sun today."

I cautiously stepped out. "So. You coming tonight?"

His hands tapped the mat by his hips. "I haven't decided."

I badly missed his company today; I needed to confront his chill. "What's been eating you, Peter? Why're you so cool to me?"

"Not cool. Bored. I'm bored with the Ralph Eckhart Show."

"Not as bored as I am."

"You're not bored. You're high on it. High and oblivious," he grumbled in his blindfold. "Now I can't walk the streets without seeing your puppy dog face on the *Voice*. 'Please take me to your heart. Please, please, please.' "

His bitterness threw me; he was not bored but angry. "Why're you pissed? What have I done?"

"Not a damn thing. Forget it." He snorted at himself for saying too much. "I have no emotion left for other people anymore. I've got my health and treatments and energy levels to think about. Let me sleep. Go talk to Nick."

"Nick's gone out."

"Yeah?" His hands tapped the mat again. "Shit." He slowly sat up, peeling the mask to his neck to peer into the apartment. When he saw that we were alone, he drew his knees to his chest, wrapped his arms around his legs and rocked for a moment.

"Did Nick ever fuck you?"

"No!"

"Too bad. He's a real good fucker."

Was that what this was about? "Peter. That was years ago. You can't be jealous of that. Nick's interested in me as a cause, a case. Not me."

"You're right. Absolutely. He's not interested in you. Forget it. You're the last person I should be striking at."

It was ridiculous to argue the personal today, but I did. "If I love anybody, I love you. I feel closer to you than I ever did to Nick."

"Love, love, love. What a load of horseshit," he grumbled. "I love you like a brother, Ralph. Or did. I can't love anyone anymore. Nick says he loves me and what he does is all for love. Even when it's unlovable." He cut his eyes at me. "He did fuck you, you know."

"No. I'd remember. Believe me." But I knew he was talking about something else.

"Didn't you ever wonder how the FBI knew you were in D.C. the night of the murder?"

"Yeah, but—we figured they saw me on a security camera in Union Station or the Metro."

"Uh-uh." He took a deep breath. "Nick. I told him. The night after we saw the obit. He knew something was up. He met the guy once, remember? So I went ahead and told him, thinking there was no harm in saying how ironical it was that harmless old Ralph happened to be in town for his boyfriend's murder."

I stepped backward, trying to see his lowered face. I stumbled against the tub of the lemon tree.

"So it's my fault too," he muttered. "But I had no idea. None. I didn't know until he told me two weeks ago that he picked up the phone that very night and told his contact, Lovelace."

"With the FBI? Nick works for the FBI?"

"He wouldn't call it that. He's an informer. Now and then. When he wants them to know something. He says he's using *them*, and I guess he is."

"No. I can't believe that. Nick's not a spy." My mind stopped at that. It seemed such a cheap, implausible fiction.

Peter looked up, his cheeks sucked in. "Believe it. I've known that part all along. When there's a zap he wants them to cover or an action he wants them to know won't turn violent, he calls Lovelace, his own private hot line. He throws them a red herring now and then, but he usually tells them the truth."

My fear jumped ahead. "*He* thinks I killed Bill?"

"No. He assumes you didn't."

"Then why—?"

"He thought you'd make a good symbol," Peter sneered. "A cause celeb. A poor lamb falsely accused. And to help it along, he called his media contacts in D.C. and told them the FBI was bringing O'Connor's killer down from New York."

I looked out at the sea of roofs, the traffic glittering like metallic blood down Seventh Avenue. The high beveled box of St. Vincent's Hospital stood uptown like a huge brick engine block. The terrace vibrated with the tremble of a subway train under the street, thirteen stories below.

"So Nick did fuck you, Ralph. And yeah, I've hated you ever since I found out. Because you let yourself be fucked, and I couldn't do a thing to stop it."

I was surrounded by open space, thrown into it. I was falling yet did not fall.

The white curtains in the sliding glass door suddenly blew over the terrace like a pair of hands, and sank down again when the door to the hall banged shut.

Peter fumbled at his mask, then let it hang and just sat there, waiting. "We're out here," he shouted.

Nick came to the sliding door. "Oh good. You didn't go. I've got a minute before I run out again, Ralph. Did you want to discuss what you're going to say tonight?"

I couldn't speak, could only stare at him, trying to see in his familiar eyes and black thatch mustache the complete stranger who'd thrown me into outer space.

"He knows," said Peter, squinting up at Nick. "I told him."

His mustache tightened around his mouth. He put his hands on his hips, looking deeply disappointed with Peter. "You couldn't wait? You had to flush it from your conscience today?"

"So it's true," I whispered. "*You* did it?"

He frowned at me, annoyed. "No. I gave it a push. That's all. I was going to tell you, Ralph. Once you were in the clear. When we could laugh about the fast one we pulled on the media."

"You told the FBI I did it?"

"No, I told them only that you were down there. The rest happened on its own."

"Except for your calls to the press," said Peter.

"All right. That too." He stepped out on the terrace, hands still on his hips, keeping Peter between us. "Just a couple took the bait, although they turned out to be enough."

"But why?" I demanded. "I don't see what you gained."

"A commotion. A noise. A way of getting us back in the news." He lost patience with my failure to understand. "I thought it'd be over by the next day. You'd be released, charges dropped, we'd get a minute of attention and a poster boy. Or something. I didn't know how far we could go. But we'd get *something*. I never guessed the media would drop a gay story as unclean even with a political murder attached. Or that the murder charges wouldn't be thrown out in twenty-four hours. I never dreamed there was anything that made you a suspect, Ralph." The words poured out while he paced and turned; he'd been preparing these words for some time. "Look, if I could set anyone up, I'd have set myself up. I make a more convincing killer. A better story too. Desperate activist with sick lover murders gay right-winger? But circumstances only gave me you."

"The papers got the idea I was an AIDS activist from you?"

"It was the one way I could make the connection."

"You threw me in the shit without knowing what'd happen?"

"It was a gamble, but it looked promising."

"You were gambling with me, Nick. Remember me?" I cried. "Your friend!"

"I had no choice. I could only respond to what was already happening. I'm sorry that the something was you, Ralph, but there you have it."

"But if I go to prison, it'll be your fault."

"You won't go to prison."

I hadn't believed I would either, but anything seemed possible now. "What makes you so sure? You were wrong about the rest of it."

"Because you didn't kill him."

"Do you know who did?"

"I don't. Sorry. All I know is that the feds have washed their hands of the case. The DA has nothing except possible motive and the fact you were in town. But a million people were in town that night. There's no hard evidence, nothing to put you at the scene of the crime. You'll drag through court for a while. But you won't be convicted."

I didn't believe him, yet I couldn't dwell on what that did to my future. "Who else knows about this?"

"Nobody. Not even Maura. I wouldn't have told Peter except he was digging and riding me about why I busted my ass for you. I thought he was afraid I was in love with you," he said with a derisive snort. "But no, he thought I was doing it out of bad conscience. That I knew who did it or maybe even did it myself. If you can believe that."

"I can," I said. "I believe you capable of anything now."

"Well, I didn't. But I had to tell him what I did do and explain why I did it. And how it was my concern for him that made me so desperate I could—"

"Don't!" snapped Peter. "Stop using me as your excuse. It makes me sick every time you say you screwed Ralph for my sake. If it was for me, you should've asked. And I'd have said no."

Nick looked at him and winced. They must have been arguing about me ever since he told Peter. "Nothing more I can say, Ralph," he muttered, his eyes still on Peter. "Except that it changes nothing about tonight."

"You still expect me to attend this thing tonight?"

He looked up without surprise. "Yes. Like I've always said, it's bigger than you. You just have to be there and say thanks."

"You'll let me speak!" It seemed the ultimate insult. "You're not afraid I'll tell everyone what you did to me? And that one of their top dogs is an FBI snitch?"

Nick remained calm. "No. Because I trust your loyalty."

"Loyalty to *you?*"

"No, loyalty to what this is really about."

"Jesus, Nick," snarled Peter. "You won't be happy until you turn us all into liars."

Nick swallowed. He could hold his own with me but not with Peter. "All right! I fucked up! What else do you want me to say? I didn't know what would happen. I grabbed it without thinking. But we've come this far. An active campaign? The front page of the *Voice?* Let's see what else we can pull from this mess. Or are you two both so hot on being pure that you'd throw it away? Go on being morally straight and utterly helpless."

"Can't make an omelet without breaking eggs," charged Peter.

"No, you can't. The egg's already broken so we should go ahead and use it. You want to damn me up and down, Ralph, you can start chewing my ass tomorrow. Right now, I have to get your videotape to the club for a sound check. I hope to see you at nine. If you don't show, we're still doing this. Your presence is not an absolute necessity. And you still need money for legal costs. Yeah, I put you in shit soup, but I'm doing all I can to get you out. You want to reject my help because it's me, that's your decision. Think about it."

He charged back inside. We heard him make a quick call—"I'm on my way"—then the front door slamming behind him.

Peter remained hunched on the mat, a bony, defeated Buddha. "You see, Ralph. I wasn't angry at you," he murmured. "Not you at all."

"No. I don't exist. I'm just a thing here. A fucking egg." I felt gutted, blank, my mind white with anger.

"What're you going to do?"

"I don't know. I don't fucking know. What about you?"

"Me?"

"He's your life. You can stay with Nick after this?"

Peter folded his arms and legs around himself. "That's my shit. You have your own shit right now."

I attacked Peter because he was still here and I thought I still knew him. But I no longer understood Peter either. "You thought Nick was the killer? You've been with him all these years and could think that?"

"Something felt wrong. But unbelievable as that was, it looked cleaner than this. Better to kill a stranger than fuck a friend." He shook his head. "Nick hates being helpless. It's made him crazy. But the clumsy bastard does love me. It's gotten lost under his shit, but it's buried there somewhere."

I hated Peter for knowing and not telling me, and then for telling and remaining bound to the man he told on.

"You still skipping tonight?" I said.

"Yes. Aren't you?"

"Skip it? Skip it? You think I should skip it." The phrase made it sound so easy. "You afraid I'll blow the whistle on him?"

"No." He was surprised I could even suggest it. "He has it coming to him if you did, but—" He grimaced. "No, Ralph. I can't tell you what to do. But the smart thing right now would be for you to wash your hands of this and just walk away."

"Walk away? Yeah. You would think that." I could not trust the judgment of a man who expected to walk away from his life in a year or two. I was so angry I could hate Peter even for that.

I walked out without a word or touch of good-bye.

28

The elegant, oak-veneered elevator should have carried me straight down to an airless, stinking cellblock. Instead, it spilled me onto a quiet tree-lined street, into sunlight made unearthly by the red fog in my head: anger, disbelief, humiliation. I thought I'd become a man with no illusions, careful, hard and suspicious. But I'd never suspected the worst. I finally had the explanation I thought I'd never get, a human face for my metaphysical *It*: Nick Rosi, who'd lain beside me in the street and alongside me in bed, who had gone beyond the shallow intimacy of sex to share his life and lover with me. I could kill him, only the urge was not just an emotion to someone already accused of murder. The consequences were too real. But I could destroy him in public. "This is a sham," I'd tell them tonight. "A hoax created by Nick Rosi." He had handed me a loaded gun and dared me to use it.

Fists jammed in my pockets, my jaw chewing at air, I must have walked at a killing pace. All too soon I was on my street and climbing my stairs. The surprise of the unlocked door barely registered. But inside, sitting at the table between two windows like empty eyes, her elbows propped around a mug, was Nancy. I'd forgotten Nancy. I wanted to be glad to see her. She stood up with a gravity that implied she already knew.

"Where have you been?" she asked.

"Up to my eyes in shit. All this time. Only I thought I knew who my friends were."

She touched my arm, apologetically. I couldn't understand why *she* needed to apologize, until I remembered Diaz's call.

I lowered myself into the chair across from her. "Oh yeah," I said suspiciously. "Diaz told me you met."

She sat back down timidly. She thought my anger was about her. "I've been out walking, Ralph. Thinking about what he told me and what I should tell you. I couldn't tell Diaz about Kathleen but I should have told you. I just never believed it would get this far."

I stopped listening. "Stupid, stupid gossip! A blind item in a footnote has you scared shitless. For fuck's sake, Nancy."

But my faith in everyone close to me had been broken. Wisdom was quick and ruthless.

"Fuck," I said. "You *are* lovers."

She closed her crepe eyelids. "Was. Were. For two months."

"When?" Nothing shocked me now. My mouth opened in a scornful grin.

"Last fall. It ended just before you came down to visit."

"You've been lying to me from the start?"

"I couldn't tell anyone, Ralph. Not even you. You can understand, can't you? A business-trip affair. Started on a business trip and continued out of town." She let it spill out, her voice pitched on the edge of tears. "I had a crush and she was touched and we both got tipsy one night and I offered her a back rub and—" She rolled her hand through the obvious. "It was frightening. Exciting. To have a smart, admirable woman suddenly admiring and exploring me. She'd never been with another woman. I was totally new to her."

I pictured Nancy nude and happy, and a twinge of envy fed my scorn.

"Then other trips, three or four. Until she sat me down and explained how she didn't feel for me what I did for her and she feared she was using me, and we should stop before it got serious. It was nothing, Ralph. Ultimately. A messy fling. An office romance like millions of office romances, gay and straight. But politics would make it something monstrous if it came out in court."

So Bill had been right. The bastard had been right.

"And you called me brainless for humping who I humped?"

She narrowed her eyes at me. She angrily drew her lips against her teeth. "It takes one to know one," she said bitterly. "At least I was in love with mine."

I struck back with, "Does her husband know?"

"Oh yeah. She told him when the book came out. Not the first time something like this has happened. Only usually it's him."

No wonder he'd resented springing me from jail. "So if he already knows, why can't you testify?"

"I never said I wouldn't. Kathleen never told me not to. But I'm afraid of what this will do to her career if it comes out."

"Then lie. You lied to me long enough."

"I could go to jail for perjury."

"Only if they have proof." I knew more of the law's cynicism than Nancy did. "Or did you take Polaroids of each other?"

She ignored my jab. "Do I lie to Diaz? He said he has to know everything that might come out."

"Why not tell him? If Jack already knows. Or would it embarrass him that another lawyer in his firm knew?" Then cold wisdom seized a worse possibility. "But that's all that worries you? That you'll hurt Kathleen's career?"

"I don't care about mine. If it were just me, Ralph, I wouldn't hesitate for a second."

"No. You're not keeping something else from me?"

"Like what?"

"Like knowing maybe it was Kathleen who had him killed?"

Her eyes opened wide, her face went slack.

I said it without horror or disgust. It was just an idea, but so brutally perfect: One friend turned me in for a murder ordered by another friend's lover. He who laughs has not yet heard the terrible news? But I wanted to laugh.

"No, Ralph. She's nothing like that."

"She was nothing like a dyke, but she went to bed with you. She had the most to lose here."

"She couldn't. She didn't. It's not her nature."

"She arranged my bail and lawyer to shut me up."

"No! She did it because you're my friend and we thought you were foolishly protecting me. If she were involved in a murder, would she do anything to help? No, she'd let you rot in jail."

"I don't know. Would she?" But I knew. She wouldn't. The idea hadn't horrified me because I couldn't make myself believe it. I had imagined it simply to cut myself and get at Nancy.

She angrily shook her head. "Ralph, I will testify. I told you I would. I'm your only alibi. But I want you to know how much is at risk here. Public humiliation and the end of Kathleen's career. But I'm not going to sacrifice you for the love of a woman who doesn't love me."

"If she did love you? Would you sacrifice me then?"

Sh hesitated. "No. I wouldn't."

"Yeah, it's pretty to think you wouldn't."

She clenched her teeth. "All right. All right," she told herself. "I deserve this. I lied to you. I turned you into an ass-hole of paranoia. If I'd told you what was happening, if I hadn't felt so threatened and angry when you came down to help—" She grabbed at explanations. "You're going to be all nerves today anyway. I wasn't going to hit you with this until tomorrow or later tonight," she said. "After your thing."

Mention of the fund-raiser knocked me from scorn into

something like shame. Her lie was the least of the crimes against me. She was not the source of my anger.

I lowered my head. "I'd rather you didn't come tonight," I said coldly.

"*Why?* I said I'd testify. I told you what I was risking. Doesn't that count for something?" She sounded more hurt by this than anything else I'd said.

"I just—cognitive dissonance," I lied. "Oh, I'll forgive you," I claimed. "In time. But not tonight."

She hesitated, trying to read the truth in my face. "Okay. If you prefer I wasn't there—"

"It'll be bad enough without you in the crowd."

"The sight of me hurts you that much?"

"Tonight it would. Yes."

She accepted my rejection as just what she deserved. "Then I'll take the next shuttle."

"If you don't mind."

My courtesy was chilling, my dishonesty cruel. My coldest cruelty was refusing to tell Nancy that her lie was not why I didn't want her there. I didn't know if I'd be there or what I'd say or what would remain afterward. Whatever happened, I did not want Nancy to know what else had been done to me.

"I didn't want to come anyway," she said. "But I thought my presence would remind us both that we were in this together and—all right. All right. If it's what you want." She stood up.

"It is. Tonight anyway. Sorry."

"Then I better be going. Good luck."

"Thank you."

"Good-bye."

I walked her to the door. I watched her descend the steps with her head and shoulders bent with guilt. What was this masochistic egotism that made us blame ourselves when we were hurt by others?

I closed the door. I fell on my bed, exhausted, hoping sleep would save me from my freezing contempt for everyone I'd ever loved and trusted. I wanted sleep to decide what I'd do about tonight. But I only lay there on my back, cold anger weakening enough for sympathy to flow again.

I slowly acknowledged just how much Nancy had offered me. She would testify, despite the risk. "Doesn't that count for something?" It did. Why couldn't I forgive her? I felt like an idiot for not realizing sooner that she had lied and Bill had told the truth—his presence added to the pain—but Nancy did not deserve my righteous contempt.

I wanted to hurt Nick, not Nancy. But Nick couldn't be hurt. And I needed Nancy, more than Nick needed me. I was caught in a chain of obligation and blame, a circle jerk of people using people. What else are other people for? I didn't know anymore.

I needed to break the circle and save myself. How? Staying away tonight while people batted my name around was too much like the rest of my life. Watching the light fade on the ceiling, I rehearsed phrases to myself. "This is a hoax. A lie. But you shall know the truth and the truth shall set *me* free. . . ."

29

An electric bass thudded and thumped in the brickwork like a bad heart. The cobblestone street by the river, a tilted zone of loading docks and stranded tractor trailers, looked more like the scene of a crime than part of the club scene. I stood outside the public lie, by the rows of posters stuck to tarred bricks. "Free Eckhart," they whispered over and over. Right, I thought.

Latecomers came up the street in isolated twos and threes without making the street look less deserted and sinister. A pair of muscle boys walked blithely past me and released a blast of dance noise before the door swung shut.

"Ralph!" a female voice shouted from the shadows.

Shoes slapped the pavement. Erica and Alec raced out of the darkness, breathless and laughing.

"Boss man!" cried Alec. "You here by your lonesome? Where's your limo and entourage?"

I'd forgotten other friends might come, less important but people who knew me in a former life. "You guys shouldn't be here," I said, hoping to change their minds. "You'll probably be the only straight people in there."

"Cool," said Alec.

"We came to do our bit," said Erica.

"And dance," Alec added with a jokey swing of his hips. "Dance for your freedom."

Erica grabbed my arm. "Don't be shy," she teased. "Here, we'll be your entourage."

Alec took my other arm and they walked me inside, goofing on their familiarity with the artificial martyr.

This is a lie, I thought. I am a lie. If I told everyone that tonight, could I make myself honest?

"We brought your guest of honor," Alec told the trio of skinheads in the box office. One of them shouted across the lobby. Veronica came over, in Ben Franklin specs rather than sunglasses tonight, and a faded ACT UP T-shirt.

"The man!" he cried. "We been waiting for you. Can't have a Ralph-a-thon without Ralph. Here, your pals can take care of themselves." He took me from Alec and Erica, who wished me luck. He steered me into the din with his arm around my waist. "Nobody but Gay Cable News came," he whispered. "But they can get footage to the biggies later. Not great door but good door. Defense fund should net two thou after costs. Oooh, you're tense," he giggled, and began to massage my shoulders. "Relax. They'll love you."

The main room was full of bodies in T-shirts and baggy shorts, not packed but dispersed in a loose bundle swaying to a factory pound of bass and short-circuiting snaps like a bug-zapper. It looked no more political than any club on a weeknight except that there were a few more women and the only go-go boys were virtual. The video screen over the stage displayed four dancers of various races and underwears stepping back and forth in separate panels; the panels suddenly rearranged themselves like cards in a computerized solitaire game. Once upon a time I had wanted to see my face up there, magnified, public, losing myself on the giant screen. But tonight I needed to regain face.

People noticed us as we passed through, a grim man getting rubbed and psyched like a boxer by his trainer. Nobody

rushed over, but there was a constant turning of heads, a cur-
dling along the edge of the crowd.

"Eckhart! Twenty bucks!" someone called out, Ned Wing
hanging on an older guy who must be his Chelsea boyfriend.
"Steep for a Monday, but we did it for you!"

Maura Morris was suddenly walking alongside me. I
hadn't seen her since the *Voice* appeared. "Hey, Ralph. You
like the piece? Front page. Good picture. Hope you don't
mind what I said at the end."

"Why should I? I'm autistic."

She laughed. "That was a little harsh," she admitted.
"But I was using you to make my point, like all that stuff at the
end. I really do think it's time we get more ruthless. Break a
leg up there." She dropped back into the crowd.

She had no idea how ruthless "we" could be. I knew
more about real life than that radical berry did.

Veronica aimed us toward a purposeful group to the
right of the low stage. There was no backstage; everyone was
out in the open: a lesbian techie in a headset; a beefy fellow
in a battery belt with a large video camera at his feet; the gay
cable reporter in incongruous coat and tie. Behind them, a
drag queen in a red dress and gold beehive sat in a folding
chair as if it were a throne. Squatting at her side, giving last-
minute advice from a clipboard, was Nick.

"Ah. Here's Ralph," he said, calmly getting up, looking
neither surprised nor alarmed to see me. He wore a mask of
pure business. "Lady Remington, this is Ralph Eckhart."

She rose, a slim, snub-nosed man made tall and stately
by heels and hair. "You brave, brave boy." She clutched my
upper arms to embrace me at arm's length, so as not to muss
her breasts. "It's an honor to lend my name to your cause."

Her dress was a Soviet flag, the hammer and sickle at her
shoulder, apparently chosen because tonight was political. If
Communism had become camp since the fall of the Soviet
Union, it should be no surprise that a murder charge could
be camp as well. It was all a bad joke. It reduced me to a joke.

Nick introduced the reporter, who smiled and shook my

hand like a politician. "A crime what they've done to you, Eckhart. A real crime."

Nick gestured at the crowd. "Good turnout, Ralph. Yes?"

"Is Peter here?"

"No. He said he wouldn't come."

"What a surprise," I said facetiously. But I was glad Peter didn't come. I needed to do this alone.

"You going to speak?" said Nick, still playing dumb.

"I'll speak. You bet I'll speak."

"Good. I hoped you would."

Was he bluffing? Did he think that little of me? "You trust me up there? You don't think I'll blow it all away?"

He showed no trace of fear. He cocked his head and weighed me with his eyes, cooler now than he'd been on the terrace. He studied me like a road map.

"Can we start?" said the woman in the headset.

"Ten minutes," Nick told her. "In case Channel Five sends someone. Do you need to take a quick leak first?" he asked me.

I did—anger did not block the anxiety in my bladder— but I suspected Nick had another motive. "Where's the nearest toilet?"

"There's one up here," said Nick. "I'll show you."

He hopped up on stage. I stepped up and followed him along the Sheetrock wall. Of course. Here is where Nick will beg or cajole or threaten. He opened a door without a knob and followed me into a dank brown room like a deep closet. He stood at the sink while I went to the toilet in the rear.

"Okay," he said. "It's not everything we hoped for tonight. But it's something, Ralph. It *is* something."

The music throbbed outside. I stared into the rusty bowl with one hand propped against the wall.

"Bread and circuses," I told him. "Without the bread. You once said that, Nick. You threw me to the wolves just to get yourself another damn circus."

"I know," he muttered. "But it's all circuses now. You saw this crowd. It's just another party to them. And they're the ones who care. They don't believe in politics. Politics is a bummer." He cleared his throat. "So go ahead, Ralph. Tell them the truth. It'll be what I deserve. You'll only be telling them what they want to hear. That it's all tricks and fakery. But you can't deny that we're in trouble and need to do something to fight back."

I couldn't piss; I couldn't even think with my dick hanging from my fly. I zipped up and came out, shouldering my way between Nick and the sink to wash my hands. In the tarnished mirror, I saw his calm dark eyes, the mustache like a guiltless frown.

"An FBI snitch, Nick? Jesus. What'll people think when I tell them that?"

"It's not like it sounds. If Lovelace didn't have me, he'd plant someone else, a foe instead of a friend. This way I put my spin on everything they know."

I rubbed my hands more furiously. " 'The best lack all conviction, while the worst are full of passionate intensity.' "

"No, Ralph. I'm full of conviction. I might use it badly, but I have conviction."

"Then maybe you're one of the worst."

"I'm not. And you know I'm not. What I did was bad. But you have to learn to tell the bad from the worse from the worst."

I shook my head at him. I quickly dried my hands.

Hurrying out on stage, I walked toward the muddy tremble of people dancing in the murk. I am here tonight to tell you how a friend threw me to the wolves. By which I mean the FBI, the media, and you.

Nick stepped down behind me. "Let's do it."

The techie spoke into her headset. The cameraman hoisted his machine and settled it on his shoulder.

The house music gave way to a pompous arrangement of "God Save the Queen." The jiggling crowd subsided and tightened and faced the stage. I assumed the tune was Lady Remington's intro, until the four video panels were filled with one large image. A clip of news footage: my arrest at the airport.

I'd never seen it before. I was stunned to see myself in

handcuffs, my shaved head bowed, two glum detectives herding me into the flashes that were dampened on tape to a flicker of fireflies. The lines dividing the panels formed a set of crosshairs over my face. A classic image of modern life, I was mocked yet glorified by the tune that was also "My Country 'Tis of Thee." Twenty seconds long, the clip was on a loop, so I approached and passed, approached and passed, repeating like a spastic video game. The crowd watched without laughing.

It was a joke, I was a joke. But under the joke were genuine pity and fear. I glanced at the man who'd thrown me into that. He didn't look at me or the screen, but worriedly scanned the crowd.

I was sorry Peter wasn't here. Nancy too. In spite of all our harsh words, *because* of our harsh words, they were the only people in the world I trusted. Their presence might enable me to think more clearly.

Lady Remington climbed the steps and strutted serenely across the stage.

The screen behind her blipped to a new channel. The electric billboard was suddenly full of Lady Remington, caught by a closed-circuit camera in the deejay booth facing the stage.

"We must march, darlings!" She thrust her fist in the air, a Black Power gesture in quotes, ironic about its irony, a double negative that read as sincere for anyone who wanted sincerity.

"We know why we're here tonight. Because one of us, a boy named Ralph, has been hit with a murder rap. *They* say he killed a right-wing closet case. Imagine. Well, I met him and he *is* butch. But murder? Butter wouldn't melt in his mouth. Although something else might."

Laughter. Jokes did not need to be funny here; they only had to sound like jokes.

"But we know what it's really about, don't we? They—you know who I mean, and I think you do—*they* say we're just a tribe of evil queens who run around killing each other. With guns or disease, they don't care, so long as they can make us look bad. Tonight would drive them cra-zeeee. A roomful of queens pulling together to help one of our own?"

This is a lie, I thought. I am a lie. But with the lie and the jokes were the myths—we are a community, we have enemies—and in the myths were grains of truth.

Lady Remington continued to joke while she read the earnest letters of support sent by gay or gay-friendly politicos. Borough President Ruth Messinger called for justice—such an odd, forgotten word. Urvashi Vaid denounced the far right for using a gay man to attack gay women and then blaming his murder on another gay man, so that homosexuality was its own punishment. "Right on, Urvashi, like we're a self-cleaning oven," Lady Remington quipped. Council member Tom Duane declared that at a time like this, when our rights were besieged in Colorado and elsewhere, when we fought for the most basic medical funding, when our very lives were at risk, how tragic, truly tragic, it was that a homophobic culture set us against each other, first in misogynistic attacks, then on trumped-up charges of murder.

Flat political rhetoric, yet it had some truth. I was caught in a lie, but the lie contained a large truth: We were in trouble. I did not know how to kill the lie without harming the truth.

"I've changed my mind," I said. "I won't speak."

"Chill," said Veronica. "All you got to do is stand there and look injured. They'll love you."

"Nick," I said. "You shouldn't want me to speak."

He gave me a surprised, sharp, worried glance. Then his fear dissolved in a grim smile, a do-what-you-will nod.

It was too late. Lady Remington was already describing me.

"Butch but not too butch. Caring but fun. Sweet but not sappy. One of us. Come out here, Ralph. Say a few words."

Veronica gave me a push and I stepped up. A sound of wind in dead leaves blew me across the stage. I raced toward Lady Remington and seized her. Startled by my embrace, she let me hide in her silk and hairspray and muscular arms for a moment. I heard the applause. Not wild applause, but concerned, even sympathetic clapping. Can one hear sarcasm in beating palms? Lady Remington gently released me and stepped back.

I stood alone with only a mike stand in front of me. My hands went into my pockets, afraid to touch anything.

A sea of heads, a lake of people. Not just the idea of people reading newspapers or the sample of pseudonyms in Gayworld, but a massed fact of actual faces. They were silent. I couldn't tell what they felt beyond courtesy and curiosity. Seeing foreheads lift toward something above my head, I turned around and saw it, a living billboard turning around to look at itself. I faced forward, yet continued to feel the electronic magnifying glass at my back.

It was a bad joke, but the joke included real emotions. It was a lie, but the lie contained a truth. The people who came to party tonight were also here for what I represented. Not for me, but for *something* I represented.

I fell back on what I'd originally intended to say:

"Words fail me. But thank you for your help. It's good to know that I am not alone."

I was not alone, and it was terrifying. To be the focus of so many eyes was like a blow to the head. It shook up more words and I automatically said them.

"I am innocent. In more ways than one. People keep talking about my innocence. But innocence is another word for stupidity, isn't it? Okay. I was stupid. I slept with a Republican."

People laughed, thinking I'd made a joke.

"But that was the least of my stupidities. The very least."

I looked for Nick, blaming their laughter on him, but I couldn't see him in my druglike rush of self-consciousness.

"But Bill O'Connor. He was the stupidest of us all."

I rode a runaway horse of nerves and panic. I held on tight and said whatever came into my head.

"He wrote a shitty book. He could be a shit himself. But he was young. Maybe he would've gotten wise as he got older. Maybe not. We'll never know. First he got flattered by the wrong people, made to feel important in ways it would take a stronger man to ignore. And then he got killed. I don't know who did it. My lawyer tells me we might never know. His getting killed doesn't mean we should forgive him. But it does change things, doesn't it?"

Their silence grew restless. I didn't know why I talked about Bill, except to keep from talking about myself. Or was I talking about myself?

"It's not like death is new to us. But he was one of us. Yes, for all his faults, Bill was one of us. And he wasn't in the closet when he died. He came out. On *Nightline*. For all the wrong reasons, but he must've known something wasn't right. So maybe he was no worse than many of us. No worse than I. In some ways. Another stupid victim. We talk like being a victim gives you clout, makes you smart. That suffering is good for you. But it can turn you into a shit. It can make you nuts."

I was only talking to myself. Here was my chance to deliver wisdom, yet I had no wisdom. I had nothing but uncertainty.

"I'm not saying hate the sin and love the sinner. I'm not sure what I'm trying to say. Sorry to be unclear. I'm not clear about any of this."

Angry with myself, I suddenly snapped, "What do you want from me anyway?" Then, more softly, "What do I want from you? Why should it matter what you think or say about me? Why should we be so important to each other? Why should other people matter? What are other people for?"

I stopped. I blinked.

"Yes," I said. "What are other people *for*?"

"Fucking!" a voice shouted.

Nobody laughed. The rest of the audience was with me, either in sympathy or embarrassment.

"But what else?" I said. "There's got to be something else. What are other people for?" I repeated. "Something besides sex and money and votes. Or we wouldn't constantly talk about each other. Are we just entertainment? Distractions? Are we just burying our own shit in other people's shit?"

There was a ripple of heads turning and whispering. I felt someone standing to my left.

"I hope not," I continued. "But I don't know what else there is anymore. I don't."

I turned and found Lady Remington beside me. She made no move to intervene, but patiently waited for me to finish.

"Sorry," I told the mike. "I'm just talking to myself up here. It must look like I'm having a nervous breakdown." Was that what was happening? "What *are* other people for?" I repeated one last time, still hoping for an answer, and still nothing came to me. "Sorry," I mumbled. "Yes. Sorry. Thank you. Good night. Sorry."

I fled across the stage, toward the glass eye of the video camera that promptly swung back to Lady Remington. She clapped her hands to stir up a delayed, uncertain applause.

"What did I tell you?" Veronica whispered. "You did fine." As if he'd noticed nothing cracked about my speech.

"What Ralph was saying," declared Lady Remington, "in his oh-so Zen way, is that we must love each other. Yes. Each other and ourselves. So we can stand firm against those who don't."

Was that what I'd been groping for? Love? No. It was too glib, too easy. A drag queen could get away with saying it, but I couldn't. Such a private word meant nothing when said in a crowd. It was only a dry wish, a vague hope.

I'd failed. I could not give them the mean, small truth about Nick, or the large, slippery truth that I'd felt before I went up. We are in trouble. Why didn't I say that? I'd said nothing. Desperate to get away from there, I ducked out from under Veronica's arm, and collided with Nick.

"Thanks," he whispered.

"For what?" I pushed his hand off my shoulder. "For talking nonsense? For being too chickenshit to say what you knew all along I wouldn't say?"

"I thought you could. I was sure you would."

Was he bullshitting me? "You did a damn good job hiding your panic."

"I was never panicked. Because I knew I deserved it."

Lady Remington continued to tease and cheer the crowd back to life, her speech covering our exchange.

I stared at Nick, sorry I hadn't hurt him yet glad I hadn't, wanting only to escape his sheepish, knowing look. "I'm leaving," I said, and stepped past him.

"Ralph? Ralph?" called Veronica in a loud whisper.

"Let him go," said Nick.

"But we're not done. Gay Cable wants to—"

I swung toward the left to avoid the crowd concentrated in front of the stage, although I didn't feel as if I were fleeing. I felt strangely unashamed, oddly relieved. The forest of faces continued to watch Lady Remington, but people along the border noticed me. They stared blankly, like they thought I'd gone mad, except for an older man with a bushy beard who sadly smiled and nodded, as if approving of what I'd said, as if he understood what I didn't.

I was almost to the door when I spotted the scarecrow figure in the back. His hands were clasped on top of his head, his pursed frown in a halo of elbows. Among the spectators along the wall, Peter was the only one watching me. When he saw that I saw him, he lowered his arms and came out.

"What're you doing here?" I said accusingly.

He sighed and shook his head. "I couldn't just sit on my ass at home wondering what I'd set in motion tonight."

"You? Oh yes. You." Each of us saw him or herself as the center of the drama.

We lingered by the door, guiltily frowning at each other, only what were we guilty about? Complicity? Helplessness?

"Does Nick know you came?"

"No. My being here isn't about Nick."

"Enough politics for tonight, my darlings," Lady Remington concluded. "We must march, but we must dance too! So. Dance!"

She clapped her hands; the music resumed. The bodies shifted, clustered and resumed dancing. They forgot about my breakdown. Or maybe they only wanted to forget. Either way, I was glad to have Peter.

Without asking where we were going, he followed me

out to the street. The silence was sudden and deep, like stepping into a photograph. I started us away from the river toward Tenth Avenue, where I knew he could catch a cab. It was too far for Peter to walk home.

"You did the right thing," he said. "Nobody would've blamed you if you blasted Nick. But this was better."

"Oh yeah? So what the hell did I do?"

"You told the truth. You said you were confused and didn't know anymore. Which ain't what one expects at a rally. And you told people to be more thoughtful and tolerant and careful." His head ducked into his shoulders. "That's what I heard anyway."

It was certainly what I'd felt up there, but—"Negative capability," I said. "I'm nothing but negatives, Peter. I didn't denounce Nick. I didn't kill Bill."

"Better to do nothing than the wrong thing."

"Is it?" Yet I was pleased to be out of there with my soul intact—my frivolous, ineffectual soul. To have had the power to do harm and refused to use it.

We walked up a slight slope, in and out of shadows, Peter setting the pace.

"I was surprised you said so much about *him*."

"Not as surprised as I was." But much of what I'd said still amazed me. "So what the fuck *are* other people for?"

I didn't expect Peter to have an answer either, but he promptly said, "They're not *for* anything, Ralph. They simply are. You have to take them or leave them."

"Yeah?" It sounded like the answer to a different question, but it would do. "Well, I wish they'd leave me. In peace. Because I'm finished with them. Every last one."

He solemnly nodded, accepting it as a perfectly natural desire. "Does that include me?"

"Oh no. Not you," I said. "But everyone else." I gladly took Peter—I slipped an arm through his arm—but what could I do for him? What could I do for anyone?

30

You can't win for losing. All I did that night was save my very private ass from a public fire. Which wasn't nothing, but it seemed a meager thing, a successful failure, a relief of failure. There are so many ways to fail.

But I still had the law in my life, my long, loveless marriage to a murder charge. I was actually pleased that I had to go down to D.C. on Wednesday for the motion to eliminate, my first appearance in court. I took refuge in that other, colder, impersonal public fire.

I rode an early-morning train in my coat and tie and polished work boots, calmly watching the endless spin of summer fields and cool green woods. It looked so peaceful out there, so open. I wondered how many more changes of season I'd see from a train window before this was over. Diaz said that today might be only the first of several pretrial hearings. He'd gone down on Monday for another case. We were to meet in superior court at Judiciary Square; our hearing was scheduled for two o'clock.

The judicial theme park of my arrest looked entirely different when I walked through it freely in daylight. The

Superior Court Building was new to me, a mammoth concrete bunker half-sunk in a terraced slope. I entered a grim
rectangular mouth at the foot of the hill. It opened into a
wide, dimly lit corridor of beige marble, a low-ceilinged mall
lined with many courtrooms. Families sat in the scoop chairs
along the walls, mothers with children, adult children with
parents, most of them black, like the population of Washington, everyone dressed in clean yet casual clothes. Only the
lawyers wore suits and ties. It was like the waiting room of a
hospital or a bus station in the underworld. People spoke in
hushed, self-effacing whispers, although nobody except the
lawyers had much to say.

The lights in courtroom 23 were off, the chairs outside
the door empty. Diaz told me to be here early to discuss our
motion, but he hadn't arrived yet, so I took a seat and waited.
Not until then, perched alone in this underground hall of
anxiety, my jail cell buried somewhere nearby, did I begin to
suffer a feeling of dread. The harsh smell of floor cleaner
matched a remembered smell from the lockup, as if the cells
hidden under my boots seeped their air into the courts. I was
amazed I'd been able to block out my raw physical fear of jail
for the past two months.

A police sergeant entered my courtroom and turned on
the lights.

The nervous quiet was suddenly broken by the banter
of a man and woman around the corner. Diaz strolled into
view, tall and bearded, sheathed in a stone-colored suit,
accompanied by a pretty blonde in a long skirt and floppy
bow tie. They smiled and talked, smiled and talked, like
old friends, Diaz teasing her with the manila folder in his
hand. He was friendlier with this woman than he'd ever
been with me.

"Good afternoon, Ralph. My client," he explained.
"Ralph Eckhart. Elizabeth Gaskins. Your prosecutor."

She nodded without looking at me and finished what she
was saying. "No way, Michael. This Baltimore thing is immate-
rial. We have a watertight case, with or without the tape.

Nothing about the police not looking into this other thing means beans. There was no prejudice. No incompetence."

"Have it your way, Beth. Just want to save your office embarrassment if this goes to trial."

"You're so damn considerate," she scoffed. "But it will go to trial. I'd reconsider my deal if I were you." She shook her wavy hair and sailed through the swinging door into the courtroom.

Diaz saw the fallen look on my face. "Don't worry, Ralph. They all talk tough at this stage." He sat down and handed me the folder. "I knew I wasn't going to convince her with this, but I hoped to plant a seed."

I opened the folder. Inside was a rough, childish sketch of a thuggishly handsome face with a crew cut.

"The Baltimore suspect," he said. "Faxed to me on Monday."

Straight brows, narrow eyes, square chin—a generic cartoon. "He looks like a dozen guys you'd see any night in a gay bar."

"Exactly. Which I'll point out if there's a witness who says they saw someone *like* you with O'Connor that night. Which I doubt or Gaskins would've mentioned it when I waylaid her upstairs. Meanwhile, you'll be happy to know your alibi is in place."

I was too absorbed with trying to believe this cartoon had killed Bill to catch what Diaz meant.

"Wenceslas came by my hotel last night," he whispered. "She told me what might come out." He wrinkled his nose. "Sticky. But we can work around it. I can keep it out of court anyway. If worse comes to worst, she can plead the Fifth. What they did is technically a crime in Pennsylvania. Not sodomy, but adultery." He shook his head. "The law works in mysterious ways. However, if the DA's office finds out about it, and they might once they investigate our witnesses and find that footnote, there's no guarantee they won't leak the story to the press."

I thought: Poor Nancy. I was safe. Thank you, Nancy. I was safe. This could go on for years, but I should be safe.

"There's nothing we can do to protect them?"

"Nothing except hope and pray the prosecution doesn't figure it out." He tapped his watch. "We better go in."

The courtroom was lit like a theater, bright lights around the judge's bench, the rest of the room in shadow. Gaskins sat at the table on the right going through her papers. A man in white shirt and tie set up what looked like an adding machine under the bench. We sat at the table on the left. It was like any courtroom scene in the movies, except that there was nobody else in the room, the jury box and other chairs staring emptily. The whole thing had the leisurely, provisional air of a play rehearsal.

"How was she?" I asked Diaz.

"Your friend? Not happy. I'll say that. Hearing how much has to be left to chance did not make her feel better. But that's not our concern. Well, not mine anyway."

The police sergeant opened a door in the pine-plank wall behind the bench. "All rise," he declared, as if to a packed room. He announced the court and presiding judge. A baggy-faced white man with a gray crew cut and many chins fluffed his black robe and seated himself at the bench. He put on a pair of half-moon glasses.

"The United States versus Ralph Eckhart?" He read from an index card with a genteel Virginia accent. "Mr.—Diaz? You have made a motion in limene to disallow from evidence the tape recording of a telephone conversation dated April 15 of this year. *Miss* Gaskins." He pointedly emphasized the archaic title. "You sent me a transcript but not the tape. I won't read it without hearing it, both to check the accuracy of transcription and the context."

"I have the tape with me, Your Honor." She held up a black cassette, a commonplace item hung with a large tag.

"Fine. No need to delay this. No need to clear the court, I see. Let's just play it and get this over with. Did either of you bring something to play it on?"

They both had. The judge chose the cassette player that Diaz took from his briefcase. The sergeant set it on the ledge of the witness stand, as if the machine were to testify, and loaded the tape. The judge gazed down his crescent lenses to the transcript.

"It's already cued to the call," said Gaskins.

"What else is on there?" asked the judge.

"Nothing. The deceased appears to have rewound the tape to the beginning so he could record the entire conversation."

"Fine," said the judge. "Let's hear it."

Diaz remained standing, leaning against the front of our table. Gaskins and I were seated. The sergeant pressed start.

The phone rang. I answered.

"Turn it up, turn it up," said the judge.

"Did you watch? Did you see me?"

"Bill?"

"Now I'm your equal. I did it for you."

Our voices sounded loud and strange in the enormous room. Through the removes of cassette player, answering machine and phone, they seemed to echo deep inside a well, as if from a long time ago, another age. As with any recording, my own voice wasn't mine, but mumbly, hoarse, alien. Bill's voice, however, was utterly, disturbingly him. His smugly cheery tone, his breathy laugh. He blindly believed that he'd set everything right by coming out on television. He assumed my desire for him was so strong that I had to forgive him. He was so oblivious, so vulnerably oblivious. The cherub in a bed, a dead cherub now. I would never be rid of him. He'd surfaced in my speech to hundreds of people the other night; today he wheedled and sighed in an empty courtroom. Would he haunt me for the rest of my life? Who was this man I did not kill?

"Do you know what I'm doing while we're talking? Here. Listen. I'm naked on my bed, pretending you're beside me."

When the judge understood what was happening, his mouth tightened, his chins began to quiver.

The court reporter clicked away at his adding machine.

"You're dead, Bill. Your right-wing buddies are going to drop you like a stone. The chatline tonight was full of gay men who can't wait to piss on your grave."

I heard myself insult the dead. But I knew my angry words hadn't killed him. I was furious with Bill all over again, yet there was sorrow too, my tear ducts prickling even as I resented him for angering me and then taping it. Why had the bastard taped it? What did he hope to preserve with my voice?

And then: "Don't you get it, Bill! You're dead! I could kill you right now, I'm so angry. Only you're already—"

My dial tone, another sharp love cry and the tape went dead.

I fell back in my chair, full of anger and sorrow and fear. Cut off like that, it sounded like a threat. Didn't it? Would strangers understand what I'd meant? I'd been so enraged that I hadn't made myself clear. Bill had struck at me from the grave. The blow made him very real; his death hurt me in every way imaginable.

Diaz peered over his shoulder as he straightened up. His deadpan face gave away nothing, but the fact that he even looked at me suggested trouble.

"Disgusting," said the judge, dropping the transcript. "It's nothing but an obscene phone call. Inflammatory and prejudicial. No jury of mine will hear such filth in my court. Motion to disallow is granted."

Gaskins jumped up. "But Your Honor—"

"I won't discuss it, Counselor. An obscene phone call that proves nothing. Anyone would be upset by it. But I won't let my court be turned into a theater for homosexual smut."

"Thank you, Your Honor," said Diaz.

He signaled me out of my chair, rushing us out before the judge could change his mind.

Just beyond the swinging door, he grabbed my elbow to stop me. He was grinning, the first real grin he'd ever shown me. "I heard Judge Carter was old-school straight and narrow," he chuckled. "I didn't mention it for fear of worrying you."

Through the window in the door, I could see Gaskins on tiptoe at the bench, pleading with the judge.

"But I never dreamed it'd work in our favor. I can't guess what a jury would've thought if that tape were played in court. You do have a temper, Ralph. But you were saved by homophobia. That's an irony even I can appreciate."

I attempted to smile. I knew I should be pleased, but it happened so quickly, and I was still full of sorrow and anger with Bill.

"Let's wait for Gaskins. I want to see how tough she talks now that she's lost a major piece of evidence."

The sergeant came to the door. "United States versus Eckhart?"

"Yes?" said Diaz.

"Judge Carter hasn't finished with you."

Diaz looked startled. He quickly resumed his smooth deadpan and we went back in.

Gaskins remained at the bench with the judge. She'd regained her grim, cool confidence. I feared that she'd convinced the judge and I'd have to hear that tape again, when my jury heard it.

"Will the defense approach the bench?" said the judge.

Diaz motioned me back into the chair I'd just left. He joined Gaskins and the judge, who handed him his tape player and mumbled something. Diaz listened to the judge, then to Gaskins. I sat fifteen feet away, but couldn't hear a word they said. Diaz kept his back to me. His right shoe began to tap against the floor. Gaskins let out a mirthless laugh like a sharp bark.

"Very well then," the judge declared, wearily shaking his head. "Will the defendant please rise?"

I stood up shakily, alarmed by his attention. I was suddenly afraid that he was sending me back to jail.

"The District has decided to withdraw the charge of first-degree murder. I don't pretend to understand this. Still—" He cleared his throat. "You're free to go, young man." He grumpily got up and turned away.

I just stood there. They *weren't* sending me back to the cells? But could it mean what it sounded like it meant?

"My client and I thank you, Your Honor," Diaz called after the judge.

Gaskins hurried out with a brisk, stern walk, refusing to look at me.

Diaz came over, his eyebrows lifted halfway up his forehead. "I don't believe it, I don't believe it," he said. "What're you waiting for? Let's go."

I followed him out. "What just happened?" I spoke softly, as if speaking too loudly could ruin it.

"They dropped your case. Just dropped it."

At the door we passed another lawyer and his client, a sullen man in crayon-colored sweats, on their way in.

"Does that mean it's all over?"

"Yes!" He broke into a new grin and laughed. "What did you think it meant, Ralph? They withdrew charges! You're a free man."

"But there hasn't been a trial."

"There won't be. Unless they turn up new evidence. Which I doubt. Or you want to sue for false arrest, which I advise against."

"But it can't be over," I said. "It doesn't feel over."

"It never does." He snorted and shook his head as we stepped out into the sun, still unable to believe it himself.

No, it couldn't end like that, with only a quick chat between a judge and prosecutor, without my ever getting a chance to speak.

We climbed into the oven of Diaz's car and sat there while the air conditioner kicked on. Diaz continued to chuckle and groan in unprofessional disbelief. "It's what I hoped it might be all along," he claimed, trying to talk away his surprise. "A screwup from start to finish. Political pressure made them hot to charge somebody. The police had only you and the DA's office pounced on that, ending the investigation. But Gaskins knew they had no case. Losing the tape gave her the excuse she needed to pull out. Without it, plus the procedural mess, they were going to look like idiots in court. She blamed the FBI, claiming they'd promised a strong witness but never delivered."

Nick. They thought they were going to get Nick? I
hadn't had a chance to tell Diaz about Nick. Now I wouldn't
have to.

But I couldn't feel joy, not with so much left unanswered.
"Will they look for the real murderer now?"

"Oh, they'll look. They might find him too. Only you'll
never know. Or, if you're lucky, six months from now, a year
from now, when this is all a bad memory, I'll call you out of
the blue to say I was talking to a DA here and they happened
to mention a junkie confessed to the O'Connor murder. Or
an ex-boyfriend you never knew about. Or even our friend,
the Baltimore suspect."

"But it's likely that I'll never hear?"

"Correct. In the eyes of the law, you're nobody. Just a
private nobody." He put the car into gear. "I need to get back
to the hotel. Where can I let you off?"

"The train station. I might as well go back." Back to what?
The cold fire that had become my life was suddenly out.

"You're not going to see Wenceslas?"

"No. I have to be at work tomorrow." I hadn't intended
to visit Nancy while I was in town. I was ashamed to face her
now without the crisis that had justified all I'd said and done.

Giddy with success, finished with me as a case, Diaz
turned into a chatterbox as he drove. "I didn't always get you,
Ralph. But you're an interesting man. I would've preferred
getting to know you over beers. Now I know you too well. The
incest taboo."

He regretted we couldn't date? Was that what he meant?
His sidelong smile seemed flirtatious after his weeks of chess-
player cool. I still didn't even know if he was gay.

"Most clients I never want to see again," he added. "But
you came through this better than I anticipated. It didn't make
you hysterical or crazy with righteousness. It didn't make you
paranoid either. You have some kind of moral ballast that got
you through. Let me just say I admire you for that."

He didn't know. He knew so much yet so little about me,
like a doctor and his patient.

We swung in front of the glaring plaster wedding cake of Union Station and pulled against the curb.

"I guess this is good-bye, Ralph." He shook my hand. "Good luck. Maybe we'll run into each other in a restaurant or movie."

"Thanks," I said. "Thanks for everything. I mean that." I opened the door. "I'd like to say it's been real. But it hasn't."

"I can well imagine. But this was quicker and cleaner than any other case I've handled. And you did well. You might not think so, but you did quite well."

I closed the door and he drove off. I stood in the hot sun, tugging at the strange tie knotted around my throat.

It was over? I'd craved this moment, ached for it, expecting to experience what a drowning man feels when he touches bottom and can get his head above water. I thought it would be like the joy of coming out of a terrible dream and realizing it had only been a dream. But I woke from a life with too much purpose into one with no purpose at all.

I wandered into the high, cool, murmuring space of Union Station. I couldn't leave Washington yet. I found a bank of pay phones and called Nancy at work. I had to tell her the good news—I needed to hear myself say that the news was good. The receptionist said Nancy was out and wouldn't be back until three at the earliest. I called her machine at home.

"Nancy. This is Ralph. You're safe. We're all safe. The DA dropped the case. There'll be no trial. I don't know where that leaves you and me. I'm going back to New York today. But I wanted to let you know that you and Kathleen are safe. And to thank you for risking so much."

But that didn't do it, did not even feel like a start. We had so much to set right between us. I needed to see Nancy before I went back, even if it meant haunting Union Station for the rest of the afternoon.

I remained wedged in the stainless-steel niche of the phone, feeling there was someone else I should call, a courtesy call I should have made long ago. I'd not been free to make it until today. I dialed information, gave the name and street, then dialed that number. A woman answered.

"Mrs. O'Connor?" My mouth was dry.

"Yes?" A timid, ladylike voice.

"My name is Ralph Eckhart. I was a friend of your son."

31

Who was the man I did not kill?

A baby with corn silk hair and tiny white teeth. He laughed and clapped his hands for a studio portrait. He was once a baby, of course, an anonymous infant. He did not begin to be Bill until he was three and wore his first pair of glasses. Eyeglasses on any toddler have an incongruous look of premature wisdom. He perched uncertainly in the arms of a happy, horn-rimmed father in air force blues and sergeant stripes.

"Ralph? More decaf?" asked his mother.

"No thank you. I'm fine, Mrs. O'Connor."

We sat in a sunny living room used only for company—waxed furniture, yellow brocade upholstery and matching drapes—looking through the white photo album in my lap.

It's always strange being with the parent of someone you've slept with. Imagine that strangeness to the tenth power.

Mrs. O'Connor had been stunned at first by my call and tardy condolences. When I explained why I couldn't respond to her card until now, she said, "Oh, I am so glad they dropped the charges. So happy for you," with an exaggerated joy that would sound sarcastic from a peer but was quite earnest. "I know you couldn't harm my son." She'd like to meet with me sometime, she said. She was sorry to hear I was going back to New York today. Suddenly, without knowing why, I wanted to see her; I needed to see her. I was the one who proposed coming by the house. When she hesitated, I expected her to make excuses, but then she said yes, this afternoon was good. She told me to take a MARC train to their Baltimore suburb and she'd pick me up at the station.

Not until I stepped out on the elevated platform did I remember Diaz's talk of relatives who took justice in their own hands. I experienced a few flickers of fear before I came out of the station and saw her: a shy mouse of a woman who stood by her car in a starched blouse, summer skirt and earrings, dressed like a widow on her first date. She smiled weakly as she offered me her petite hand. "I can't thank you enough for coming, Ralph." She buried her confusion in courtesy, as baffled as I was over what we hoped to achieve with this meeting.

Mother and child sat on a beach, grinning at the camera. Father and son waded hand in hand into the lapping waves. The young couple took turns posing with their offspring.

After Mrs. O'Connor served me coffee and coconut cake, after we ran through the formalities of offering each other sympathy, she brought out the photo album. Like any family album, it was mostly smiles, a routine happiness where the faces expressed less than the clothes or furniture.

A five-year-old boy wore long beads, a clown-smear of lipstick and a gingham dress.

"Halloween," she explained. "He chose it himself. He wanted to be a hippie girl. Should that have clued us in?"

I was startled she could mention *it*. "Not really. All kids like to dress up." Would Lady Remington have spoken more kindly of Bill if she'd seen him like this?

Only after that photo did I see Bill in his mother. She had her son's chestnut eyes. It was disturbing to look up and

find his eyes timidly watching me from a small face with lipstick and pale brown bangs. Her hands were tightly clutched
in her lap.

Yes, this was what I needed to come down from the thin
air of public insanity, I told myself, this was why I'd come
today: for the stony privacy of a mother's grief. I wanted to
finish with anger and say good-bye to Bill in sorrow. Here is
the home chord, I thought. Here is where I will end the story,
if there came a time when I could tell it. Two shy strangers sat
in a living room used only for visiting clergy and salesmen
and thought their private thoughts over photos of the dead.

An eight-year-old in an Easter suit and clip-on tie. A
group photo of a Little League team, Bill looking glum
among the happy faces. His father stood at the back, a cocky,
beaming coach.

"Oh, he hated baseball. Just hated it," said Mrs.
O'Connor. "He and his father could not see eye to eye on
that."

Bill was an only child. Unlike my family, there were no
siblings to relieve the claustrophobia of the album. The
photos became fewer. There were many of a dog, a smugly
grinning collie.

"Rusty. It broke Bill's heart when he had to put her to
sleep. Billy too."

She and Mr. O'Connor disappeared from the album.
Bill continued to be represented by school pictures, his
gawky, skinny face growing into his teeth and glasses. The
cute trumpet player in a scarlet band uniform had a full, kiss-
able mouth. He was never fat. I'd assumed he'd been a large,
overweight kid, but he didn't put on height or weight until
later. After the pompous photos of high school and college
graduation was a print of the picture that I'd seen in the
American Truths, Bill shaking hands with Ronald Reagan—I
recognized Jeb Weiss in the shadows, puffed up like a proud
parent.

"He met the president. We were so proud of him. He
wasn't president then. But still."

The rest of the page was empty, the facing plastic-sheathed page blank, an abrupt white absence. I closed the album and set it on the table. "Thank you," I said.

"He was a good kid. A real good kid." She kept her hands knotted in her lap, her elbows pressed to her sides. She blinked at a brightness in her eyes. "I know he liked you very much."

I shifted uncomfortably. "He told you about me?"

"He said he'd met someone he really liked. When he brought you by the house that night, I knew it had to be you."

I needed to shift the subject elsewhere. "He talked to you about that part of his life?"

"Quietly. When his father wasn't around. I knew, and Billy knew that I knew. So all I had to say was, 'Be careful,' and he understood what I meant. And all he had to say was, 'I met someone.' We're not one of those families who have to name everything under the sun."

It was all too familiar. My family was much the same.

"What did you like most about Bill?" she asked. As if there were a hundred things I liked.

I couldn't give my usual glib answer about sex or kissing. "He was happy," I said. "Yes. He was cheerful. It was nice to be around someone who was so happy and confident about his future." It didn't seem like much, but it was true.

"Yes, he could be happy, couldn't he? There was a time in school when he wasn't. But later, when his work took off, he was very happy." She lifted her chin as she considered that. All emotion seemed frozen inside her, a slight melt leaking now and then into her eyes or voice. If she'd hoped meeting me would enable her to express her grief, my visit must be disappointing.

"I should maybe be heading back," I said. It was after four. I still had to call Nancy.

"What? Oh yes. Right." She smoothed her skirt over her knees. "I should take you to the train before my husband gets home. He wouldn't understand you being here."

"Probably not," I said. I didn't understand either.

She did not get up but sat there frowning, as if trying to remember something else she wanted to say. She gave her head a shake. "Would you like to see Billy's room before we go?"

I didn't, but it clearly meant something to her. "Yes. That would be nice."

I followed her up a short flight of carpeted stairs. We entered a boy's bedroom, but cleaner and neater than any boy would keep it. The room jumbled together different ages of Bill, a sort of Bill museum. Cowboys chased cattle through the folds of a curtain. His Towson State diploma hung over a spotless desk; he had lived at home while he went to college. A striped bedspread covered the narrow, solitary bed.

Mrs. O'Connor stood in the door, shyly watching me, as if waiting for me to understand what this room meant. Motherly grief? Eternal love? It suggested that she expected Bill to come home any day.

I went to the bed. There were actual sheets and blankets underneath. A crazy idea came to me, a ludicrous impossibility, but I lowered my face to the pillow. I sniffed the bedspread, then drew back the spread and smelled the pillow-case. It was clean, with no scent of a sleeping head.

"I still launder them every week. When I do our own bed." She spoke apologetically, as if finding it natural that I'd want to smell the ghost of her son.

Of course he was dead. I'd seen the police photos. But Bill had such a persistent life after death—on tape, in print, in Internet—that for a split second I'd wondered if his people had faked his death, conveniently disappearing him after his confession, making an artificial martyr of Bill just as my people had done to me.

I sat on his bed, shaken and embarrassed, glancing at the books on the shelf fixed into the wall over his desk: college texts, Ayn Rand paperbacks with concave spines, some Mencken, a laptop, a one-volume Shakespeare.

"The terrible things they said about him," said Mrs. O'Connor. She stood by the door, caressing a trace of dust off the top of the dresser. "That he hated women. He didn't. He loved me, I think."

"He did," I said. "He told me himself how much he loved and admired you."

"Really? He said that?" She sounded close to tears; she closed her eyes. When she opened them again, she could not look at me but gazed forlornly at the bookshelf.

I couldn't tell her that Bill's problem may have been that she was the only woman he knew and loved. I shyly followed her gaze and found myself looking at the laptop. A battleship gray laptop with an air force emblem in the corner.

I stood up and went to it. I eased it off the shelf. It was a Powerbook, with the same decal that I'd seen at the Plaza Hotel. I carefully set the machine on the desk. "This was Bill's?"

She stood very still, watching me without alarm or surprise. "Oh yes. He must have left it here his last visit."

"The police said it was stolen."

"Did they? You sure? Maybe it was his other computer."

I lifted the lid. I turned it on and an electric piano chord chimed. The earlier thought lingered—he is still alive—while my new knowledge slipped into place.

I rolled the mouse and found the file. The direction on how to use a chatline came up. "Thersites," I said.

"I beg your pardon?"

I looked at her. "Thersites," I repeated. I spelled the word for her. *"You,"* I said.

"Whatever do you mean?"

My heart raced but I remained cool and careful. I would not scare her off this time. "You and I spoke. On a chatline. Last month. I thought I was talking to a ghost. But it was you."

She swallowed. She looked down. "I was curious. And I missed him. I wanted to know what his life was like. For a week or two, I used to plug it in and visit around and talk to people. After his father went to bed. When I couldn't sleep. Excuse me. My throat's quite dry. Would you care for something to drink?"

She turned and hurried down the stairs.

I remained at the desk, rolling the mouse and letting myself think the rest of it: Mrs. O'Connor knew I didn't kill her son because she'd known all along who had.

I heard her voice down below, whispering on the phone. I went out to the hall, then stepped slowly down the stairs, hoping to make out what she was saying. Before I could, she'd hung up.

I found her in the kitchen, standing at the wall phone by the breakfast nook, her eyes blank, her face very pale.

I don't want to know, I thought, I don't want to know.

"So you and I spoke by computer," she said. "Small world. Small, small world," she chanted brightly. "And now we meet eff to eff. Face-to-face? Right?"

"Who killed him, Mrs. O'Connor?"

She lowered herself into a chair. "Nobody killed him." She tilted her head against the yellow flowers on the wallpaper. "It wasn't like that. It was an accident."

She was so distraught that I wanted to take her hand, but couldn't. I slipped into a chair facing her and said, "Accident?"

"My husband and I—" She took a deep breath. "My husband, Bill. He was furious when Billy told the world what he was. You have to understand. He's a different generation. He'd been singing Billy's praises to his pals when the book came out. He was so proud that Billy was going to be on Ted Koppel. But when Billy did what he did—Lord. It was all I could do to stop him from jumping in the car that night and driving straight to Billy's with blood in his eyes. He was humiliated, furious over what people would think of *him*. He already knew. We never talked about it but he knew. Ever since we came home one weekend and found Billy with some white trash he'd picked up on his paper route. Which had been awful. Just awful."

Her eyes focused on air, as if she saw a movie there. Bill had never hinted that his hustler idyll ended badly. Her voice continued in an affectless, hypnotic whisper.

" 'Right is right and wrong is wrong, and you don't shout

your wrongs from the rooftops.' That's my husband's philosophy. We went over the next night. When he'd cooled down. Just to talk. Just to let Billy know we were displeased. And it would've gone fine if Billy had showed some remorse. But he was *proud* of what he'd done. Proud?" She couldn't understand it. "You should know. My husband is a loving man. But he has his pride. He has his temper. They were at it like cats and dogs. Bill shouting. Billy sneering, throwing more fuel on the fire. But I was able to calm them. Just barely. I told Bill it wasn't the end of the world, and Billy he should see his father's point of view. It looked like it was over. I thought it was over when Bill asked what the TV people were like. I went to the kitchen and washed Billy's dirty dishes, to calm my nerves, I was so upset.

"Then I heard them at it again. In the bedroom this time. I froze. I couldn't move a muscle. Even when I heard the pounding, an awful, awful pounding, I just stood there, heartsick. Then I heard Bill shout, 'Get up. Stop playing possum. Get up. Get up.' "

She whispered the words that must have been shouted.

"I ran in. Bill stood in the room pointing his finger and shouting, 'He called me a loser. The little . . . B called me a loser.' That's all he could say for himself, standing over Billy on the floor. 'Tell him to get up. Tell him he can't scare me.' He said it over and over while I got down and shook Billy and felt for a pulse or breath or something. I still had on the rubber gloves from the kitchen. I didn't think to take them off, like I was afraid to touch him. Bill couldn't understand what he'd done, beating his son's head against the wall. If only it hadn't been such an old apartment! The walls so thick and solid." She drew a sharp, pained breath. "He'd grabbed him by the scruff of his shirt and slammed him against the wall. Over and over. Until something—broke. His face was all—" Her trembling hand touched her own face. "Billy had hit his face against the wall before the side of his head started banging it. His face was all blue and deadlooking."

I sat bolt upright in the chair. My hands were ice cold, my skin drawn tight, my hairs stood out like nerves. I whispered, "And then you and your husband made it look like a robbery."

"We had to. It made sense at the time. It did!" she insisted. "What else could I do? I couldn't let Bill go to prison. I'd lost my son. Did I have to lose my husband too?"

"So you took the TV and suitcase and jewelry and—" It was so cold-blooded, so ruthless. "And you undressed him? You took off his clothes to make it look like sex?" Nausea filled my throat as I pictured it: the man and wife stripping their son's corpse.

She screwed her eyes shut. "It made sense! It's what he told us to do. It makes me sick to remember it. It made me sick then. My own son, who I undressed a thousand times when he was a baby? To undress him for that?"

Her pain was so deep that it put her outside judgment. Split between horror and pity, I suddenly caught what she'd said.

"He? What he, Mrs. O'Connor?"

Her eyes popped open. "My husband," she said. "It was my husband's idea."

"No. You said 'told us.' How did your husband know to make it look like a trick?"

Her neck muscles tightened. "How should I know? I never knew he could kill his own son. Married to him thirty years and yes, he had a temper and could hit. But I could never imagine that."

But I knew who'd told them. I could make a good guess.

"And you've told nobody?" I said.

"No. Oh, a priest. In confession. Not my own but a different parish. I said someone I loved killed someone else I loved and I was protecting them, but someone else was accused of the crime."

"What did he say?"

"He told me to go to the police. For the sake of my soul and the innocent man. But I couldn't. Not yet. When you called today and said you were free, I thought: It's over.

Nobody else'll get hurt. Everything'll be all right. But it's not all right or I wouldn't have found myself hoping you'd figure it out."

"You never told Jeb Weiss?"

"No," she said. "Billy's friend? No. Why should I?"

"It was his apartment. He's smart. He'd know what to do."

She hesitated, her eyes darting and shifting, as if she were trying to hear something in her head.

The front door loudly jerked open.

I jumped up and stepped back, facing the hall. It had to be the murderer. It was too late to flee. Should I play dumb? My hands closed into fists.

He stumbled in from the hallway, a weary, burly man with a red supermarket blazer on his arm. A bow tie hung at his open collar. He was startled to find someone in the kitchen with his wife. But hadn't she just phoned him?

"Hello?" he said. "Sorry. Didn't know we had company." He automatically smiled at me before he turned and saw his wife.

"This is Ralph Eckhart," she told him. "The boy arrested for Billy's murder."

He stared at her, then swung his heavy face at me. The blood rushed into his neck and cheeks. "What the hell are you doing here? Haven't you brought us enough pain?"

Here he was, the killer himself, yet all I saw was an unhappy middle-aged man in glasses. I was afraid of him, but it was like the residual fear and respect I felt for my own father. "I didn't kill your son, Mr. O'Connor. And you know I didn't."

Mrs. O'Connor sat still, her eyes fixed on her husband.

"I want you out of my house this minute! Or I'm calling the police!" He turned on his wife. "Damn it, woman. What're you doing talking to this man? Do you have any idea what you're doing?"

"Bill. He knows." There was a hint of triumph in her voice.

The color went out of Mr. O'Connor's face. "What're you talking about? Nothing to know."

"He knows about the accident."

"What accident? What did you tell him? What did she tell you?"

"Everything," I said. "How you beat him against a wall and then made it look like a robbery."

"That's ridiculous. Nobody would believe that. You're a fool to believe her."

She glared at her husband. "The newspaper said he choked to death from his head injury. He may have lived if we'd called an ambulance."

"We don't know that! You make it worse by thinking that!"

"I wanted to call an ambulance," she said plaintively. "But you insisted we call Jeb, that Jeb would know what to do."

"He was dead, Helen! Already dead! You have to accept that!"

"No!" she cried. "You wanted him to be dead. You decided he was dead. Your own flesh and blood." Her anger flared up. "But I was the one who had to undress him. You wouldn't. You could kill your son but were too manly to undress him. My child. Who I'd undressed until he was old enough to undress himself."

"Shut up, woman! Shut up! Do you want to go to prison? Do you want us both to go to prison?"

His words hit her like a slap. "No," she said softly. "But I can't live with this either. I thought I could but I can't."

You want to know everything, and then you do and it's overwhelming. I was a spectator to a nightmare in broad daylight. They were monsters, yet I felt pity as well as fear for them, even Mr. O'Connor, who had cried so freely at his son's funeral.

The doorbell rang. We were suddenly back in a house in the suburbs, in a kitchen with a purring refrigerator.

"Jeb," murmured Mrs. O'Connor. "I called him as soon as I understood how much the Eckhart boy knew."

Mr. O'Connor charged out to answer the door. Mrs. O'Connor remained in her chair.

"Mrs. O'Connor? Mrs. O'Connor?" I whispered.

She closed her eyes, refusing to admit I was still here, terrified by everything she'd told me.

There was a rapid exchange of whispers in the hall. Then Jeb Weiss strolled into the kitchen, short and wide in his gray suit but no tie; he must live in gray suits. The smile over his chin beard was bizarrely warm and chipper.

"Ralph, right?" he said, pretending not to be sure, feigning friendliness like a psychiatrist come to save a family from a psychopath. "There, there, Helen," he said, laying his hand on a shoulder. "It's all right. Not to worry. What's done is done."

I stared at him, thinking: I'd been right all along. I'd been wrong but I'd been right: Jeb Weiss *was* involved. I could despise him without pity.

"He came busting in here!" charged Mr. O'Connor. "Talking garbage to my wife and getting her all upset!"

"Calm down, Bill. No cause for alarm," said Weiss. He saw the hate in my eyes. "A tragedy, Ralph. A terrible tragedy."

"That you made even worse," I said.

"Now, now. Don't think like that," he chided. He spoke to me as he spoke to the O'Connors, like pets. "We should leave these poor people in peace. Can I give you a ride back to D.C.?"

"What? You going to bump me off too?"

He only chuckled. "Give me some credit, Ralph. I'm nothing like that. I only want to explain the situation."

"I want to call the police."

"All in due time. But let's talk first. You're sore over what happened to you, and for good reason. We need to talk."

I hated Weiss, but I wasn't afraid of him. I needed to escape this nightmare house. The temptation to know the rest of the truth, his truth anyway, was strong.

Mrs. O'Connor withdrew deeper into herself. "I can't live with this," she mumbled. "I can't, I can't."

"Get him out of here!" shouted Mr. O'Connor. "Before I forget where I am and lose it." He struck the counter behind him with his fist. "I can, you know. You know I can!"

"Cool down, Bill. We're going. Aren't we, Ralph?"

I had to get out of there. Mrs. O'Connor couldn't protect me and it was two against one here. Weiss was at least sane. "Okay."

"Step aside, Bill. We're leaving," said Weiss. O'Connor obeyed him.

Weiss followed me down the hall and out into the daylight. Birds twittered over suburban lawns and there were children playing down the street. My fear was cool, distant, not quite real. I peered into his car to make sure that no thug sat in the backseat waiting for me.

"Get in, Ralph. I'm not going to bite," said Weiss. "I just want to talk."

I could have kept walking, down the street to the highway and a pay phone, but I had to hear the rest of the story. I climbed into a smell like new shoes. It was not just a Lexus like Bill's, but the Lexus that Bill had driven. As we backed out the driveway, I rolled down the electric window, wondering if I could shout for help from a moving car.

Weiss drove with both hands lightly on the wheel, resting his head in chewy black leather. "Sad, sad story," he began. "Those poor people. The tragedy they suffer. You should've heard them the night they called and told me what happened. It would've broken your heart."

"Why didn't you tell them to call the police?"

"I had to protect them. Wouldn't you want to protect them?"

My fear did not silence me. He wasn't stupid and I gained nothing by playing dumb. "You weren't afraid how it would look that Bill was killed by his own father? Family values and all that? It could make you and your friends look bad."

"Yes. There was that to consider," he admitted with a smile.

"So you took their private tragedy and turned it into political capital."

"On the contrary. I needed to keep other people from making capital out of it." He maintained a sarcastic calm, daring me to believe him.

"And then you stuck the crime on me."

"Now *that* was an accident. Believe me, Ralph. Although I admit it was a happy accident from our point of view. You made a beautiful symbol. But I had nothing to do with that. I never mentioned you to the cops. A little bird told them Bill had been traveling with a rough-looking radical who must be the murderer."

"Ren Whitaker?"

He smiled again. "Maybe. Just maybe."

"What does he know about this?"

"You can never tell what Ren does and doesn't know. Cagey little fellow. He's tight with someone in the D.C. prosecutor's office, but his influence goes only so far. When the FBI hand-delivered you, however, D.C was sure they'd found their man. Where the FBI got their tip, I don't know, but that wasn't me either. All I did was keep mum. So there was no conspiracy, Ralph. Half knowledges and sins of omission, accumulated. Nasty, but no court's going to convict anyone. Except the O'Connors."

"You're an accessory. You just said so."

"They'd have only your word in court. I'll call you a liar. You have reason enough to lie. Helen was upset today, but she'll settle down again. She won't want to hurt me."

If she could hate her husband, she must hate the man who'd trapped her with this crime. Except hatred left her traumatized and unpredictable.

We were on the interstate now, surrounded by cars coming home from work, a floating crowd sealed up in public privacies. A highway sign assured me that we were headed toward Washington, but I suddenly felt trapped, not just because there were no stoplights where I could jump out but because Weiss remained so calm, so unafraid of what I knew. He kept his eyes on the road, his lower lip tucked under his upper lip to form a soft beak like he was smiling to himself.

"What do you intend to do with me?" I nervously asked.

He chuckled. "No, Ralph. The question is, What are you going to do with the O'Connors? They're my only concern. I'm hoping you and I can reach an arrangement."

"Money?"

"If money will sweeten the deal. But I assume empathy will be the operative factor. You had a taste of jail. Can you imagine how that would affect Bill Senior? Or what the shame of being dragged through the papers would do to Helen? Nice people. Both of them. Would you want to hurt two nice people?"

"There's been nothing but nice people involved. And look what happened."

"Yes. Painful. Very." His beard wiggled as he worked his jaw back and forth. "Don't think that I'm a heartless man, Ralph. I'm not. I liked Billy. He was good company. It broke my heart, what happened. When I flew into town that morning and knew how I'd find him, it upset me more than you can imagine." He shook his head. "No, I was a better father to him than Bill Senior ever was. His sex life didn't concern me in the least. A few years from now, it won't concern anyone else. But when in Rome—" He shrugged. "He should've kept his mouth shut. That was your doing, you realize. Knowing someone like you confused him. Before he met you, he felt exactly as I do, that it was nobody's damn business. But you changed him, Ralph. You made him feel bad for being in the closet."

The clever bastard was trying to make me feel guilty. "You're saying it's my fault his father killed him?"

"No. I just want to point out your involvement."

His cool logic was a smoother, more insidious version of Nick's, with no strong emotion to tangle him in knots.

"You should meet a friend of mine," I said. "Only he's an amateur where you're a pro. And he had good reasons for pulling the shit he pulled."

"We all have our reasons."

"What're yours?"

He shrugged. "I'm no fanatic, Ralph. But I like winning. I like being at the center. I enjoy being part of the future."

"But this could fuck your future."

"Not mine. Only the O'Connors'."

"Uh-uh. Ren Whitaker and the rest will drop you in a minute for fear of how this can hurt them."

He frowned, then touched the signal and changed lanes.

"Where we going?" I asked.

"Wherever you like. I was thinking we can continue this at my apartment."

The scene of the crime. Was he really as invulnerable as he pretended? I decided to call his bluff. "No," I said. "Let's go to the Willard Hotel."

"What's there?"

"Michael Diaz. My attorney."

Weiss snorted humorously. "Don't think for a minute that I'll tell him what I just told you, Ralph."

"Then you can drop me off there. I need to talk with him before I go to the police."

He did not scare. "You have an ace in the hole. You should use it to get something you want."

"But there's nothing I want that you can give me. I'm going to Diaz and we're going to the police."

"Are you absolutely sure about that?"

"Yes."

"Sorry you feel that way, Ralph." He took his foot off the gas. We drifted toward the breakdown lane. "I tried to reason with you. Tried to let you know what was at stake here. You want to hurt those poor people, so be it. But I'll be damned if I'll deliver you to the cops."

We slowed down alongside a coffered concrete bulkhead. We were in a sunken stretch of highway, a six-lane canyon with an overpass up ahead. Traffic exploded past on our left, the elongated shadows racing across the concrete wall.

My senses were alert, my mind quick and emotionless. I watched his hands, ready to grab them if he reached under the seat or dashboard for a weapon. If he shot me here, would any of the people rushing past see it?

He hit the brake and the car slammed to a halt.

"Go on. Get out," he said.

He kept both hands on the wheel.

"You heard me!" he snapped. "Get out damn it!" His smoothness was gone. He was helpless, furiously helpless. "Just get the fuck out of my car!"

I opened the door and jumped out. I slammed the door. "See you in court!" I cried even as my body leaped back, my muscles still expecting him to run me over. The Lexus shot straight ahead, spitting gravel. No, he wasn't a killer and didn't know what else to do with me.

I stood in a hard corridor of concrete and orange sunlight, the rush-hour traffic roaring by. I took deep breaths of burned, poisoned air. Emotion poured up like adrenaline: a fear I didn't know was so strong until I was safe enough to feel all of it; and an overwhelming awe like joy. I fell against a pebbled cement panel, wanting to laugh at the overload, then letting go with a dazed comical moan.

My God, I thought. My God. I had all the pieces of my metaphysical It, my malevolent God. And they were all human: shockingly, pitifully human. I alone had all the pieces: Weiss, the O'Connors, the police, the FBI and Nick. A logjam of half-truths, fuckups and bad faith. What did they mean? What could I do with them? Knowledge gave me power and terrible responsibility.

I would go to Diaz and we'd go to the police. My pity was not so sentimental as Weiss hoped. The law would deal with the O'Connors. I wanted to go after Weiss. I'd enlist Nancy there, and maybe Nick and Maura, if they could play by my rules. We were starting over. One more time. Had I learned nothing from all I'd been through? Could I actually jump back in? Would we be able to change anything now that I had the truth?

I walked sideways up the breakdown lane, jabbing my

thumb at the blind machinery racing past, an insignificant, solitary figure stranded in the middle of nowhere. But I was not alone.

I was alone.

I was not alone.